WILD CARDS CONTINUES . . .

Originally begun in 1987, long before George R. R. Martin became a household name, the Wild Cards series earned a reputation ~~~~~~~~~~~~~~~~~~~~~~ for its smart reimagining ~~~~~~~~~~~~~~~~~~~~~~~~ with *Lowball*, the Wil~~~~~~~~~~~~~~~~

D0428024

"Martin has a~~~~~~~~~~~~~~~~~~~~~~~~~~~~~~ of writers. . . . Progressing through the decades, Wild Cards keeps its momentum to the end."
—*Locus*

"Emotionally powerful. Wild Cards deals up the variety of short fiction without losing the continuity of a novel."
—*The Seattle Times*

"Readers eager to find the very best in superhuman storytelling cannot afford to pass up the Wild Cards books—they're simply too important to the genre. *Lowball* has the hallmarks of being the start of a major turning point in this ongoing alternate history."
—*SFRevu*

The Wild Cards Series

A WILD CARDS MOSAIC NOVEL

LOWBALL

Edited by

George R. R. Martin

&

Melinda M. Snodgrass

Written by

Michael Cassutt | David Anthony Durham
Melinda M. Snodgrass | Mary Anne Mohanraj
David D. Levine | Walter Jon Williams
Carrie Vaughn | Ian Tregillis

TOR®

A TOM DOHERTY ASSOCIATES BOOK
NEW YORK

LOWBALL

A Tor Book
Published by Tom Doherty Associates, LLC
175 Fifth Avenue
New York, NY 10010

www.tor-forge.com

Tor® is a registered trademark of Tom Doherty Associates, LLC.

ISBN 978-0-7653-6862-1

Our books may be purchased in bulk for promotional, educational, or business use. Please contact your local bookseller or the Macmillan Corporate and Premium Sales Department at (800) 221-7945, extension 5442, or by e-mail at MacmillanSpecialMarkets@macmillan.com.

First Edition: November 2014
First Mass Market Edition: November 2015

Printed in the United States of America

0 9 8 7 6 5 4 3 2 1

Copyright Acknowledgments

"The Big Bleed" copyright © 2014 by St. Croix Production.

"Those About to Die" copyright © 2014 by David Anthony Durham.

"Galahad in Blue" copyright © 2014 by Lumina Enterprises, LLC.

"Ties That Bind" copyright © 2014 by Mary Anne Mohanraj.

"Cry Wolf" copyright © 2014 by David D. Levine.

"Road Kill" copyright © 2014 by Walter Jon Williams.

"Once More, for Old Times' Sake" copyright © 2014 by Carrie Vaughn.

"No Parking . . ." copyright © 2014 by Ian Tregillis.

For Fred Ragsdale

A WILD CARDS MOSAIC NOVEL

LOWBALL

The Big Bleed

by Michael Cassutt

Part One

Prologue

SINCE HE WAS ELEVEN, when the terrible thing happened, he had been called Chahina instead of Hasan. Chahina was a most unusual name for a Berber boy, but fitting, translating loosely as "Wheels" or "Transport." At the age of eleven, Hasan had been brutally transformed into a joker who resembled a small motor truck.

His body had doubled in size and mass—during the feverish transformation he had eaten enough food for ten Hasans—becoming cube-like, with a swale on his back and a hunched, neckless formation where his head and shoulders used to be.

His hands and feet had become horny pistons with flat, circular "hands" that cracked off every few months—or, he learned, with wear—yet remained a part of him, like bracelets around a girl's wrist. Chahina learned that if he locked his four piston-like appendages just so, the free-rolling circular "hands" could act like . . . well, like wheels.

Wheels that allowed him to move down a city street or a dusty Moroccan highway much like a truck, with one obvious difference.

Chahina used his back legs to propel himself forward, giving him the appearance of a truck with a broken suspension as he swayed from side to side—

"Ah," said one of his customers, a burly Dutch weapons smuggler named Kuipers, seeing Chahina in action for the first time, "you are like Hans Brinker!"

Chahina's lack of comprehension must have been clear, even on his grille-like face.

"A skater," Kuipers had said. And, looking like a demented clown, had mimed the side-to-side motion of a boy on blades on ice.

Hans Brinker? Chahina wasn't sure . . . but from that day on he referred to his movements as "slip skating."

And, over the past eleven years, he had slip-skated his way to a decent career as a transporter of illegal substances, contraband, and, yes, weapons, from one point to another, usually at odd hours in great secrecy, frequently on less-traveled routes. His ability to combine stealthy movement with common sense won him many fans in the criminal underworld of northern Africa and southern Europe, so much so that when one of his primary customers expanded his operations to the United States, Chahina was "invited" to come along, traveling as—what else?—Deck ballast on a freighter.

Once he had adjusted to the rigors of life in New York and environs as an illegal joker immigrant, Chahina had grown to appreciate the relative ease of his new smuggler's life. Roads were better. Law enforcement was usually more predictable and honest (Chahina did not break speed limits, and so never got stopped).

And there were no hijackers! Chahina's time in America had been lucrative; the future was promising.

But on the evening of Monday, May 7, 2012, he made a mistake.

Chahina frequently looked down on human drivers and their vehicles, finding them an inferior breed, each half useless without the other. He, after all, was both brains and automotive brawn.

But there were times he wished he had a bit of navigation help, so he would have avoided that wrong turn coming north out of Tewksbury, where 519 and Old Turnpike overlapped: he had wasted ten minutes going west on OT when he should have continued north.

Normally this slight detour wouldn't have been a problem, but Chahina had a deadline: by eight P.M. he was to deliver his cargo to the customer on the edge of Stephens State Park. . . . The address did not appear to be either a commercial property or a residential one, but rather an open field.

In order to make up lost time, Chahina broke his self-imposed rule about speed limits, a risky move because in order to go faster, he had to make more exaggerated slip skates.

He noted the startled reactions of a pair of oncoming drivers, but knew from experience they would simply assume he was some foreign-model truck with unusually sleek, rounded lines. And possibly an intoxicated operator.

(One thing that night trips forced on Chahina was the addition of "headlights," in his case, literally: he had to strap lamps to the outside rim of each eye for basic illumination, and to ensure that he looked like a truck to other vehicles. There was no quicker way to draw attention from highway patrol than to be racing down a rural road with no lights. . . .)

What Chahina hated most was what he'd been driving through almost every day for the past two months . . . and that was rain.

First of all, it was simply uncomfortable. Chahina's transformation to joker had left him looking like a vehicle—and naked, which was a shocking situation for a boy who had never worn any garment more revealing

than a T-shirt and long pants in public. His older brother
Tariq had helped him sew canvas "trousers" that covered
his nether regions and looked, to other eyes, like the fabric enclosing the cargo beds of real trucks. Chahina had
improved on this early solution, however, fabricating
better-fitting and vari-colored "trousers" to suit any en-
vironment. Tonight's, for example, were plain gray.

But they weren't waterproof, and Chahina slip-skated
along with the uncomfortable feeling that he had just sat
in a puddle while rain spattered his neck and back.

Worse yet, the rain made it more difficult to see. And
it almost destroyed traction. (His "hands" and "feet" had
none of the radial grooving found in tires.)

The rain had started fifteen minutes after he'd left
Staten Island, before he even crossed the Goethals Bridge
from Staten Island into New Jersey.

It never got heavy—but it didn't take much to make
things uncomfortable for Chahina.

Fortunately, his load was just two dozen plastic containers. A little moisture wouldn't hurt them.

Safely out of Hackettstown now, just passing Bilby, the
developments gave way to old farms and woods.

What little traffic willing to brave the rain vanished
with the loss of daylight. Wheels took a breath and skated
harder. He knew he was pushing both speed limit and energy reserves—why hadn't he eaten more? His roommates
were always teasing him about what he consumed, and
how much. . . .

Suddenly there was a man lying in the road—!

Wheels rode right over him. It was much like the impact on a suburban speed bump . . . if the bump squished
like a human body.

And it *hurt*. Calloused as they were, his wheels were
essentially bare hands and feet. Hitting that body was
like stubbing your toe on a curb.

He lost traction, lost control, skidding and sliding like

a drunk on an icy sidewalk until he hit a left turn a hundred yards farther up the highway—

And slammed into a ditch backed by trees.

The impact flattened his nose. He had not felt such pain since the time—pre–wild card—that Tariq had punched him for stealing a candy bar.

He was so stunned he wasn't sure how long he sat there, head down, rear high, leaning to his right. With darkness, it was impossible for him to measure time. Had it been a few seconds? Minutes?

He sure hoped it wasn't an hour.

Extricating himself from the ditch took patience. He was like a football player with a cracked rib: every attempted movement was painful.

Eventually, however, he had himself upright . . . and had used his good left front "hand" to push himself out of the ditch far enough to let his back "feet" find traction.

It was only when he was finally upright, on the highway surface, that he realized he had lost one of the containers he carried. He couldn't see it anywhere; even if he could, he was not capable of picking it up and replacing it.

It was like losing a tooth—but likely to be far more painful, once he met his customers.

Well, Wheels had lost items before . . . had been beaten and otherwise mistreated. But he knew it was better to show up with nineteen of twenty items than to try to avoid the confrontation completely.

There was another matter, however.

Slowly, painfully, Wheels skated a dozen yards back down the highway, to where he had run over the body . . . there was little he could do to help the victim, assuming he lived. And now time was truly critical.

But Wheels had been maltreated so many times in his short life. He couldn't bear to just . . . skate away—

Suddenly there were lights far to the south . . . another vehicle!

Wheels did not want to answer questions, nor did he want to be seen anywhere near a body in the middle of a road.

He turned and slip-skated into the rainy night.

Those About to Die . . .

by David Anthony Durham

Part One

MARCUS FLUNG ASIDE THE manhole cover. He pulled himself partway through and leaned back to check his cell phone. There. Finally. He had bars again! It wasn't the only problem with living in the tunnels and sewers below Jokertown, but the fact that cell phone service was spotty was one of the most annoying.

One voice mail. One text.

The message was from a girl who had been sweating him. He didn't know why he'd ever given her his phone number. She was a nat. Kind of average looking, with flat blond hair and too much smile for her face. She had approached him at Drakes in the Bowery last week. Grabbing his arm, she admitted out of nowhere that she had a snake fetish. "I just love serpents. Venomous ones the most." She had made him horny, but not exactly in a good way.

He pressed delete.

The text was from Father Squid. Marcus smiled. It always amused him to imagine the good father texting. It couldn't have been easy for him to hit the little buttons, considering that his fingers had suckers all over them. The text read: RMBR PRCNT. 5PM.

"I'll be there," Marcus said. "Not that it's going to do any good."

Marcus liked the priest well enough, but the old guy tended to get worked up about things. He'd roped Marcus into helping him look for so-called missing jokers. A few days into the search, Marcus was beginning to feel like there wasn't anything to it. Sure, some guys had gone awol, but they weren't the sort of guys anyone was too upset to see vanish. Why the priest cared so much Marcus couldn't fathom.

Flipping the phone shut and slipping it into his chest pocket, Marcus rose out of the sewer hole. He was normal enough from the waist up. A young African-American man, well built, with muscles that cut distinct lines beneath his fitted T-shirt. Hair trimmed nice, like someone who cared about their look, thick gold loops in his ears. Below the waist, however, he was one long stretch of scaled serpentine muscle, ringed down the twenty feet of tapering length to his tail. His garish yellow and red and black rings flexed in a hypnotic fashion as he carved a weaving course forward.

He didn't stay earthbound long. He surged up into a narrow gap at the alley mouth, curving from one brick wall to the other, creating a weave of tension between the two. Once out of the shadows of Jokertown's urban canyon lands, the spring sun shone down. The heat of it poured power into Marcus's tail. He pulled his shades out and slipped them on. He knew he looked fly. A couple years ago he thought his life was over. Now, things looked and felt a whole lot different.

As he skimmed along the edge of a roof, a voice called up from the street below. "IBT! Hey, IBT!"

Marcus peered down at a plump woman in a black T-shirt.

"I'm your number one fan, baby. Check it." She directed two stubby fingers at her chest. The bright pink letters IBT stretched taut across her T-shirt. She clearly had more than two breasts pressing against the fabric.

The guy beside her jabbed toward him with a finger. "You da man, T!" he said, stomping the ground with an oversized foot.

Marcus waved. He peeled back from the edge and carried on. "You da man, T," he mimicked. "What's the deal with shortening everything?" he grumbled aloud. "'T' means he's calling me Tongue but being too lazy to even say the whole word. The name is Infamous Black Tongue," he announced to the sky, then thought, *And IBT's all right, I guess, if you're in a rush.*

He found it a little strange that it wasn't his tail that gave him his moniker, but he had gotten a lot of early press for the concussive power of his tongue to deliver venom. Made an impression, apparently.

That reminded him of something.

He cut away from his intended route long enough to perch looking down on the graffiti-scarred wall of a building facing an abandoned lot-cum-urban garden. The wall had been repainted in one massive mural, a tribute to Oddity, whose cloaked and masked shape dominated the scene. IBT featured in it, too. Down by the far end, he rose up on powerful coils, half engulfed by licks of flame. One hand stretched out toward Oddity to accept the keys the vigilante legends were offering him. The other hand was smashing the dirty cop Lu Long across his dragon snout.

Marcus cocked his head. Squinted. They'd done some good work since last he saw it. They had his tail down pretty well. The color pattern of his stripes was mixed up, but he doubted anybody but himself would notice. The only thing he didn't really like was his face. He looked too angry, too full of teeth-gritting rage. Father

Squid had warned him that when he became a public figure his image wouldn't be his own anymore. Here was proof, sprayed large.

♣

He hit the street just down from the precinct. In the half block he nodded in response to several greetings, received an overly enthusiastic high five from a lobster-like claw, and autographed a furry little boy's Yankees baseball cap. He tried to protest that he was an Orioles fan, and not a baseball player in any event. The boy was insistent, though.

Father Squid waited for him on the precinct steps. Though it was warm, the tall, broad-shouldered priest wore his thick robes, as usual. He stood with his hands tented together on his chest, as if in prayer. He almost looked tranquil, except for the way his fingers tapped out his impatience. "Have you any news, son?"

Marcus shook his head.

"No sightings?"

"Nope."

The priest leaned close, the scent of him salty and fishy. The tentacles that dangled from his face seemed to stretch toward Marcus, as if each of them was keen to touch good news. "What about that abandoned apartment?"

"I checked it out. No sign of Wartcake."

"Don't call him that. Simon Clarke is the name his parents gave him."

Marcus shrugged. "I know, but everybody calls him Wartcake. When I ask about Simon Clarke nobody knows who I'm talking about. So I always have to say Wartcake, and then they go, 'Oh, Wartcake, why didn't you say that in the first place?'" He met the priest's large, dark eyes. "I'm just saying."

Motion inside the precinct didn't exactly freeze when

Marcus and Father Squid entered, but a hush fell across the room. One after another, pairs of eyes found Marcus and followed his progress toward the captain's office. Officer Napperson glared at him from behind his desk, looking like he was wishing him dead with just the force of his eyes. Another guy in uniform put his hand on his pistol, fingering the grip.

Father Squid strode with lumbering determination. Marcus kept his eyes on the priest's back. He tried to keep his slither cool, but the scrutiny made him nervous. He couldn't figure the cops out. Most of them treated him like a criminal they were itching to bust for something. That didn't stop them from using him, though. Officer Tang once gave him a tip about a guy the cops couldn't touch, some politician's brother who liked getting rough with joker hookers. Marcus had caught up with him one night and given him the scare of his life, enough to keep him out of Jokertown for good. He'd caught, venom tagged, and gift wrapped three perps who had been sparkling with Tinkerbill's pink aura. Ironic, considering that he'd spent a long evening tinkling like a fairy himself.

He'd even played dominoes in the park with Beastie a few Sundays.

None of that changed the chilly reception at the moment.

Deputy Inspector Thomas Jan Maseryk sat at his desk, head tilted down as he studied a stack of reports. He lined through something with a red pen, wrote a note.

Father Squid knocked on the doorjamb.

Without looking up, Maseryk said, "Hello, Father. The way you waft the scent of the seashore makes me hungry for cotton candy and foot-long hot dogs."

"There are two more missing," Father Squid said. "Two more, Captain. Do the disappearances merit your attention yet? If not, how many must vanish before you take notice?"

"We take all complaints serious—"

"You've yet to grasp that something is truly amiss here. Shall I name the vanished for you?"

The deputy inspector plucked up the page and deposited it in the tray at the corner of his desk. Exhaling, he leaned back and stretched. His deeply lined face was stern, his graying hair trimmed with military precision. "If you have anything to add to what you offered last time, see Detective Mc—"

"Khaled Mohamed," Father Squid cut in. He counted them on his suckered fingers. "Timepiece. Simon Clarke. Gregor. John the Pharaoh. These are not prominent people. They're loners, ruffians, users, abusers. All of them male. They may not be the pillars of our community, but they're still God's children. Maseryk, I won't allow you to ignore them."

The captain's face could've been carved in stone. "Unless someone made you mayor while I wasn't looking, I'll ask you to refrain from threatening me. As I said, Detective McTate will be—"

"I want a commitment from you personally."

"My work is my word." Peering around the priest, the deputy inspector nudged his chin at Marcus. "What's he got to do with all of this?"

"Marcus has been doing the work that the department hasn't. He's been combing the streets, day and night, looking for the missing, asking questions, trying to piece together some explanation."

"And?" Maseryk asked.

"I haven't found anything yet."

"Wonder why that is?" Maseryk ran his eyes over the reports again, as if bored of the conversation. "Maybe it's because a few drifters and grifters and petty criminals going missing is as everyday as apple pie. The fact these guys are gone isn't exactly a hardship for the community." He shot a hand up to stop Father Squid's response. "I'm not saying we're ignoring it. Just that there may be nothing to this. You want our full attention? Bring us something real. Some solid proof that anything at all is going on here. Without that, you're on a back burner. Good day, gentlemen."

♠

Marcus wasn't exactly an adventurous eater, but the scent wafting from the Elephant Royale got his long stomach grumbling. The sprawling restaurant featured outdoor seating, which relieved Marcus. More space for the tail.

The owner, a Thai man named Chakri, greeted Father Squid with a wide grin and flurry of back patting. A slim man dressed smartly, the only sign of the virus in him were his eyes. They were two or three times larger than normal. Round and expressive, they sparkled a deep green, with flecks of gold that reflected the sunlight.

"You've had success with your search?" Chakri asked, as he seated the two jokers at one of the curbside tables.

"I'm afraid not," Father Squid said. "We've been on our own. Very little help from the police. We will continue our efforts, though."

Marcus curled his tail under him, trying to keep the tip of it out of the way of passersby.

"You a good man, Father," Chakri said. "I do this: I tell my people to keep a lookout. Deliverymen. Grocers. Shippers. They're out early, up late. They see something they tell me. I tell you."

"Thank you, Chakri," Father Squid said. "That could be very helpful."

"No bother. Now . . ." He blinked his large eyes, changing their color from green to vibrant crimson. "What would these good men like to eat?"

Having no idea, Marcus let the priest order for him. Soon, the two of them sipped large glasses of amazingly sweet tea. Marcus tentatively tried one of the fish cake appetizers. They didn't look like much, but man they were good!

Father Squid said, "For a long time I couldn't eat Thai food. Reminded me too much of . . ." He paused and cleared his throat. "Of things I didn't want to remember. That's before I met Chakri. His kind, generous nature is a balm. As is his cooking."

Marcus plucked up another fish cake. "You fought in Vietnam, didn't you? What was it like?"

Father Squid blew a long breath through the tentacles around his mouth. "It's not something I discuss. War is madness, Marcus. It takes men and makes them animals. Pray you never see it yourself."

Typical old guy thing to say, Marcus thought. Why did people who had experienced all sorts of wild stuff—war, drugs, crazy sex—always end up saying others shouldn't experience the same things themselves?

Marcus's cell phone vibrated like a rattlesnake's tail in his chest pocket. He glanced at it. "I should probably take this."

Father Squid motioned for him to do so.

"IBT, my man!"

Slate Carter. Talent agent. Marcus had never seen him, but he had to be white. No black guy would butcher street slang with such gusto.

"Waz up, G? You got that demo for me?"

Looking slightly embarrassed, Marcus twisted away from the table. "Hi, Slate. Um . . . no, it's not ready yet. I'm not sure it's such a good idea any—"

"Don't blaze out, bro! I explained it all to you already. You got the look, the initials, the street cred, the vigilante backstory. You even beat down a crooked cop! That's our first video, right there."

"But—"

"You know what I've done for NCMF, right?"

"Yeah," Marcus admitted. Of course he knew. Slate never failed to mention his most famous client.

NCMF was a rapping joker who happened to be the spitting image of an extinct early humanoid known as *Paranthropus boisei*. Nutcracker Man. Dude could drop some serious rhymes. His latest video was a concert reel, him stomping around the stage before a frenzied crowd, long arms pumping and swiping. The crowd would ask, "What's your name?" He would answer, "Nutcracker, Motherfucker!" His rapping style was all natural flow. It never sounded like he was rapping. He was just talking, cursing, shouting. Somehow it all came out fast and funky. "NCMF but I don't crack nuts! I crack butts. That's right, I crack butts. I tear them open like I'm going extinct!" He proceeded to simulate his butt-cracking prowess with the backsides of a number of dancers. "I crack butts!"

"You and I are gonna blow that away," Slate promised. "You gonna explode like Jiffy Pop! Shoot me that demo and we'll make it happen. You feel me?"

Marcus did. He was a twenty-year-old virgin, after all. Visions of bottles of Krug spurting fizz over bikini-clad dancers, SUVs bouncing and chants of "Gz Up, Hoes Down" . . . well, such things did have a certain appeal. He had conceded only one problem. A big one. He'd just never managed to actually say it to Slate.

Snapping his phone closed, Marcus muttered a curse.

Father Squid asked, with a raised eyebrow, "Something amiss?"

"That was an agent."

"What sort of agent?"

"Talent. He represents musicians. Rappers mostly. He reps Nutcracker M—" Marcus caught himself. "Well, that . . . guy, with that song. You might've heard it."

Father Squid frowned. "That one . . ."

"Anyway, Slate is legit. He thinks I could be a rap star. Blow up like . . . Jiffy Pop."

"I didn't know you were a musician."

"Neither did I." Marcus cut his eyes up at the priest's

face, and then took a sip of his iced tea. "I mean, I'm not. Slate keeps asking for a demo, but . . . I can't rap. I tried. I got videos on my cell phone, but, man . . . I suck."

"I can't say that I'm disappointed to hear that."

"He's just after me 'cause I got a tight image, you know?"

"You have a measure of fame. With it comes responsibility. You understand that, right?"

"Yeah, you talk about it all the time."

The father dropped one of his heavy hands on Marcus's shoulder, the suckers on his palm squeezing. "I remind you because I care. Because I see a life of great promise ahead of you. I doubt very much that rapping would be fulfilling your potential. Marcus, if your card hadn't turned, where would you be now?"

"In college, I guess."

"Then you should be there now. The fact that you're a joker need not change that."

Marcus shifted uncomfortably. He couldn't imagine slithering across the quad of some campus, all the nat students staring at his tail. It might have been his future once, but college didn't seem possible anymore.

"Perhaps we can use your celebrity status for something other than making vulgar music," Father Squid said. "And you can do something other than dispensing vigilante justice. You do much good. I won't deny that. But where is the line? What happens when you err? When you hurt an innocent by mistake? What happens if you lose the bits of yourself that are kinder than your fists and muscles?"

The main dishes arrived.

The priest stuffed a napkin under his tentacled chin. After thanking the waitress, he continued, "Your life need not be defined only by the physical abilities the wild card has given you. That's why I'm going to set up a college fund in your honor. I think quite a few people would be willing to contribute to that."

Marcus hid the wave of emotion that rolled over him by digging in to his curry dish. Part of it was fear. Fear of wanting to strive for something that nats strove for. Fear of failing, of all the eyes that would watch him, critical and cold. Part of it was surprise that anyone would want to invest in his future that way. His parents didn't. Nobody in his old life did.

Father Squid chuckled. "I should have warned you it was spicy."

"Yeah," Marcus said, wiping at the moisture in his eyes, "spicy. It's almost got me crying."

The Big Bleed

Part Two

"DID THAT HURT?"

Jamal Norwood stared in pain and horror at the wound on his left forearm. Pain because, yes, it hurt to have the extra-large needle jabbed into his arm, to feel the blood being sucked into the giant, toy-like syringe. Even the withdrawal was slow and jagged. What, this guy couldn't have used a new needle? Or a small one?

"Yes!" Jamal couldn't help sounding surprised at his frank answer, and a bit ashamed of himself. The grunting, high-pitched squeal hardly matched the image of a buff former movie stuntman turned SCARE agent.

The doctor, a centaur in a lab coat, frowned. "Sorry," he said. His name was Finn and he came highly recommended, not that Jamal had done much in the way of due diligence. He had needed a quick, quiet consult . . . and the Jokertown Clinic seemed to be the best place.

Now, of course, with the crude, industrial-sized instruments, Jamal was revising his opinion. "It's not your fault, Doctor," he said, rubbing his arm. No, it was entirely Jamal's problem. Hence the terror: he was Stuntman! His whole ace power was bouncing back from damage that would have severely injured, or killed, another human being, nat, ace, or joker.

And quickly! Being dropped from a forty-story building and flattened? Stuntman would bounce back within hours.

In past experience, a pinprick would have closed as soon as the needle point touched his skin. In fact, Jamal couldn't remember the last time he'd had blood taken.

Or needed to.

"Hold on to this while I get something better," Dr. Finn said, placing a cotton ball on the wound and closing Jamal's arm on it.

Jamal wanted to tell the man no, no need.

But there was need: it felt as though his blood was gushing . . . it felt as though the cotton ball had already been soaked through.

What the hell was happening?

♦

The spring of 2012 had been one of the warmest in New York history. When Jamal and the rest of the SCARE team arrived in late March for the presidential primary, they had expected a typical spring: cold, raw days interspersed with warm ones, rain, trees beginning to bloom.

Well, they found the rain, that was certain.

But the weather had been tropical . . . high temperatures, equally high humidity, and rain every day. New York streets, never in great shape in good years, were transformed into a collection of terrifying potholes and cracked pavement.

Jamal's immediate boss, Bathsheeba Fox, also known as the Midnight Angel, was a good Christian belle whose default setting was to accept "God's will" when it came to fouled-up situations. Jamal suspected that Sheeba felt glorified by the opportunity to protect the Holy Roller, the Reverend Thaddeus Wintergreen—the first ace to run for the presidency—from the increasing numbers of people who (in Jamal's opinion) quite understandably wanted this Mississippi shithead dead. Sheeba would gladly have called down her personal Sword of the Lord on any member of the SCARE task force who dared to offer a discouraging word. . . .

Yet even She Who Must Be Obeyed had stood in the rain yesterday, her signature leather outfit showing cracks from wear, her jet-black mane a sodden, tied-up mess, her minimal makeup smeared, as she looked up at the sky and said, "You know, this kind of sucks." Which summed up the whole New York tour . . . bad weather leading to ill temper all around. SCARE had assigned Jamal and Sheeba to provide coverage for Wintergreen. It didn't matter that the Roller had zero chance of winning—Senators Obama and Lieberman and Attorney General Rodham were divvying up the delegates there. Known to millions from *American Hero* (that goddamn show again!), the Roller was drawing huge crowds wherever he went, and a goodly percentage of his fans resided on Homeland Security, Secret Service, and SCARE watch lists.

The Holy Roller detail had been a death march of long hours spent in grim factory gates, high school gymnasia, and an amazing number of cracker churches—more in the state of New York than Jamal would have believed. Each event required the SCARE team to engage in tedious "interfaces" with local police and sheriffs, plus the endless interviews, follow-ups, crowd scans.

It could have been worse, Jamal thought: he could have been assigned to cover one of the Republican candidates, but with Romney running away with the contest, SCARE's very own Mormon, Nephi Callendar, had come out of retirement to provide "interface" with that campaign—sparing Jamal Norwood and the others.

Even though they'd avoided involvement with the Republicans, a greater challenge loomed: the Liberty Party and its national standard-bearer, Duncan Towers, a blow-dried blowhard who made the Roller seem rational. So far Towers had been protected by the Secret Service and his own personal security force, but with the Dems moving on to California and what might yet prove to be a brokered convention, Sheeba's team had been ordered to stay in New York to provide "advance" work for Towers and Liberty.

Jamal devoutly hoped that the assignment would be a short one. He had joined SCARE because he was bored with Hollywood and determined to rehabilitate himself after the debacle of the first season of *American Hero*. What better way than to fight terrorists in the Middle East?

And that had been satisfying. But it was now five years in the past. . . .

Until the morning of May 8, 2012, he had a firm plan to resign from SCARE the day after the November election. He wanted to make more money; he wanted to enjoy his work again. (A friend had sent him a script titled *I Witness* that might work for television.) Jamal didn't particularly want to become the sole male lead of an action-adventure network series; that was a good way to make a lot of money and ruin your life. Nevertheless, going back to Hollywood and being thrown off tall buildings was a step up from a Sunday-night town meeting in Albany. And *I Witness* might wind up on cable . . . less money, but fewer episodes. The biggest lure was that going back to Hollywood meant he could rebuild his relationship with Julia—

"Any ideas on what this might be?"

Finn shrugged. "Joker medicine is still the Wild West." Jamal let the joker reference go uncorrected. "There's no reason to believe it's anything . . . dire at the moment."

"Wow, Doc, way to reassure a brother."

The words obviously stung. "Sorry," he said. "It's just . . ."

"We don't get a lot of aces in a place like this," Jamal

said, sliding off the table. "And at these prices, no wonder." The doc had obviously never heard the old wheeze.
Or maybe he was just freaked out by the unique nature
of Jamal's problem.

Either way, it was time to get out of here.

As a special agent for SCARE, Jamal could have taken
his problem to a facility higher up the scale than the
Jokertown Clinic. Two things argued against that move,
however: a visit to, say, Columbia Medical or Johns Hopkins or especially the New Mexico Institute would have
surely come to the attention of Sheeba and the higher-
ups at SCARE. And Jamal Norwood wasn't eager for
that.

Besides, Doc Finn and the Jokertown Clinic had more
experience dealing with wild card–related matters than
anyone on the planet. They were likely Jamal's best bet
to find out what was wrong with him.

He had just received a promise from Finn for a follow-
up report within forty-eight hours when his phone
beeped. Sheeba the Midnight Angel herself. "Jamal," she
said, her Southern accent and perpetual air of exaspera-
tion stretching two syllables to three, "where are you?"

"A personal errand," he snapped. "Does it make any
difference why I'm off duty for an hour? If you need me
somewhere, now, I'm on my way."

"Yeah, well . . . we have a DHS incident in New Jersey.
Some kind of toxic spill."

"Why is that our mission?"

"They don't tell me why, Jamal, they just tell me. DHS
is shorthanded today. Tell me where you are and we'll
pick you up on the way."

He improvised. He was still largely unable to visual-
ize lower Manhattan—had they been uptown, say,
Seventy-second Street, it would have been easier. But

here? "Uh, corner of Essex and Delancey," he said, naming the only two major streets he knew.

"See you in ten minutes," Sheeba said.

Jamal grinned. It wouldn't be ten minutes. The Midnight Angel's metabolism ran hot, requiring at least half a dozen meals every day. (What would it be like when she hit menopause? he wondered. Would she slow down? Or would she blow up like a fat tick?) The moment she hit the street, she would see some food cart, and that would add ten minutes to the trip. And beat hell out of Sheeba's per diem.

Which would allow Jamal Norwood to find the corner of Delancey and Essex.

Jamal liked to run, as long as he was in gym gear, wearing sneakers and on grass or at the very least a track. Running down a hard and broken Manhattan sidewalk in suit and dress shoes was not only far from his idea of decent exercise, it was too damned slow, especially with the afternoon crowds.

It was also too damned public. He caught a startled double take of recognition on at least two faces, and heard one construction worker hollering, "Yo, Stuntman!"

He pretended not to notice. He kept hoping that his exposure on *American Hero* would fade. No luck, alas.

It took him thirteen minutes to reach the corner of Essex and Delancey from the Jokertown Clinic. And when he did—

He was on the northeast corner, about to cross with the light, when something flashed in his peripheral vision. A battered white van made a hard left headed south, so close to the corner that Jamal and the other pedestrians could feel the slipstream. "Shit goddammit!" a young man shouted.

Jamal glanced at him—a mistake. What he saw was an

African-American joker, his upper half human-shaped, his nether regions more appropriate to a giant snake . . . if a giant snake adorned itself with rings of yellow, red, and black.

The social protocols required Jamal to say something. "Hey."

He hoped to disengage at that point, but it was too late. "Hey, you're Stuntman!"

Busted for the second time in a few minutes. *American Hero* had fattened Jamal's bank account, undeniably a good sign, and had led to his meeting Julia, a jury-is-still-out sign, but in most other ways had proved to be a disaster.

Especially when it came to anonymity. Working in Hollywood had exposed Jamal Norwood to the perks and the price of fame, and it had quickly become obvious that the price far outweighed the perks. "Guilty."

"Marcus!" the kid said, indicating himself. "What are you doing here, man?"

"Just . . . going from point A to point B." This joker wasn't likely to be satisfied with that, but it was all Jamal was offering. Maybe an autograph, if really pressed.

"Oh, wait," the kid said. "Yo, Father!"

Christ, now what? Jamal had barely formulated the thought when Father Squid appeared out of the crowd. Jamal realized that, in addition to cooking food and auto exhaust, he had been smelling the sea. Father Squid was the source: big, tentacle-faced, wearing a black cassock, he also reeked of brine. The good father turned to Jamal. "Stuntman himself! What are you doing here? Thought you were working as a secret agent or something."

"Something like that," Jamal said. "Protection for candidates."

The priest laughed long and loud. "Shielding the Holy Roller! What a task that must be!"

"Maybe that's why they don't know shit about anything going on in the streets," Marcus said.

"Charity, Marcus," the priest said.

Jamal was annoyed. "What's he talking about?"

One of Squid's tentacles uncurled in the direction of the nearest telephone pole. In addition to the usual long-past concert and job postings, the pole held three different homemade posters, the most prominent showing a joker named John the Pharaoh under the heading, *Have you seen him? Missing since May 1!*

"What's going on?" Jamal said.

"A bunch of jokers have disappeared," Marcus said. "I can't believe SCARE doesn't know about this."

"SCARE might," Jamal said. "My *team* doesn't."

"That sucks," Marcus said.

Squid placed a calming tentacle on Marcus's shoulder. "The local police aren't stepping up. We can hardly expect the Feds to do what Fort Freak won't."

"How many have there been?" Jamal said. After five years with SCARE, he was finding it easy to slip into an investigative role.

"At least half a dozen," Father Squid said.

"That's a big number," Jamal said, feeling alarmed. SCARE should know about this—

Suddenly Marcus started. "Who's that?"

A black Ford Explorer pulled up across the street. Jamal's phone buzzed.

"My team." He turned to the priest. "I'll make sure someone looks into this."

"You can reach me at Our Lady of Perpetual Misery."

"I know the place." As he turned to cross the street, he hoped he had gotten away without making too many promises. Squid and Marcus made him nervous.

He would not have believed that the sight of a black Ford Explorer with the Midnight Angel in the front seat would ever have made him happy.

♣ ♦ ♠ ♥

Galahad in Blue

by Melinda M. Snodgrass

Part One

OFFICER FRANCIS XAVIER BLACK—known to his fellow officers as Franny—came whistling through the doors of New York's 5th Precinct ready to defend truth, justice, and the American Way in Jokertown. Only to be viciously elbowed by Bugeye Bronkowski.

The blow was so hard and so unexpected that it sent Franny stumbling into the chairs lining the walls of the waiting room. Mrs. Mallory reached up and stopped his tumble before he landed in her lap. Louise Mallory was a diminutive woman whose hulking joker son Davy ran with the Demon Princes. But Davy wasn't too bright, and he certainly wasn't very lucky. He was constantly getting arrested.

Franny righted himself and looked at Sergeant Homer Taylor, currently manning the front desk. But Wingman didn't say a word. Bugeye stomped through the gate and back into the precinct. "What's up his ass?" Franny asked Homer.

Wingman gave his drooping wings a shake that wouldn't have looked out of place on a dying bat. "Couldn't say,"

he said, in tones that indicated he knew exactly what
had precipitated the assault.

Franny let it go and turned back to his rescuer. "Thank
you, Mrs. Mallory, sorry I . . . stumbled. Here to bail out
Davy?"

"Yes, that boy just keeps getting into hijinks."

"He does that."

"CO wants to see you in his office," Wingman grunted.

It was never a good thing when a patrolman was called
into the brass's office. Franny's stomach became a small,
hard knot against his spine. He wished he hadn't eaten
such a big breakfast.

As he moved through the bullpen Franny became aware
of the eyes. Everyone was staring at him. There were a few
disgusted head shakes and several people looked pointedly away. *God, what have I done?*

Beastie, all seven feet of him, fur, horns, and claws,
stumped up to him, and laid a hand on Franny's shoulder. The brown eyes gazing down at him were sorrowful
and sympathetic. "Oh, Franny, dude."

Nothing else was forthcoming. Beastie mooched on.
Franny made his way to Deputy Inspector Maseryk's
office. At his knock the nat yelled a *come in*. Franny
obeyed.

"Sir."

"Sit down, Black."

Franny took the proffered chair, but found himself
perching on the edge as if preparing for flight.

"You took your lieutenant's exam."

"Yes, sir, I know I'm not technically eligible to be promoted, but I figured I could get in some practice."

"Well, you aced the damn thing." Maseryk's tone
didn't make it sound like a compliment.

"Good?" Franny said diffidently. When there was
no response he added an equally uncertain, "Thank
you?"

"The damn brass down at One Police Plaza have decided in their infinite wisdom to promote you early."

Franny sank against the back of the chair. It was all becoming horribly clear. This was why Bugeye had hit him. Resentment curdled his gut—how was it apparently everybody in the precinct had known about this before *he* did? He gave voice to none of that however. "That seems . . . ill advised," he managed.

"To put it mildly."

"So, why—"

"Because we've been taking a beating over the corruption that's been uncovered in the two-oh."

"Oh."

"The damn press just won't let up so the brass decided to give them a new narrative. All about *famous captain's son steps up*." His tone underscored the irony. "But a story about a flatfoot isn't news. A promotion, that's news . . . and fortunately the media vultures all have ADD. They'll stop writing about the two-oh and write about *you* until another scandal comes along."

Franny's first impulse was to refuse, to not be a hand puppet for the Puzzle Palace, as the plaza was sometimes called. Balanced against that was the drive to live up to his father's memory. To be not just a good cop, but maybe a great one. He had always wanted to make detective. His work thus far didn't involve much investigation. It involved a lot of intimidation and running after people. Plainclothes, no more walking a beat; that's when he realized he'd miss his beat and the people who depended on him—Mr. Wiley who ran the mask and cloak shop, Tina who managed the Starbucks, Jeff the bellman at the Jokertown Hyatt who spent most of his day out front carrying luggage and parking cars so he watched the world go by, and often reported what he saw to Bill and Franny.

Bill! Shit! How would his partner react to this?

He also had to acknowledge that he was ambitious. *You aced it.* The captain's words danced through his mind. Damn right he had. He'd gone to law school, passed the bar on the first try. No, he couldn't refuse. Franny stood and held out his hand. "Thank you, sir. I'm honored. I'll try to live up to your expectations."

"You've already failed in that regard. I thought you'd have the good sense to turn it down." Maseryk shuffled through papers. "Okay, I'm pairing you with Michael Stevens."

"But he's a nat too."

"I'm aware of that, but his partner just got transferred, and nobody else was willing to be broken up just to accommodate you. I'll fix it as soon as I can, but for right now you're with Stevens. Next, we've got a situation. Jokers have gone missing. Mostly loners, people without family or roots in the community. I think it's a tempest in a teapot. People like that drop off the radar all the time, but Father Squid is busting my ass over it, and we don't need another media feeding frenzy. So, as of now you're in charge of the joker investigation."

"Is Michael going to work with me on that?"

"No, Michael has a real case to investigate. Go find your desk."

"Yes, sir. Should I go home and change?"

"I wouldn't if I were you. Wait until tomorrow to rub their noses in it."

Franny slunk out of the office. Before he found his desk and new partner he went to find his old partner. Bill would be expecting him to join him on patrol . . . or not. Maybe Bill had gotten the word like everybody else.

He found the big Chinese-American officer in the locker room. Bill clipped his nightstick onto his belt, and turned when he heard Franny's footsteps. They looked at each other, each waiting for the other to speak. Bill slammed the locker door, and headed for the door. "I won't be going out with you today," Franny said.

"I heard," Bill said in a high-pitched, squeaky voice, so at odds with his massive form.

Since no congratulation had been uttered, Franny had at least hoped for noncommittal. Instead there was ice edging Bill's words. "Look, I didn't ask for this."

"Didn't turn it down either."

"Would you?"

"No, but I've got eleven years in on the force, not two. I've taken the lieutenant's exam three times. But you get promoted, and you're not even one of us."

"Yeah, I'm a nat. Why don't you just say it?"

"Not that, you moron."

"What then?"

"You're not Chinese."

"What?" Franny said, not following the logic at all.

"We've got jokers in this station. We've got aces, but we're on the edge of Chinatown, and only two of us are ethnic Chinese, and only a handful of us speak Chinese. How are you going to investigate crimes in my neighborhood when you can't even speak the language?"

"Get a translator."

Bill snorted. "Yeah, that's gonna work real well."

"Look, Bill—" But the big man turned his back on Franny and walked out of the locker room.

Back in the bullpen, Franny located his desk. It backed up to another desk, which belonged to Michael Stevens. The cops at the station loved to gossip and leer about Stevens—two live-in girlfriends and ace daughter. *And I can't even get a date,* Franny thought. SlimJim McTate gave him an encouraging smile and handed him a file. "Here's the list of missing jokers."

Franny had just started to look through them when he became aware of someone staring at him. He looked up to find Apsara Na Chiangmai standing at the side of his desk, smiling down at him. Apsara was the file clerk for the precinct, and the most beautiful girl Franny had ever seen. Dark hair hung to her curvaceous ass, and her oval face had skin as smooth and perfect as old ivory. He'd tried to ask her out back when he first started work at the Five, only to be turned down. It had been done with charm and a smile, but it had still been a shutdown. Now here she was. She drew in a deep breath, preparing to speak, which thrust her amazing rack almost into his face. "Detective Black, I wanted to offer you my congratulations," she said in fluting tones.

"Ah . . . oh . . . thanks."

"Would you like to ask me out?"

"Ummmm . . ."

Ties That Bind

by Mary Anne Mohanraj

Part One

DETECTIVE MICHAEL STEVENS WALKED into the Joker-town precinct and paused, blasted by noise that didn't help his pounding head. It had been a shitty day even before he came into work. Michael had woken with a raging hard-on, but he'd somehow slept through his alarm. Both of his girlfriends were already up and dressed, and his daughter was up too and hollering for her breakfast, so there was no chance of persuading one of the women to come back to bed, even if he hadn't been late. And then Minal had gotten distracted by Isai pissing all over the kitchen floor, so the eggs had gotten overcooked, and if there was one thing Michael hated, it was dry eggs. Also, piss on his kitchen floor. Isai was supposedly done with potty training, but sometimes, she got distracted. He'd finally escaped the family drama and taken the subway to work, jammed between a guy covered in spikes and a woman who smelled like rotted meat. Michael had entered into the precinct with a sigh of relief, only to be greeted by this wave of noise slamming at him, like a steel spike jackhammering on his head.

Not a wild card–powered wave, just the normal morning frenzy at Fort Freak. What you'd expect in a station where a handful of underfunded cops tried their damnedest to keep the peace in an increasingly strange and difficult borough of New York City. Perched on the front desk, where she had no business being, Apsara leaned over, making sure that the desk sergeant had a full view of her generous assets. Hey, sweetheart. Got something for me? Her voice loud enough to carry over the noise. Darcy the meter maid was just leaving the room, thankfully—he didn't need to hear her ranting about law and order and a civil society again.

Sure, that was why Michael had become a cop, to protect and serve. In the deepest parts of his soul, that desire was what pulled him through his days, the need to be a great cop, to prove himself. He'd grown up watching his folks struggle just to make ends meet; he'd promised himself that someday he'd have a job that was more than just a way to put food on the table and clothes on your back. Michael had never loved school, but he'd gritted his teeth and plowed through. He'd spent late nights over his books at the scarred Formica table in his mother's kitchen, while she cooked bi bim bop and they waited for his dad to come home from his second job. Michael's folks had skipped vacations, skipped meals, even skipped Sunday church sometimes because they were embarrassed by their threadbare clothes. Clothes they hadn't replaced because the money had gone to pay for Michael's grammar school uniforms, his high school books, his college application fees.

He owed them so much that it stuck in his throat, love and gratitude tangled up with resentment. Michael had been determined to pay them back for it, and eventually he had, at least a bit. When he'd made detective, the pay bump had been enough that he could finally put the down payment on a condo for them, and help them out every month with the mortgage. He'd worked as hard as he could to rise above, to be better than everyone else—a better student, a better cop, and now, a better detective. Michael Stevens was determined to be the best damn cop on the force. But unlike Darcy, he didn't need to talk about it all the time.

The door banged open and a kid scuttled in, shrieking. Really shrieking, in a voice pitched three octaves above normal. The hammering in Michael's head escalated along with it, and he fought the urge to cover his ears with his hands. That wouldn't look professional, but damn, if someone didn't shut that kid up—oh, thank God. Beastie had him, and was covering that horrible mouth with one warm furry paw. There were days when Michael wondered why he didn't just walk away from all the crazy here. He was a nat—untouched by the virus, at least so far. After the success they'd had a few years ago in taking down the Demon Princes, he could have transferred to any other city he wanted, left the freaks and weirdos behind to protect normal citizens instead. Michael could have risen through the ranks, become a captain, maybe more. He'd thought about going to D.C., applying to join the CIA or SCARE. But in the end he'd chosen to stay in Jokertown.

Michael slipped a hand into his jacket pocket to reassure himself that it was still there—yes. The visible manifestation of his reason for staying. A small red velvet box, holding a bit of captured sparkle—two of them, in fact. One box with two rings, for the two women who drove him crazy on a nightly basis. They were the ones who held him here—one joker girlfriend, one ace, both of them happy to share him, which was perhaps the strangest of all the strangenesses in his life. Minal, with tiny nipples that covered her torso, front and back—she looked ordinary enough when dressed, and walking the street, she could pass for normal. But her wild card burned within her, and just a brush against her torso was enough to set her simmering. No wonder she'd been such a popular hooker, back when she'd made her living walking the streets. Any other woman would have been insanely jealous. But his girlfriend Kavitha just smiled and dragged Minal off to bed, sometimes inviting him along. Maybe it was her ace powers that made Kavitha so self-confident?

When she danced, her brilliant illusions turned real enough to walk on, real enough to fight with. They'd learned that the hard way, two years ago, when their daughter had been kidnapped by a Jokertown gang. Kavitha had been a pacifist—she still was, in most ways. She did work for the Committee on occasion now, always stipulating that she would only use her powers for peaceful endeavors. But Kavitha had fought like a tiger that day, when their daughter was at risk. Michael didn't know if being an ace had anything to do with her welcoming attitude toward Minal; he was just grateful. In another city, their family would have garnered way too much attention. In Jokertown, Minal was just one freak among thousands, and their threesome was unconventional, but more the kind of thing that got you harassed by your buddies, rather than got you fired.

Besides, where else would they raise their ace daughter? Where else could Isai fly free when she transformed into a giant creature with the body of a lion, the head of an eagle, and a wingspan wider than six parked cars? Cleveland? Last year, Isai had started kindergarten, and had become the public school's problem for seven straight hours of the day—and somehow, the school had coped, which was a minor miracle in itself. Michael didn't know how they'd manage otherwise, with Minal finally in culinary school, and Kavitha performing most nights and leaving town periodically for the Committee's bizarre projects.

Michael had never asked for so much strangeness in his life—he'd just wanted a great, normal life. Solid career, beautiful wife, a couple of kids and a house of his own. That would have been plenty for him. But having found love, twice, how could he walk away? He was lucky, as the guys at the precinct kept reminding him. Today was a stunning May day, the prettiest they'd seen in months. The perfect day for a proposal, the back of his brain whispered. Michael was a half-black, half-Korean tough guy who'd fought his way up from the wrong side of town; he could handle a proposal. The question was, could he handle two?

"Hey, sweetie—you forgot something!" Minal had come up behind him, was tapping him on the shoulder and handing him an insulated bag. He felt his heart thump hard, once, at her wicked grin. That grin wasn't going to cure his headache, but if Michael could get half an hour alone with her, he was sure Minal would be able to help him out. Sadly, that wasn't going to happen anytime soon. The inevitable chorus of hoots and catcalls rose from the guys (and some of the gals).

"Hey, baby!"

"What'd you bring for me?"

"Something hot and sweet, I bet!"

"I need something spicy!"

Usually Minal would banter back, but today she was already late for her class. She smiled at the gang, dropped a kiss on Michael's cheek, and then was out the door again. She let the battered wood slam shut behind her, leaving him to face the music alone.

Michael knew how to handle this. It'd been two years since he'd come out to his old partner and the rest of the precinct about the threesome; he had this down. "Aw, you guys are just jealous," he said loudly. That quieted them down, because it was true. Not only due to the sexy bi babe whose curvy body had just walked out the door, but also due to the incredible scents rising out of the little carrier. The insulation might keep the rice and curry warm, but it wasn't nearly strong enough to keep the scent of Indonesian *rendang padang* trapped inside the bag.

Slow-cooked beef, simmered in coriander, curry leaves,

ginger, cloves, lemongrass, coconut milk, and he wasn't sure what else, but he didn't care. Minal was taking a Southeast Asian class this semester, and Michael was grateful. Her curries were almost as good as his Korean mother's, and the rest of the precinct was jealous. Any cop knew that while it was nice to come home to some sweet loving after a long day, it was more important to keep your stomach well fed—that's what would keep you going when the night got long and crazy. Donuts could only carry a man so far.

Finally, his day was looking up.

He carried the food over to his desk, and almost dropped it when he saw Franny sitting across from him, at his partner Sally's desk. "Hi, Michael!" the kid said, his voice just a little too cheerful.

♠

Two minutes later, Michael was in the captain's office, wondering how hard he'd have to beg to fix this. "Captain, please. You have got to be kidding me? The kid?" Just minutes ago, life had seemed so good. He'd been happy enough to propose, for God's sake. He was finally making some progress on his smuggling case, and he had a smart, sexy partner to work with him. Last week, Sally had taken down a mugger with a sneaky Jiu-Jitsu move that might not be academy-approved, but which was nonetheless impressive. And even though she was tough as hammered nails, Sally was also willing to flirt with the nerdy art insurer if it would get them a lead for their case. She had been the perfect partner—and now she was gone, and Michael was about to be thoroughly screwed. And not in a good way.

Maseryk frowned. "This isn't your decision, Michael. And it's not up for debate. Sally deserved that promotion to One Police Plaza, and I'm sorry for the short notice, but they needed her on something urgent. We'll throw her a racket at the bar Friday night; you can say your good-byes then. I'm promoting Black to be her replacement." He shrugged. "The truth is, the brass uptown dictated his promotion, and I don't like it any more than you do. The kid doesn't know shit. I've sidelined him on a dead-end case; you focus on that art ring you and Sally were handling."

"But sir—" Michael knew he was pushing, but he couldn't just let it go.

But Maseryk was already turning away, back to the mound of papers on his desk. "Enough, Michael. End of story. You can shut the door on your way out."

Michael just barely managed not to slam the damn door. He came perilously close, though, shutting it with a solid thud.

"Whee-oh! I remember that sound." His father was in the hallway, up on a ladder, fixing a light and grinning down at him. "What crawled up your ass, son?"

God, not this too, not today. When would the old man retire? "Dad. I don't need this right now."

His father peered down at him through thick glasses. "You mad 'cause the kid got promoted?"

"You know?" Shit. It would've been nice if the CO had told him first, instead of informing his dad the janitor. The old man should just retire—he was old enough now that his dark skin stood out shockingly against the pure white of his bushy eyebrows.

"Son, you know how fast gossip moves through this place. Everybody knows, and I can tell you that no one is happy about it. Poor kid."

Michael snapped out, "He's jumping the queue. He's too young. He's a goddamned smart aleck who is completely full of himself."

His father cackled. "Reminds me of someone else I know."

"We are nothing alike." That would have come out

better if it hadn't sounded quite so whiny. Michael bit his tongue.

His father nodded serenely. "Yessir, whatever you say, sir. I know better than to argue with my superior officer."

There was nothing to say to that.

The old man continued, "When are you bringing those three pretty girls of yours over for dinner? I haven't seen my granddaughter in four whole days. Your mama was thinking Saturday would be nice. She's got plans for jambalaya, and she wants to teach Minnie the recipe."

Michael sighed. "Don't call her Minnie, Dad. You know that's not her name."

His father frowned. "I'll call her what I like; I'm old enough, and I've earned the right. She don't mind. When are you going to call her your wife, that's what I want to know. You ever gonna put rings on those gals' fingers?"

Not him too. It was bad enough listening to the voice in his own head. His parents had been harassing him to marry Kavitha, before Minal moved in—they'd been blessedly quiet on the subject for the past two years. But apparently, his grace period had ended. "I can't marry both of them, not legally." He wanted to, though. He was pretty sure.

The old man snorted. "Did I ask what you could do legally? Do you think we give a damn what the law says? Your mama is dying to throw a wedding for her only child, boy, and if you know what's good for you, you're not going to make her wait much longer." The old man hesitated, and then said, in a softer voice, "Her heart's been acting up again, you know."

Michael's own heart squeezed once, painfully. "I can't talk about this now, Dad." He had a case to solve. Now wasn't the time. He wasn't sure when it would be the right time. "We'll come for dinner, okay? Tell Mama." Maybe he'd propose this week; maybe he'd be bringing two fiancées to dinner on Saturday. Michael loved them, he did. But two wives? It wasn't the life he'd planned for.

His father shook his head. "All right. You be nice to that kid. The whole station's going to give him hell, he doesn't need to get it from his partner, too." Then he turned back to the light above their heads, leaving Michael to face the long walk back to his desk. No more Sally at the desk facing his; that was Francis Xavier Black's desk now.

Terrific.

The Big Bleed

Part Three

AFTER A TORTUROUS COMMUTE from Manhattan, Sheeba and Jamal had arrived at the spill site close to sundown, the worst possible time to conduct a visual investigation. *Too bad we aren't making a movie,* Jamal thought. It was the golden hour, that last bit of the day when directors and cinematographers preferred to film the kissing scene or something equally romantic.

Not that Stuntman had been involved in many such scenes. But he had frequently found his shooting days rearranged around the need to have the crew ready for golden hour. "Something funny happened here," Sheeba said, demonstrating her unfailing ability to state the obvious.

What was your first clue? Jamal wanted to ask, but didn't. Surely it couldn't have been the Warren County Emergency Services unit parked halfway onto the shoulder of the two-lane asphalt road, and the crime scene tape delineating two squares—one large, one small—in the ditch.

The drive from Manhattan had taken twice as long as it should have. Sheeba Who Must Be Obeyed had elected

to follow her Navstar, overruling the obsessive freak behind the wheel who kept insisting that it was taking them
around three sides of a square. "Couldn't we have booked
a helicopter?" Jamal said, only half joking.

"Unavailable," Sheeba snapped, meaning she had actually made the query.

The extra minutes they spent stuck in traffic allowed
Sheeba to recount—largely for Jamal's benefit—the flurry
of text messages, e-mailed maps, and other communications that resulted from one simple fact: sometime last
night a vehicle had gone off this lonely New Jersey highway and spilled a container of ammonium nitrate.

"Why did it take so long?" Jamal had asked, not, he
thought, unreasonably.

"No one found the container until noon today," Sheeba
said. Her voice suggested that there was something lacking in the moral fiber of the residents of Warren County,
New Jersey, that they would fail to note a container of
dangerous material by the side of one of their roads.

Feeling a bit like an actor in a bad action movie, Jamal
had felt compelled to persist: "And why are we chasing
this and not DHS?"

"One of the locals said the whole thing felt joker-like."

"Some kind of keen perception?" Jamal said. "The
smell, maybe—?"

"The crash site."

And so, yes, here they were, in the company of a pair
of Warren County hazardous materials types, and Deputy Sheriff Mitch Delpino, a tall, hunched nat around
forty who wore a gunslinger's mustache that clashed with
his old hippie manner.

"It appears a vehicle went off the road here," Delpino
said, spreading his hands and gesturing, as if the tracks
could possibly have been mistaken for anything else.

"And it should have wound up nose-first in that ditch,"
Sheeba said. "It's pretty deep. How do you suppose it got

out?" She turned to Delpino. "Any calls for tow trucks
out here last night or this morning?"

Delpino glanced at Jamal, as if to say, *you poor bastard, having to work with this*. "Yes, we checked with all
the services. No one got a call out here or anywhere near
here in the past forty-eight hours."

Jamal said, "Officer, assuming this truck was carrying
something illegal when it ran off the road, how likely is
it, do you think, that it would call a legitimate service
whose destination could be traced?"

Delpino allowed himself a smile so faint that only Jamal
could see it. "Quite unlikely."

Jamal turned away and let his eyes adjust again. There
was something odd about the tracks where they crossed
the mud. "Any insights into what kind of tires were on
this truck?" he said.

Delpino stepped forward like a grade schooler eager
to recite. "These are not tire tracks," he said. "They are
narrower than any commercial U.S. brand or any European one we know. And there's no tread."

"In fact, it looks as though they were thin and solid,
like wheels on a kids' wagon," Jamal said. "It does sort
of feel like a joker thing."

Ten yards off the road, its passage still obvious from
crushed vegetation, a yellow plastic barrel sat upright in
the weeds. "Was this how you found it?" Jamal said.

"It was on its side," Delpino said, which was a good
thing: neither haz-mat specialist seemed eager to talk. "It
hit and rolled. You can't see it from here, but there's a
small crack on one side. Some fluid spilled." He smiled.
"Which we were able to identify as ammonium nitrate,
which is why we called you. Well, DHS."

Sheeba reasserted command at that moment. "So
strange truck rips along, loses a barrel, and then goes off
the road? Seems wrong, somehow."

"How so?" Delpino said.

Sheeba's phone jingled. As she held up her finger, Jamal answered for her: "The logical sequence is, vehicle goes off the road first, spills its cargo . . . then gets out of ditch with no obvious help." She gestured at the crash site. "With all the rain, there would be tracks if another vehicle helped out the first one."

"So we have a mystery," Jamal said. "First step, though, is to secure that material."

"Where do you want it driven?" Delpino seemed eager to have this case off his plate as soon as possible.

"Let me check." Jamal reached for his phone. "They'll probably want us to cordon the place off. . . ."

Before he could make the call, however, Sheeba rejoined the conversation. "Get this," she said, clicking off her phone. "Highway 519 is already cordoned off between Bergen and Hackettstown. New Jersey Highway Patrol." Sheeba turned to Delpino. "What do you know about this?"

"Not a thing. Traffic here is light; the spill is minuscule. And we really don't have the authority—"

Jamal looked down the road. Several sets of headlights burned. "Looks like an accident scene." Christ, now he was stating the obvious. All these months with Sheeba must have affected him.

"What are the odds of two unrelated accidents at the same time on this stretch of road?" Sheeba asked. She turned to Delpino. "Do you know anything about this?"

"Not a thing. I got a call from dispatch just before noon and came straight here. Called in the haz-mat unit before one." Delpino hooked a thumb toward the haz-mat truck. "This is Warren County." He tilted an index finger toward the scene two hundred yards away. "One of those vehicles says 'New Jersey Highway Patrol.'"

"Shoot," Sheeba said, "not this again. Different jurisdictions."

Jamal said, "The bane of SCARE's existence. Wherever

we go, we have to make sure the local PD and the highway patrol and the sheriffs are all in the same loop . . ."

Sheeba finished for him. ". . . and they never are!"

"Why don't I go?" he said. It would be informative, and would get him away from Sheeba as her blood sugar drove her to more frequent rages. He chose to walk. The cars weren't that far, he needed the exercise, and it saved him from a pointless discussion about being sure to bring the Explorer back. Maybe Sheeba suspected his eagerness to drive away and never look back.

Walking also allowed him to show up more or less unannounced, without adding that big movie moment of the black Explorer arriving at a crime scene.

Which is clearly what this was: a New Jersey State Police prowler half blocked the road, its flashing cherries clearly visible in the twilight. (Even in bright sunlight, the SCARE team would have seen them from the truck spill site, except that there was a small hill between the two locations.) A coroner's van was next to it.

The yellow chalk figure in the middle of the highway told Jamal much of what he needed to know: they had found a body. And, from the apparent height and shape— not that a chalk outline was remotely reliable—some kind of joker.

As Jamal approached, he saw and felt eyes turning toward him, especially those belonging to one of the New Jersey cops, a tall guy with his right arm in a sling.

Stopping an appropriate distance away, he hauled out his shield. "Special Agent Norwood, SCARE." As if the black suit didn't give him away.

"Gallo," he said, clearly not happy with Jamal's presence. "What brings SCARE to New Jersey?"

Jamal jerked his head back up the highway. "We've got a crime scene. Ah, Federal issues. Controlled substances." He quickly described the crash and the cargo. "And this might explain one problem we've found."

"You think they're related?" Gallo's whole manner

suggested skepticism, but, then, he could barely see over the hill to the next site.

As patiently as possible, Jamal explained the mystery of the crash-spill sequence. Perhaps because he began to concentrate on crime scene matters, or possibly because he had already made it clear he didn't like a) Feds or b) aces or c) both, Gallo began to unbend. "We've got a DB here, male, joker approximately thirty years of age. Found here early this morning."

"Cause of death?"

"Now, that's an interesting question. First cut is, hit by a vehicle." Gallo nodded toward the coroner's unit. "But they say, not so fast. Indications are he was dead before that. Autopsy will tell us, I imagine."

"And the time?"

"That we've got: twenty hours ago, give or take a couple."

"But last night."

"No question."

"We don't have two crime scenes here. We have one in two parts."

"What do you want to do about it?"

Jamal thought about it. Have SCARE take it over? Their team numbered two and not only had to beg for any resources beyond an extra cell phone, but was at the mercy of DHS for its schedule: they would surely be detailed to a political event tomorrow. "Leave it where it is," he said. "We'll take custody of the ammonium nitrate. You figure out what happened with our dead joker." He reached for a business card and found one in the clip where he carried his driver's license and a single credit card.

Gallo took it, but didn't offer one of his own. Which was fine with Jamal. Then, possibly realizing that he had been less than helpful, he said, "Agent Norwood, you got any ideas what this might be?"

At that moment, rain began to fall.

"We get reports of wiretaps or signal intercepts about vital 'deliveries' about five times a week," Jamal said, wondering how long it would be before the gentle drops turned to a downpour. He could hardly expect Gallo to offer him a ride up the road. "They never amount to much."

"Until the day they do."

That sounded serious. "You heard anything?"

Gallo was shaking his head. "It is a little strange, though. Dead joker in the road, nasty shit spilled."

"Well, let us know if the autopsy turns up anything we need to know."

Gallo never turned back. Maybe he was eager to get in out of the rain, too.

Jamal retreated up the hill, back to the SCARE team. As he walked, he called Sheeba to report what he'd seen, trying to leave out Gallo's bored unhelpfulness. What else did he expect from the New Jersey State Police, anyway?

Naturally, Sheeba told him they were about to leave, could he hurry? Apparently coming to pick him up wasn't part of the plan. The instant he hung up and prepared to pick up his pace . . . with the Explorer and the Warren County team in sight . . . he suddenly felt weak, as if hit by a blindsided tackle.

He actually had to stop and bend over, trying to catch his breath. What the hell was happening to him? Blood loss, that was it. He had had blood taken—you were supposed to eat when that happened, or just take it easy.

The weak moment passed. It was only when he was feeling better and walking that he allowed himself to remember that the warning about weakness after blood work was for people who had been transfused . . . who had given a pint of their blood.

Not a few ccs.

♣ ♦ ♠ ♥

Cry Wolf

by David D. Levine

GARY GLITCH SCURRIED ACROSS rooftops, the evening air cool on his face as he bounded from one roof to the next across alleys and streets, unnoticed by the people below.

If anyone had seen Gary, they might think he was strange-looking even for a joker. Four feet tall, with skinny arms and legs and huge ears, he resembled an animated sock monkey more than a human being. And if they should happen to see him leap twenty or thirty feet, landing with a muted clang on a fire escape or access ladder and continuing without pause, they might really start to wonder just what sort of creature he was.

Gary tried hard to keep that from happening.

Tar paper, concrete, and shingles flew past beneath his boots as he made his way quickly uptown, heading for the ritzy residential neighborhood north of Houston Street. The pickings were usually pretty good there on a weekday night.

Reaching a fancy apartment building where he'd often had good luck, Gary scrambled up the fire escape to the roof, then quivered on the parapet, peering down into an air shaft. There was a lesbian couple here who could be counted on for a good show. Alas, tonight their window was dark and silent.

Three more of Gary's usual perches yielded nothing, even after many long minutes of watching and listening. Finally, frustrated, he decided to take a bit of a risk. Dashing four long blocks to an apartment building on St. Marks Place, Gary crept quietly down the downspout to a ledge near an open rear window.

Gary didn't really like this spot. There was only one place where he could perch and see into the room, and it was illuminated by a streetlight and in full view of a dozen nearby apartments. But the view was worth the risk: the Trio were in full flagrante delicto.

The man—black and lanky—rocked enthusiastically behind the raised ass of the skinny brown woman, whose face was buried between the thighs of the other woman. The one whose entire torso was covered with writhing pink nipples. All around the three of them whirled a nimbus of light, gold and orange and red. It pulsed in time with their gasps and moans. Gary's throat went dry and his own breathing quickened, matching the rhythm of the three on the bed.

Then a slithering crunch came from above. So unusual was the sound that Gary pulled his attention away from the Trio.

Gary's eyes literally popped out of his head, extending a good three inches, as he saw just what had interrupted him.

A huge black snake-man was racing down the fire escape toward him, well-muscled arms reaching out to snatch him from his ledge. Twenty or thirty feet of black-and-yellow-striped snake tail extended behind his human upper body.

Gary shrieked and scrabbled away, barely avoiding the snake-man's grasp. Fingers clinging to the gaps between bricks, he scampered right up the wall.

But the snake was nearly as fast. "You've peeped your last, peeper!" he called as he climbed, his colorful snake body doubling back on itself.

Just before the snake could snatch him from the wall, Gary reached the parapet of the roof and clambered over it. But a loose bit of metal on the parapet's flashing caught his foot and he went down, falling face-first onto the tar paper. He lay stunned, expecting the snake to catch up with him at any moment.

"Freeze!" came a new voice, echoing up from the alley. "IBT, what the fuck?"

And the snake did not arrive.

Hauling himself to his feet, Gary risked a glance down into the alley. The black man from the Trio, still naked and glistening with sweat, was leaning out of the window Gary had just vacated, training a handgun nearly as impressive as his God-given equipment on the snake-man.

The snake put his hands up as ordered. "I'm on *your* side, man! I was on patrol, and I saw *that* little fucker peeping in your window!" He pointed right at Gary.

The man turned his attention to Gary, followed by his gun. Their eyes met over the gunsight. But then both of them were distracted by a lightning-fast motion.

Taking advantage of Mr. Trio's momentary diversion, the snake-man launched himself into the air. A moment later his whole coiled body landed with a meaty thud on the roof.

"Gotcha!" he cried, lunging inescapably at Gary.

Gary shrieked and vanished.

◆

Back in his apartment, cartoonist Eddie Carmichael clutched his misshapen head and moaned. He preferred to bring his creations back to the apartment before erasing them; making them disappear where they were gave him a horrendous pain behind his eyes. But it was better than the alternative. If Gary had been killed—and the descending snake-man would certainly have smashed him to bits—Eddie would never be able to manifest him again.

Shivering with pain and adrenaline, Eddie took a Percocet and a sleeping pill and dragged himself into bed with his clothes on. But, despite the drugs, he lay awake for a long time.

He'd tried to quit peeping so many times. It was wrong and sick and twisted and disgusting, and someday it might get him into real trouble, but no matter how hard he tried he always started doing it again.

It was the only good thing the wild card virus had ever done for him.

The next morning Eddie was awakened by the bell of his cheap-ass landline telephone. "Hello?" he bleated, once he managed to get the receiver to his ear the right way around. The headache was still there.

"Eddie Carmichael?" A male voice, young and hesitant. "The artist?"

"Yeah . . ."

"This is Detective Black at the Fifth Precinct. We need a sketch artist right away. Are you available?"

"Uh, yeah." The response was automatic. As a freelance artist, he couldn't afford to turn down work, and forensic art paid well as contract assignments went. He hauled himself upright. It was ten minutes after eight in the morning. "I can be there by nine."

"Could you make it eight-thirty?"

"I'll do my best."

Eddie hung up the phone, then cursed with great sincerity as he hauled himself from the bed into his rolling desk chair, which he used to scoot himself to the bathroom.

Eddie's chair was the single most expensive thing in the whole apartment. It had seventeen different points of adjustment, and over the years he'd tweaked them all until the chair fit his twisted, asymmetrical body perfectly. It was the only place on Earth he could be truly comfortable.

The rest of the apartment, all three hundred and twenty square feet of it, was little more than an extension of the chair. He could roll from one side of it to the other with a good hard kick, all of the work surfaces and most of the storage were reachable from a seated position, and even his child-sized bed was higher than normal so he could lever himself in and out of the chair with a minimum of effort.

And then, of course, there were the drawings.

Every single square inch of vertical surface—walls, doors, cabinets, even some of the windows—was covered with Eddie's drawings in pencil, colored pencil, charcoal, and Sharpie. He added, subtracted, and rearranged them nearly every day, to reflect his latest work and current mood.

Not one of them had anything to do with the endless round of single-panel gags, greeting cards, advertisements, and other illustrations he did to pay the bills. Those lived only on the drawing board, and only long enough to satisfy the client. Once they'd been mailed off, he forgot them as quickly as possible.

The drawings on Eddie's walls were all of his own cast of characters. Twitchy little Gary Glitch; slick and sleazy Mister Nice Guy; The Gulloon, a bowling-pin-shaped gentle giant; voluptuous LaVerne VaVoom; hyperactive Zip the Hamster; and many more cavorted across every surface. They were crude in every sense of the word, executed quickly with Eddie's trademark shaky line and generally engaged in activities that would shock most people's sensibilities.

Sometimes he told himself that the sick, exploitative,

sexist situations his characters got into were okay because they were only ink on paper. Just drawings, not hurting anyone. Sometimes he even believed it, a little.

None of Eddie's cast of characters had ever been or would ever be published. But in some ways they were all the family he had.

Eddie's mother had been killed by the same wild card virus outbreak that left him a joker. His father had died of a stroke—or the strain of caring for a hideous, deformed child as a single parent—just a few years later. But thanks to his cast of characters, one of the teachers in the group home had spotted and nurtured his artistic talent. Eventually his work brought him enough money to move out of the group home and live independently.

But independence for a freelance artist was always a precarious thing, and he really needed this paycheck if he was going to keep the wolf from the door. So once he had taken care of business in the bathroom and swallowed another Percocet, he gathered his tools and materials, threw on some clothing—keenly aware of the stink of his unwashed body—and hauled himself down the two flights to the street.

With his hunched, diminutive stature, Eddie's view of the heavy Canal Street pedestrian traffic was mostly butts and thighs. But he could still feel the pressure of eyes on the back of his neck, see the small children who pointed and gaped, hear the disparaging comments . . . he couldn't fail to know just what his fellow New Yorkers thought of him. Even his fellow jokers. Did they think the virus had left him deaf as well as ugly, malformed, and in constant pain?

Yes, ugly, even by Jokertown standards. Though he'd been hearing that Joker Pride crap for his whole life, he couldn't buy into the idea that "everyone is beautiful in their own way" applied to him. His head, one arm, more than half his torso, and both legs were hideous masses of deformed flesh, with lumpy pink skin like an old burn scar and tufts of black hair sprouting here and there. Even his bones had been warped and twisted by the virus into a parody of the normal human form.

And yes, despite his best efforts, he did have an odor. Thank you very much for noticing, ma'am. Was it his fault his warty, craggy, twisted body was so hard to keep clean? Bitch.

As if he needed a reminder of why he got all his groceries and other purchases delivered.

Grimly Eddie stumped onward. His right hand, the good one, gripped his four-footed cane, bearing more than half his weight on every other step. Every few minutes he paused to rest.

♠

Finally he reached the station house, Fort Freak itself. Three labored steps up to the door, which opened even before he'd begun to fumble with his portfolio and cane. A massive pair of legs stepped aside, and a deep voice rumbled, "Morning, Eddie."

Eddie tipped back his hat and looked up at a furry face, the smile inviting despite its fearsome fangs. "Morning, Beastie." Beastie Bester was one of the few people in the precinct who didn't seem to mind Eddie's appearance. "Haven't seen you in a while. What brings you in today?"

"Dunno. I got a call from a Detective Black." He shrugged. "It's work."

After signing in with the winged desk sergeant—and enduring the indignity of standing on a box to reach the desk—Eddie clipped a temporary badge to his lapel and waited. Officers in blue polyester bustled in and out, their belts crowded with guns and handcuffs and other cop equipment.

Daniel in the lions' den, Eddie thought, and loosened his tie.

The first time he'd come to the police station he hadn't slept a wink the night before. But he'd come anyway—no one knew what his characters got up to at night, and his fellow freelance artist Swash had insisted that the job was easy and the money good. And, indeed, he'd gotten nothing from his occasional forays into cop territory but a few modest paychecks and a paradoxical sense of civic pride. He could even boast that his work had helped to put away some very nasty characters.

If, that is, he had anyone to boast to.

" 'Scuse me," said one of the cops, a shapely redheaded nat with a detective's badge clipped to the waistband of her skirt, and Eddie shuffled out of her way. But despite her surface politeness, as she pushed past he saw that her nose wrinkled in distaste. Eddie thought about what Mister Nice Guy might do with a redhead like her and a leather strap.

"Eddie Carmichael?" Eddie jerked his eyes up to see a pale nat in a cheap suit. "I'm Detective Black." He was young, even younger than Eddie, and had a soft voice that Eddie recognized from the earlier phone call. "You can call me Franny. This is my partner, Detective Stevens." Stevens was a tall, black nat in a dark suit. He was slim, with prominent ears . . .

Jesus Christ. It was Mr. Trio.

"Whoa," Franny said, catching Eddie's shoulder with one slim hand. "You okay?"

"Yeah, I . . ." He swallowed hard. "I just had a tough time getting here this morning." He wiped his face with his handkerchief. "I don't deal well with crowds."

"Maybe you should sit down."

Franny helped Eddie to a seat, then fetched him a

paper cup of water. He took it with shaking hands, trying not to look at Stevens. "I'll be all right."

If the situation weren't so terrifying it would almost be laughable. Called in to sketch his own creation! But there was nothing, absolutely nothing, to connect him to Gary Glitch. As long as he kept calm and did his job—maybe not too good of a job, but not so bad as to attract attention—he could just collect his paycheck and that would be the end of it. The hardest part would be pretending that he'd never seen Stevens before.

No, the hardest part would be *not* drawing Gary Glitch as though he'd drawn the character ten thousand times before.

"What's the case?" Eddie asked, struggling to keep his voice level.

Franny shrugged. "Missing persons. Sort of."

"I, uh—oh?" Eddie fumbled with his portfolio and cane to cover his confusion and relief. "What do you mean 'sort of'?"

"It's not much of a case," Franny admitted.

"It's the best you deserve," Stevens muttered under his breath, so low that Franny couldn't have heard it. *Oh, really?*

"We aren't even really sure anyone has actually gone missing," Franny explained as he led Eddie through swinging doors and across the crowded, noisy wardroom, where too many desks were crammed together under harsh fluorescent lighting and a miasma of stale vending machine coffee. "Very few of the supposed missing persons are, you know, anyone that anyone would miss. But now we've got a witness—someone who claims he saw some of the missing jokers getting snatched off the street." They paused outside an interrogation room and looked through the one-way glass. "For all the good he does us."

Slumped in a plastic folding chair on the other side of the glass was one of the most pathetic-looking jokers

Eddie had ever seen. His head resembled a wolf's—a mangy, flea-bitten, ragged-eared cur of a wolf. The fur was matted and patchy, with a lot of gray around the muzzle; the watery, red-rimmed eyes stared wearily at nothing; and the lolling tongue was coated with gray phlegm. The rest of him was essentially human, with a stained and tattered Knicks T-shirt stretched across a swollen beer gut. Dandruff and fallen gray hairs littered the shoulders of his filthy denim jacket.

Stevens crossed his arms on his chest. "His name's Lupo. Used to tend bar at some swank joint, he says, but that was a long time ago. Now he's just another denizen of No Fixed Abode."

"He was passed out behind a Dumpster," Franny continued, "and woke up just as the supposed kidnappers were leaving the scene. Didn't get a very good look at the perps, but maybe enough for a sketch."

Eddie was dubious. "I'll do what I can."

Franny sighed. "I sure hope so, or else this case is just going to fizzle out."

At the sound of the door, Lupo's head jerked up like a spastic puppet's, his eyes wide and feral. Eddie let the detective precede him into the room.

"It's just me, Lupo," Franny said.

Lupo's muzzle corrugated as Eddie entered, his eyes narrowing and his ears going back. Though the wolf-headed joker was no rose himself—he stank of garbage, cheap wine, and wet dog—his beer-can-sized muzzle probably gave him a keen sense of smell. "What's *that*?"

Love you too, Eddie thought.

"This is Eddie Carmichael, the forensic artist," Franny said. "He's going to draw some sketches of the men you saw last night."

With some reluctance Lupo pulled his eyes off of Eddie and stared pleadingly at the detectives. "I tol' you, it was dark. And I don' remember stuff so good anymore."

Stevens gave Lupo something that Eddie figured was

supposed to be a reassuring smile. "Mr. Carmichael is a professional, Lupo. He'll help you to remember." He looked sidewise at Eddie, his hard glance saying *Right?*

Eddie froze for a moment, remembering those cold cop eyes looking over the barrel of a gun at him, then shook away the memory. "That's, uh, that's right."

"Well then." Stevens stood. "I'll leave you two to this oh-so-important case while I get back to some real detective work." He looked pointedly at Franny. "If you need any help . . . don't call me." And then, without a backward glance, he left.

Eddie swallowed, his heart rate slowing toward normal. There was something weird happening between the two detectives, but as far as Eddie was concerned, he felt like he'd dodged a bullet for the second time in twenty-four hours.

Hauling himself up into a chair, Eddie unzipped his portfolio. He pulled out a sketchpad, a fat black 6B pencil, and a battered three-ring binder of reference images, but to begin with he just laid them all flat on the table. "There's nothing magic about this process," he said, beginning a spiel he'd used a hundred times. But this time he was trying to calm himself as much as the witness. "I'm going to ask you some questions, but you'll be doing most of the talking. All right?"

Lupo's ears still lay flat against his head, but he nodded.

"So, just to begin with . . . how many of them were there?"

"Three, maybe four. They had this poor asshole with four legs all tied up carrying him toward a van. I only saw the front, couldn't get no plate—"

"Um, actually," Franny interrupted, "he doesn't need to know about the crime. That's my department."

Eddie nodded an acknowledgment at the detective, then returned his attention to Lupo. "All *I* want to know is what they looked like."

A wrinkle appeared between Lupo's eyebrows, and the

pink tip of his tongue poked out. "Well, they were all guys . . . or really ugly women." He smirked. "This one big guy seemed to be ordering the other ones around."

"Tell me about him."

Lupo spread his hands like he was describing the fish that got away. "Big."

Eddie sighed. "*How* big? Six feet tall? Bigger?"

"I dunno. Six four, maybe?" The lupine joker squeezed his eyes shut and clapped his hands over them, bending his head down. "I used to be good at this," he muttered into the table's scarred Formica. "When I was tending bar at the Crystal Palace, I knew every regular customer. What they liked, how they tipped, everything."

The name of the bar struck Eddie like a lightning bolt. "You tended bar at the *Palace*?"

Franny just looked at Eddie. He was a nat, so he couldn't possibly understand how important the Crystal Palace was. Eddie himself could only dream of what the place had been like—he'd been only five when the place had burned in '88—but here was someone who'd actually worked there!

Lupo raised his muzzle from the table. "Yeah. I was the number two guy in the whole place—I was in charge whenever Elmo wasn't there."

Eddie felt as though he were in the presence of one of the Founding Fathers . . . or, at least, the decrepit, wasted shell of one. "Did you know . . . Chrysalis?"

Lupo's leer was an amazing thing, the long black lip curling up to reveal an impressive array of discolored fangs. "Yeah, I knew her." He sat up straighter, his eyes seeming to focus for once, though what they were focused *on* was something beyond the walls of the interrogation room. But after only a moment, he slumped in his chair again. "Not that she ever gave me the time of day."

For a moment Eddie actually felt sorry for the battered, alcoholic wolf-man. But then Franny cleared his throat meaningfully, and Eddie reasserted his professional demeanor. "So, the big guy, the one who was ordering the others around. Was he white? Black? Chinese?"

"Joker." Lupo nodded definitively. "His skin was kind of gray and slimy."

"All right." Eddie bit his lip. This would make his job easier in some ways, a lot harder in others. "How many eyes?"

They talked for half an hour before Eddie laid pencil to paper. It was always a good idea to get the subject thinking, forming a good strong image in their own mind, before beginning the actual sketch. He drew vertical and horizontal guidelines, dividing the page in equal fourths, then began to rough in the shape of the suspect's face. "You said his head was kind of narrow. Like this?"

"I dunno." Lupo stared uncertainly at the oval. "Maybe a little pointy on top."

"And the eyes, big and wide-set." He lightly sketched in a couple of ovals.

"Bigger. Wider."

Another half hour and the general proportions of the face were sketched in. The suspect was an ugly sonofabitch, no question, with no nose to speak of and a wide mouth full of pointy teeth. Now it was time to crack open the binder of reference images.

Most sketch artists used one of several standard reference books of facial features; some even used computer software. But in this, as in so many things, Jokertown was different. Eddie's binder, based on one Swash had loaned him when he was studying for his exams, included plenty of photos of actual jokers, but also animals, sea creatures . . . even plants, fungi, and rocks.

Eddie licked his thumb and flipped through the binder until he came to a page showing dozens of pairs of eyes. "Any of these look familiar?"

Lupo studied the page for a long time, tongue tip sticking out. "Could be any of 'em." He poked vaguely at one pair. "Those, I guess."

"Uh huh." Eddie's pencil scribbled in the eyes, big and black and dead, then began to sketch in the structures around them.

It went like that for a long time. Usually a sketching session would be over in less than two hours, but Lupo had gotten such a poor glimpse of the suspects, and his mind was so scattered and fogged by alcohol, that the process was slow and frustrating for both of them. Franny had excused himself before the first hour was up, asking Eddie to call him when he was done. Lupo slurped cup after cup of vending machine coffee; Eddie drank Coke.

Finally, some time in hour four, Lupo's replies to Eddie's questions had turned into little more than a mumbled yes or no, and Eddie's back, hip, and shoulder were screaming from hours in the cheap plastic chair. "All right," he said at last, tearing the final drawing from his sketchbook and tacking it to the wall. "Last chance. Is there anything in any of these drawings that does *not* match your memory of the suspects?"

There were three of them. The big guy, the leader, was a fish-faced joker, all eyes and teeth; the other two were nats. To Eddie the sketches all looked pretty generic— even Fish-Face could have been any of a hundred jokers Eddie had seen on the Bowery in the last year—but they were the best he could do with the information he'd been given. There may or may not have been a fourth snatcher, but Lupo's recollection of him was so hazy Eddie hadn't even attempted a sketch.

Eddie-the-commercial-artist itched to tear these pre-liminary sketches up and do finished, polished drawings. But Eddie-the-police-sketch-artist knew that composite drawing had its rules, and one of them was that what-ever came out of the session with the witness had to be used as-is, with no subsequent cleanup, revision, or improvement.

"They're okay, I guess." Lupo scratched behind one ear, then shrugged. "I'll let you know if I remember anything else."

"Uh huh," Eddie grunted noncommittally, and used the phone on the wall to call Franny. He'd probably never see Lupo again; it might be months before he got another call from the police department. And the way his back and hip felt right now, he might wind up having to spend this whole paycheck on chiropractic. Maybe he should take his name off the list for police artist work?

But no, he realized . . . as frustrating as it was to work with random, unobservant idiots like wolf-boy here, and as humiliating and painful as it was to haul himself out of his comfortable little apartment, it did his heart good to help track down crooks.

It kind of balanced out his karma. He hoped.

A knock on the door, then Franny entered. "So . . . how did it go?"

Eddie gestured at the sketches tacked to the wall. "We got three of 'em, anyway. Lupo didn't get a good enough look at the fourth." *If there really was one*, he didn't say.

The detective looked over the sketches, then turned back to Eddie and Lupo. "These are great," he said. "I'm sure they'll be a big help."

"Thanks." Eddie began collecting his scattered reference materials, pencils, erasers, and sharpeners.

"So what happens now?" Lupo asked, not unreasonably.

Franny shrugged. "You're free to go. But you're a witness, so don't leave town. We'll leave a message at the White House if we need to contact you." Eddie knew the White House Hotel, one of the Bowery's few remaining classic flophouses. Fifty jokers sleeping on sagging beds in one big room.

"I thought I might, y'know, go into a safe house?"

The detective shook his head. "I'm sorry."

Lupo looked back and forth between Eddie and Franny, the whites showing all the way around his big brown doggy eyes. "I told you before, they might've seen me! I know what they look like, and they know it! As soon as I'm back on the street, they'll snatch me too!"

Franny spread his hands, palms up. "There's no budget for it."

Now Lupo was really panicking, ears laid flat against his head. "Can't I get *some* kind of police protection?"

Franny laid a hand on his shoulder. "I'm sorry, Lupo, really I am, but we just don't have the people for it. I can put in a request, but . . ." He shrugged. "Don't get your hopes up."

"Oh man . . ." Lupo put his head in his hands.

Eddie felt bad for the mangy wolf-man, but there was nothing he could do about it. He cleared his throat and held out his time card and pen to the detective.

"Oh. Sorry." He scrawled a signature across the bottom of the card. "Thanks, Eddie. You've been a big help."

"You're welcome." He leaned in closer to the young detective and spoke low. "Say . . . I know it's no business of mine, but is there something wrong between you and Detective Stevens?"

Franny swallowed, and at that moment he looked nearly as miserable as Lupo. "It's nothing you can help with. Thanks for your concern, though."

"Well, whatever it is, I'm sorry." Eddie struggled to his feet, taking one last look at the sketches on the wall. "I hope you get those guys soon."

"Me too."

◆

After the long day he'd had, Eddie wasn't even up to ordering dinner from the New Big Wang Chinese Restaurant down the street. He opened a can of soup and heated it up on his tiny two-burner stove, meticulously washing and stowing the pot, bowl, and spoon when he was done.

Then he rolled his chair over to the drawing table and began to work.

Sometimes he did four-panel strips, sometimes book-length stories. Tonight it was a single large panel, Mister Nice Guy disporting himself across the page with a collection of anonymous, pneumatic women. Eddie worked rapidly, sketching the characters' forms loosely in pencil before dipping his ink brush and bringing them to detailed black-and-white life.

One of the women resembled the redheaded detective from that morning, only with much larger breasts. Mister Nice Guy had her tied up. She smiled around a full mouth, looking up at him as he patted her head.

Eddie's fingers tightened on his brush and his mouth twisted into a sardonic grin as he detailed the woman's thumb-sized nipples.

♥

After Eddie had finished the panel, cleaned his brushes, and taped the new pages up on the wall above his bed, he settled down in his chair with a small sketchpad and a black fine-point felt-tip.

Eddie tapped his fingertips together, pondering options and possibilities. Then he began to draw. With just a few quick lines, a familiar form began to take shape on the pad in his lap.

As Eddie sketched, something like white smoke began to swirl in the air, condensing and thickening, spiraling downward into a hazy bowling pin shape about seven feet tall. Bulbous arms and legs coalesced from the mist, a small head, an enormous cucumber schnoz.

Eddie looked up from his completed sketch of The Gulloon to see the same character looming over him in person, his big clodhopper boots pigeon-toed on the scuffed vinyl of Eddie's floor. He raised one hand and gave Eddie a little three-fingered wave. The Gulloon didn't talk.

Through The Gulloon's eyes Eddie saw himself, a hunched warty excrescence of a joker, but that didn't last long. The Gulloon turned away, clambered up onto the kitchenette counter, and squeezed through the finger's-width gap that was always left open at the bottom of the window. With an audible *pop* he reappeared on the other side, pausing a moment on the fire escape to mold himself back into his usual shape. Then he ambled down the fire escape ladder toward the street.

Eddie himself remained in his chair, conscious and aware, but he closed his eyes to block out the view of his apartment. It was easier that way.

The Gulloon wasn't a rooftop peeper like Gary Glitch; he liked to lurk in the shadows until he saw a pretty girl, then follow her home and look in her window. The big guy was surprisingly quiet on his feet. But tonight there was little foot traffic in Jokertown, and what there was all seemed to be heading in one direction. Curious, he joined in the flow.

Their destination was the Church of Jesus Christ, Joker, at the door of which Quasiman stood handing out flyers. The Gulloon took one. "HAVE YOU SEEN US?" it said, above a grid of sixteen photos. Every one of them was a joker.

The Gulloon, one of Eddie's first creations, was kind of funny-looking even for a joker . . . smooth and round and, frankly, cartoonish. But this crowd seemed preoccupied enough that he felt he could step out of the shadows without attracting too much attention. And, though he did get a few curious glances, no one in the crowd of winged, tentacled, and scaled jokers seemed too perturbed by his appearance. He entered and descended the stairs to the community hall.

The room was filling up fast. The Gulloon stood at the back of the crowd, between a bull-like man and an enormous joker who seemed to be made of gray rock, and edged back into the corner so nobody would touch him. The strange material that made up Eddie's characters' flesh and clothing felt kind of like Styrofoam, stiff and light and fragile.

As The Gulloon shifted around, peering around the heads of those even taller than himself, he spotted the snake-man—Infamous Black Tongue, that was what he was called—in the crowd. But though even the easygoing Gulloon tensed at the sight, Eddie reminded himself that the snake was just as welcome in the church as any other joker, and he had no reason to suspect The Gulloon of anything. Still, The Gulloon kept one eye on him as the crowd took their seats.

The murmuring crowd quieted as Father Squid rose and stood at the lectern. "Thank you for coming tonight," he said, the tentacles of his lower face quivering with each consonant. "As you know, Jokertown has been suffering a series of disappearances. It's said that some jokers have been snatched from the street. Others have simply vanished." He looked down at his hands, which rested on the lectern before him in a prayerful attitude. "Sadly, this is not unusual in our community. But the numbers are higher than usual, and many suspect that these disappearances are related."

Father Squid raised his head, and there was fire in his eyes. "We will not stand for this any longer." Though the joker priest was old, his muscles going to fat, Eddie didn't envy anyone who got in his way. "We will band together. We will be vigilant. And, if necessary, we will fight!" The crowd applauded. "Now, not all of us are fighters." A few in the crowd chuckled at that. "But all of us have a part

to play. You have seen the flyers with the photos of the
disappeared. If you have any information as to their
whereabouts, or any clues as to what has become of
them, call the number at the bottom. And if you should
happen to observe a kidnapping in progress, or even anything vaguely suspicious, call the same number. Better to
raise a false alarm than to let even one more joker vanish." He looked out sternly at his congregation, and a few
"Amen"s were shouted. "We will now open the floor for
testimony, remembrance, and ideas."

Joker after joker now took the podium, telling tearful
stories about the vanished ones, or proposing strategies
that seemed to Eddie completely ineffectual, or express-
ing fear and concern for their own lives. But The Gulloon
kept his eye on Father Squid, who stood to one side with
his still-powerful arms crossed above his substantial belly.

Eddie wasn't a religious man, and he wasn't a member of Father Squid's congregation. But he was a joker.
And watching Father Squid standing there, looking over
the crowd, he knew that the old pastor would do anything in his power to protect every joker in Jokertown.

Even him.

No matter how much of a worthless little shit he
might be.

♠

Eddie got an assignment from the J. Peterman catalog
drawing men's shirts for their incredibly fussy art
director—a royal pain, but the job paid really well.

He didn't peep at all; he didn't draw any salacious
cartoons; he tried hard not to even have any impure
thoughts. Instead, he drew a long, hallucinatory fantasy
story involving Gary Glitch and Zip the Hamster on a
cross-country road trip. But after a couple of days without peeping he woke up from a lucid, lurid dream of The

Gulloon peering into basement windows, only to realize that it wasn't a dream. Eddie hustled his character back to the apartment and dispelled him immediately.

It was far from the first time he'd manifested his characters while sleeping. In fact, that was how he'd started. He hadn't realized the dreams of his characters wandering his own neighborhood had been the manifestation of a wild card talent until one of the other group home residents described a really strange-looking joker she'd seen peering in her window. But ever since he'd started peeping consciously it happened only rarely.

But now it was starting again. As Eddie stared at the spot on the floor where he'd dismissed the easygoing Gulloon, he wondered what Mister Nice Guy or LaVerne VaVoom might get up to if he couldn't keep control of them.

For that matter, what if they'd *already* gotten up to something? He didn't always remember his dreams.

He spent the rest of that night staring at the ceiling and worrying.

◆

"Morning, Eddie," Beastie said, strolling up to the station house door. It was exactly eight in the morning and Eddie had been nervously shifting from foot to foot on the sidewalk for twenty minutes. If he'd been built for pacing, that's what he would have been doing. "So Lupo convinced Franny to call you in again?"

Eddie took off his hat to get a better look at Beastie's face. "No, I'm—I'm here as a concerned citizen. I was wondering if there had been any other sightings in the, uh, the monkey-faced Peeping Tom case."

Beastie shrugged. "Haven't heard of any such thing."

That was a relief, but something else Beastie had said nagged at Eddie's mind. "Wait, what was that about Lupo?"

Beastie rolled his eyes. "He's been in here every damn day, hoping for some kind of protection, but after a while he figured out that wasn't going to happen. Now he's telling anyone who will sit still that he's remembered more details about the snatchers and demanding another session with the sketch artist. Some of us are starting to wonder if he really saw anything in the first place."

Eddie considered the question. "I think he really did. He was a little fuzzy on the details, but I don't think he was making it up or hallucinating."

A rough, growling voice interrupted the conversation. "Oh, thank God you're here!" Eddie looked up to see Lupo running down the sidewalk toward him. Beastie spread his hands in a *see what I mean?* gesture. "I mean that, Eddie," Lupo panted as he came to an unsteady halt, hands on knees, before the station house steps. "I literally thank my Higher Power that you are here. I was beginning to think no one was listening to me."

Eddie shook his head. "I'm not here because I got called back for you. I don't think I've ever gotten called back on the same case. Memories fade with time. You have to get them when they're fresh."

"This *is* fresh, Eddie. I saw him again! The fourth snatcher!"

Eddie and Beastie looked at each other. "When?" Eddie asked.

"Just this morning."

"Really?" Beastie asked, not quite condescendingly. "The timing is awfully convenient."

Lupo raised a hand. "Swear to God." The raised palm was scrubbed and pink, though lines of dirt remained ground into its creases. "I saw him on Bond Street, just around the corner from my hotel." The whites showed all around his eyes. "They're looking for me, Eddie! They know I saw them, and now they're going to snatch me too!"

Beastie didn't seem convinced. "You're absolutely sure it was him?"

"Look, I know I haven't always been the most reliable witness. But my mind is much clearer now. I haven't touched a drop in two days." Lupo crouched down, bringing his head to Eddie's eye level. "You gotta give me another shot, Eddie."

"It's not my decision." Eddie looked to Beastie. "But for what it's worth . . . I believe him."

Lupo's heavy, lupine head swiveled between Eddie and Beastie. "I can give you a good description of the fourth snatcher now. Please." His big brown eyes were impossibly sad and soulful. "Please?"

Beastie sighed. "I'll pass the information up the line."

Lupo and Eddie sat on a hard bench outside the wardroom door while Beastie went in to talk with Franny. This wasn't exactly how Eddie had planned to spend the morning, but if he could get another few hours of composite sketch work out of it he wouldn't turn the money down. Anyway, pulling himself away from the desperate, pleading wolf-man would have seemed rude.

"I'm a new man, Eddie, I swear. You'll see. I was all messed up last time."

Eddie had to admit that Lupo was not only cleaner, he seemed more alert. And his voice, though still sounding a bit odd because of the shape of his mouth, wasn't at all slurred. "You're really serious about this."

"I've never been more serious in my life. There's nothing like the fear of getting snatched to make a man sit up and take notice of what's going on around him." He sighed. "Or what's going on inside him. I've made a mess of my life, I admit it. Maybe this is the wake-up call I've needed. I hope it isn't too late."

"It's never too late," Eddie said, though Lupo looked

to be sixty or seventy . . . not an easy time of life to make a fresh start. "Even for people like us."

"People like us?"

Eddie winced, sure he'd crossed a line. Not even jokers liked to be equated with an ugly lump of flesh like him. "Sorry . . ."

"No, no, I'm not insulted. Just surprised to hear you say it. You're an artist, a professional . . . I figured you for an East Village type, not a J-town boy like me."

At that Eddie snorted. "Hardly. I live in an efficiency about a mile from here. Heart of Jokertown."

"No shit? Why haven't I seen you around the neighborhood?"

"I don't get out much." *Not in person, anyway.* Eddie cleared his throat. "I hear things, though. Rumors. Some kind of monkey-faced Peeping Tom, looking in windows at night. Maybe a whole gang of Peeping Toms. Have you heard about anything like that?"

"Not lately." Lupo's lip drew back, exposing yellowed fangs. "But two years ago . . . I was staying at my sister's place, and she came screaming out of her bedroom saying that some big-eared little bastard was on her fire escape watching her undress. I couldn't get the window open, but I got a look at the guy before he escaped." His hairy hands balled into fists. "I might be a joker, I might be an alcoholic, I might even have sold a few things that didn't exactly belong to me, but I'd never stoop that low. If I ever catch that little asshole . . ." He smacked a fist into the opposite hand, and Eddie realized there was still some serious muscle under the ex-bartender's fat. "He'll be sorry."

Eddie was ashamed to admit that he had no idea which of the many women he'd peeped in on had been Lupo's sister. The incident didn't stand out from so many similar ones in his memory. "Sorry to hear about that," he said aloud.

"You wouldn't believe the shit that goes down in

Jokertown." He blinked. "Or maybe you would. How long you lived here?"

"Almost ten years."

"So you never saw the Palace before the fire?"

"No. I've heard about it, though. Was it really as crazy as they say?"

"Crazier." He grinned, an evil thing full of yellow teeth. "One time I was damn near killed by a panda bear. A panda bear! In a bar! Where else but the Palace?"

He went on like that for a while, sharing fascinating anecdotes about people and places that were nearly legends to Eddie, until the wardroom door opened and Franny emerged. "Beastie tells me you saw the fourth snatcher?" he said to Lupo. He seemed half hopeful and half dubious.

"It's true! Swear to God!"

Franny didn't look convinced. He turned to Eddie. "You've been talking with him. Do you believe him?"

Eddie nodded. "I do, actually."

"Would you be willing to do a few more sketches?"

"Sure, if you're paying. But I don't have my stuff with me."

The detective set his jaw and did his best to look decisive. "All right. Come back in an hour and I'll try to find you an interrogation room."

After Franny left, Lupo said, "Thanks for standing up for me."

"You're welcome. And thanks for the stories."

♣

The second session went much more smoothly than the first. Sober, Lupo turned out to be as keen an observer as he'd claimed to be, and in less than an hour they had a good sketch of the fourth snatcher, a hulking blond nat with a broken nose. Lupo also remembered some more details about the other two nats—one had a badly scarred

ear, the other a tattoo on his left wrist that Franny identified as a Russian gang mark. "This will be very helpful,"
he said. "It might not hold up in court, but if we can use
it to pull in a suspect, that's a start."

Behind the detective's back, Lupo gave Eddie a
thumbs-up.

Eddie didn't even want to admit to himself how good
that small gesture made him feel.

♠

That night, instead of peeping, Eddie sent Mister Nice
Guy out to prowl the streets on foot, peering at faces.
Eddie had not been allowed to keep a copy of the sketches
he'd made, but after so many hours with Lupo he knew
the snatchers well, especially Fish-Face.

Mister Nice Guy had no trouble blending in with the
street traffic in the shabby joker neighborhood near
where the snatch had taken place. Pale and big-nosed
he might be, but he was humanoid enough to pass for a
joker as long as no one bumped into him.

It felt weird to just be walking around on the sidewalk
like a normal person, not skulking and sneaking, and not
the subject of stares and comments. By comparison with
Eddie a cartoon character was normal, at least in Jokertown.

The people on the Jokertown streets at this hour were
a mix of types, fashionable bohemians as well as drunks
and thugs. A joker couple strolled down the sidewalk
tentacle-in-pincer, their clear affection for each other
making them cute. A trio of teenaged nats crept about,
hesitant and frightened, pointing and giggling when they
thought no one was looking. A muscular joker strode
past them, heads high and chins up, his four-eyed glare
forcing them to silence. But none of them resembled any
of the snatchers.

As he walked, Eddie tried to think himself into the

snatchers' shoes. Where might they have taken the struggling joker after tying him up? Where else might they be hanging out right now, preparing for another snatch? Were they even now closing in on Lupo, the only witness?

There were so many places to watch.

Fortunately, Eddie could be in more than one place at a time.

Back in the apartment, he opened his eyes and sketched up Zip the hyperactive hamster. A vibrating football-sized furball of nervous energy, Zip barely paused after being created, immediately bounding to the countertop and through the gap in the window. He tore across rooftops in the direction of the White House Hotel, hoping to catch Lupo there or nearby.

It took effort to maintain two characters at once, but it felt good, like the stretch he felt during an intense chiropractic session.

And he was doing it to help other people, for once. To try to catch the snatchers, prevent another snatch, protect his friend.

No. Protect an important witness.

No one could consider lumpy, ugly Eddie a friend.

Zip dashed through the night under a cloudless spring sky, the wind cool on his fur.

◆

Saturday night. Eddie was out in force, with Mister Nice Guy barhopping and The Gulloon wandering back alleys. Gary Glitch was keeping an eye on Lupo, who sat on a bench in Chatham Square chatting with some of his buddies.

It had been three days that he'd been patrolling instead of peeping, staying up until two or three A.M. every night, but what sleep he'd gotten had been deep and dreamless. At night he felt alive, moving his characters around

Jokertown like chess pieces, scanning and searching the crowds for the snatchers' faces.

Switching his attention among three different characters, all of them moving and active, was a challenge. Sometimes he realized that he'd left one standing stock-still, unobservant, defenseless. When he discovered these situations his heart pounded, but so far none of his characters had gotten into any serious trouble because of it.

It seemed that just about any kind of appearance or behavior was acceptable in Jokertown at night. If only it wasn't so hard for Eddie to move around, he might even . . .

Suddenly something tugged at his attention. It was Gary Glitch, hidden under a bush a few yards from Lupo's bench.

One of the passing faces seemed familiar. In fact, that same face had passed this spot a few times recently.

Eddie sent Gary scampering across the cold sidewalk, through the soft spring grasses, and up a tree to where he could get a better look at the burly, frowning pedestrian loitering on the far side of the park's play structure.

He seemed to be keeping a covert eye on Lupo as he paced the sidewalk behind the playground, sucking on a cigarette.

He was a nat, big and muscular, Caucasian with an ash-blond buzz cut.

He had a badly scarred ear.

Gary clambered down the tree and crept across the grass to another bush, just a few feet from the guy. He didn't *exactly* resemble the sketch that Eddie had made of the second snatcher, but then again he didn't exactly *not* resemble it. The sketch was pretty generic—it had been drawn while Lupo was still under the influence—and though the scarred ear was a strong identifier, in this part of town knife scars weren't that uncommon.

Eddie wasn't sure what to do.

There was little he *could* do, anyway. Eddie's characters didn't have a lot of physicality to them; they could make noise, maybe lift a few things as long as they weren't too heavy, but they were too fragile for fighting.

He'd keep an eye on the situation. Maybe if it seemed that Lupo were in danger he could have Gary shout a warning.

With another part of his attention, Eddie started Mister Nice Guy and The Gulloon moving toward Chatham Square. But neither of them was as fast as Gary; it would be half an hour or more before they arrived.

A burst of chat and laughter from Lupo's bench drew Gary's attention. Gary saw Lupo stand up, shaking hands and high-fiving his friends, then zip up his jacket and set off in the direction of the White House.

The muscular stranger took a drag on his cigarette, ground it out under his boot heel, and moved off in the same direction.

Keeping out of sight as much as possible, Gary followed.

As the stranger walked—loitering, in no visible hurry, but nonetheless managing to stay within a block of Lupo—he pulled out a phone and muttered a few words in what sounded like Russian. A few minutes later Gary saw him nod to another man across the street.

Fish-Face.

He wore a black leather jacket, scarred and torn at the elbows, and the streetlight gleamed on the silvery, slimy skin of his bald head. His eyes were big, black, and dead, exactly as Lupo had described, though Lupo had failed to mention the fin-like ears and had, if anything, underestimated the toothy horror of the fishy joker's mouth. He was bad news, no question.

Fish-Face and Scarred Ear stayed on opposite sides of the street, leapfrogging each other as they moved along in Lupo's wake. Lupo, oblivious, was enjoying the cool spring air, ambling along, stopping from time to time to chat with friends on the street. He had a lot of them.

Eddie didn't know what to do. The snatchers were big, strong, and probably experienced fighters, there were two of them, and they had the advantage of surprise. If Gary let Lupo know he was being tailed, whether quietly or by shouting, Eddie didn't doubt that Lupo would turn and try to fight them—and get himself snatched.

Could he defuse the situation by attracting the attention of passersby? Hardly. It was nearly two in the morning, on a side street in the Bowery, and the few passersby were most likely as plastered as Lupo on a bad day.

Back in the apartment, Eddie opened his eyes and looked at the phone that sat near his bed. All he had to do was dial 9-1-1.

But Eddie's voice and phone number would be recorded, and sooner or later he'd have to explain how a crippled stay-at-home joker could be an eyewitness to a crime—a *potential* crime—more than a mile away.

Gary Glitch could pick up a pay phone, if he could find one, or dash into an all-night convenience store and raise the alarm. But Gary Glitch was wanted for peeping, and with his distinctive face and build Stevens would recognize him immediately. If Gary ever came to the attention of the police, Eddie might have to retire him permanently.

While Eddie fretted, Lupo continued to make his way home. He was now a block from his hotel; the two thugs following him were now on the same side of the street. Half a block behind Lupo and closing in fast, they were no longer making an effort to conceal themselves. Lupo was oblivious, whistling an old disco tune as he strolled along.

If Eddie was reading the situation right, there probably wasn't much more than a minute before Lupo got snatched. Something had to be done, and fast.

Mister Nice Guy was just a couple blocks off, The

Gulloon a bit farther away, but they were moving too slowly to offer assistance in time. Only Gary was close enough to do anything, and Lupo hated him.

Eddie had an idea, but it was going to be tricky.

As Mister Nice Guy hurried to meet up with the snatchers before they reached Lupo, The Gulloon lumbering along as quick as he could, Gary Glitch scrambled down a fire escape and dashed across the silent street to tug at Lupo's sleeve. "Hey, dog-breath!" he sneered. "Remember me?"

Lupo's hackles literally rose at the sight of the little cartoon. "You're that big-eared asshole who peeped in my sister's bedroom!" He raised a fist, murder in his eyes.

"Yeah, that's me!" Gary said with a smirk. "And I bet you can't catch me this time, either!" He turned and scrambled away, leading Lupo away from the two snatchers.

With an inarticulate growl, Lupo took off after him.

Two blocks away, Mister Nice Guy rounded a corner. He saw Gary running away, Lupo following him, and the two thugs running after Lupo.

Mister Nice Guy set off after the two goons. He wasn't as fast as Zip or Gary, but like them he was capable of inhuman feats. He lengthened his stride, his legs stretching to ten or twelve feet long as he hurried to catch up with the thugs. The pace was tiring but he wouldn't need to do it for long.

Gary scrambled on hands and feet down the cold gritty sidewalk. He could easily escape by scurrying up the side of some building, but if he did that Lupo would give up the chase and then get caught by the thugs. So Gary hurried along with frequent glances over his shoulder, fast but not too fast, carefully keeping himself in Lupo's sight. It was even more exhausting than running full-tilt.

Back in his apartment, Eddie sat in his chair with fists clenched and sweat running down his sides. With everyone moving so fast it was hard to keep track of who was where. Feet shuffling on the linoleum, he maneuvered his chair across the floor and pulled a New York street map from a shelf.

Meanwhile, The Gulloon plodded along. Eddie couldn't spare much attention for him so he just kept going in a straight line.

Loping with his impossible stride, Mister Nice Guy soon caught up to the two thugs. They didn't hear his cartoonish footfalls coming up behind them.

Three more giant steps and he was well past them.

Then he brought himself to a sudden boinging halt, extending one ten-foot leg across their path.

This was going to hurt. Eddie knew Mister Nice Guy's fragile material would crumble like paper under the impact of two thundering brutes, but he hoped it would stall them. He braced for the impact.

But as soon as he saw Mister Nice Guy's extended leg, Fish-Face shouted, and tried to stop himself. Big and strong though he was, Fish-Face's reflexes were merely human, and in trying to stop he stumbled and fell, tripping Scarred Ear in the process.

Mister Nice Guy pulled back his leg like a retracting tape measure, a fraction of a second before the thugs fell across the place where it had been.

"Gotcha!" cried Lupo.

Eddie jerked his attention back to Gary Glitch, who stood frozen like a scared rabbit in the wolf-man's path. Eddie had forgotten to keep him moving while Mister Nice Guy was dealing with the thugs. With a squeak Gary jumped up, barely dodging Lupo's grasp, and ran at top speed down the street.

But Eddie couldn't afford to ignore Mister Nice Guy for long . . . Fish-Face and Scarred Ear were disentangling themselves and in a moment they would be all over him.

That was exactly what Eddie wanted. He put Mister Nice Guy's thumb to his nose and blew an enormous raspberry.

Enraged, Fish-Face leaped up from the sidewalk. But his grasping hand closed on thin air as Mister Nice Guy swerved out of the way, his body curving into a parenthesis. Scarred Ear growled and tried to grab him in a bear hug, but he ducked that too, bending like a balloon animal.

The two snatchers weren't as dumb as they looked. They charged him simultaneously, from opposite directions. But Mister Nice Guy leaped straight up in the air at the last minute, grabbing onto the horizontal bar of a streetlight as the two thugs collided where he'd been.

That bought Eddie a moment to look in on his other characters. Gary was still running full-tilt with Lupo in hot pursuit, and The Gulloon was still plodding along, so far away from the action that he might as well be on another planet.

Eddie couldn't just keep his characters running forever. They might be cartoons, but they still tired . . . or maybe it was just Eddie who was getting tired. Either way, he had to find a place to stash Lupo pretty soon. The thugs had intercepted Lupo on the way to the White House, so they must know he roomed there. Fort Freak was too far away, and anyway the cops wouldn't take Lupo seriously.

There was only one place in New York City that Eddie knew was safe.

No. He couldn't possibly.

But he had to do *something*.

Eddie bit his lip and redirected Gary on a southbound trajectory.

Toward his own home.

Even as Gary ran, though, Eddie realized none of this would make any difference if the two snatchers lost interest in Mister Nice Guy and took off after Lupo again.

Lupo wasn't that far ahead of them, and they could easily catch him before Gary reached Eddie's door.

Eddie returned his full attention to Mister Nice Guy, who was still hanging on the streetlight. Below him the two thugs had recovered their feet. But instead of either giving up on Mister Nice Guy or screaming at him, Fish-Face was just smiling up at him—the most disturbing toothy grin Eddie had ever seen. Meanwhile, the other thug was talking in Russian on his cell phone. What the hell?

Then Fish-Face reached out and grasped the lamppost in one gray, slimy hand.

And a horrible, juddering electric shock surged through the metal and into Mister Nice Guy.

Mister Nice Guy shrieked, his body vibrating and his bones becoming visible through his flesh. His hands clenched the lamppost in an uncontrollable spasm. The pain was incredible. Eddie gasped and curled up like a prawn in his rolling chair, and Gary and The Gulloon both collapsed where they were.

But pain was something Eddie dealt with every day. When the electric shock stopped, Eddie was still alive, still conscious, and still in control of all his creations.

And really pissed off.

Fish-Face seemed disappointed that Mister Nice Guy hadn't dropped off the lamppost like an overripe fruit. He reached for the post again.

Before he could touch it, Mister Nice Guy stretched out his arms, legs, and torso like a striking lizard's tongue, socking Fish-Face right in the jaw with both feet.

It wasn't much of an impact—it probably hurt Mister Nice Guy more than it did Fish-Face—but it was such a surprise and came from such an unexpected direction that it sent the joker tumbling over backward. Mister Nice Guy landed on the sidewalk beyond him, his extended legs coiling like springs, and bounced away into the night.

The other thug just stood there agog for a moment, until Fish-Face snarled something at him. He put the phone in his pocket and began running after the escaping cartoon.

Exhausted and stunned from the electric shock, Mister Nice Guy wobbled on his boinging, Slinky-like legs. But he couldn't slow down now. He headed north . . . back the way he'd come, and directly opposite the direction Gary was leading Lupo.

He risked a look over his shoulder. Both thugs were following him. Good.

Eddie switched his attention to Gary Glitch, who still lay where he'd fallen when Fish-Face had shocked Mister Nice Guy. Gary looked up from the pavement . . . to find headlights and a blaring horn bearing down on him. He yelped and scuttled away, fingernails tearing on the asphalt . . . reaching the curb just in time. But before he could catch his breath, Lupo was in the crosswalk and closing fast. Gary shook himself, looked around, and scrambled off toward Eddie's apartment as fast as he could.

Now Eddie, still dazed from the shock, was running *two* characters just fast enough to keep ahead of their pursuers. It was an incredible strain. Even with two fingers on his map he was having trouble keeping track of them. But he couldn't just make them vanish . . . he had to lead Lupo to his apartment, and at the same time he had to keep the two thugs as far away from him as possible for as long as possible.

God, he was tired.

By now Gary was only two blocks from Eddie's apartment door. He looked behind to make sure Lupo was still following.

Lupo was. But there was also someone following *him*, and gaining. A big blonde with a broken nose. The fourth snatcher.

How the hell—? But then Eddie remembered that the

bald thug had made a phone call not long after Lupo had gotten away. Gary ran faster, hoping Lupo could keep up.

But even if he could . . . they were all heading straight for Eddie's home. He needed help, and fast. If only he had Zip in play . . . Could he handle four characters at once?

Eddie opened his eyes and reached for his sketchpad.

It wasn't easy drawing Zip while also keeping his other characters in motion. But finally the hyperactive little hamster coalesced into existence on Eddie's kitchen floor. He shook himself, then squeezed out through the window and shot off across the city toward Fort Freak. Zip had no criminal record, and with his speed he could plausibly claim to be a witness to the situation going down near Eddie's apartment.

Assuming he could make himself understood, and that the cops would listen to a football-sized manic hamster with a squeaky machine-gun voice. Eddie had to hope that Jokertown cops were prepared to handle a crime report from *anything*.

Then Eddie's attention was jerked back to Mister Nice Guy, as Scarred Ear picked him up by the neck. Fish-Face was there too, grinning a vicious, toothy grin. Electricity began to crackle . . .

. . . and The Gulloon, who'd been plodding along unattended this whole time, slammed into all three of them. He wasn't going very fast, and he didn't actually weigh very much, but he was *big,* and he sent the whole group tumbling like bowling pins.

Eddie took the opportunity to direct his attention to Zip, who had just arrived at Fort Freak. Even at this hour the station was brightly lit. Zip careened in the door, past the desk sergeant, and into the wardroom, looking for Beastie, or Stevens, or . . .

There! Detective Black!

"Franny!" Zip squeaked, waving his little paws. The detective looked around, his gaze passing well over the hamster's head. Zip stuck two fingers in his mouth and let out a piercing, almost supersonic whistle. "Down here, fuckhead!"

That got his attention.

"It's the snatchers!" Zip squeaked like a CD on fast-forward. "The snatchers! They're chasing Lupo! You have to come right away!" He gave Eddie's address.

And Mister Nice Guy looked up to find Fish-Face's heavy boot coming down toward his head.

Eddie swore and made both Mister Nice Guy and The Gulloon vanish. Clutching his head from the pain, he returned his attention to Gary Glitch and the wolf at his door.

Gary had just reached Eddie's apartment building. With a great effort he squeezed his way under the front door and collapsed, panting, inside.

Lupo came charging up. Seeing Gary through the glass, he pounded on the door with both fists. Eddie paused with his finger on the door buzzer. What the hell was he doing?

"You peeping asshole!" Lupo yelled, his voice muffled by the thick security glass. "I'm gonna get you if it's the last thing I . . ."

Behind Lupo, Gary saw the fourth kidnapper.

Eddie pressed the door buzzer and sent Gary scrambling away, up the steps.

Lupo snarled and snatched the door open, tearing after Gary.

Gary paused for just a moment on the first landing, looking back, hoping against hope . . .

. . . but the door, swinging gently closed on its hydraulics, did not click shut. A moment later it slammed open again, revealing the big nat. Lupo, hearing the noise behind him, turned.

And then the whole scene was flooded with red and blue lights and a voice on a bullhorn. "You! At the door! This is the police! Stop and put your hands up!"

The man stopped in the doorway. But he didn't put his

hands up. Instead he turned and ran, vanishing into the night. "Halt!" cried the bullhorn. But the pounding footsteps kept going. The flashing lights followed.

All was quiet and still for a moment. Then Lupo turned back to Gary, who still stood stunned on the landing. The wolf-man's lips curled back and his fists clenched.

Eddie pressed the intercom button. "Forget about him, Lupo!" he shouted. "It's me you need to be talking with."

Lupo looked around, then noticed the intercom grille behind him. The door was still easing shut. "Eddie?"

"Yeah."

"You know this little fucker?" It hurt Eddie's already-throbbing head to hear Lupo's grating voice simultaneously through Gary's ears and, with an echoing delay, through the intercom.

"In a manner of speaking." Eddie swallowed. "Please, just listen to me."

Lupo gave Gary a vicious glare, but he stepped to the closing door and stopped it with one foot. "I'm listening."

"Look, the situation's kind of complicated and I'm not proud of it, but right now the important thing is this: the snatchers are real, and they're after you. But I . . . but my *friend* here"—he made Gary wave—"he led you away from them, while some of my other, uh, friends, distracted the thugs and called for help."

"How do I know *you* aren't in cahoots with the snatchers?"

"If I were, would I have given Franny those sketches that looked just like them?"

"Urr . . ." Lupo growled, looking uncertain.

As Gary looked down the stairs at Lupo, Eddie wondered what the hell he was doing. How could he let this alcoholic, wolfish joker into his own home? He might work with the police sometimes, but he wasn't a cop—he wasn't sworn to serve or protect anyone.

But still . . . saving Lupo from the snatchers had felt so

good. He'd never dreamed that an ugly, twisted little joker like himself could have such a big impact on the world.

And Lupo was, if not a friend, at least someone who had treated Eddie like a human being. Eddie pushed the intercom button again. "I swear I am not a snatcher, Lupo. But the snatchers *are* still out there." He released the button, paused, swallowed, pushed it again. "If you come upstairs, I'll . . . I'll keep you safe for a while, until we can get this mess sorted out."

Lupo blinked, his big brown eyes shining in the vestibule's harsh fluorescent light. "You'd do that for me?"

"Yeah."

Lupo considered the idea for a bit, then stepped inside and let the door close behind him. "Okay."

Gary led Lupo up to Eddie's apartment. Lupo regarded the little cartoon with clear suspicion, but followed quietly, trudging heavily up the stairs. It was only now that Eddie realized just how exhausted Lupo must be after that long chase.

What a pair they were.

Finally the cartoon and the joker stood outside Eddie's door.

Eddie hesitated, the brass doorknob cold in his hand. He hadn't let another human being into his apartment in over five years.

He turned the knob.

Galahad in Blue

Part Two

APSARA SASHAYED INTO THE bullpen. Every male and even a few females paused to watch her progress. Everything was in motion, hips swaying, hair swinging, boobs bouncing. Last night that rack had been pressed against Franny's bare chest, the hair wrapped around him mirroring her arms' embrace. Franny was glad the desk hid his involuntary physical reaction. It was like being sixteen again. *Next,* he thought, *I'll break out, and my voice will start cracking.*

As she drew closer Franny could see the beautiful oval face was set in lines of worry and alarm, and the dark eyes were wide. Franny suppressed the desire to sigh. Looked as if her phi—otherwise known as her pissant wild card power—was giving her hell again. As soon as she got close enough for him to be able to see it, her dark eyes filled with tears. She was the only woman he'd ever met who could cry and stay beautiful. No red nose, no snot on the upper lip. Franny steeled himself for whatever crisis had arisen.

"Frank." Once they'd started dating she stopped calling him Franny. "I need to talk to you. Someplace private."

Her voice trembled a bit, and cynicism gave way to actual alarm. Maybe something serious had happened.

He led her outside because there was no place in the cop shop that he would have considered truly private. They settled on a bus stop bench. Franny shifted to face her. "Okay, honey, what's wrong?"

"My parents," she wailed. "They're coming to visit."

Blinking in confusion Franny asked, "Isn't that a good thing? You said you really loved your folks."

She nodded vigorously, tears flying off her outrageous eyelashes. "I do, but I told them I was a cop."

"Well, you are sort of a cop. I mean, you work for the precinct."

"No, a real cop. A *decorated* cop. With a badge. And a uniform. And a gun."

Baffled, Franny stared at her for a few moments. "Why? Why would you do that?"

"Because they love me so much, and they're so proud of me, and I haven't done anything to earn that. If they find out I'm just a file clerk they'll put on a brave face, but they'll be so disappointed, and . . . and I just can't bear that." Her voice broke on a tiny little sob. Instinctively Franny gave her a hug and patted her on the back as she wept.

"Okay, I get the whole parent/child issue, I've got the famous cop father thing going on, but I'm not seeing how I come into this."

As if a spigot had been turned the tears ended. She straightened and took his hands in hers. "So, I rented a uniform from a costume store, and I took an old retired badge out of storage and I've asked for a few days off, and you could do the same and we could be partners, and take my folks along like they did when that Hollywood actor came to town last year," she ended in a rush.

Franny pulled his hands away and held them up palms out. "Whoa, whoa, whoa. First off, I can't take time off right now. I'm in enough trouble as it is, and I'm not going to put back on my uniform and go out on the street with an untrained file clerk and a pair of civilians. That's a good way to get *us* fired, and *all* of us hurt or worse. And didn't you sleep with that actor guy?" he added, jealousy making him resentful even though they hadn't been together back then.

"What if I did? I was with Moleka then, not you, so you shouldn't care."

"It's the pattern, Apsara, that's what bothers me."

The bus farted up and with a creaking of brakes came to a stop in front of them. Four jokers flopped, crawled, and hopped off. The doors stayed open, and then the driver yelled, "You gettin' on or not?" They shook their heads. "Then get off the damn bench!" The doors rattled shut and the bus pulled out, baptizing them with a blast of diesel fumes. Apsara and Franny retreated, coughing.

"So, you're not going to help me," she said once she caught her breath.

"If by help you, you mean play cops and robbers with you and your parents, then no, I'm not going to help you."

"Will you at least keep my secret?"

"Are you going to be prancing around in this uniform?"

"Yes." The word was defiant, an out-and-out challenge.

"You know it's a crime to impersonate a police officer," he said, still sparring, but more feebly now.

"I'm not going to arrest anybody. I'm just going to wear the uniform at dinner, and we'll stay away from Jokertown so no one will see us." She paused and looked up at him, big eyes pleading, the corners of her perfect lips drooping. "Please, Frank, let me make them proud."

"I don't know, and why do you need me along for this?"

"I need you to talk about all the cases I've solved. If you bring it up then it won't look like I'm bragging."

"And what cases would those be . . . exactly?"

"Well, there was The Stripper for starters, and you wouldn't be lying because I helped you catch that guy."

He didn't love the reminder. He had just started working at the precinct when he'd solved the case of the teenage ace whose power was to blow a kiss and have the clothes disappear off the object of his gallantry. Bruce Cordova. That was his name. Some of the guys at the precinct had thought it would be hilarious to have Bruce remove Franny's clothes day after day after day. It had been . . . for them.

And Apsara *had* helped catch The Stripper. She had been the luscious bait walking down the street. Franny had gotten only the smallest look at her attributes that day because he'd been busy arresting Bruce. Of course now he saw those attributes almost every night. He felt a stirring in his crotch. Apsara saw his boner forming. She gave a sly smile, and pressed up against him. "Please, Frank."

All his resistance collapsed. "Well, okay, but so help me God, if you try to act like a real cop . . ."

"Oh thank you, thank you. You are the *best* boyfriend." She rained kisses on his face. Franny finally caught her lips, and they shared a long deep kiss until the whistles and catcalls from passersby on the street drove them apart.

Road Kill

by Walter Jon Williams

GORDON WISHED HE HAD more time to examine the body. Not just to find out who killed the victim, but to find out how the joker was put together.

It looked as if there were extra attachment points on the biceps brachii, for example—the normal two on the scapula, plus another, stronger attachment to some kind of disk-like rotating bone, equipped with a nasty ten-centimeter spur, which seemed to float somehow off the head of the humerus. When the biceps contracted, not only would the forearm rise but the spur would rotate forward, as if aimed at an enemy. So if the joker raised his fists in a boxing stance, say, the spurs would roll forward, and he could impale an enemy by shouldering him in the clinch. Or he could grab an attacker and pull him close, and the very act would throw the enemy onto the spur.

And if the arms were relaxed, the spur would rotate backward to protect the head from a surprise attack from the sides or rear.

There were spurs on the knees as well, but these looked like an anatomically simple extension of the tibia. There were also some scars to suggest there had also been spurs on the heels, but these had been amputated at some point to allow the subject to walk normally.

Gordon thought that the wild card was sometimes capable of great beauty, even genius, in its adaptation of human anatomy; but it was also capable of forgetting that someone apparently designed as a street fighter might also need to walk.

Gordon would have liked to dissect the shoulder just to understand the mechanism. But that wasn't part of his job.

His job was ascertaining cause of death, here in his morgue annex in the basement of the Jokertown precinct, a room that smelled of antiseptic and plastic body bags and the bitter-cherry scent of death, where deformed bodies lay on steel tables coated in blue-gray porcelain, and where police officers paced as they drank coffee from paper cups and waited for information.

"So," said Detective Sergeant Gallo, "it was the hit-and-run did him in?"

Gallo stood a respectful distance from the body, by the door. He wanted to be in the room during the autopsy, but he didn't have a compulsion to stand right by and watch the pathologist at work. Maybe he didn't like corpses, Gordon thought, or maybe he'd seen so many that he was no longer interested.

Which was not something that could ever be said of Gordon.

"No," Gordon said. "He was dead by the time the vehicle hit him."

"The vehicle hit a corpse," Gallo said.

"The vehicle was pretty unusual," Gordon said. "It had slick tires—the prints on the victim's body and clothing were absolutely featureless, no tread marks at all." He looked at Gallo and blinked. "What uses slick tires besides a drag racer?"

Gallo shrugged. He was a tall, broad man, dark-haired,

blue-eyed. His right arm was in a fluorescent red fiber-glass cast and carried in a sling, and he wore a black leather jacket on the left arm and thrown over the shoulder on the right. His pistol was tucked into the sling for ease of access.

"Coulda been a drag racer, I suppose," he said. "Though it wasn't going very fast when it hit the victim. But if the vic died from the beating, there's no point in chasing down the driver."

"It wasn't the beating," Gordon said. "El Monstro didn't kill him."

Gallo was startled. "Who?"

"El Monstro."

Gallo was New Jersey State Police and not from New York, so he wouldn't have had a chance to meet El Monstro. Certainly the joker was hard to miss—nearly eight feet tall, horned, with chitinous armor plates covering most of his body—and plates on his knuckles as well, plates that left a very distinct imprint.

"His real name's José Luis Melo da Conceição Neto," Gordon said. "Brazilian kid, raised in Jokertown. I testified on his behalf about fourteen months ago, in an assault case." Gordon gestured with one hand at the distinctive bruising on the dead man's upper arms and torso. "El Monstro pretty clearly left these marks. Nobody else has fists like that."

Gallo reached for his notebook, juggled it one-handed for a moment, then put it on one of the counters that surrounded the room. "Can you give me that name again?"

Gordon did. "Neto isn't really part of the name," he said. "It just means 'grandson'—grandson of the original José Luis Melo da Conceição."

Gallo wasn't used to writing left-handed and it took some time to get the name down.

"He was a nice kid," Gordon said. "He'd be about nineteen now. Works a couple jobs, trying to support a disabled mother and get through NYU. I was able to show the court that he suffered at least half a dozen defensive injuries before he put his assailant in a coma with a single punch. The assailant had a history of violence and robbery, so El Monstro walked."

"He walked all the way to Warren County," Gallo said, "where he killed this other joker."

Gordon shook his head. "No," he said. "He didn't kill this John Doe."

Gallo's tone turned aggressive. "If the truck didn't kill him, and your El Monstro didn't beat him to death, what the hell did put his lights out?"

Gordon looked up from the body. "SCD," he said.

Gallo stared at him in disbelief. "Sudden cardiac death? You're telling me the John Doe had a heart attack?"

"Not a heart attack. Cardiac arrest caused by aortic valve stenosis." Gordon gestured toward the victim's heart, which was sitting in a plastic container on the counter. "His aortic valve narrowed to the point where the heart couldn't pump enough blood into the aorta, which caused the heart to pump faster and faster until it went into ventricular fibrillation, and then . . ." Gordon made a vague gesture. "Asystole, cardiogenic shock, loss of circulation, death. It happens pretty fast, sometimes within seconds."

"What caused the, ah, stenosis?"

"At his age, it was most likely congenital. Happens to men more often than women."

For the first time Gallo approached the body and looked at it thoughtfully. "So he got beat up by this El Monstro guy."

"The wounds were antemortem, though not very far in advance of death."

"And then the vic has SCD, and drops dead on the road, apparently, and was then hit by a drag racer?" The fingers of his left hand reached into his cast and scratched the fingers of his right. He looked up. "He can't have been pushed out of a car or something?"

"No drag marks. No skid marks." Gordon shrugged. "Lividity hadn't developed when the vehicle hit him, so he was run over less than twenty minutes after death."

Gallo shook his head. "This is the worst case of bad luck in all history," he said. He made a disgusted noise. "What was he doing on Route 519? Rural New Jersey, for cripe's sake!"

The victim wasn't, technically speaking, Gordon's business. New Jersey had its own forensic pathologists. But jokers weren't very common in northwest New Jersey, and when the body turned up beaten, run over, and naked except for an athletic supporter and a pair of Adidas training pants, it had been taken to Jokertown for an examination by a specialist in joker bodies.

By Otto Gordon, M.D., known to his colleagues as Gordon the Ghoul.

Gordon adjusted his glasses. "You sure there weren't any prizefights in the vicinity?" he asked. "Cage fights? He'd been through a beating."

"Nothing in that area but dairy farms. We didn't see any crowd leaving, any sign of anything unusual."

"Footprints? Tire tracks?"

"Zilch. And certainly no sign of anyone like El Monstro."

"Well." Gordon shrugged. "Let me stitch up the body, and you can take it home. I'll send you the report when it's done."

"And I'll liaise with NYPD to see if we can pick up this Monstro guy."

Gallo left to do his liaison work. Gordon closed the Y-shaped autopsy incision, made sure the plastic containers with the victim's organs were properly sealed and labeled, and then called his diener, Gaida Hanawi, to help shift the victim back into the body bag he'd arrived in.

Gallo returned along with the uniformed trooper who had driven him into the city from Warren County. Gaida and the uniform began wheeling the body out to the loading dock, past a couple local cops who looked at him in surprise. The trooper's sky-blue jacket with its gaudy yellow patches and the gold-striped black trousers were a considerable contrast to the more severe dark blue uniform of the NYPD.

"How'd you hurt your arm, anyway?" Gordon asked.

"Hit by a vehicle when I was trying to make an arrest," Gallo said. The uniformed trooper snickered.

"Shut up," Gallo told him.

"It was a skateboard," the trooper said. "The detective got hit by a kid on a skateboard, and now I have to drive him everywhere."

"Fuck you," Gallo said.

"Kid got away, too."

"Fuck you twice."

They went to the loading dock, and loaded John Doe onto the vehicle from the Jersey morgue. "I'll be glad to get out of here," the trooper said. "These jokers give me the creeps."

"Moriarty," Gallo said, in an exasperated tone. The trooper looked at him.

"What?"

Gallo rolled his eyes toward Gordon. The trooper looked skeptical, then turned to Gordon. "You're not a joker," he asked. "Are you, Doc?"

Gordon considered the question, and then gave a deliberate laugh, *heh heh heh*. "If only you knew," he said. He went back into the clinic, and as the door sighed closed behind him, he heard Gallo's growling voice. "Jesus Christ, Moriarty, the guy looks like a praying mantis on stilts, and you don't think he's a fucking joker!"

Gordon returned to the morgue and looked at himself in the mirror. Tall, thin, hunched, thick glasses beneath short sandy-brown hair. Praying mantis on stilts. That was a new one.

He returned to the morgue and found Detective Black waiting for him. Franny Black was dark-haired and ordinary-looking and young—too young for his job, or so Gordon had heard it said. He was the son of one of Fort Freak's legendary officers, and he had so much pull in the department that the NYPD had violated about a dozen of its own rules to jump him to detective way early.

This hadn't made him popular with his peers.

"Okay," Franny said. "Now you're done entertaining the folks from out of state, maybe you can do what you're actually being paid to do, which is work on stiffs from this side of the Hudson." He gave a snarl. "What about my Demon Prince body?"

Franny wasn't naturally this belligerent, or so Gordon thought—he was just talking tough in hopes of acquiring a respect that most of the cops around here weren't willing to give him. "The Jersey body might be yours, too," Gordon said. "Have you checked Father Squid's list of the missing?"

Franny's eyes flickered. "You have a copy of the list here?"

"No. Father Squid keeps dropping off handbills, Gaida keeps throwing them away. She likes a tidy lab." He cocked his head. "But," he said, and flapped a hand, "when a mysterious joker appears in Jersey, he had to have come from somewhere."

Franny seemed impatient. "Maybe," he said. "But how about the Demon Prince?"

Gordon indicated a body laid out on a gurney and covered with a sheet. He'd looked at it earlier and seen that its wild card deformities had made the banger uglier, but not necessarily tougher. "I only had a chance to give your victim a preliminary inspection," he said. "But it looks like the murder weapon was oval in cross-section, tapering to a point from a maximum width of about point seven five centimeters."

"Like a letter opener?" Franny asked.

"I'd suggest a rat-tail comb."

Franny frowned to himself. "Okay," he said.

"Your perpetrator is between five-four and five-six and left-handed. Female. Redhead. Wears Shalimar."

Franny for his notebook. "Shalimar," he repeated, and wrote it down.

"Your victim," Gordon said, "had recently eaten in a Southeast Asian restaurant—Vietnamese, Thai, something like that. Canvass the restaurants in the neighborhood, you'll probably find someone who's seen him with the redhead."

Franny looked puzzled. "I thought you said you'd only done a preliminary," he said. "You've already got stomach contents?"

Gordon shook his head. "No. I just smelled the nuoc mam on him—the fish sauce."

"Fish sauce." Scribbling in his notebook.

"High-quality stuff, too," Gordon said. "Made from squid, not from anchovy paste. I'd check the pricier restaurants first."

"Check." Gordon lifted the sheet, revealing the pale corpse with its tattoos and wild card callosities. "You can give it a whiff if you like. Check it out for yourself."

A spasm crossed Franny's face. "I'll trust you on that one, Doc."

"I'll let you know if I find anything else."

The subsequent autopsy revealed little but the bùn chả in the stomach and some gang tattoos, not surprising since the victim was a known member of the Demon Princes. The question for Franny was going to be whether the killing was gang-related, or something else—and since rat-tail combs were not a favored weapon of the Werewolves, Gordon suspected that the homicide was more in the nature of a personal dispute.

Gordon and Gaida zipped the body up into its bag, put the bag in the cooler, and then it was time to quit.

"I'm heading uptown tonight," Gaida said. She was a Lebanese immigrant, a joker, who wore her hair long to cover the scars where her bat wing–shaped ears had been surgically removed. "Going to take in *Don Giovanni* at Lincoln Center."

"Have a good time," Gordon said.

"You have plans for the weekend?"

"The usual." Gordon shrugged. "Working on my moon rocket."

The diener smiled. "Have a good time with that."

"Oh," Gordon said, "I will."

Gordon hadn't mentioned to Sergeant Gallo that he owned a house in New Jersey, a two-bedroom cabin in Gallo's own Warren County where Gordon went on weekends to conduct his rocket program. Though Gordon followed all precautions and did nothing illegal, it had to be admitted that he kept a very large store of fuel and explosives on his property, and he figured that the fewer people who knew about it, the better. Especially if the people in question were the authorities.

He took the train to Hackettstown and picked up his Volvo station wagon from the parking lot near the station. On the way to his cabin he found a nice fresh piece of roadkill, a raccoon that probably weighed twelve or fourteen pounds. It was a little lean after the long winter but would make a fine dinner, with cornbread-and-sausage stuffing and a red wine sauce. He picked up the raccoon with a pair of surgical gloves, dumped the body in a plastic bag, and put the bag in his trunk. Once he got to the cabin he put the raccoon in his refrigerator. He'd cook it the next day, when Steely Dan came by to help him make his rocket fuel.

The raccoon was boiling in salt water when Steely Dan arrived at mid-morning. Dan was, so far as Gordon knew,

the only joker in Warren County, and he lived there because he had family in the area. Steely Dan was short,
squat, ebon, smooth, and shiny, as if he were made of
blackened, polished steel. He had no body hair, he was
very strong, and his head was literally bullet-shaped.
Children tended to think he was some kind of robot.

He'd been on *American Hero* in its fifth season, but
had lasted only two episodes.

Dan worked at auto repair, and he brought useful skills
to Gordon's rocket program. He had built the steel cells
used to synthesize sodium perchlorate, and also scav-
enged lead diodes from an old auto battery, which
would have been messy if the job had been left to Gordon. The synthesis of $NaClO_4$ was easy enough; but then
any residual chlorides had to be chemically destroyed lest
the subsequent addition of ammonium chloride turn the
compound into a highly unstable chlorate. The oxidizer
itself, ammonium perchlorate, was created through a
process of double decomposition, then purified through
recrystallization. And because NH_4ClO_4 could be ab-
sorbed through the skin, Gordon and Steely Dan both
had to wear protection even though the danger to the
thyroid was slight.

Gordon didn't know if Steely Dan even had a thyroid.

At the end of the long afternoon Gordon had a substantial quantity of ammonium perchlorate, a pure white
powder that when mixed with aluminum powder and a
few minor additives would form solid rocket fuel, the for-
mula used by the Air Force in the boosters of their Hor-
net shuttle.

The operation was carried out in the old barn, amid
the scent of musty old hay and rodent droppings. By the
end of the afternoon, the ammonium perchlorate was
safely transferred to steel drums, then pushed on a hand-
cart to Gordon's storage facility, a prefabricated steel
shed in the middle of a meadow, and surrounded by
berms of earth pushed into place by a neighbor with a

bulldozer. If anything unfortunate should befall the shed, the force of the explosion would go straight up, not out into the countryside.

Which was good, because of what Gordon kept there. The aluminum powder that would turn the ammonium perchlorate into flammable mixture. Kerosene. Tanks of oxygen. Syntin, which had driven the Russians' Sever boosters into space. Hydrazine and nitrogen tetroxide, which were not only explosive in combination but also highly toxic.

Gordon hadn't quite worked out what fuel he wanted to take him to orbit, so he was keeping his options open.

The stuffed raccoon had been sizzling in the oven for two hours. Gordon sautéed new potatoes to serve with it, and he'd made a pesto of ramps, which were the only local vegetable available at this time of year; he served the pesto on linguine, with a sharp parmesan made by one of the local dairy farmers. With the meal Gordon offered a robust Australian shiraz, which Steely Dan preferred in a ten-ounce tumbler, with ice.

"Damn, man," Dan said, after tasting the raccoon. "That's amazing. It's kinda like pork, isn't it?" He had a half-comic strangled voice that contrasted with his formidable appearance.

"Tastes more like brisket to me," Gordon said. He lowered his face over the plate and inhaled the rich aroma.

"This is a first for me," Dan said. "If my family ever ate varmints, that was way before anyone can remember."

"I hate to let an animal go to waste. The whole license business is ridiculous." New Jersey required a license to prepare roadkill, which Gordon thought was simply weird. *Who thought of these things?* he wondered. And who would actually enforce such a law?

"So," Steely Dan said, counting on his fingers, "I've had squirrel here, and possum, and rabbit."

"Venison," Gordon pointed out. "There's a lot of road-kill venison out there."

Steely Dan jabbed at Gordon with his fork. "Is there anything you won't eat?"

"Rat. They can transmit Weil's disease—and believe me, you don't want that."

"I never heard of Weil's disease, but I believe you." Steely Dan took a generous swig of his shiraz.

Gordon chewed thoughtfully, and then remembered the previous day's autopsy. He looked at Steely Dan, and saw himself reflected in the joker's glossy skin. "Do you know any other wild cards living in this area?" he asked.

"Besides yourself?" Steely Dan said. And, at Gordon's blank expression, said, "You are a wild card, right?"

Gordon ignored the question and explained about the unknown joker found on the road nearby. Steely Dan was surprised.

"Just up 519 from here," Gordon said.

"That's weird," Steely Dan said.

"You haven't heard of any, say, sporting events involving wild cards?"

"In Warren County?" Steely Dan shook his bullet head. "Man, that's nuts."

"Murder isn't exactly the most rational act."

Steely Dan's smooth face contorted into an expression of amusement. "Unlike trying to shoot yourself into space," he said.

Gordon grinned. He raised his glass. "Ad astra," he said.

♣

Gordon had been involved with amateur rocketry since he was in his early teens. He had been an Air Force brat, and every air base had a model rocketry club where Gordon could find like-minded peers. He and his friends had built rockets and explosives while consuming vast amounts of science fiction, mostly stuff that had been in the base library for years, if not decades.

Gordon remembered George O. Smith's *Mind Lords of Takis,* Leigh Brackett's *Journey to Alpha C,* Dick's *Radio Free Skait,* "Skait" being the secret, anagrammatical name of Takis, at least according to Philip K. Dick. All books that shared the common assumption that it was only a matter of time before Earth's scientists succeeded in duplicating Takisian starship technology, leading an unshackled humanity to spread into the galaxy. (Though in the Dick, it turned out that humans were grub-like creatures groping along on a burned-out planet, and all human history an illusion implanted by sinister Takisian telepaths.) All these renderings of smooth, efficient Takisian technology made rocketry seem a little quaint, but Gordon was willing to settle for what he could get, at least until someone handed him a starship.

In fact Gordon still belonged to an amateur rocket club, the American Rocket League, which had a big meeting in the Nevada desert every year to fire off boosters that required the participants to have a Federal explosives license, and which regularly climbed higher than fifty miles, right to the brink of space. Gordon was not alone in wanting to send himself into orbit. He liked to think he was farther along than most of them, however.

The fact was that Earth physicists had failed to decode Takisian technology, despite regular claims of breakthroughs that seemed loudest at every budget cycle. Ever since 1950 scientists had promised whole armadas of starships in ten or twenty years.

In the meantime the Air Force and its Space Command shared Earth orbit with an underfunded Russian program. Each operated as secretly as they could, each spied on the other, each put up thousands of communications and spy satellites, each may or may not have weaponized near-Earth orbit. There was no exploration of the Moon or Mars or any of the bodies that had held the imagination of early-twentieth-century writers. Everyone was waiting for his starship. No one got them.

It was beginning to look like the solar system might be all humanity ever got. And now it was the turn of Takisian starships to seem like a quaint, old-fashioned chimera, while rocket technology was beginning to seem like the most contemporary thing in all the world. With the military program in stagnation, it was civilians who were driving rocket innovation now. There was even a cash reward now, the Koopman X Prize, for the best, cheapest, and most practical design.

Gordon figured he was an underdog in the race, but then so were the Wright Brothers. So was Jetboy. Sometimes an underdog could surprise you.

♠

Sunday was a cool, blustery day, with low clouds that scudded urgently along, dropping lashings of rain. Steely Dan picked Gordon up in his pickup truck for a run into Belvidere, where Gordon had a delivery waiting. This was a scaled-down version of an aerospike hybrid rocket engine, a working prototype of a larger design that had never been built. Gordon had bought the prototype when the subcontractor had gone out of business following the cancellation of the Air Force project.

Gordon was beginning to think that hybrid rockets were maybe the way to go. A hybrid had certain inefficiencies, but the aerospike design would more than make up for that. He'd have to work out a way to perform static tests with the new engine, some way that didn't involve setting his property on fire or blowing anything up. He'd have to build more berms, or maybe big trenches. And he'd have to get some HTPB, or make some. . . .

As windshield wipers slapped back and forth, Gordon and Steely Dan discussed the technical details on the ride to Belvidere. Around them the low mountains were green with new spring growth.

One of the nice things about living in rural New Jersey was that the lady who owned the express company was willing to open on a Sunday so that Gordon could collect his delivery. She even fired up her forklift in order to load the rocket engine on the back of Steely Dan's Dodge Ram. The engine came with a good deal of plumbing and electronics, and these were packaged separately, and Gordon and Steely Dan strapped the containers into place around the engine.

"You've got the plans, right?" Steely Dan muttered. "Even with a schematic this is going to be like working a jigsaw puzzle."

After the cargo was strapped in, Gordon bought Steely Dan lunch in a diner. People stared: they weren't used to jokers. This reminded Gordon of the dead joker who had been found nearby. "Let's go look where that victim was dropped," Gordon said.

He knew the place only approximately, but there wasn't anything to look at anyway—just as Gallo had said, there wasn't much around but dairy farms and woods and tree-covered ridges. Holsteins either endured the drizzle or clustered under shelter. Then a different sort of facility loomed into sight around a curve, and Steely Dan slowed without being told.

There were a series of long, low buildings, some of them new, some older and maybe repurposed from another use. There were spotlights on tall metal masts. Surrounding the compound were two forbidding twelve-foot chain-link fences, each topped by dense coils of razor wire.

The place looked more secure than some prisons Gordon had seen. "All it needs is a guard tower in each corner," Steely Dan said.

There was no sign out front, so the place wasn't an enterprise that sold to the public. A fifty-yard-long gravel drive stretched from the highway to the gates, and Gordon could see a small metal sign on the gate.

"Turn down here," Gordon said.

Steely Dan brought the truck to a halt at the driveway entrance. "You sure?" he asked.

"Yeah. What are they going to do, arrest us?"

"They could hit us with fucking baseball bats."

Gravel crunched under the Ram's tires as Steely Dan steered it toward the front gate. He brought the vehicle to a halt, and Gordon stepped out and regarded the facility.

Cold wind rustled up the back of his jacket. He heard dogs barking. There was a wet animal scent in the air. Gordon looked at the rusted sign on the front gate.

IDS
CANINE BREEDING
AND TRAINING FACILITY
UNIT #1

Gordon had no idea who or what IDS was. There was a rubber squeeze bulb hanging outside the gate, with a wire that led to the nearest building. Gordon squeezed the bulb, and he heard a metallic clatter from inside the building. A chorus of dog barks rose at the sound.

A door slammed behind him as Steely Dan left the pickup truck. His bullet head was shrunk in his jacket, and his eyes scanned uneasily back and forth.

"What are you gonna do?" he asked.

"I'm going to tell them I want a puppy," said Gordon.

"Yeah," Steely Dan said, "they're for sure gonna believe that."

A man came out of the building. He was tall and wore

a scowl on his face. He seemed fit and wore green-and-brown camouflage fatigues with lace-up military boots. The only piece of apparel that didn't look government issue was a wide cowboy belt, with a buckle in the shape of a longhorn bull's head.

"Yeah," the man said. "You need something?"

Surprise rose in Gordon at the man's Eastern European accent. "You breed dogs, right?" Gordon said. "I was thinking of getting a dog."

The man didn't reply. His eyes moved from Gordon to Steely Dan, and then his expression turned thoughtful.

"You do sell dogs, right?" Gordon prompted.

The man's eyes didn't leave Steely Dan as he answered. "We breed and train dogs for the military, police, customs, and border guards," he said. "We only sell to government agencies."

"Oh," Gordon said. "Sorry to bother you."

The man pointed at Dan. "Wasn't he on the television? *American Hero*?"

"Yes, that's right."

The man raised a fist and made a muscle. "Very strong, yes?"

Gordon nodded. "Yes. Very strong."

The man said nothing more. Gordon and Steely Dan returned to the truck, backed out onto the highway, and headed for Gordon's cabin. The man stood behind the gate, watching them the entire way.

◆

There was only one dead joker in the morgue on Monday morning, a straightforward shooting, and Gordon went upstairs to the squad room to deliver a copy of the autopsy to Harvey Kant, the detective in charge.

Kant was the most senior detective at the precinct and had been there at least forty years. If anyone had told him it was time to retire, he'd ignored the advice. Rumors were that he was holding something, or several some-things, over senior members of the department, and they'd decreed he could stay as long as he liked.

Kant was brown and scaled and looked like a heav-ily weathered dinosaur. He dressed in a frayed suit of polyester-blend gabardine and smelled strongly of cigars. He ignored the autopsy photos, glanced at the written report, then put both in their jacket and tossed it on his desk. Because he held a detective rank equivalent to lieu-tenant, most of the cops just called him "Lou."

"Nine millimeter," he said. "Fits the Sig found on the scene." He gave a sound like a cross between a snarl and a hacking cough. "Another goddamn drug shooting," he said. "I'm gonna be chasing my own ass for days on this one."

"Hey Doc!" Franny Black crossed the room smiling. He carried a tall clear plastic coffee go-cup from Café Mussolini down the street.

"I wanted to thank you about that description you gave me the other day," he said. "Redheaded woman, five six?"

"You found her?" Gordon asked.

"Sure did. She was hostess in the third Vietnamese res-taurant I visited. And I'm glad you told me she was left-handed, because that was the hand I was watching when she drew the rat-tail comb out of her purse and tried to stab me."

"Glad you didn't end up on my slab," Gordon said.

"Yeah, Franny." The new speaker was the rail-thin De-tective McTate, known as Slim Jim, who had followed Franny into the squad room. "You're lucky all around. The doc here gives you a perfect description of the perp, and you get credit for the bust."

Franny flushed. For a cop, Gordon thought, he flushed rather easily.

"How's the search for El Monstro coming along?" Gordon asked.

"El Monstro? He's vanished." Franny shrugged. "I don't know how a joker eight feet tall can just disappear, but that's what happened."

"The family?"

"His mother's in a wheelchair and doesn't speak English. The father's dead." Franny's eyes narrowed. "But the sister's hiding something."

"But not her brother?"

"Not in that little bitty apartment, no."

Kant eyed Franny's coffee. "What's that you're drinking, Fran?"

"Iced peppermint macchiato," Franny said in all innocence.

"Yeah." Kant nodded. "All us detective he-men like us our peppermint macchiatos."

Franny flushed a deeper shade, and he turned to Gordon. "Thanks, anyway," he said, and faded in the direction of the men's room.

Kant's lipless mouth stretched into a grin as he watched Franny's retreat, and then he looked at Gordon. "Sometimes the information you dig up is uncanny," he said. "Sometimes it's useless." He picked up the jacket with the weekend's homicide. "I mean, yeah, I know the guy was shot, thanks anyway. And sometimes . . ." He shook his head. "Remember when you told me that the perp was six feet six and armed with a club?"

Slim Jim was grinning. "I ain't heard this story," he said.

"I was lookin' for a fucking Neanderthal," Kant said.

"I didn't see the crime scene," Gordon explained. "Nobody told me about the—"

"About the ladder," Kant said. "The perp was four foot nine and killed the vic by dropping a bowling ball from a ladder."

Slim Jim guffawed.

"If I had seen the crime scene photos," Gordon said, "I would have seen the ladder."

"I spent ten days looking for the Terminator," Kant said, "and instead I was looking for a munchkin."

"If I don't have all the information," Gordon said, "I can't—"

He looked up and saw a group of uniformed officers coming into the squad room to report to Kant on a door-to-door survey of the area around the crime scene. Among them he recognized Dina Quattore, the telepathic ace attached to the K-9 unit.

Oh, he thought. *That would work.*

"You turned investigator now?" asked Dina Quattore. "Maybe I should buy you a freakin' Sherlock Holmes hat."

She was in Gordon's Volvo station wagon, heading toward the dog-breeding facility. Dina was a New York cop out of Fort Freak, a short, buxom woman with curly black hair. Gordon had talked her into joining him on her free afternoon, and she was out of uniform, dressed in jeans and a baggy nylon jacket that covered the pistol she wore on her hip.

"I just got curious about this place," Gordon said. "They claim they're a dog-training facility, but I think there may be other things going on in there."

"What kind of other things?" Dina asked.

"A joker was found dead near there."

"Uh-huh," Dina said. "Doc, it's the Sherlock Holmes hat for you."

Gordon was clearly stepping outside his sphere. Despite what might be seen on television, real-life forensic pathologists and profilers and crime scene investigators and other specialists did not actually confront suspects, participate in car chases, or get involved in shootouts. Gordon's job was to perform autopsies. Sometimes he'd be called to the scene, sometimes he'd testify at a trial, sometimes he'd hear about an arrest, and often he never ever found out about the disposition of a case. His focus was normally confined to the morgue.

But he couldn't help but notice that there were some unaccounted-for anomalies here in Warren County. The dead John Doe was one, and the IDS facility was another. Maybe the two belonged together.

He'd done research on IDS. They had no web page, no listed telephone number. They had a business license in New Jersey, with the address of the facility.

It wasn't even clear what IDS stood for.

"Also," Gordon said, "the man at the facility was a Russian or something."

Dina snickered. "I hope you give me my share of credit when you crack the spy ring."

"Just look at the place," Gordon said. "Tell me it's legit."

He slowed the Volvo to a crawl as they approached the compound. Dina looked out the window in silence as the buildings moved past. "Pull off the road once we're out of sight," she said, her voice suddenly serious.

"What are you getting?"

Dina shook her head. Her eyes were closed in concentration. Gordon drove on till the compound was hidden behind a stand of silver maple, then pulled onto the shoulder and parked. Dina led Gordon across a roadside ditch partly filled with water after the last rain. The humid, cool air was filled with the scent of spring flowers. Gordon and Dina walked slowly through the trees until they had a view of the IDS facility, and then Dina bent her head, her face set in an expression of fierce concentration.

Dina, Gordon knew, was a telepath. She could read the thoughts of others at a distance.

But not humans. Dina could only read dogs. That's why she worked with the K-9 unit. NYPD Public Relations called her "K-10." Everyone else called her Dina.

Water dripped down Gordon's collar as he waited. Then Dina straightened and shook her head. She tapped her nose. "You know what I'm smelling?" she asked. "Semtex."

"Plastic explosive."

Dina nodded toward the compound. "They're training bomb-sniffer dogs right this minute," she said. "Other dogs are being trained to find drugs." She shook her head. "Man, that chronic must be twenty years old, it's a miracle they're not training the dogs to find mold." She began walking back toward the car. "None of the dogs seem unhappy, and none are being mistreated. And if there are explosives and controlled substances used to train the dogs, that explains the high security." She looked at Gordon and laughed. "Sorry to destroy your detective fantasy."

Gordon shrugged. "It's better to know," he said. He opened the passenger door for her. "Dinner's on me," he said.

Dina started to get into the car, then hesitated. "No offense, Doc," she said, "but does that mean you're doing the cooking?"

Gordon blinked at her. "Sure."

Dina gave Gordon an uncomfortable look. "You know," she said, "my taste in food is pretty conventional, when all's said and done."

"Game is organic," Gordon said, "and it's lean. Free-range. It's better for you than anything you'll find in a supermarket."

A stubborn expression entered Dina's eyes. "Doc," she said, "I've eaten your chili."

Gordon surrendered. "I'll take you to a restaurant."

Dina's smile was brilliant. "Thanks."

He took her to a place in Belvidere with a view of the Delaware. He didn't know whether she was on a low-carb diet or whether her tastes in food were more like a dog's than those of a human; but Gordon watched Dina devour a fourteen-ounce rib eye while taking only a few bites of her salad and baked potato.

The conversation was pleasantly professional, ranging from weird crimes to weird autopsies. An older couple at a nearby table asked to be moved when Dina described a cadaver one of her dogs had found.

Gordon found himself enjoying Dina's company. She was a very attractive young woman, and he was far from immune to her allure.

Most men, he supposed, would be wondering what Dina looked like naked. Gordon had no such questions, for the simple reason that he already knew the answer. He'd seen more naked women, of every size and age and description, than the most accomplished seducer. There were no mysteries left—not even cause of death, because he always found that out.

That the vast majority of the women he met were dead put him at something of a social disadvantage with living females, but not as much as most people might think.

Beauty did not leave with death. The human body was a marvel of intricate design, the highly crafted product of millions of years of evolution. Contained within its morphology were membranes as delicate as a spider's web, a muscle as powerful and enduring as the heart, a structure as diffuse and ephemeral as the lymphoid system. The musculoskeletal system was a glory of complexity, the interaction between muscles and bone producing everything from a champion athlete to a shy girl's smile.

The human body was as varied and wonderful as the surface of a planet.

The wild card added to the wonder: sometimes its

improvisations were brilliant, sometimes merely chaotic. It subverted every single cell—or enhanced it. Or both.

Gordon lived a fair percentage of his professional life in a constant state of awe.

After dinner Gordon joined Dina on the train back to New York.

"You know," she said, "everyone at the precinct thinks you're a joker."

He looked at her in surprise. "You think I'm not?"

"You've been around some of my dogs," Dina said. "They can usually smell a wild card—the metabolism's generally tweaked some way that causes the difference to come out the pores."

"I've noticed that myself," Gordon said.

"I think you're just—" She laughed. "Skinny and very tall."

Gordon nodded. "Good observation, there, Officer."

"And another thing," she said, tapping his arm. "You make a terrible Sherlock Holmes."

I guess, Gordon thought, *I'll have to settle for being Wernher von Braun.*

They left the train at Pennsylvania Station and ran into the usual Penn Station crowd: commuters, street people, and pimps waiting for the arrival of runaway teenagers from Minnesota. Gordon saw Dina to a cab. "Dinner again some time?" he said.

She smiled up at him. "I feel like I need a booster seat sitting across the table from you," she said.

He shrugged. "I'll have the waitress bring you one."

Dina nodded. "Okay. Give me a call."

Well, he thought as he watched her drive away, *that went well.*

♣

There was a lot of yelling from Interrogation Room Two. A woman kept wailing, "He was a good boy!" and a man's voice was uttering threats against the city, the department, and probably everybody else.

Gordon looked around for Detective Kant and saw only Detective Van Tranh, the vibrating ace who failed utterly to rejoice in his nickname of "Dr. Dildo."

"Kant sent for me," Gordon said.

Tranh waved in the direction of the interrogation room. "Your Jersey John Doe got identified," he said. "He's one of the missing on Squid's list. Franny and the Lou are trying to calm the family down."

"And I'm supposed to help with that?"

"You're supposed to explain the medical evidence," Tranh said. "So far, the family isn't convinced."

Gordon stepped toward the door, then hesitated. "I should go back and get my autopsy report."

"Fran's got a copy."

"Okay." Gordon walked to the door, knocked, and entered the small room where Kant and Franny were being shouted at by the grieving family.

Gordon had met his share of bereaved couples over the years, but he had never encountered quite so much drama stuffed into two people. They were both broad and tall and took up a lot of space, and they made so much noise that they seemed to occupy the whole room. Mrs. Heffer cried, wailed, asked God to punish her, and kept insisting her son was a good boy. Mr. Heffer suspected conspiracy, refused to believe a thing he was told, and banged the table as he uttered threats. "My son did not have a heart attack!" he shouted as he kicked a chair. "He worked out all the time! He studied Brazilian Jiu-Jitsu!"

"It wasn't a heart attack," Gordon attempted. "It was sudden cardiac death."

Mr. Heffer beat himself on the chest with a fleshy fist. "My son did not have a heart attack!" he screamed.

"Aortic valve stenosis is not uncommon in young men—" Gordon began.

"Not uncommon," Mr. Heffer repeated scornfully.

"What the hell does that mean? You're contradicting yourself already!"

"People were always making trouble for him!" Mrs. Heffer said. "Tommy was a good boy!"

Mr. Heffer waved a fist. "My son was kidnapped!" he said. "Why else would he be way the hell out in Jersey?"

Franny opened his notebook and readied his pen. "Do you know anyone who might want to kidnap Tom Junior?" he asked.

Heffer stared at him in utter scorn. "That's what you people are supposed to find out!" he said. He beat his chest again. "How the hell would I know who kidnapped him? Do I look like I hang around with kidnappers?"

"Kidnapped!" Mrs. Heffer burst into tears. "He was probably kidnapped by that communist from down the street."

"Communist?" Confusion swam into Franny's face. "What communist?"

"He runs the tobacco shop," Mrs. Heffer said. "He sells poison to the kids!"

"How do you know he's a communist?" Franny asked, and then they both began shouting at him.

Gordon decided to interrupt with the one fact that might be relevant. "Tom Junior didn't smoke," he pointed out. The lungs had been pink and healthy.

"Damn right Tommy didn't smoke!" Mr. Heffer said.

"He was a good boy!" Mrs. Heffer wailed.

Perhaps it was the mention of tobacco that spurred Harvey Kant's action. He drew a large cigar out of his gabardine jacket, snapped open his lighter, and brought the flame to the cigar's tip. He puffed noisily and with great satisfaction, blowing out clouds of smoke. Mrs. Heffer sneezed. "Hey!" said Mr. Heffer. He pointed at the No Smoking sign. "You can't do that in here!"

"I'm the lieutenant," Kant said. "I decide who smokes and who doesn't."

Within a few minutes Kant had succeeded in gassing

the Heffers into silence, after which he gave them the information necessary to claim their son's body from the New Jersey morgue.

Mr. Heffer managed to summon an echo of his earlier belligerence. "Jersey!" he said. "What's my boy doing up there?"

"It's the Jersey cops' case," Kant said. "That's where he was found."

Heffer sneered. "Why in hell are we talking to you, then?" he said.

After the Heffers left, Gordon stood with Kant and Franny in the squad room. Gordon's head swam, though he couldn't tell whether it was from the cigar smoke or the Heffers' shouting.

Kant took a last draw on his cigar, then crushed the lit end against his scaly palm.

"Right," he said, and turned to Franny. "Tommy Heffer was kidnapped here and dumped in Jersey, the CO gave you this case, so liaise with the Jersey cops. Now—" He handed Franny the victim's file. "In spite of what the mom said about his being a good boy, the vic had some scrapes with the law—drunk and disorderly, fighting, vandalism. He was never formally charged with anything, so he doesn't have a record per se—but you can start by talking to the other kids who were arrested along with him."

"They're not kids. One of them is this guy Eel," Franny argued.

"I know you're the the big celebrity cop, but I'm the lieutenant." Kant grinned. "So talk to the kids."

A muscle in Franny's jaw moved. "Yes, sir," he said.

"Good boy." Another gesture with the cigar. "The vic studied Brazilian Jiu-Jitsu," Kant said. "And El Monstro was Brazilian. So there's a connection, maybe, at the Jiu-Jitsu school."

Franny looked dubious. "El Monstro was working at least two jobs as well as going to college," he said. "I doubt he had time to train in martial arts—especially as he didn't need to. Anyone attacking him would just bounce off. And Eddie said some of the guys sounded Russian."

"Check it anyway," said Kant.

Kant ambled back to his desk. Franny looked at the file folder in his hand, and his lips tightened. "Fran?" Gordon asked.

Franny jerked out of whatever thoughts were distracting him. "Yeah?"

"When you see the Jersey cops, could you not mention I have a house out in Warren County?"

"I didn't know you had a place out there. But sure, okay." Franny frowned. "Why?"

"I go out there to relax and work on my own stuff. I don't want to be the guy they call on weekends when their own medical examiner is drunk."

Which was true enough, though the shed full of rocket propellant had a lot more to do with why he preferred to remain invisible to his neighbors.

Franny nodded slowly. "Sure. That makes sense."

"Thanks. See you later."

Gordon returned to his basement morgue and finished helping Gaida bag the shooting victim, after which Gaida went to lunch and Gordon signed off on the last of the paperwork while gnawing on a log of homemade pemmican. He heard a knock on the door and looked up to see Dina Quattore. "Come in," he said.

Dina was in uniform, curly black hair sprouting from beneath her peaked cap. The radio at her hip hissed and squawked.

"Just wanted to let you know another stiff is on its way," she said. "Elderly street joker, walked in front of a bus while drunk, stoned, or otherwise impaired."

"Am I needed at the crime scene?"

"No. Plenty of witnesses to what happened."

"Okay." Gordon capped his pen and offered his plastic container of pemmican. "Care for some?"

Dina approached and peered at the dark brown pemmican logs. "What is it?"

"Pemmican."

"And what's that?"

"Ground venison," Gordon said, "rendered suet . . ."

"Wait a minute!" Dina yelped. "You're offering me a roadkill meat bar?"

"It also has dried fruit, nuts, and honey," Gordon pointed out. "Very nutritious. Everything your Mohawk warrior needs on the trail—good for quick energy, and you can store it for years."

"How many years has this—?" Dina began, then shook her head. "Never mind. I'll stick with the turkey sandwich I got at Mussolini's."

"Bring it and we'll have lunch, if you have the time."

Dina considered this. "You may not have the time, with the stiff coming."

Gordon shrugged. "The deceased won't be in a hurry."

"True that." Dina went upstairs to her locker, then returned with the plastic-wrapped sandwich and a can of Diet Pepsi. She parked herself on a plastic chair near the X-ray machine, then began to unwrap her sandwich. She looked at him from under the brim of her cap.

"Is it true what they say about you?" she asked.

"Depends," Gordon said. "What do they say?"

"That you build rockets?"

He hadn't realized any of the police officers actually knew that. Gaida, he thought, must have talked. Still, there was no reason to lie. "Yes," he said.

"How big?"

He preferred evasion. "Different sizes," he said.

"Gaida says you're going to shoot yourself to the moon," Dina said.

"Well," he said. "I'd need help." He told her about the

Koopman Prize, and how anyone with a decent design was eligible. Dina chewed her turkey sandwich thoughtfully, then took a sip of her Pepsi. "I'm trying to figure you out, Doc," she said.

Gordon considered this. "I don't know that I'm particularly mysterious."

"You're not hidden," Dina said, "but I'm not sure how all the parts fit together."

Gordon had never considered himself as a collection of randomly ordered parts and had no answer to this. He took a bite of his pemmican and chewed.

Dina took off her cap and hung it from the X-ray machine. "You know," she said, "I think you're some kind of goofy romantic."

"Uhh—" Gordon began, uncertain. He had never categorized himself this way.

"Yeah!" Dina said, suddenly enthusiastic. "You cut up bodies as part of your crusade for justice! You want to plant the flag on another world!" She pointed at the pemmican. "And you recycle dead animals!"

Gordon blinked. "I usually autopsy them first."

She frowned. "Okay," she said. "That's disturbing."

"I learn stuff," he said.

He was about to object to being called a romantic and say that he was interested in the way jokers were put together in the same way that he was interested in the way rockets were put together—but then it occurred to him that if Dina thought of him as a romantic, that might say good things about her intentions toward him.

"Anyway," Dina said. "I'd like to see the rockets."

"Okay." Pressing his luck seemed a good idea. "This weekend?"

"I've got family stuff on Saturday," she said. "How about Sunday?"

"Sure."

"I can take the train out, and you can pick me up at

the station. I'll see the rockets, and then you'll take me out to dinner."

"Great."

"At a restaurant," she added.

"If you like."

Gordon decided that being a romantic was working for him. Until the weekend, when he found that Steely Dan had gone missing.

♠

"Another joker vanished," Franny said. He looked around Steely Dan's living room, his pen paused over his notebook without anything to write. "Another element in the series," he said. "And this time, the crime happens in New Jersey. And you think that dog-training facility may have something to do with it?"

Gordon followed Franny as he prowled into Dan's kitchen, where a half-eaten breakfast of eggs and sausage sat on the dinette next to a cold cup of coffee. If there'd been a knock on the door while Dan was eating, he'd have left his breakfast and walked to the door to open it . . . and then what? A clout on the head, a jab with a Taser? Dan was strong, but his skin only looked like blackened steel. He was as vulnerable to a weapon as any nat.

"That Russian at the facility was very interested in Steely Dan," Gordon said. "Kept staring at him."

"Jokers get stared at," said Franny. "More in the sticks than anywhere, I imagine." He frowned. "The Jersey cops looked into that place when Tommy Heffer turned up there. But it's legit—they even sell their dogs to the Jersey state cops."

"They could have a legitimate business on top of whatever it is they're really up to," Gordon said.

"Maybe," Franny conceded. "But there's no grounds for a warrant."

"I suppose not," Gordon said.

If only Dina had sensed something.

And the weekend started so well, he thought. Normally Friday was one of his busy days, for the simple reason that a lot of people got killed on Thursday night. The reason the homicide rates jumped on Thursday was that Friday was usually payday, and by Thursday people were starting to run short of money.

The usual scenario ran something like this:

1. Mommy wants to use the remaining money to buy Little Timmy's school lunch on Friday.
2. Daddy wants to use the money to buy beer.

Therefore:

3. Daddy beats Mommy to death, takes the money, and gets drunk.

Unfortunately Daddy is usually unable to reason out the next couple of steps, which are:

4. Daddy ends up in prison, and;
5. Little Timmy gets lost in the foster care system, which mightily increases the odds of Timmy becoming an angry sociopath who perpetuates the cycle of violence into the next generation.

The other high time for homicide was late Saturday night and early Sunday morning, where the motivation might also be money, but was usually sex and/or love.

However, on this particular week in May, the bliss of a beautiful spring seemed to have descended on New York, and all the Daddies had decided they didn't need the beer after all and taken all the Little Timmys of the city to the park to play catch, and Gordon was finished with his work by one in the afternoon. So he gave himself and Gaida the rest of the day off and took the train to Warren County, where he spent the rest of the afternoon loading model rockets with his homemade APCP and firing them into the mellow May sky.

On Saturday Steely Dan was scheduled to come round in the afternoon to help plot a static test facility for the aerospike engine, but he hadn't turned up. Gordon called his home and mobile with no result, then called the garage where he worked. His boss said he hadn't come in for work on Friday, and that he'd called Dan's cell phone without getting an answer.

Steely Dan lived in an old shiplap farmhouse that came with twenty acres of decaying apple orchard. Gordon drove there, found Dan's truck and car in the garage, and pounded on the door without result. That's when he called Franny Black, and Franny called the Jersey police, who still hadn't turned up.

New Jersey loved its jokers, that was clear.

Franny had found Dan's spare key under a rock in the garden, and he'd let the two of them inside. "No sign of violence," Franny said, prowling into Dan's bedroom. "Nothing obviously stolen. No sign of abduction at all."

Frustration flared in Gordon's nerves. "I can tell you one thing," he said. "Dan didn't do Brazilian Jiu-Jitsu."

"Christ." Franny rolled his eyes. "That lead went nowhere," he said. "Just like I told him it would."

"Any leads on El Monstro?"

Franny shook his head, and tapped the butt end of his pen against his jaw. "Jokers," Franny said. "Dogs. Jokers and dogs. Dogs and jokers." He waved a hand in frustration. "I don't get it."

"What I get about the Jersey cops," Gordon said, "is that they care more about the dogs than the jokers."

Franny hesitated, then put a hand on Gordon's arm. "I'll find your friend."

"Let's hope," Gordon said, "that he's not found stretched out on a road somewhere."

♦

The Jersey police did eventually show up, but Gallo had the weekend off and wasn't among them, and Franny had to explain everything from the beginning. Gordon lacked the patience to hear it, so he went back to his cabin and for lack of anything better to do took one of his rockets out of the barn and put it on the launcher. He pressed the igniter into the solid fuel at the base of the rocket and connected it to the nine-volt battery and remote receiver. He then stepped to a safe distance, flicked the rocker switch on his remote control to ON, and saw the LEDs shift from Safety to Armed. He poised his thumb over the Fire button, looked at the rocket, made sure his binoculars were in his other hand, and pressed the button.

Gordon raised his binoculars to his eyes as the rocket flew straight and true for six or eight hundred meters, then ran out of fuel, popped its parachute, and drifted home to Earth.

He watched the launch without pleasure. After the rocket drifted silently to its meeting with the lush New Jersey meadow, Gordon stared at it for a long while, frustration building in his heart, and then he put the rocket gear back in the barn and carried his binoculars to the car. He drove to the grove of silver maples from which he and Dina had observed the IDS facility, parked, went into the woods, and settled down to observe the compound.

The NYPD would call Gordon's operation a "plant." Everyone else in the world called it a "stakeout."

Observation didn't reveal much. A trainer exercised half a dozen German shepherds on a dog run inside the compound. Both the dogs and the trainer seemed to be enjoying themselves. Occasionally Gordon saw people walking from one building to another. He was too far away to recognize any of them. He coped with the tedium by planning a more scientific investigation of the compound. He'd visit a spy store in Manhattan, he decided, buy some boom mikes, a video camera with a telephoto lens, a capacious hard drive capable of holding twenty-four hours' worth of images.

If Steely Dan's distinctive silhouette appeared on any of the video, or his distinctive strangled-puppet voice on audio, that would suffice for a warrant. Or so he imagined.

Gordon was working out the finer details of this fantasy when he heard a car slowing on the highway behind him. He turned and his heart gave a lurch as he saw a white panel van pulling up onto the highway shoulder behind his Volvo.

Moist earth squelched beneath his feet as he ducked behind a hackberry bush, then raised his binoculars. He could see only the dark silhouette of a driver behind the windscreen. The driver seemed to be peering around, looking for the Volvo's driver. Gordon huddled into himself on the far side of the hackberry.

After thirty seconds or so the driver gunned his engine, then pulled the van back onto the highway. Gordon watched as he drove past, then turned into the IDS facility.

I believe I have been busted, he thought. If the driver had got his license plate, they could have his ID in short order. He'd been in newspapers with one thing or another, and all they'd have to do to get his picture was Google his name.

Maybe Dina was right, and he really sucked as an investigator.

♥

Sunday afternoon with Dina wasn't a success. The day was gray and overcast, with scattered showers, and

Gordon was too distracted by Dan's disappearance to play host. Though Dina actually seemed interested in the rockets and the big aerospike engine sitting unassembled in the barn, Gordon himself couldn't raise his usual enthusiasm. As he loaded one of his bigger rockets with APCP, he told Dina about his plan to stake out the IDS facility, and asked what kind of cameras and detectors would be best.

"I'm not an expert on any of that stuff," Dina said. "You should ask some of the detectives back at Fort Freak—Kant or somebody. They're used to running plants."

"Franny Black is supposed to be in charge of the investigation."

"Little Mister Golden Drawers. The Spy from the Commissioner's Office." Her face gave a little twist of distaste, and then she gave the matter more thought. "It doesn't have to be you running the plant," she pointed out. "You don't need a warrant to surveil a place, or to point a shotgun mic out a window. Franny could do it legally." She cackled. "And the rest of the precinct would love it if he spent all his time out here."

Gordon nodded. "I'll talk to him."

Dina gave another laugh. "And if Franny weren't so wet behind the ears," she said, "he'd know that while he can't get a warrant to visit IDS to look for a missing joker, there are agencies who have a job inspecting places like IDS. There has to be some Jersey state agency who has the right to walk in and make sure the dogs aren't being abused." She thought for a moment, her eyes staring into space, and then she snapped her fingers. "Office of Animal Welfare," she said. "I've worked with them a couple times. I can make some calls for you."

"I'd appreciate that."

She looked at the rocket. "How far can that one go up?"

"A couple miles."

Dina was startled. "Seriously?"

"Sure. Three stages, it'll go high. I have to make sure there aren't any aircraft around."

Her eyes narrowed. "You got rockets bigger than that?"

"Sure. But I'm a lot more careful about firing them off. Some of them, I have to go to Nevada."

She grinned. "Area 51?"

He gave her a blank look. "Where?"

"Never mind."

"I go to Black Rock," Gordon said.

She smiled, shook her head. "That's great," she said.

Gordon had the feeling he'd just missed something.

He shouldered the five-foot-long rocket and they walked out into a meadow wet with spring showers and fragrant with the scent of wildflowers. Dina followed, carrying the launch rod that supported the rocket while it was on the ground. Gordon readied the rocket and connected the battery. After they retreated to a safe distance, Gordon listened for any approaching aircraft and heard nothing beyond the sough of the wind. He took the control out of his pocket, pressed the rocker switch to ON, watched the LEDs shift to Armed, and then handed the control to Dina.

"Be my guest," he said. "Just press the red button."

A delighted smile flashed across Dina's face. Gordon decided he liked the smile a lot. "Really?" she asked.

"Sure." He readied his binoculars.

Dina looked from the control to the rocket and back. "Do I do a countdown or anything?"

"You can do a countdown," Gordon said, "recite a poem, sing 'The Star-Spangled Banner.' Whatever you like."

"Three. Two. One." She flashed the smile again. "To the Moon!" She pushed the button and the rocket hissed upward.

The staging worked flawlessly, with no tip-off, and the

first stage tumbled back to the ground while the second stage pierced the low cloud and disappeared. Even the hiss of rocket exhaust faded. There was a distant pop as the third stage separated and—Gordon trusted—ignited. The scent of burnt propellant tinged the odor of spring flowers. The second stage, trailing streamers, drifted down through the cloud layer and landed fifty feet away. And then the third stage arrowed down, aimed like a spear at the ground.

"Oh dear," Gordon said, and then the falling stage impaled the turf with the sound of a wet slap.

Gordon and Dina walked to the third stage, which had crumpled beyond repair. "Parachute failure," Gordon said.

"Maybe we'll make it to the Moon next time," said Dina.

"We'll send up a really big one," Gordon said. "I'll get Dan to come out and . . ." His voice trailed away as he remembered that Dan had gone missing.

Dina touched his arm. "We'll get him back," she said.

Gordon wasn't comforted. *Dogs and jokers,* he thought. *Jokers and dogs.*

Gordon decided to take Dina to dinner amid the bustle and excitement of Phillipsburg, the county's largest town. Because they were taking the train to New York and wouldn't be coming back, Gordon locked the cabin and closed the gate on the road as they left. Rain drummed down, and Gordon turned on the wipers.

"So there's something I've been meaning to ask," he said as he pulled from his rural route onto Highway 519. "Do you think you're a romantic?"

Dina was surprised. "Me?" she said. "I don't think so."

A burst of rain clattered on the roof. "With your skills," Gordon said, "you could be a dog trainer, or a dog whisperer, or whatever they're called. Or you could have a famous dog act and travel around the world putting on shows. But instead you wear a uniform and work in a dangerous part of town and catch criminals." He grinned at her. "Isn't that a romantic thing to do?" *At least as romantic,* he thought, as *cutting up dead bodies.*

Dina knit her brows in thought. "Those other jobs you mention," she said, "they don't come with pensions."

Gordon looked at her. "Are pensions romantic?"

She grinned. "I hope so," she said. "I plan on living happily ever after with mine." She waved a hand. "With the NYPD, I've got a pension, I've got a decent paycheck, and what I do isn't really dangerous—I just follow a dog around. The only problem I have is finding an apartment that'll let me keep dogs."

"You've got dogs of your own?"

"Yeah. Two rescue dogs. They were abused."

"Bring them next time you come," Gordon said. "They'll like the country."

She gave an unexpected scowl, and Gordon was startled at this reaction to his invitation; but then he decided she was thinking of the abuse her dogs had suffered. Then her head whipped around, and Gordon realized that they were passing the IDS facility, visible as a floodlit glow in the rain. "Stop!" she said urgently.

"What?"

"Stop. Now."

His mind whirling, Gordon slowed and pulled to the side of the road. Dina's eyes remained focused on the IDS compound. Her hand scrabbled for the door release.

"I've got to get closer," she muttered.

"Wait," Gordon said. "What's going on?"

But she was already out of the car, her jacket pulled over her head. Gordon set the parking brake, opened the door, and followed. Cold rain needled his scalp and spattered rainbows on his glasses. He blinked and pursued Dina's dark silhouette outlined by the floodlights.

She slowed and Gordon splashed up to her, his shoes half submerged in a puddle. Dina was hunched over, her jacket still pulled up over her head, both hands pressed to her forehead. Suddenly she straightened.

"They're in there!" she said. "The captives!"

Gordon's heart lurched in his chest. "What?" he said. He stared at her through glasses pebbled by rainfall. "How do you know?"

Dina made a frantic gesture, pointed at her head with both forefingers. "I'm seeing through a dog's eyes!" she said. "I'm looking right at them. Dan's in there with the others!"

"Others?" Gordon said.

Dina frantically started digging into her jacket pockets for her phone. "Gotta call Franny!" she said. "Get a warrant!"

Her words were buried beneath a torrent of barking. The chain-link fence rattled and bowed under the impact of heavy German shepherd bodies. And then Gordon was dazzled by a battery of floodlights switching on, brilliant halogen beams burning into his eyes . . .

"STAY WHERE YOU ARE," said an amplified voice. "YOU ARE TRESPASSING."

"Fuck this," Dina muttered. She grabbed Gordon's arm. "Back to the car!"

She turned as electric motors rolled open the front gate and three dogs raced out, barking. Heart hammering, Gordon readied himself for a doomed sprint to the car. Dina spun again, gestured with the hand that had pulled the phone from her pocket. The dogs slowed, seemingly puzzled. Then two of them stopped and sat down on the wet ground. The third walked timidly up to Dina and sniffed her hand.

She was in telepathic contact with the dogs, Gordon realized.

"Can you control them?" he asked.

"Not control," she said. "But I can fill their minds with happy thoughts."

"Um, good," Gordon said. His limbs twitched, wanted to run. "What do we do now?"

"Go to the car. But slowly. You don't want to run, because that might activate the pack instinct to chase you down."

"Okay," Gordon said. He began easing backwards toward the Volvo. Dina moved with him.

Lightning sizzled overhead. In the sudden searing brilliance, Gordon saw two men walking out of the IDS gate. One of them had a rifle, the other a pistol. They moved forward onto the floodlit driveway. "You stop there!" one of them called. He was the man Gordon had spoken to earlier, and he wore a cowboy hat against the rain. He brandished his rifle. "We'll shoot!" he warned.

"Uh," Gordon said, uncertain. "Do we run now?"

He heard steel enter Dina's voice. "Not . . . just . . . yet," she said.

The dogs' ears pricked up, and they turned to look at the two advancing men. One of the dogs rose from its sitting position and took a few steps toward the two, and paused in a hunting posture, leaning forward, one forefoot raised.

"Nobody move!" said the man in the cowboy hat. He raised the rifle to his shoulder as he and his comrade advanced. Neither of them seemed to have noticed their dogs' uncharacteristic behavior. *Maybe*, Gordon thought, *Dina isn't filling their minds with happy thoughts any longer.*

All three dogs were on their feet now, moving low to the ground as they advanced on the two armed men. And then one of them gave a savage growl and hurled itself at the throat of the man with the rifle.

There was a shot that went nowhere and the man went

down. The other two dogs were bounding to their prey, and the man with the pistol started shooting.

"Now we run!" Dina said, and she and Gordon both turned and began racing for the car. Dina's legs were a lot shorter, but she was fast, and pulled ahead.

There were more shots, followed by an agonized canine howl. Dina gasped and pitched forward onto her face.

Gordon's nerves gave a jolt. He splashed to a stop, turned, bent over Dina, looked for the bullet wound, asked if she was all right. Her eyes were open and staring. Her face was blank. He could hear her breathing heavily but there was no response.

Gordon shuddered as more shots cracked out. He gave a desperate glance in the direction of the gate, and through the rain beading his spectacles saw that both men were on the ground. Two dogs lay stretched out on the driveway, and one of the men wrestled with the third.

Gordon grabbed Dina by the jacket collar and began hauling her toward the car. He was all too aware that he was underweight and not very strong, and was thankful that she was so small. He was dragging her headfirst over the ground, and he realized he could injure her neck, so he tried to support her head with his forearms.

He was gasping for breath by the time he got her to the Volvo. He groped behind him for the door handle, found it, and swung the door open. The dome light flashed on, silhouetting them perfectly for any shooter taking aim. . . .

Actinic light flashed from the heavens. Thunder roared. Gordon took a deep breath, bent his knees, and heaved Dina's head and shoulders up onto the passenger seat. Hot pain shot through his back. He grabbed Dina's hips and tried to shove her center of gravity up into the car.

Normally he had help moving limp bodies around. Normally it was from slab to gurney, or gurney to slab. Normally he didn't have to wrestle someone into a bucket seat, or avoid slamming her into the stick shift or getting her jammed against the console.

"Give me some help here!" he told Dina. "Just pull yourself into the car!"

Dina's eyes stared blankly from her lolling head. He seized her feet and tried to shove them up into the Volvo.

A shot jolted Gordon's nerves, and he heard the bullet hit pavement nearby. Shoving the limp body was clearly not working, and Gordon dropped Dina's feet and ran around to the driver's side. He threw himself into the station wagon, grabbed Dina's collar with both hands, and tried to haul her toward him. Pain lanced through his back again as he heaved her over the central console. Her head hung in his lap in a swirl of wet, curly hair.

Another shot cracked out. There was an urgent bang somewhere in the car as the bullet struck home.

Gordon reached under Dina's shoulder and shoved the gearshift lever into drive, then stomped on the accelerator as he cranked the wheel hard over. The Volvo made a screaming U-turn on the highway, and Gordon steadied the vehicle as a flash of lightning showed him the way home.

The car's acceleration had swung the passenger door closed onto Dina's feet, which were still dangling out of the car. He switched the dome light off to make himself a poorer target, then put his fingers on Dina's throat. Her pulse was strong, just a little elevated. He could hear her respiration. He hadn't seen or felt any blood.

But there had been shots, and she'd collapsed. That was pretty good evidence that she'd been hit somewhere. He drove to his cabin, opened the gate on the road, drove through, and locked the gate behind him. He despaired of dragging Dina into the house, so he drove behind the house, unlocked the barn door, and drove into the barn.

At least he'd have a dry place to make an examination.

Gordon took some of the plastic sheeting he'd draped over his rocketry gear and laid it on the ground next to the passenger door. Then he pulled Dina out of the car and laid her on the sheet. He performed a careful examination and could find no wound.

He had a medical bag in the cabin in case there was an accident with rocketry material. He unlocked the cabin's rear door, fetched the bag, and returned.

Pulse stable. Blood pressure normal. Respiration normal. Pupils responded normally to light. There didn't seem to be anything wrong with Dina other than catatonia. Which, it had to be said, was really, really wrong.

She'd been in mental contact with the dogs, he thought. She'd been getting them to attack their trainers. And then the shooting had started. The dogs, he thought. The dogs had been shot, presumably killed. And Dina had been in their heads when that happened.

Maybe the shock had been too much.

He put the blood pressure cuff back in his bag, then touched her throat. The skin was chill and clammy. He should get some blankets and insulate Dina against hypothermia.

Then call an ambulance. Then call Franny and the state police and get a warrant and go crashing into IDS to free the captives. Officer down. It was one of those calls which would result in immediate action by the authorities. And Dina certainly was down.

He unlocked the rear door of the cabin and went into the hall closet for the scratchy wool trade blankets he kept there. Returning with the blankets under his arm, he saw headlights flash across the front windows.

Gordon walked across the darkened room to the living room window and peered past the drawn curtain. He saw a large panel van parked by his gate, and a man silhouetted against the headlights peering at the house.

Gordon's heart lurched. He remembered that one of the IDS people had seen his car when he'd surveilled the compound the previous day, that they probably had his license number and ID by now.

They might have recognized his car, even in the rain. They might have just come straight here. Gordon backed away from the curtain and went to the back door. He locked the door behind him and sprinted to the barn.

Dina was as he'd left her. He put a pair of blankets over her, and her head rolled as, for a moment, her eyes fluttered open and seemed to focus. "Doc . . . ?" she said in a hoarse whisper, and then her head fell back and her eyes closed again.

Gordon knelt and opened one eyelid. The pupil narrowed in the light, but it didn't focus. She'd lapsed into coma again.

Gordon's nerves leaped as he heard a roaring engine, followed by the crash of his gate going down in front of the panel van. He stood, looked down at Dina, looked at his car. It seemed futile to try to drag her into his car again, especially as all that he could hope for would be a car chase that he could well lose. He bent again, felt under the blanket, and took Dina's gun and holster from her belt. He looked at it for a moment as the faint scent of gun oil floated to him, and then he put the holster on his own belt, feeling foolish as he did it.

What was he going to do, start a Western gunfight? These were professional bad guys, kidnappers. They'd shoot him down.

He looked again at his car. He had to draw the pursuit away from the barn.

And he knew exactly where to take them.

He went to the steel cabinet where he kept rocketry supplies and opened it. He took a battery, a set of a half-dozen igniters, a wireless receiver, and his controller. Then he turned off the lights in the barn and got in his car. He put the rocketry gear on the passenger seat.

He waited till he heard a crash as the front door of the house went down, and then he started the Volvo, gunned the engine, and backed out of the barn in a storm of power. Gravel rattled against the car as he swung around, snapped on the lights, and put the transmission in drive. Gordon stomped the accelerator again, wove through a line of evergreen, and took off down the two-rut trail that led across the meadows.

He figured there was no way the bad guys could avoid seeing his departure.

He'd gone a quarter mile before he saw the lights of the van coming after him. Lightning illuminated the rolling terrain, helped him chart his course. The Volvo bucketed up and down as it leaped along the trail, brush beating on the grille, rocks cracking against the floorboards.

The station wagon slithered down a slope and hit what seemed to be a shallow pond between it and the next slope. The tail kicked out, and the wheels spun as Gordon tried to correct. Forward motion died in mere seconds. Gravel hammered against the rear panels as the wheels spun uselessly.

Gordon grabbed his rocket gear and bolted from the car. Rain drummed on his skull as he splashed through standing water and began to run up the nearest slope. Brush clawed at his legs.

The van crowned the slope behind him and dove toward his stalled car. Gordon panted for breath. The van splashed into the same lake as the Volvo and came to a halt, wheels spinning. Two men jumped out and charged the Volvo, finding no one inside.

A flash of lightning turned the scene into day as Gordon crowned the slope, and Gordon heard a pair of shouts as he was spotted. But the flash had illuminated something else—the berms that surrounded the shed filled with rocket fuel.

Gordon dragged himself forward. He dragged himself up the nearest berm, then ran down the steep slope and slammed to a tooth-clattering halt against the steel door of the shed. Breath heaved in and out of his lungs. He wasn't used to running. He wasn't used to panic, or to fighting, or being soaked to the skin.

Better use his brains then, he decided.

He fumbled at his belt for the key to the padlock on the door, then opened the lock and threw it over his shoulder. He tore open the door, ran inside, and reached for the tank that held the syntin, the Soviet liquid rocket fuel. He opened the valve and the fuel began to drain, filling the shack with a rich hydrocarbon scent. Gordon dropped an igniter into the fuel, put the battery on the concrete floor nearby, twisted wires around the terminals, and ran back into the open. He left the door invitingly ajar, ran around the building, and scrambled up the far berm. At the top he tripped and fell, and as he lay sprawled in the grass at the foot of the berm he heard an accented voice say, "He's in there!"

Gordon got to his feet and felt pain shoot through his right ankle. He lurched toward the grove of hawthorn at the far end of the meadow.

As he ran he looked at the remote control in his hand and pushed the rocker switch to ON. The LEDs flicked from Safety to Armed. He heard the door to the shed go booming back on its hinges as the intruders stormed inside, and he heaved in a sobbing breath and pressed the Fire button. He was faintly surprised to find that the berms worked exactly as they were supposed to.

"The perps were blown into their constituent atoms," Gordon told Dina two nights later. "The crime scene guys weren't able to find a single piece of remains."

Dina seemed impressed. "I have to say that once you make up your mind to do something," she said, "you're damned thorough."

"You'll have to speak up," Gordon said. "I'm still a little deaf."

The shed had exploded and then kept exploding, going on for several minutes at least. Gordon had watched from the shelter of the hawthorns as one blast after another rocked the peaceful meadow and sent flame reaching toward the low clouds overhead.

It had to be admitted that he'd put a lot of oxidizer in that shed.

For their dinner Gordon had taken her to Au Pied de Cochon, the New York incarnation of a well-known Parisian brasserie. The linen was crisp, the waitstaff efficient, and the tulip-shaped lights cast a fine mellow glow over the dining room with its dark wood paneling. The restaurant offered proteins in substantial quantities, which given Dina's carnivore instincts seemed appropriate.

"I hope you'll forgive me for not going with you to the hospital," Gordon said. "I didn't know how to fix you, and I wanted to be there when the captives were freed in case they needed a doctor."

Dina affected thought. "Maybe I'll forgive you," she said. "I'll have to think about it."

"I was there when you woke up," Gordon pointed out.

She'd come to herself about noon on Monday, demanding her clothes, meat protein, and her gun. No permanent harm seemed to have been done to her, and she could remember nothing of the time she'd been in a coma. "You were the first person I saw," said Dina. "You get points for that."

"At least the sight didn't send you back into a coma."

She laughed thinly.

"When the first cops turned up at the facility," Gordon said, "they saw three dogs shot dead in front of the gate and the corpse of a man who'd had his throat ripped out. It was an obvious crime scene, and they no longer needed a warrant to go in, but they felt a little leery of going in by themselves and called for backup, and while they waited Franny Black showed up with about half the detectives from Fort Freak." He grinned. "They were toting some serious firepower and a lot of attitude. Harvey Kant even had a tommy gun that must have dated from

Lucky Luciano's day—which, by the way, made me wonder just how old Kant actually is. So our guys just brushed the Jersey cops aside and stormed the place."

Gordon laughed. "They were serious. For some reason they thought you were being held captive in there."

Dina's eyes narrowed. "Who gave them that idea?" she asked.

"They must have misinterpreted my phone call," Gordon said. His face was deadpan. "Our guys were too late. The compound had been emptied. At least three computers were carried away, but they did manage to pull up a few names off envelopes and bills. But they did find Steely Dan and two kidnapped Jokertown residents held in some kind of steel-lined underground cells in the rearmost building." He shook his head. "It was like some supervillain's headquarters from the movies."

"I'm surprised they didn't put them in dog cages," Dina said.

"Dog cages aren't strong enough for Dan or any other wild card with extra strength," Gordon said. "He would have ripped his way right out. The perps needed a custom facility."

"But what was it for?"

"Even the captives didn't know." All Steely Dan knew was that he'd gone to answer the door, and there had been a couple of guys there with stun guns. They'd tased him into helplessness, then bound him, thrown him in a van, and driven away.

"They were fed regularly. They weren't mistreated beyond being held against their will." He looked down at the gleaming tableware laid out on either side of his fine china plate. "The brass are thinking they were to be used to train dogs to kill people," he said, "but I've been thinking. Maybe they were being held for . . . medical experiments."

Dina gave a canine growl that came very close to

raising the hairs on Gordon's neck. "That ain't right," she said.

"Maybe if we can ID the body, or if the latent fingerprints tell us anything . . ."

"That dead guy was Russian or something, right?" Dina said. "If he was a crook, maybe the Russians can tell us who he was."

"Maybe." Gordon spread his hands wide. "So now the Jersey cops are involved, and the NYPD, and the FBI because there was a kidnapping. And FBI and ATF are both investigating my shed, because they're half convinced I'm a terrorist."

"'Blown to constituent atoms,'" Dina quoted. "Where's their evidence?"

"Well," Gordon said dubiously, "there's the big rocket engine in the barn. They might make something of that, I suppose."

She gave a laugh. "At least you're not a joker. They'd put you with the Twisted Fists." He looked at her. She looked back at him, then frowned. "You aren't a joker, right?" she said.

The police at Fort Freak had every reason to think he was a joker, because there it was in his file, the fact he'd tested positive for the wild card. In fact he'd been struck by the virus on the island of Okinawa, where his Air Force father had been stationed. Gordon had been in the hospital, out of his mind with fever, vast tumors growing everywhere on his skin, his heart thundering as his blood pressure crashed into the basement . . .

American military hospitals come equipped for all sort of contingencies. They'd given him the trump, which in those days had only a thirty percent chance of success. And it had worked, reversing the chaotic wreckage the wild card was making of his body. He'd test positive for the rest of his life, but in fact he was a nat. A nat with his height, his weight, and his olfactory sense on the extreme edge of normal, but a nat nonetheless.

"Am I a joker?" he repeated. "No, I'm not."

She screwed up her face as she looked at him, as if she wasn't quite sure whether or not to believe him. Then she picked up the menu. "Maybe we'd better order." Dina frowned over the menu, which did not include an English translation. "Well," she said, "I know what *porc* means."

"*Cochon* also means pig," Gordon added helpfully.

"What's *panés*?"

"In breadcrumbs."

The waiter stepped forward with his smile and his pad. Gordon ordered calf's face for an appetizer, followed by pig's knuckle braised in spices. Dina had onion soup for a starter, followed by—her finger traced the words on the menu as she spoke them aloud—*queue, oreille, museau et pied de cochon panés,* the pork dish coated in bread-crumbs.

Gordon didn't tell her that she'd just ordered the ear, tail, snout, and foot of a pig. Foreign cookery, he thought, should come with its share of surprises.

If she didn't like it, he decided, he'd buy her a hot dog from a vendor. Or maybe two.

The Big Bleed

Part Four

"IT LOOKS LIKE OUR terror plot is stalling out," Jamal said.

They had returned to the Bleecker after a Holy Roller speech in Harlem, a mercifully brief and trouble-free event, if you ignored the reverend's disconnected ramblings and his signature "roll-up," which never failed to win laughs . . . and lose votes.

Roller had gone to ground, and the SCARE team had been released. Upon returning to their ops center, after a slow, nasty drive through the apparently never-ending rain, Jamal had found an update from the Analysis Team at Riker's.

"We didn't find ammonium nitrate?" Sheeba said, collapsing her tall frame into her desk chair. No matter what he thought of the Midnight Angel's leadership style or personal habits, these maneuvers still fascinated Jamal. It was like spying on a whooping crane or some other long-legged bird bending to snatch a fish from a lake . . . improbable, a bit awkward, but endlessly watchable.

Especially when you happened to be bored and

exhausted—and eager for any kind of distraction. "Oh, it's am nitrate," Jamal said. "A dangerous amount, too."

"So, good for us, right?"

"No. The shipment doesn't connect. Homeland Sec has no lead on a source for it, and more to the point . . . no buyer. It's an orphan."

"Would they know every buyer or potential terrorist in and around New York City? I mean, look at our watch lists. . . ." They bore hundreds of names, Jamal knew.

"That's what took a few days. They did a big search and crosscheck, and found no one who seemed to be in the right place to get hold of the shipment."

"That still doesn't answer my question. What about the guy DHS *doesn't* know?"

"They've got an analysis staff that interfaces with every agency on the planet—"

Sheeba suddenly stood up—another impressive physical display. "Are you working for them or us? You're defending these guys and their lack of information!"

"I'm just telling *you* what they're telling *me*!"

Sheeba had started to pace. "Maybe I should call Billy Ray." Another surprise: on the infrequent occasions when Sheeba admitted that she spoke to her husband Billy Ray, aka Carnifex at SCARE HQ, she usually said "the home office" or "our nation's capital."

Never his name. Maybe Sheeba wanted to go home, too. Back to a normal life. Whatever that was, for aces. "We have other options," Jamal said. "New Jersey State Police were at the site. I do know that the body somehow wound up here in Manhattan, Fifth Precinct."

"I suppose we could call them," Sheeba said, clearly unenthusiastic about either.

"It's end of day and we'd just get run around," Jamal said, struggling to his feet. "Fort Freak's not far from here. Why don't I just go over there?"

Sheeba blinked. "Now. In the rain."

"I have an umbrella," he said. He glanced toward the window, and, not particularly caring about the truth, said, "And it's letting up."

And, what the hell, he might actually learn something at Fort Freak.

♦

To his amusement, his ruse about the weather turned out to be true. The rain had let up, which allowed him to dangle the umbrella from its wrist strap . . . and use his free hand to hold his phone.

It was the end of the workday, when lower Manhattan's buildings released their daily captives. But Jamal found the sidewalks blessedly empty . . . perhaps the threat of additional downpours was keeping people inside. Even the traffic seemed lighter.

No matter—Jamal was free to walk and talk to Julia, the one activity in his day that gave him pleasure, even though it had become increasingly difficult to arrange of late.

Part of it was the time difference, of course. Jamal was three hours ahead. Then there was the SCARE schedule along with its mandatory group dinners.

The real problem, however, was Julia's schedule. If she was at the club, she was unavailable from nine P.M. Jamal's time until two or three in the morning—and those were the times he could talk.

She would sleep from five A.M. his time til early afternoon. Her physical situation required that amount of sleep.

So in the past couple of weeks they had taken to saying hello during a brief window between five and six P.M. New York time.

It was a hell of a way to run a relationship.

Not that it was like any relationship in Jamal's undistinguished history. He had had several long-term arrangements, including one that was headed toward marriage until Jamal booked a film shooting in Mexico, where the combination of insane hours, high stress, unnecessary amounts of tequila, and an actress named Mary-Margaret had contributed to some relationship-toxic behavior on Jamal's part.

Even his bad long-term relationships were a long way in the past . . . thank you again, SCARE. He wanted to keep this one alive. More precisely, he wanted to follow this one wherever it was going. But his first call went straight to voice mail, which was annoying.

Two blocks later—deeper into Jokertown now, where, given the surging population on the sidewalks, the freaks did not seem deterred by the nasty weather—Jamal tried again. Still nothing.

Julia never went anywhere without her phone. It was her one piece of essential gear. In the four months that they'd been seeing each other, she had never ignored two calls in a row. At worst, the second attempt resulted in a "Busy, call u in a few" text. Which she always did.

What could be wrong? Worse yet, what could he do about it?

"Something I can do for you?"

The Fifth Precinct desk sergeant—Sgt. Homer Taylor according to the oxidized nameplate—was a joker. On the short side, lighter-skinned than Jamal, as if that had mattered since 1946, with droopy wings shaped like those of a giant bat. He also possessed a bland, possibly even pleasant expression, so it was hard for Jamal to get a read on his tone. Was that a genuine question, or some kind of challenge?

Jamal elected to play it straight, displaying his badge. "Special Agent Norwood, SCARE."

Taylor's wings fluttered—a sign of recognition? The

joker cop turned to the ancient assignment board. "Crash in New Jersey . . . we have a DB in New Jersey that belongs to our Detective Black." There was something in Sergeant Taylor's voice that Jamal could not quite identify . . . a hint of scorn, perhaps, or, to be charitable, possibly just amusement.

"Okay, I know this is risky, but is Detective Black available?"

Taylor shot him a look; his turn to wonder whether Jamal was zinging him. "Actually, not at this moment. If you'd like to leave a number—?"

Jamal was already sliding his card across Taylor's desk. "So, as we used to say in the 'hood, I'm SOL."

Taylor waggled the tiny piece of paper. "Right now. But I will personally see that he gets your name and number. Best I can do."

"There's no officer or sergeant who could talk to a Federal agent?"

"It's mid-shift, Mr. Norwood. If people can be on the street, that's where they are. And it's been a busy day in Jokertown. Detective Black will respond, just not this five minutes."

Jamal suddenly felt tired and angry, never a good combination. He turned away, suddenly unsure of his next move. Which allowed him to consider Fort Freak.

The ancient brownstone was like a police museum. The phones were thirty years old at least; even the rings sounded analog, not digital. Even weirder was the joker-heavy nature of the few staffers he could see, from a human-sized rat to a big tabby cat—

"Not one of these officers has any information for me."

Taylor sighed. He was big in girth—Bill Norwood would have called him a perfect lineman, except for the wings. "Normally, yes. But incidents in New Jersey are outside our jurisdiction. I understand it's a bit unusual for even Detective Black to be involved."

Jamal knew he was being slow-rolled, and fairly skillfully. "Thank you, sergeant," he said. As he turned away, his cell rang—Julia!

No. . . . "Is this Jamal Norwood?" a voice said. It took Jamal a moment to realize that it was Dr. Finn from Jokertown Clinic.

Jamal did not want to have a conversation inside Fort Freak, so he hustled out the front door. The instant he emerged he was assaulted by the gamy, fishy, and oily smell of the East River. How had he missed it earlier? Probably because the rains had cleared the air, however temporarily. "Hello, Doctor," he said, hoping his voice sounded stronger than it felt. "What's the word?"

"The best I can say, Mr. Norwood, is confusing."

"Help me out with that."

"I'm sorry." Jamal could easily imagine the joker medico pawing the carpet with his hooves. He himself was pacing, as if sheer movement could make a bad thing better. "You are showing symptoms of what, for lack of a better term, I would have to call a degenerative . . . situation."

"Is that better or worse than a disease?"

"It could be better. You could be suffering from the ace equivalent of an injury, even an allergy, that might be treatable."

"But I could also be suffering from, what, ALS? Parkinson's?"

"Those terms don't apply."

"But the analogy—"

"Fits, yes. What we need are more tests."

Standing in the lonely entrance to Fort Freak, with the drone of New York all around him, awash in the vibrations and smells of Jokertown . . . and feeling much as he had felt all his life . . . Jamal found it difficult to know what to say next. Beyond the initial churn of his stomach when he realized that Finn's message was not, *"Found it. Antibiotics for a week and you're good."*

"More tests . . . that's never good."

"Let's concentrate on the positive, Mr. Norwood. I would like to see you as soon as possible, however."

"I'll call your office first thing to set up an appointment," he said. "Thank you, Doctor." He hung up . . . and then, like the delayed blow of a tackle, it hit him.

He could die. Worse than that—if anything would qualify—he might fade away slowly, horribly, first losing mobility . . . then hands . . . bodily functions.

Finally unable to breathe, helpless. *No bounceback from that shit, right, Stuntman?* He really wanted to talk to Julia . . . why hadn't she called? Maybe it was best that she hadn't; they were hardly in a stable, long-term relationship. She didn't need to deal with this—not while it was so uncertain—

"Agent Norwood?"

Jamal turned. It took him a moment to remember that he was at Fort Freak . . . getting stiff-armed. Now, here was a good-looking young man, late twenties, in a white shirt and loosened tie, out of breath. "I'm Franny Black."

"Oh, Detective Black. Call me Jamal."

Franny held up Jamal's card. "Sergeant Taylor just gave me this. I'm glad I caught you."

If not for Finn's call, you wouldn't have. "What do you need?"

"What else? Information."

Ten minutes later, Jamal had heard enough bizarre information about missing jokers and phony dog-training academies in New Jersey that he had been able to wrap Finn's news into a small box and put it high on his mental shelf. "That must have been tough," he told Franny. "Having to tell the Heffers about their kid."

Franny sat back. They were at his desk in the corner of the second-floor squad room, a space so low rent it made SCARE's nasty hotel-room ops center seem state of the art. "It was. Especially because . . . I didn't have anything good to tell them. No reason. Nothing."

"So you don't get used to it."

"First time I've done it."

Jamal was surprised. "You're a detective!"

"Pretty much just happened. I only had a couple of years in uniform, and my partner usually took the lead . . . on everything."

"What's a nat doing at Fort Freak, anyway?"

"The more I think about it, the more it feels like unresolved father issues."

Jamal had to laugh. "Copy that."

"So what does SCARE want with my dead joker?"

Jamal hauled out a hard copy of the DHS report on the ammonium nitrate, and his own notes on the crash site. Franny nodded at the DHS paper, but sat up when he read Jamal's material. "This sounds familiar," he said. "The unusual wheel base, the lack of treads . . ." He turned to his crusty keyboard and fat old computer monitor.

"Is that thing steam-powered?" Jamal said.

"I'm lucky I have one at all." As he clicked through various documents, Franny nodded to the other desks in the squad room. Sure enough, Jamal realized: maybe a third of them had computers.

"How the hell do you catch anyone?"

"Sometimes they show up at the front door and beg to confess." Franny smiled, then turned the monitor so Jamal could see it. "Maybe this is your guy."

Jamal looked at the screen, which showed a page from a typical police profile of a suspect. A black-and-white picture showed what struck Jamal as the strangest-looking front end of a vehicle he'd ever seen. "His name's Chahina, aka Wheels. He's a joker built like, and apparently able to move like, a truck. Early twenties, new to our shores."

"What's Wheels done?"

"He's been stopped for an amazing number of moving violations in the boroughs and in New Jersey. All dismissed." Franny smiled. "For a truck driver, he seems to have a great lawyer."

"Really."

"It's the ACLU, apparently. Wheels keeps getting cited, the ACLU gets him off because they contend vehicular laws apply to vehicles, not—"

"Automotive jokers."

"It's a funny old world sometimes."

Jamal held up his phone. "Is there somewhere—?"

"Don't tell me you want to link this data? Or have me e-mail? You're in Fort Freak, Jamal." Franny pressed several keys. Across the room, a printer wound itself up. "But we can get you a hard copy of the file. We have indeed reached 1994 here."

"Looks as though he's worth talking to. Does it say where he lives?"

Franny clicked to a different page. "Where else? Jokertown."

♠

Julia finally called. "Sorry, sorry, have I said I'm sorry?"

"I sense that you're feeling a bit apologetic."

It was four hours after Jamal met with Franny Black at Fort Freak. He had returned to the Bleecker and used the hotel's business center to scan the papers on Wheels, then e-mailed them to Sheeba before meeting her upstairs.

Dinner had been substantially more interesting, with Sheeba popping up from the table to talk to her husband Billy Ray in Washington, then to connect with other federal agencies in the New York area. Finding out that Wheels was a foreign joker just changed everything, but the excitement of the discovery had worn off for Jamal. Finn's news—or lack of good news—played like a heavy-metal bass line through his every thought.

Now Jamal was flat on his back, unable to sleep, counting the potential good days he had left to his life, when his phone buzzed.

"Did I tell you my parents were in town?"

"You did not." Julia was not a Los Angeles native: she had grown up in rural Idaho, which could not have been a treat for a joker girl.

"So you're off tonight?"

"Heck, no." One of Julia's many charms was her choice of profanity, which was so tame it could have come from a 1940s movie about hot rods and malt shops. "I just ducked into the office here. The folks did keep me busy earlier, though."

Jamal tried to picture them, but his brain conjured up the grim farmer and wife from *American Gothic,* so he judged that a fail. He wasn't even sure of their names. "Are they staying with you?"

"Oh, God, no." Julia laughed. And Jamal should have known better.

In a weak moment, in conversation with his mother, Maxine, Jamal had let it slip that he was "seeing" someone, and uttered her name, Julia Jackson.

But Maxine had pressed for information, as moms will. So Jamal had let it slip: "She's a joker."

Silence on the line. "She looks perfectly human," Jamal said.

"That's a relief," Mom had said, laughing. "I thought you were going to bring home a white girl."

Needless to say, the meeting had yet to take place.

Jamal hated that memory. It wasn't just that it demonstrated how tricky any relationship with Julia would be . . .

It also reminded him of his own problems on *American Hero,* the mess with Rustbelt.

Put it away!

◆

Yes, Julia Jackson was a joker . . . the size of a Barbie doll . . . maybe a bit taller. ("All my friends kept wanting me to kiss their Kens, but he was just too short." "Did the word 'creepy' ever enter into that?" "Not then and not much since.")

Jamal had met her, he liked to say, "between Riyadh and New York," which suggested something out of a romantic novel—meeting on the QE2, perhaps—but was really only a joke: they had met when Jamal took leave in Los Angeles after the SCARE-up in the Middle East.

Whether it was the long absence, or some yet-to-be-understood sense of real accomplishment, he returned to his home city feeling like King Shit. Well, why not? He was fit, good-looking, well-spoken, well-dressed, and, best of all, famous.

Which was better than being rich, because everyone assumed famous people had money.

With his friends Brett and Roland, he had gone to Gulliver, a new club on Ventura Boulevard. "Can you believe this?" Roland had said. "Going out in the Valley!" Roland was an over-the-hill snob who lived in a new, retro-fitted tower in the heart of Hollywood. Jamal, who still had a condo even deeper into the Valley, had no such reservations. In the relatively short time since *American Hero*, Ventura Boulevard had sprouted all kinds of new restaurants and clubs, and Jamal was happy to sample them, especially since he had limited time at home.

And word was that Gulliver had exotic joker flavor to its staff or design. Since Brett was sure, at some point in the evening, to suggest a follow-up trip to a joker-staffed gentleman's club, Jamal hoped this place would satisfy his friend's urge, and allow them to experience the ideal night out: which meant staying in one place.

The first phase of any night out, ideal or less than, meant checking out the women who were entering or already present when the trio arrived at Gulliver.

"Thursday night is ladies' night," Roland kept saying.

"Meaning it's Jamal's night," Brett said. He was the white guy in the trio, a friend from high school. Like Jamal, he had been a good athlete who, thanks to lack of height, got no respect or opportunity. Unlike Jamal, he had not been hit by the wild card.

Of the three, Jamal was the most likely to come out of any club with a number, if not an actual woman on his arm. Jamal had realized long ago that he needed Roland and Brett, or two guys a lot like them, to make this happen. Women were warier around a man alone. . . .

The bar was filled with actress wannabes and some never-weres busy posing and chatting, along with any number of middle-aged hotties celebrating birthdays.

The only men in the place—aside from those obviously attached to various women—were huddled at the bar like nervous teenagers at a school dance. "I'm not seeing the joker angle," Brett said.

"Well, maybe you're not looking at it the right way," Jamal said. The interior of the place was done up like a medieval village, with "stone" walls, battlements, wooden chairs and tables . . . all of them scaled in such a way to make even Jamal feel like a giant.

Confirmation arrived in the form of the hostess, a beautiful blonde in some kind of medieval-style dress with a pretty-definitely-not-medieval-style hemline. She possessed flawless milky skin and had eyes so blue they were almost purple. As they say in Hollywood, she was actress pretty, not just girlfriend good-looking.

He would have been attracted to her in any case: any male who could fog a mirror would have. Her only flaw, if the word applied, was that she was about a foot and a half tall. "Dinner or bar?" she chirped. Her voice was pitched a little high, but no worse than Betty Boop.

Brett grinned, thinking he was perhaps forty percent cuter than he actually was. "Both."

"Any particular order? Or shall I surprise you?"

"Surprise us," Jamal said.

"This way." To Jamal's amazement, the tiny waitress hopped onto a ramp behind her podium, then fluttered across the floor. Of course: the inverse square law (which Jamal knew from the Tak World movies), which doomed giant aliens invading Earth to muscle failure and early death, worked in Julia's favor. She could practically fly . . . like a cartoon fairy.

Within seconds they were seated, giants in a Lilliputian village. Menus arrived via a joker doing a creditable impression of a troll. But Jamal and his friends were watching Julia flutter away. "I hope no one steps on her," Brett said.

The meal passed with the usual amount of chat and teasing, most of it aimed at Jamal and his adventures in Africa. When they had paid and were heading out, Julia called to them from her stand. "Don't tell me I scared you?"

"What are you talking about?" Jamal said.

Julia indicated a couch in the corner of the crowded library-bar. "It's been waiting for you for fifteen minutes."

"We already ate," Brett said.

"I know, darling," she said. "It was dinner first, then bar. Surely you remember."

"Actually," Jamal said, "we hadn't. But we do now."

And they proceeded to spend two more hours in Gulliver, having one of the most enjoyable evenings Jamal had had in years . . . laughing, meeting half a dozen new people, including four women. "A new low," Brett said, grinning. He had not only gotten a phone number, at one point Jamal had spotted him kissing a woman he had just met. . . .

"Julia's good," Roland said as they were leaving.

And so she was. But Jamal had not tried to get her number that night—indeed, had not considered it—even though Roland had noted his interest at beer round number three. "Jamal's got tone," he said. Roland liked military technology. "Tone" was a cockpit signal that told a fighter pilot he was locked onto a target.

"Get serious!" Brett had said. "You are . . . not a match." He made a face and pantomimed a big finger penis bumping up against his scrunched fist.

"Relationships aren't always about the act, my friend."

As they left, Jamal made sure to pass by the hostess station, where he was rewarded with a Julia smile, and: "Come back soon."

"We just might," Brett said.

"Not you, big boy," Julia said, her smile dazzling. "You seem nice," she said to Roland, and here she looked directly—eye to eye, thanks to the height of the podium—at Jamal. "I meant *you*."

He went back the next night . . . with Roland. And came away with Julia's number. "Call me between one and four," she had said.

And he had done that. They had talked for two hours, until Julia said, "Oh my God, you charming, distracting bastard, I've got to get ready for work."

They had spoken again the next day—and the next— and three more times, before seeing each other in person again.

When they did have their first actual date, to see some English movie about another star-crossed couple in love, Jamal had driven to Julia's address in Studio City. It was on a side street behind Republic Studios. In their first extended conversation, Julia had said she lived in a "tree-house."

It turned out to be the literal truth: the address drew Jamal to a tiny A-frame built into a notch of an ancient oak tree, six feet off the ground.

There was an access ramp winding around the trunk. And a rope. Jamal wondered again at Julia's strength: he was in shape and there was no way he could have climbed the equivalent height. . . .

She emerged and, mercifully, took the ramp. Jamal had

wondered about the protocol of walking with Julia—let her go at her own speed, two of her steps for every one of his? Or—

"You may pick me up," she said. Which, most carefully, he did, allowing her to rest in the crook of his arm.

"Shouldn't you be calling this a dollhouse instead?"

She slapped him on the arm with surprising effect. "Don't start with the short jokes."

"A serious question, then." They were almost at Jamal's car.

"One serious question."

"Don't you worry about . . . ?"

"What?"

"Hawks."

Fortunately, she laughed. "I have Mace, baby! So don't get any ideas."

He had helped her into the passenger seat. "The belt—" Was as likely to crush her as protect her, he was about to say.

"It's okay."

"You've done this before."

"This is not my first date, correct." He had the car in motion when she said, "Not to get ahead of ourselves, but, sexual relations are likely to be nonstandard."

"Not a problem."

"So you say. Now."

"As you said, we're a little ahead of ourselves."

She smiled over at him. "I have some work-arounds."

The work-around turned out to be the phone.

It was just a natural extension of their soon-to-be-daily catch-ups, almost always between the hours of two and four Pacific Time, when they talked work, books, movies, people, SCARE, and sleep schedules and then—

What they would like to be doing with each other, to each other. How it would feel. How it would look. Taste.

It turned out to be surprisingly easy . . . and even more surprisingly, satisfying.

Which was the big reason why Jamal hated missing Julia's calls.

This one turned out to be a huge fizzle, however, mostly because Julia started it by saying, "How are *you* doing?"

Now was a perfect time, and Julia was the perfect person, for Jamal to unburden himself about his health problems. Instead, he offered a curt "Fine."

"Now I know something's wrong," she said.

"Work is what's wrong." This had the virtue of being true while avoiding her question.

"Tell me."

So he gave her the short version—his boredom with the campaign, his Sheeba fatigue, the ammonium nitrate shipment, joker truck mystery, how they were going to grab Wheels later tonight. "Isn't some of that, what do you call it, classified or special access?"

"Probably," he said. "If they're bugging us—"

"—Hah! We're already in jail!" They both laughed. And then she said, "They need me—"

"I know," he said. "Thanks—"

"Now listen," she said. "Because I was so hard to reach, you get a pass this time. You can lie by omission. But next time we talk—tomorrow—tell me what's *really* wrong, okay?"

Galahad in Blue

Part Three

"PUT A FORK IN it and call it done," Captain Mendelberg said.

Franny stared down at the precinct's joker captain. Her
bloodred eyes seemed to glare back, and her high-set, fin-
like ears were waving slowly, the bright blood vessels in
the lacy flesh as red as her eyes. She swiveled her chair
around and turned her back on him. "We'll find something else for you to do."

"I assume you're talking about the missing joker file,
ma'am," Franny said.

"Well, what else would I be talking about? The case is
closed."

"Respectfully, I don't agree, ma'am."

"Oh, cut the crap, you sound like a fucking Boy Scout,
or worse, a fag in some Brit movie. This case is closed.
The perps were using the missing jokers like poodles
to train their attack dogs. Gordon blew 'em up. End of
story."

"They were Russian, ma'am."

"And the Russian mob isn't all over New Brighton?"

"None of the mob guys had ever heard of them."

"So, they were a new mob." A vein was pulsing in Mendelberg's temple.

"That doesn't make any sense. The bosses would have heard if someone was trying to move in."

"Do you know what this means, Black?" Mendelberg said and pointed at her ears. They were now motionless and stiffly upright.

"No, ma'am."

"It means I'm really pissed. The case is closed. Now get out."

Franny returned to his desk, stomach acid churning and an incipient headache lurking behind his eyes. He knew police forces were overworked and understaffed, and a simple explanation was a godsend, but this was malfeasance in his opinion. There were just too many unanswered questions. He was on thin enough ice with his promotion to keep pursuing this himself, but he knew someone who could. And who probably had better resources than he had.

He picked up the phone and called Jamal. It went right to voice mail. Franny returned the phone to its cradle, and sat drumming his fingers on his desk. Make another call and this time leave a message? If Captain Mendelberg found out, his ass was grass—a local cop calling in the Feds was one of the cardinal sins. He thought of the strained and frightened faces of the jokers they'd freed from the pens at that dog-training facility. Fuck it. They were wrong to close the investigation. He called Norwood's cell, and this time he left a message.

"This is Black over at the Fifth. I need your help with something."

He went back to the Warren County files.

He went to Mary's Lamb for lunch. Bill had introduced him to the restaurant when they'd walk the beat together.

It only served breakfast, but the food was cheap, plenti-
ful, and delicious—perfect for a cop on a budget, and it
kept them in touch with the people they were protecting. A win all around. It was owned and operated, not
surprisingly, by Mary, a joker whose true shape could
only be guessed at because her large form was swathed
in a cloak and she always wore a mask.

"Cherry almond muffins today, Franny," Mary said as
she lumbered past. Her voice had a strange, burring rasp.

"Sounds great. Let me have a Denver omelet with a
side of ham, and coffee too."

"You got it."

The coffee and muffins arrived. He broke open a pastry
and it added its steam to the pennant floating over the
coffee cup. The mingling odors of coffee and warm baked
goods had his stomach grinding. Slathering the muffin
with butter and jam, he leaned over to Tim at the next
table, who was reading the *Jokertown Cry*.

"How'd the Jets do?" he asked, referring to Xavier
Desmond High School's baseball team.

Tim tilted the paper so Franny could see the photo
and the headline. "We're in the playoffs," he said with
pride. The pale green cilia that filled his mouth quivered
from the puffs of air carried with the mumbled words.

The plate of ham arrived, and he dug in. The bells over
the door gave an agitated ring as it was pushed violently
open. Franny, along with everyone, else looked up as the
door banged into the wall.

Abigail Baker strode in. Her mouth was set in a tight
line, and her brow furrowed. Franny reflexively checked
to see if he had done something to piss off the girl, but
since he hadn't seen her in months he couldn't think of
anything. Of course, Abigail was just enough of a drama
queen to have gotten upset about something that happened ages ago.

His mental trashing of the girl didn't help. Franny's
heart still raced and his breath went shallow when he saw

her. He reminded himself that he had a girlfriend now. An irritating girlfriend.

Could she be walking over to him? *Nah, it had to be somebody else on this end of the room.* He had had a crush on Abby from the first moment he'd seen her naked and angry on a Jokertown street, another victim of The Stripper.

She couldn't be walking over to him.

Liked her even when she insulted him.

Could she?

Liked her when she shot him down when he'd asked her out.

She was still coming his way.

Kept liking her even when she took up with that part-time small-time crook, Croyd Crenson.

Speculation ended when she pulled out the chair on the opposite side of the table and sat down.

"Hi," Franny began, then had to cough to clear the muffin crumb that had lodged in his throat.

She didn't waste time on social niceties. "I need your help," she said in her clipped British accent.

She needed his help? *Oh, holy shit.*

"Why aren't you asking your lowlife boyfriend?" his mouth said, before his brain engaged and thought better of it.

She reared back in her chair, and she flashed her eyes at him. "Are you not an officer of the law? Isn't it your *job* to bloody well help people?"

He discovered that shame had a funny taste. It laid on the back of his tongue and seemed to burn. "Uh, yeah. Sorry. So, this is official?"

Now she looked uncomfortable. Horribly uncomfortable. "Umm, not exactly."

Franny opened his mouth to make another smart-ass remark only to be completely unmanned when she started to cry. Soundlessly, shoulders shaking, tears sliding down her cheeks. Unlike Apsara she didn't cry beautifully. Her nose turned bright red. He thought she looked adorable.

He bounced out of his chair like he'd been shot from a catapult, came around the table, and knelt at her side. He slipped an arm around her heaving shoulders. "Oh, God, Abigail, Abby, I'm sorry. What's wrong and how can I help?"

Franny noted that the other patrons in the restaurant had politely looked away, engaged pointedly in conversations with their breakfast companions, or buried themselves in newspapers or e-readers. He was struck again by the courtesy and sensitivity of jokers. More than any other humans they understood the need for privacy and empathy to another's pain. "Come on," he said, lifting Abby out of the chair. "Let's take a walk."

"But you haven't finished your food," she sniffed.

"It's okay." He threw a twenty on the table and guided her out of the restaurant.

The sidewalk was filled with people, nats and jokers on their lunch hour. He tried to think of someplace private to talk. Only one thing came to mind. "Uh . . . look don't take this wrong, but my apartment is just a couple of blocks away." She just nodded. His arm was still around her shoulders, and Franny noticed she wasn't pulling away so he left it there. He looked down at the flash of multiple earrings climbing up the curve of her ear.

They climbed the four flights of stairs past the sounds of televisions, and a crying baby, and the smell of frying liver and onions. He really wished Mrs. Fortescue didn't make liver so often. He let Abigail into his apartment, and she stepped away, head turning as she inspected his space. Franny followed her gaze; touching on the small flat-screen TV and the Xbox. At the leather recliner facing said TV. At the TV tray off to one side of the chair. For art he had a framed print of a Fredric Remington painting, *The Stampede*. Franny decided the place looked tawdry and ordinary and like a sad, single guy lived here, which was the absolute truth. "You like cowboys?" Abigail asked.

"Well. Yeah. My dad had a huge collection of Louis L'Amour books. I read 'em all."

"Because he made you or because you wanted to?" Abigail asked.

"He died before I was born. I wanted to."

Her face was a study in embarrassment. "Oh. Sorry about that." Her fingers writhed through her hair, making it even more spiky and tousled. "My being rude, I mean. Sorry about your dad too. I mean, being dead and all. Oh, Christ, I'm making such a muddle of this."

"It's okay. It's not like I ever knew him to mourn him. I've actually got *two* chairs at the table in the kitchen. Want some coffee? Or tea?"

"Tea, please."

She followed him into the postage-stamp-sized kitchen, and settled at the tiny two-person table. He filled up two cups with water and stuck them in the microwave to boil.

While the mugs twirled like dancing partners Franny sat down across from her, and put on his best *you can trust me, I'm an officer of the law* expression. "So, what's wrong?"

"It's Croyd."

Great. Just great. She was going to talk about her boyfriend.

She gulped down another sob, cleared her throat, and composed herself. "He hasn't slept for weeks, he's cranked out of his mind, and . . ."

"I take it you're about to tell me the worst part," he said.

She sniffed. "He's got this barmy notion that this joker, I suppose it's actually two jokers because they're twins and they're not so much conjoined as they just share a lower body, anyway, Croyd thinks they're part of this gang that's been kidnapping people, and they're coming for him next. You see, he woke up a joker this time so he feels very threatened and fragile . . . emotionally fragile I mean because he's hideously strong, with skin like rock, and when he makes a fist his fingers disappear and they become like giant sledgehammers. . . ."

Franny pictured his soft nat body going up against *hideously strong* and *rock skin,* and *sledgehammers.* It was not a pretty picture. He rose abruptly, and dumped tea bags into the two mugs. Handed one to Abigail.

". . . He could really hurt someone if he had a mind to, and I'm afraid he does right now. Not that he would. He's usually very good about controlling his impulses, but when he hasn't slept . . ."

"Is there a point in here somewhere? Are we coming to it soon?" he asked.

Abigail's fingers twisted and knotted in her lap. She tore them apart and pressed her palms against her cheeks. "So, he's planning to kill them—him." The final words came out in a rush.

Now it was his turn to run his hands through his hair. "Jesus." He stood and started pacing. "Why didn't you report this at the precinct?"

"Because I don't want him arrested, and I don't want him to hurt anyone, and he's bound to fall asleep soon."

"You actually heard him say he was going to kill them?" She nodded. "So, what did you think *I* could do?"

"I thought maybe you could help me . . . put him to sleep. Or help me lock him up until he does fall asleep."

"In case you've forgotten—I'm a nat. No powers."

"Your colleagues at the precinct said you were very clever and—" She broke off abruptly and turned bright red.

"And what? What else do they say about me?"

"You mean it?"

"Yes."

"That you're an ambitious prick, and you'd knife anybody, even a friend, to get ahead."

That hurt. Enough to completely cancel out the grudging compliment. "I didn't want the promotion," Franny said, a refutation not to the woman in front of him, but to the universe at large.

"All right. And what does that have to do with the price of tea in China?" Abigail asked.

"Sorry, it's been . . . well never mind, I won't bore you with it." He gave himself time to think by draining the last of his tea, refilling his cup with water, and setting it back in the microwave. "Do you know where Croyd is holed up?"

"Yes."

"And do you know where I can find these jokers?"

"They're working as shills at Freakers trying to get hapless tourists in the door."

"Okay, I see two approaches. We help put Croyd to sleep, or we get the jokers out of town. Or maybe we do both, a two-pronged attack."

"I've tried dousing his food with sleeping pills, but I have to be careful because he's very paranoid right now, and the couple of times I succeeded it hasn't done a damn thing. And I'm out of pills. I got them when my mum came to visit and they only gave me thirty, and I used quite a few of them during *that* nightmare, so I only had about seven to use on Croyd, and I didn't want—"

He stopped the seemingly inexhaustible flow of words. "Maybe we need something stronger than sleeping pills."

Dr. Bradley Finn, head of the Jokertown Clinic, agreed to see them. Finn was a man in his fifties with silver-streaked blond hair, and a small paunch that pushed out the material of the Hawaiian shirt he wore beneath his white doctor's coat. The middle-age spread that was affecting the human torso wasn't echoed in the body of the palomino pony that made up the rest of the good doctor's form.

"Yep, you've got a problem," he said after hearing their story. "We've had occasions where we really, really needed Croyd to go the fuck to sleep, and we've tried everything, even horse tranquilizers. Nothing pharmaceutical works. His wild card decides when he's going to sleep, aided and abetted by Croyd."

"But that doesn't make any sense," Franny said. "How can he use speed to stay awake, but drugs can't put him to sleep?"

"Damned if I know," the doctor said. "Ask the virus."

Franny and Abigail exchanged looks. The doctor sensed their disappointment and her desperation. "Look, I've known Croyd for a long time, and I was able to put him to sleep back in the eighties—"

"How?" Abigail demanded.

"Brain entrainment and suggestion, but it takes time, and he was motivated. He'd promised some girl he wouldn't go out with her cranked."

Franny risked a glance at Abigail. Her face was set as she tried to hold back any reaction. "Problem is when he's in this state he's very paranoid—"

"No shit," Abigail interrupted the doctor.

"And this time he doesn't want to go to sleep because he feels threatened," Finn added.

"You're not telling us anything we don't already know," Franny said.

"Bear with me. In addition to being paranoid he's also very suggestible." A faraway expression crossed the doctor's face as he looked at a memory, and he gave a soft chuckle. He then gave himself a shake. "Point is, if you can get close enough to him you might be able to convince him to go to ground, or obsess about something else until the virus does put him to sleep."

"Thank you, Doctor." Franny stood and shook hands with the joker.

They walked out of the clinic accompanied by the sound of clashing bedpans, and the squeaking wheels on carts, moans and cries from patients, and incomprehensible gabble over the intercom. Franny felt like his clothes were absorbing the smells of alcohol, old coffee, overcooked peas, and sickness.

Outside he said, "I'm going to go talk to these jokers. You keep an eye on Croyd, and warn me if anything changes. Here's my card and my cell phone number."

Abigail started to walk away, then paused and looked back. "Thank you," she added softly.

♠

The entrance to Freakers was between the spread legs of a neon multi-breasted joker woman. Standing at the entrance was the joker . . . jokers. Franny could see why Abby had been a bit vague. From the waist up they looked like two aging bodybuilders, but their torsos plunged into insanely wide hips set atop two pile-driver legs that culminated in extra-wide feet encased in black wingtips.

The torso on the right wore a T-shirt that read REPENT OR BURN! The one on the left screamed out BLOW ME! The man wearing the religious T-shirt also held a Bible in one hand. "Do not enter this den of iniquity!"

The twin with the goatee rolled his eyes. "Come right in. Feast your eyes, and grow a chubby—"

"Actually, I want to talk to you guys." He flashed his badge. "Detective Black."

"What? Why?" said Religious, suddenly dropping the bombastic tone.

Franny paused, realizing he needed to tread carefully here. If he named Croyd the twins might actually go to the cops, and that would upset Abby. He also realized he didn't even know their names, and he couldn't spin a tale when he so obviously had no idea who they were. He took out a notebook and pen.

"Full names," he rapped.

"Rick Dockstedder," said the twin with the goatee, and jerked his thumb at his brother. "He's Mick."

"Look, I've got a tip that you boys ruffled some feathers. Might be a good idea for you to get out of town for a couple of weeks until it blows over."

"Whose feathers?" Rick asked.

"We can't," Mick said. "Our mother's sick. She's at the Clinic, and her surgery is tomorrow."

"Ovarian cysts," Rick offered.

"Mention not the private, female parts of our mother," Mick cried.

Rick smacked his brother on the back of the head. "Jesus, you are such a tool."

"Take not the Lord's name—"

"And we gotta feed her cat," Rick interrupted the latest religious eruption from his twin.

"And she needs my prayers," Mick added, and shot his brother a smoldering look. That elicited another eye roll from Rick.

Franny toyed with arresting them on some trumped-up charge and putting them in protective custody, but there would be awkward questions from his superiors. What settled it was the knowledge that he'd want to be there if *his* mom was sick.

He temporized. "Well, just keep a close eye out. Maybe get off the streets and just spend your time at her apartment and the clinic."

"Who's after us?" Rick asked again.

Franny shook his head. "I'm not at liberty to say. It could compromise an informant and an investigation." He started to walk away.

"You sure you don't want to come in?" Rick called.

"I don't think so."

"Bless you, you are a good man, and your purity will surely be rewarded," Mick shouted.

Rick smacked his brother on the back of the head then gave Franny a sly smile. "It's roast beef special today. $8.99."

He had had to cut short his lunch, the price certainly recommended it, and the dancers were very . . . flexible.

The Big Bleed

Part Five

OPERATION RE-PO WHEELS COMMENCED far too early the next morning. That is, three A.M. Which figured: Jamal had left the planning to Sheeba. She was a big fan of special operations stories, where the raids always took place in the middle of the night, when the target was likely asleep or otherwise weakened. And the streets were emptier.

They gathered in their ops center, joined by a young FBI agent Jamal had never seen, a nat named Gunn—surely fodder for a million jokes ("Is your first name 'Lone'?")—who was a little pudgy, pale, and clearly from the accounting side of the Bureau.

"We'll have your unit and two of ours," he said, pointing to locations on the streets bracketing their target's residence. He smiled. "If Wheels rolls, we'll be ready for him." Gunn was also, as Jamal soon realized, one of the annoying compulsive punsters.

Sheeba had reverted to Big Sister mode, had brought coffee for all of them. Of course, she had probably stopped off at a Dunkin' Donuts to upload a dozen for herself.

Jamal took a sip, and regretted it. The coffee was nasty. They did have several key operational details to get straight before they got too close to their target.

Nevertheless, Sheeba's briefing was, well, brief: name, images of Wheels. Rap sheet vitals, mostly suggesting he wouldn't be armed. "How could he be?" Gunn said. "He hasn't got arms."

Sheeba had a question. "What about Fort Freak? Do we bring them in?"

"Speaking of knuckleheads," Gunn said.

Jamal quite agreed that Fort Freak was a collection of knuckleheads, but so was every other police department he'd worked with at SCARE. And, to be fair, not everyone at Fort Freak was equally useless: Francis Black had actually made this raid happen. "Actually, we should have."

"Doubt they'll be able to do much at three A.M.," Sheeba said.

"Or at any A.M.," Gunn said.

"I have to let Franny know," Jamal said. "Let me text him."

"He won't appreciate it at this hour."

"He'll be even more unhappy finding out we staged a raid in his precinct after it's done."

They finished up the basics: address, type of building, the likelihood that Wheels lived on the ground floor ("Thank God for small favors," Sheeba said). Rules of engagement. Where Wheels would be taken—the federal lockup on Rikers—and by whom (Jamal with the FBI team).

Gunn had already departed when Jamal asked, "How do we haul him in?"

"What do you mean?" Sheeba said. "We will have the wagon—"

"The guy is literally the size of a truck."

"I will, ah, remind them the moment we're done here."

"Yeah," Jamal said, "remind them to bring a flatbed and chains. Tell them to think King Kong."

Jamal and Sheeba grabbed their vests and weapons. As they were leaving, Jamal noted that one of the computers was live, Skyping. "Big husband is watching?"

"He's interested."

That was a surprise. Sheeba had been so skeptical of Wheels's value as a target that Jamal assumed that Billy Ray felt the same way. Maybe not.

Or maybe he was just afraid of having his team screw up.

Jamal had spent considerable time traveling into, out of, and around Manhattan wondering who lived in its buildings. The fancy Upper East Side towers held no mysteries, obviously: the rich, often the foreign rich. Upper West Side, yuppies, families, more diversity.

One thing they had in common? No jokers.

But everywhere else . . . the East Side near the FDR, Eighth Avenue and Fifty-second . . . in all those grim brick buildings with their tiny metal entrances, those windows above the awnings, the places where the smells of food from the restaurants below had to be overwhelming . . .

And in the worst places. The old tenements on the Lower East Side and TriBeCa and SoHo and Jokertown. Worker storage units, obviously, but Jamal had no idea what the workers looked like.

Well, tonight he would.

The Explorer glided down narrow streets wet and shiny enough for a Ridley Scott commercial. There were few inhabitants to be seen . . . the master of one all-night news kiosk, a skinny man who looked to be homeless who was nevertheless sweeping the sidewalk in front of a closed Le Pain Quotidien, an amazingly tall tranny hooker leaning against a door, a three-legged joker hobbling God knew where. . . .

None of them spoke for several minutes, not until the Explorer made the turn from Grand onto Ludlow. "Okay," Sheeba said, "we've got our warrants."

The phone buzzed in its dashboard mount. "FBI is on station." Sheeba pulled the Explorer to a spot in front of a fire hydrant, the only open one on either side of Ludlow Street. That moment, at least, felt like a movie production—

"Do we have to wear the jackets?" Jamal said. The last item they had to don were blue Windbreakers with the word SCARE written on the backs in huge yellow letters.

"Yes. That was the one thing Billy made me promise: wear the jackets!"

Wheels's building was a typical tenement, pre–World War II, six stories tall, decayed, soot-covered. "How many jokers you figure you'll find here?" Jamal heard himself ask. "And just how the hell are we supposed to get around back?"

Sheeba held up an iPad with an illuminated street map: it showed a narrow alley to the south of the actual address that ran to a courtyard of sorts in the back. It was so narrow that it wasn't visible from half a block away.

The alley was SCARE's route. The FBI would hit the front door. The backup team would stand off to the north, ready to move laterally, should Wheels slip the leash.

Sheeba closed the iPad and left it in the car. "Showtime," she said. "Isn't that what they say in Hollywood, Jamal?"

"We say 'action.'"

But the reminder was apt. He had not been able to shake the feeling that this was a movie . . . except that on movie sets, things moved slowly and deliberately. It wasn't unusual to spend six hours rigging and rehearsing a single stunt.

Now they were just walking quickly up a dark Jokertown street at three A.M. Up ahead, Jamal could see the three FBI agents approaching from the opposite direction.

Sheeba had her hand to her earpiece. "Turning into the alley," she said quietly.

And they did.

"Tight quarters," Jamal said. The alley was so narrow that Jamal felt as though he could have touched the walls merely by spreading his arms.

Sheeba was thinking the same. "How the hell does Wheels get in and out?"

"He sucks in his gut," Jamal said.

In the courtyard, forty feet away, the edge of an ancient garage door—the kind that opened like a vertical accordion, not a roll-up—glimmered in the yellow light from apartment windows. As they got closer, about to turn the corner, Jamal and the others could see a second door next to the first, and a single floor of truly ancient rooms above both. It was quiet enough that they could hear their shoes scraping on the broken pavement. No music. Then, a voice from around front: "Open up! FBI!" And the sound of a door being forced.

Still no response in the courtyard. "Which one is he in?" Jamal asked.

"One way to find out," Sheeba said, striding toward the first.

A siren started grinding from somewhere out on Ludlow. In seconds, it was a full howl. Sheeba stepped back, trying to talk loud enough to be heard by the FBI, but not so loud that she spooked Wheels. "What's going on?"

She listened. Then shook her head in disgust. "Fire station!"

Sure enough, a fire unit, siren blasting, cherries flashing, rolled south to north down Ludlow, rousing the neighborhood. Windows lit up in the apartment building, and much worse, in the garage unit. The right-hand garage door opened and—with no warning rev of an engine, and no lights—a vehicle emerged. It skewed into a right turn in the small courtyard, then executed a left into the alley.

Sheeba was in the courtyard and managed to skip out of the way. She held on to her radio, screaming, "He's in the wind!" Jamal started chasing the vehicle down the alley.

Reaching the street, Wheels pulled up short, obviously wanting to be sure he wasn't rushing into traffic. The hesitation allowed Jamal to jump for the truck bed.

Which, as it turned out, was like trying to mount a wild horse.

It was . . . alive, sweaty human flesh. Nothing to grab on to—and the smell! Like a locker room mixed with oil-stained garage. All Jamal could think to do was shout, "FBI! You're under arrest!" (He had enough presence of mind to know that SCARE would mean nothing.)

All this warning did was spur Wheels to motion. The joker managed to turn on four appendages, like a show horse in an arena, aiming left, facing directly at Gunn and his FBI partners.

Who had to dodge behind parking meters and between cars as Wheels picked his way down the sidewalk. Being flung from side to side, Jamal stretched his arms and legs, bracing himself against the "walls" of the "bed." Then Wheels hit the street and began a sickening rock-and-roll motion as he gained speed. Jamal could only think, *the son of a bitch is getting away—!*

But up ahead, a black Escalade pulled into the street, a blocking move by the second FBI team. "Give it up, man! We've got you!" Wheels didn't hear or didn't understand. He slewed into an impossible turn and tipped his right side toward the front of the Escalade. The joker managed to avoid hitting the FBI vehicle. Not so Jamal, who was flung into its grille. As he felt himself getting airborne, he dug his nails into Wheels's "bed," the equivalent of scratching a man's back.

The last sound Jamal heard before slamming into the Escalade was Wheels's anguished cry. Jamal bounced onto the street, landing on his side. He felt as though he'd been punched at the same time someone twisted his arm and kicked him in the leg.

There was no bounceback. Just Jamal Norwood half conscious, in horrifying pain.

Those About to Die . . .

Part Two

"ARE YOU SURE ABOUT this?" Marcus asked. He slithered along beside Father Squid, having to work at it to keep up with the furiously striding joker. "Meeting in the middle of the night and all? Don't sound right to me."

Under streetlights, into shadow and out, along parked cars and down alleys, the priest marched like a man on a mission. "We can't let this opportunity escape us," the priest said. "This could be the key to everything. It's the lead I've been praying for. God always responds to us, Marcus. Sometimes he even provides us the answers we seek."

The priest turned unexpectedly, heading east on Water Street. Marcus had to carve around and shift it to catch up. "Okay, but . . . who called and what did he say?"

"I don't know who he is, but he mentioned Chakri's name. Said he'd heard I was looking for information about the disappearances."

"You sure that's not been solved already? I mean, the dog-training—"

"Was a sideshow, Marcus! Breaking that up was a rare

success on the part of the police, but not all of the missing were found at the kennel, and it hasn't stopped the disappearances. Two more went missing just this week. There remains something sinister at work."

Dryly, Marcus asked, "Which makes it a good idea to be going to meet some guy in the middle of the night?"

He knew he was pushing the skepticism, but he'd been hoping that the case was indeed closed. He'd had enough of this. Cruising around the city at night, looking for creeps nobody really wanted to find anyway, getting nowhere. There were other things he could be doing.

He checked the time on his phone. 11:13. It wasn't actually that late. Early enough for a few good hours at Drakes. His thumb caressed the screen. He itched to replay the video greeting the snake-loving nat girl had sent him. She was persistent. He had decided to meet up with her there just before Father Squid had called him.

He thought to himself, *Option One—meet up with blond girl that did some very weird things with a garter snake in a video. Option Two—follow a fishy-smelling, tentacled joker priest on the wild-goose chase to meet some unknown dude.*

"If you had heard the man's voice," Father Squid was saying, "you'd have no doubts. He had reason to be nervous about reaching out, and yet he did so anyway. His line of work is not entirely legal."

"Great." Marcus put as much sarcasm into the word as he could.

"He runs a chop shop. He dices up stolen cars, gets new ones in every night. Earlier this evening a vehicle came in that wasn't stolen. It wasn't even new. It had little value, and yet the owner wanted it painted and detailed. Disguised."

"You think it's this van Lupo and Doctor Gordon saw?"

"Why else would someone go to an illegal establishment to have work done to an old vehicle?" He turned

and set his dark eyes on Marcus. "We just need to con-
firm it. Then we call the police into action. They wanted
tangible leads? We'll give it to them."

"Yeah, but the guy's not going to want the police anywhere near his chop shop."

"We're meeting him in the East River Park. He is taking great risks, as you must now see."

As they passed a fenced basketball court lively with
late-night play, a lanky nine-foot-tall joker shouted, "Hey,
IBT, ball's up!" He tossed a basketball over the high
fence.

Marcus caught it. The court was crowded, jokers and
nats mixed together, shirtless guys with cut abdomens,
groups of girls milling around, bottles tilted in the air.
Speakers boomed out the ubiquitous, deep-throated lyrics
of Nutcracker Man's latest release. It was tempting. He'd
never been much of a ball player before his card turned,
but he had some skills now.

"This is no time for ball playing," Father Squid said. He
snatched the ball away and spun around long enough to
hurl the ball back over the high fence and right through
the hoop. If the ring had had a net it would've whooshed.
The priest acknowledged the impressed exclamations
with a raised hand, but he kept moving.

Marcus tore his eyes away from the crowd. As they
called after him, he followed the striding, hooded figure
of the priest toward the dark shadows of the East River
Park.

♥

"That's it," Father Squid said. "Just where he said he
would be."

The van sat under a thick copse of trees on a dead end
street in the park. As they got nearer, Marcus noticed a
lone figure standing a little distance away, illuminated by
a streetlamp just behind him. He could see him clearly,

but kinda wished he couldn't. He was a thin man, naked except for a cloth wrap around his privates. His bald head and boney chest and pigeon-toed legs all glistened with a sticky-looking moisture. He ran one hand over his abdomen, streaking the sticky stuff. The man walked forward to meet them.

The name came out of Marcus's mouth all by itself. "Gandhi?"

"That supposed to be an insult?" Expecting a Hindi accent to complete the look, Marcus was disappointed. The guy's voice was pure Village, a bit nasally and dipped in sarcasm. "I'm no Gandhi. Just a joker, like you."

A gust of air blew in from behind him, draping a pungent medicinal scent over Marcus. He covered his nose with his hand. He'd heard of this guy. "Vaporlock," Marcus said, "you don't chop cars. Petty burglary's your deal, isn't it?"

The joker chose to ignore that. "I said for the kid to come by himself."

"I saw no reason to send Marcus alone," Father Squid answered. "I am a man of God. I am no danger to you. I could not, however, know that you were not a danger to us. I could not send the boy into harm's way alone."

"That's real like . . . fatherly of you, Father," the guy said. "Annoying, too." He rolled his eyes and said, as if speaking to someone other than the two jokers, "He was supposed to come alone. But no, there's two of them!"

"It doesn't matter," Marcus said. "Just show us the van!"

The guy chewed the corner of his mouth. "All right. Why the hell not?" He gestured toward the vehicle with a glistening finger. "That what you're looking for?"

It wasn't much to look at. A battered, off-white cargo van. Dent in the side, hubcaps missing, gang tags etched in the coating of grime on the back door, half a Yankees sticker on the bumper. New York plates. "Wait till you see what's inside," Vaporlock said.

Marcus's long stomach tensed with unease. He could've been at Drakes, getting stroked by an average-looking blond girl with a thing for shiny scales. Instead, he was about to look into the back of a parked van. Images from serial killer documentaries flooded his mind. Father Squid, however, sounded resolved as ever. "Open it." He crossed himself and glanced at Marcus. "Prepare yourself, son."

Vaporlock got a grip on the latch with one moist hand. His free hand slid up his chest, cupping a handful of gook. "It's nothing like what you're thinking." He yanked on the handle.

Inside was one of the ugliest jokers Marcus had ever seen.

Huge black eyes, tiny ears, no nose at all. The guy hissed, drawing his lips back from a bristle of needle-thin teeth. All of this supported on a muscle-bulging weight-lifter's body. Before Father Squid could draw back, the joker punched him. The blow knocked the big priest's head back, but it wasn't the impact of the fist that really hurt him. It was the electric sizzle that accompanied it. Father Squid shook with convulsions. His eyes rolled back and he fell.

Before he hit the pavement, Vaporlock snapped his hand out and shoved the palmful of gook up Marcus's nose. The scent exploded in his head. His vision blurred. Tears sprang from his eyes. As he crumbled to the ground beside the priest, he heard the joker say, "Told you I was no Gandhi."

Ties That Bind

Part Two

THE RINGS WERE STILL in Michael's pocket days after he thought he'd be proposing. He walked in the door at home, exhausted and late for dinner, to be met with chaos. Happy chaos, for the most part—Kavitha had her latest show mix blasting, and was slowly twisting in the living room, sending out happy sparkles, rainbow coruscations. She must have just gotten back from the studio; she was still dressed for rehearsal, in a black leotard and long flowing skirt, her eyes darkened with kohl, her hair piled high, in elaborate braids. Kavitha looked gorgeous, like an Indian queen from a storybook, and once again, Michael wondered why she'd picked him. A woman that beautiful could have had her pick of guys—a doctor, a lawyer, a Wall Street trader. But instead Kavitha had gone for a skinny black cop. He should count his blessings. Isai was dancing around her mama and laughing, trying to catch the lights. Minal was, for a change, not at the stove—dinner was clearly over, with a clutter of dirty plates still on the dining table and the scent of curry lingering in the air—but was sprawled across the sofa instead, smiling and watching the show.

And, surprisingly, they had a guest.

Some guy was in the easy chair, his back to Michael, so that for a minute, Michael couldn't place him. Was it unenlightened of him, that for that minute, Michael's pulse rate quickened, and he felt a surge of possessiveness? A strange male in his territory, among his women. The adrenaline rushed through him—and then drained away a moment later, as the boy turned. It was only Sandip. What was he doing here?

"Brother!" the boy said, enthusiastically bounding out of his chair to wrap Michael in a hug. Michael hugged back, wincing a little.

Why did teenagers have so much energy? He was tempted to correct Sandip—after all, the kid was Kavitha's brother, not Michael's. But on the other hand, the boy was only jumping the gun a bit—if Michael ever actually managed to propose, then Sandip would be his brother, in law at least. Frightening thought. Did that mean he'd have to take on familial responsibility for this wild child? Kavitha smiled approvingly at him, still twisting in the center of the room, her body a long, lean poem of grace and beauty. His throat tightened. For her, okay. He could watch over Sandip. And he was honestly fond of the boy—Sandip had some of the same passion that Michael had felt at that age, the same need to prove himself. Although Sandip was more culturally directed, toward his own Tamil Sri Lankan people. Not the safest of passions.

"It's good to see you, man. What are you doing in town?" Michael hadn't seen Sandip in months—it only cost a couple hundred to fly down from Toronto, but that was a lot for a seventeen-year-old working odd jobs. "You finally checking out colleges?" Sandip was still living at home, and had decided to take a year off between high school and college; his parents weren't thrilled.

"Can't I come to visit my sister? See my adorable niece?" Sandip turned and stuck out his tongue at Isai, delighting her—she grinned and returned the gesture. In that moment, he looked closer to twelve than seventeen.

Kavitha slowed her spinning, long enough to say, "You know, I'd be happy to take you up to Columbia tomorrow. They have a great poli sci department." She smiled hopefully at her little brother.

Sandip groaned. "Aw, let it go, okay? I don't want to study politics, like some geek—I want to be in it, making shit happen."

Michael's pulse quickened. God, if the kid was getting involved with the Tamil separatists—that shit was dangerous. There were quite a few, up in Toronto; some people just couldn't accept that the war was over, like it or not. And yes, the Tamils back in Sri Lanka were getting treated like shit, again, but that wasn't a reason to return to the killing. On that subject, Michael and Kavitha were in complete agreement. But this hothead—the kid was just like Franny, wanting to skip the work, jump the queue. It wasn't right, and it wasn't fair. "You need to grow up, Sandip. Go to college, learn something about how the world really works." Michael snapped the words, and laid a warning hand on Sandip's arm.

The boy hesitated, and for a moment, Michael thought he had managed to get through to him. But then Sandip's face hardened, and he shook off Michael's hand. "You're not my father, bro. And I'm not an American—you don't need to police me."

Damn it. He'd come on too strong, as if he were questioning a suspect. Michael gentled his tone. "Sandip, I wasn't trying to—"

Sandip flung up a warning hand. "Yeah, *machan*, I don't need this kind of crap from you. I just came here to get a meal, see my sister and my niece. Minal Acca, thanks for the food—it was delish. I gotta get going. Later."

"Sandip, wait!" But it was too late. The kid had already grabbed his leather jacket and was out the door, slamming it behind him.

Kavitha came to an abrupt stop in the middle of a spin, her eyes wide. "Michael. What the hell just happened? Where's Sandip going?" Minal was sitting up on the sofa now, and Isai came running up to Michael. He bent down and scooped her up into his arms, bending his head down to smell the sweet child scent of her. Almost five, and she still smelled like a baby, vanilla and cinnamon mixed together.

"Uncle Sandip went away?" Isai asked, her eyes wide and confused.

"He'll be back soon, sweetheart," Michael said, forcing a smile. "He just went for a walk."

Typical teenager—Sandip would probably walk the streets for hours, but he'd be back when he got hungry and tired enough. Isai snuggled down into his arms, reassured. Kavitha seemed less convinced, but she let it go for now. Tension still lingered in the air. Probably not the best time to break out two engagement rings. Besides, he was starving, and the food smelled great. Michael smothered a twinge of guilt. The kid would be fine.

They were in bed that night, the three of them, Isai safely asleep, when Sandip's call finally came. Michael had just shifted over to the middle of the bed, to take his turn for some extra attention. Minal's mouth was moving on his, her hands tangled in his tight black curls. Kavitha was sliding down the bed, her body slick with sweat. When they were together like this, warm and sweet and hot as hell, that's when Michael realized how lucky he was, how all he wanted was for this sweetness to go on forever. That was why he'd bought those rings in the first place. But today had been a rotten day, and right now, he couldn't think about getting married. Maybe later; proposing in bed could be romantic, right? But right now, all Michael wanted was to forget himself in their bodies for a while. Kavitha was just lowering her mouth onto him when the phone rang. Michael groaned.

"I'm sorry," Kavitha said. "When people call at this hour it's usually important . . . or bad." And she was up, rolling out of bed, picking up the handset and walking out of the room, still gloriously naked. Her tight dancer's ass lifting and releasing with every step.

"Sandip? Where the hell are you?" Michael was relieved the kid had finally called, but damn, his timing sucked.

Minal grinned at him sympathetically. "Don't worry, sweetheart. I think I can keep you occupied until she gets back." She rolled over so that her body was braced above his, and Michael slid his hands up her hips, feeling his dick get painfully hard. There, just above his fingertips, the nipples started. He'd tried to count them more than once, with fingers and lips, but he never got very far. Tonight would be no different. She was just lowering her lush body down to his when Kavitha started yelling from the hall. "What? What are you talking about? Sandip, don't be an idiot!"

Michael groaned, and reluctantly slid out from under Minal. Cop training—respond to trouble. There was a phone extension in the hall; five steps had him there, picking it up, hearing Sandip ranting. "I don't need school, I don't need Amma and Appa, I don't need you! I got a job, sis. I've got people who appreciate me and my skills!"

Kavitha spat out, "What skills?"

Sandip snapped, "Wouldn't you like to know? I'm not a little kid anymore. I can do shit."

What kind of mess was the kid getting involved in? Michael tried to intervene in the sibling shouting match. "Hey, no one doubts you have skills, Sandip. We just want you to come home." He'd come on too strong before; Michael tried to keep his voice calm and coaxing this time.

But to no avail—the kid was too far gone, practically screaming into the phone, "I'll come home when I'm ready! When I've proved myself. Then you'll see. You'll all see!"

Kavitha said, "Sandip, shut up and listen to me!"

"Go to hell, sis!" And then the click—they'd lost him. Well, that was a terrific end to a truly crappy day. Michael stood, naked in the hall, staring at an equally naked Kavitha. This night really hadn't gone the way he'd planned. Now what was he supposed to do? Wander the streets looking for his girlfriend's brother? The kid was almost an adult—surely he could manage in Jokertown for one night? Minal came out of the bedroom, wrapped in a blanket, and leaned against the doorway, her face worried.

"Was he calling on his cell?" Michael asked. They could track that at the station.

"No," Kavitha said, shaking her head. "His cheap phone doesn't work in the States. He must have used a pay phone."

Damn it. The kid could be anywhere. "Look, I'm sure he'll come back in the morning." He wasn't actually sure of that, not anymore.

"I have to call my parents," Kavitha said.

"Of course you do," Minal agreed. She came forward then, wrapped an arm around Kavitha and clumsily draped the blanket around both of them.

"I thought they weren't talking to you?" Michael asked tentatively. It was something they didn't talk about much.

Kavitha's face was stark, wiped clean of all expression. "They'll talk to me for this," she said flatly.

Michael groaned inwardly. It was going to be a long night. "I'll make you some tea." It was something to do, at least. He didn't know why it was that both women always wanted tea when they were upset, but after all this time, he'd learned that much, at least. Tea wasn't going to find the kid, but maybe it would give them the strength to start looking.

The Big Bleed

Part Six

"WE CAUGHT HIM," SHEEBA said. "And he's singing."

"Good," Jamal croaked.

"But it's not what anyone expected." She went on to relate the details of an exotic smuggling and manufacturing cartel, only the product wasn't heroin or meth. "It's *food*."

"Get the fuck out of here."

"There's no need for that language. The product is illegal—endangered species used for entrées, magic mushrooms, other stuff that isn't supposed to be imported because it could get loose and wipe out indigenous plant life—"

Jamal tuned out at that point. The only relevant thing he heard was: "Everyone at HQ is happy with our results," implying that Carnifex had not been entirely enthusiastic about the mission—no surprise there. "And now that that's behind us—"

"That's it?" Jamal said. "No follow-up?" Jamal Norwood was sitting up in a bed at the Jokertown Clinic. He had been taken first to St. Vincent's, but the single attending there was over-burdened (there had been a bad fire several blocks away, with four people brought in suffering from burns and smoke inhalation), and claimed to know nothing about aces.

Loaded with painkillers, Jamal had waited, conscious or dozing, for four hours until an ambulance arrived to move him to Jokertown Clinic and Dr. Finn.

Who examined him yet again, and again just shook his head. "This obviously can't be considered part of your . . . syndrome."

"Is that anything like illness?"

The joker doc smiled. "We still don't know that whatever is . . . afflicting you doesn't have, say, an environmental trigger. So, no, syndrome, not illness."

"Not yet."

"Do you want to be ill, Mr. Norwood?"

"Have you added shrink to your job title?" Jamal had snapped. "Consider this a firm 'no.'"

Finn wanted to keep him for the day, for observation. And in truth, Jamal was not eager to be discharged. He was *finally* feeling bounceback, and was confident that he would be a hundred percent in a day . . . but he wanted that figure to be closer to sixty percent before he chanced the streets.

And told Julia. And his parents. Because each notification would be as good as telling the recipient that something was seriously wrong with Jamal Norwood—because his ace power should have put him back on his feet within the hour.

Not forty-eight.

The door hadn't even closed before Sheeba slid onto the corner of Jamal's bed and, assuming what must have been her idea of a motherly manner, said, "What's wrong, Jamal?"

He saw no benefit to denying the obvious: the Midnight Angel had worked with him for years. She knew how Stuntman was *supposed* to bounce back; she'd seen him hit harder. So he gave her the quick version.

"Why didn't you tell me? I can't let you back on active duty in this state, Jamal."

"Okay, Sheeba, two things." He was getting angry. "One, I'm not fit for duty today and could probably use another twenty-four hours off. Fine.

"But, two, I *am* bouncing back. A nat would be out of duty for months, maybe crippled for life. So whatever rules you're trying to access . . . they just don't apply." He smiled. "Don't make me charge you with discrimination."

Sheeba was so shocked she actually stood up and struggled for a response.

Jamal spared her. "I'm kidding," he said. "Really, really kidding."

But maybe he hadn't been kidding. He owed his whole SCARE career to his win on *American Hero* . . . and he owed that win to his confrontation with Wally Gunderson, the ace known as Rustbelt, a big, goofy, iron-skinned hoser from Minnesota, a world without African-Americans or anyone other than white Lutherans. Rusty had bugged Jamal from the moment he showed up at the *American Hero* house . . . he was too obviously trying to be nice, too simple. No one was really like that. No one outside of a group home, that is. And in one of the contests, with cameras rolling, Jamal was convinced he had heard Rusty come out with what he was really feeling, the words, "I'm gonna beat his black ass."

Or so he remembered it after all these years. It wasn't as though he had ever watched any footage of *American Hero* since the day it ended for him. . . .

Jamal had confronted him. Rusty had denied it, of course, but Jamal had been shaken . . . enough to lose. Days later, with what his mother would have called more charity, he realized it was possible Rusty had said "black ace." Which wasn't really objectionable, though whenever a white person threw "black" into a sentence, it was usually loaded—

"What do you want, then?" Sheeba was asking him.

Jamal realized that he had her on the run—which was exactly where he wanted her.

"Look, let me see how I feel when they turn me loose. I'll tell you in the morning," he said.

She nodded, patted the bed while smiling wanly. "Just get better."

♠

Jamal Norwood's wild card had turned his first year out of USC, when working as a junior stuntman on a bad movie. But there had been a harbinger.

It was a JV football game between Loyola and Cathedral. A Friday in early October, it was raining, cold, miserable. The moment he got off the bus, Jamal wanted nothing more than to have someone postpone the game.

No chance. Big Bill Norwood and every coach who ever lived said the same thing: football is violence and bad weather. (Jamal had Googled that quote later, and found that it wasn't complete. "Football was violence and bad weather *and* sex and rye." He still wondered what rye was.)

In spite of the mud and wet, the game turned out great, for Jamal. He'd returned the opening kickoff sixty-five yards. He might have reached the end zone except that he slipped getting past the Cathedral kicker . . . and landed on his butt.

He had made four solid runs on that drive, only to see Trey Lackland, the QB, take the ball for the touchdown. On the second drive, however, Trey sent him on a deep post pattern. Jamal had shot out of the backfield around the right end, faked the safety toward the sideline, then cut into the middle. He could see the other safety heading toward him, but Trey's pass was already in the air . . . long, but Jamal had simply stuck out his right hand. The point of the football buried itself in his palm; his momentum allowed him to quickly draw the ball into his chest.

And he ran fifty yards into the end zone, untouched, his first receiving touchdown ever.

He was on his way to the best game of his life. On the sidelines, he glanced toward the stands. With the nasty weather, the crowd was sparse . . . it was easy to find Big Bill Norwood on his feet, cheering. Cheering in a way he had never done before tonight.

When Jamal returned to the field on offense, he was pumped, eager for another pass play, or even a run. True, Trey's lack of game sense had left the team with a field position right between the hash marks, which is to say on the most chewed-up part of the field (would it have killed him to run plays to the right or left, where there was grass?).

But Jamal was eighteen . . . he was fast and furious. He could make this work.

The call was a forty-two dive right, a handoff to Jamal with the idea that he would bust through a hole on the right side of the offensive line. Trey's handoff was clean, but the hole collapsed. In a third of a second, Jamal turned to his right, paralleling the line, planning to simply go around it. Easy if you're fast—

—but not if you're turning on mud. And get hit by a defensive end going one way through your left ankle, and a linebacker the other way above your left knee.

Jamal heard his knee crunch even before he felt the pain.

Which still managed to be instantaneous and over-powering. Jamal had hit the ground as the ball squirted out of his hands, recovered by Cathedral and returned for a touchdown . . . something he didn't learn for a day. Because he was howling in pain, trying to put his left leg in a position where it wouldn't hurt. Wouldn't be swollen. Would function again.

He was foolish enough to try to stand. He failed. By then Trey and Mosicki the trainer and one other player had reached him. They waited for a stretcher to carry him off. The diagnosis—several torn ligaments in his left knee, specifically the anterior cruciate, which allowed a runner to make cuts and sharp turns.

Surgery was recommended, though not for several weeks, until the swelling subsided enough for a doctor to determine the seriousness of the injury.

Basic recovery for a healthy eighteen-year-old male would have been six weeks. Jamal Norwood was running and making cuts again in three. Of course, the season had long ended. Over the rest of Jamal's senior year, there was some talk around the Norwood house about that surgery . . . but since basketball was out, and Jamal found no difficulty competing in the 100, the 200 and the 4x100 in track . . . it just went away.

It wasn't until five years later, once he had become Stuntman, that Jamal Norwood began to wonder if that injury had triggered his first bounceback.

Whatever. Now he was on the other side.

◆

Jamal was still in the hospital gown, about to get dressed and get back to what was left of his life and career, when Detective F. X. Black appeared in the door. "How are you doing?"

"If I wasn't an ace, I'd be fine." Well, that was largely a lie. But since he didn't know anything for sure . . .

"When do you get released?"

"The moment you're gone."

"Hey, I can—" Franny hooked a thumb toward the door: *I can beat it out of here.*

Jamal waved that away. "It will only take a few minutes. Besides, there was something I needed to tell you."

Franny listened with growing amusement. Finally he said, "All this chasing around for some . . . magic mushrooms?"

"Not magic, just illegal. And not just mushrooms. All kinds of exotic foods. It's a huge deal to the Department of Agriculture." Jamal laughed at the image in his head. "I can just see *those* guys on a raid now, in their official Windbreakers with 'AG' written on the back. They probably wore green."

Franny shook his head. "Well, that's just fucking great. The big Wheels caper turns out to be about food, not bombers or kidnappers."

"It is, as we say in the law enforcement biz, a dry hole."

"Yeah, well, my hole just got reamed by one of my captains about my end of this little investigation. I am to forget the Warren County incidents forthwith and completely."

"Don't you still have a building—that dog-training joint?"

"You noticed that." He was as angry as Jamal had seen him. "According to everyone on the planet but you and me, there's no connection! These dead guys don't show up in any Fifth Precinct files, which means that they might as well not exist. Even if we had some info on any of them for any reason, they're not locals, which is about all we deal with. They're just . . . no-name hoods from another land, someone else's problem. Fuck." As he spoke, Franny had taken the file folder he carried, opened it up, and started dropping pages into Jamal's trash can, one by one.

"What's that?"

"My files on the hoods."

"Don't you archive those things?"

"I wasn't supposed to have them in the first place."

"Well, even so, throwing them away here isn't smart. . . ." Jamal had the folder fished out of the can and was presenting it to Franny before he realized: "You're not throwing it away. You want me to take it."

Franny smiled. "Thank you."

"Assuming I agree to spend five more minutes on this thing, which isn't automatic . . . what the hell do you want me to do?"

"Run the names through your database. SCARE must have access to FBI, DHS, CIA, Interpol, and, fuck, the Jetboy Junior Club, right?"

"Yes, but—"

"Look, maybe these three guys were just wannabe mobsters though they had a few kidnapped jokers stashed in cages. My captain has made up a story, but truthfully none of us have any idea why. And, naturally, my boss has made it clear that she doesn't want me proving her guess wrong and making her look bad, so I should just back off. That's bad enough. But just suppose, though, that they are deep-cover terrorists, the kind that always seem to bite us on the ass. They're dead, but they must have come from somewhere, must have been working with someone."

"I'll do what I can."

♥

He woke, as usual, before his alarm. He had his right arm over his head . . . when had he started sleeping like that? He blinked. Oh yes, it was Wednesday. Tuesday he had spent in the Jokertown Clinic.

He had come home, spoken to Julia briefly—she was at work—and yet, in a few moments, managed to terrify her with a description of his symptoms.

Good work, Jamal. That conversation convinced him to defer the parental notification for a day or two.

Then, feeling as though he was probably seventy percent bouncedback, he had collapsed in bed.

Now, this morning, ten hours later, he couldn't seem to move. Not with any ease.

He fought the panic. *Listen to me, whatever you are!*

You are not a degenerate disease! You are only accumulated injuries!

Okay, he told himself. *Whatever.* Maybe he was suffering from *something* (and when was that useless piece of shit Finn going to give him some good news?). Obviously it didn't help to have a vicious close encounter with a joker sized and shaped like a small truck—

Build yourself up. Bounce the fuck back.

Breathe. Stretch.

Take a moment and think. Listen to the city coming alive around you.

Where are you? Where have you been?

Where do you want to be?

He had a condo in Toluca Lake, so close to the Warner, Universal, and Disney studios that he could have walked there . . . and a short drive from Republic, Columbia, and Paramount. He hadn't seen it in two months. His parents were checking up on it, making sure there weren't letters jamming the mailbox, that the plants got watered.

He'd gotten so used to life on the road, to hotel rooms, the lonely breakfasts and nasty coffee, because he couldn't stand another buffet, the piled-up laundry, and the street roar, even on the twelfth floor. He wasn't entirely sure, but he believed that it was quiet at his condo. Maybe there was some freeway drone. Surely the planes taking off from Burbank Airport. . . .

What troubled Jamal was that he couldn't remember!

But that wasn't a sign of diminished capacity—he hoped, anyway. That was entirely due to living on the road for most of the past four years.

He took another breath. He seemed to be better.

Roll to your left . . . elevate with hands and arms, not your middle—

He was sitting up.

Then, miraculously, he was standing. Heading for

the bathroom and feeling as though he were seventy years old.

Forty-five minutes later he had showered—and conducted a survey of the bruising on his legs and right side—shaved, and dressed. After a yogurt and cereal breakfast, with one cup of coffee, he was functional if nowhere near good. Maybe back to where he was last night. His phone carried no new messages from the Angel or anyone at SCARE. No surprise there; as far as they were concerned, he was off the grid. Nothing from Franny, either, which was nice: no "reminders."

Why not check out the cop's information? What else was he going to do with his time? He opened his laptop and set it on the foot of the bed. (The desk was the wrong height . . . he had developed a severe case of lower back pain using the computer in that position during his first week at Bleecker Towers.)

He logged in, going through the tedium of entering his password. (Clearing the cache was not only a habit, but a requirement.) Then called up a multi-agency search, able to access the master DHS watch list, FBI and ICE and even Interpol.

While the page was loading, he opened the file Franny had given him—pages of standard police narrative as well as crime scene photos—and flipped to the list of names.

"Gornov, Dennis Timofeyevich." Thirty-six, Russian, from the sound of it, and from the ID photo. Blond, born to be a thug. Search.

New window: "Krekorian, Sev." Armenian. Twenty-seven.

"Rafikov, Zakir." That sounded Kazakh. Forty. New window.

God, these names. The African-American community

had a few brain-twisters and Jamal was generally good at them . . . but today, especially, he kept having to look at his notes and re-type. Jamal's laptop wasn't new or fast, and the Wi-Fi connection in the Bleecker was iffy. So it took several moments for the database searches to turn up results. The wait was worth it. U.S. agencies and Interpol *all* had files on the men. All had made border crossings in questionable circumstances or with suspect associates. Jamal quickly noted one surprising commonality: All three were ex-KGB.

Suddenly Jamal felt sicker than he had since getting slammed by Wheels on that Jokertown street. This wasn't some random, small-time crime. When you found three Russian hoods, you were likely to find half a container ship filled with contraband, or de-stabilizing weapons. Or even a goddamned nuke.

And these clowns were kidnapping jokers. Why? Potential suicide bombers, maybe? People who could be blackmailed into doing bad things? Jamal fumed. This was important information—

—but not necessarily to SCARE, not yet. Especially with the team so concentrated on candidate protection . . . and the dismaying results of the search for Wheels so unrelated to terrorism. And tomorrow he'd be going back on Holy Roller detail.

He dialed Franny at Fort Freak.

Galahad in Blue

Part Four

IT WAS GOING TO suck to tell Father Squid that the precinct had closed the case on the missing jokers. Especially since Franny wasn't sure he was a good enough actor to cover his own misgivings about that decision. But it had to be done. The priest deserved that much respect. Franny also wanted to talk to the priest about Croyd. Maybe enlist his help. If anyone could get through to the paranoid ace it might be the man who embodied, at least in Franny's mind, the conscience of Jokertown.

He also figured a morning spent at mass wouldn't be amiss—he'd certainly been afflicted by impure thoughts about both Apsara and Abby, and a corrosive anger toward his fellow officers and his captain. He promised himself he'd go to confess on Saturday, but for now he could try to find some peace among the polished wood and the smell of incense. He still found it hard to look at the joker Jesus crucified on a DNA helix, but he'd never been all that comfortable with the nat Jesus on his cross.

He turned the corner and was startled to see a crowd spilling out of the church doors onto the sidewalk. He mentally reviewed the liturgical calendar, but couldn't think of any particular saint days or holidays that would have caused the crush. Some people spotted him and reacted.

"*Oh thank God!*"

"The police."

"Now we'll get some answers."

Franny pushed through the people. From inside he heard Quasiman's voice stretched with anxiety. "No Father! No Father!"

The hunchback stood in the center aisle twisting his fingers together and shaking his head so violently that the trail of drool that perpetually ran down his chin flew onto nearby people.

"What's going on?" Franny asked.

"Oh thank heavens." It was Mrs. Flannery, an energetic joker woman in her fifties who ran the altar guild with ruthless efficiency, and made certain the altar was always decorated with appropriate flowers. She was clutching a bouquet to her chest right now with her misshappen hands. "Officer Black, we can't find Father Squid. Poor Quasi is so upset, and he has a hard time talking at the best of times. I know Father thinks he's getting better but—"

"Mrs. Flannery, you need to focus. What do you mean you can't find Father Squid?"

"No bed. No sleep. No eat. No Father," Quasiman burst out. As Franny watched a portion of the joker/ace's left arm phased out and disappeared. He seemed unaware of the loss.

A gnawing pain settled into the pit of his stomach. "Show me," he ordered.

The entire crowd lurched into motion. Franny held up his hands. "No, if there's evidence we have to preserve it. Quasi, take me to the rectory. The rest of you stay here, and figure out when you saw Father Squid last."

Quasi lurched off with Franny following close behind.

The priest's bedroom was spare and very orderly. Franny remembered that the man had been a soldier in Vietnam, and the room reflected that military background. It didn't take long to search and produced nothing. Father Squid's office showed the same organization. There were multiple versions of the Bible on the shelves and works by great religious teachers. The desk's surface held only a blotter, a notepad, and a pen holder. The notepad held a few notes that seemed to pertain to an upcoming sermon.

"Quasi, when did you last see Father Squid?" The joker stared at him and drooled, the saliva dripping onto the front of his T-shirt and forming a dark patch. Franny considered the last time Father Squid had come to the precinct. He had been with IBT. "Quasi, do you know where I can find IBT?" Drool. "Marcus." Drool. "Infamous Black Tongue?" Drool. "The big snake?"

There was a flicker of comprehension in the dull eyes. "With Father."

"Okay, when was that?"

But Quasi was gone. The office held only Franny and questions. As he walked back into the church Franny wondered if Quasi had gone to wherever his arm currently resided. Another time, another dimension, another galaxy . . . who knew? The hunchback, maybe, but he wasn't saying.

The parishioners had been busy in his absence. They were on cell phones, calling friends and relatives in Jokertown, and there was a small amount of information. A security guard had seen the priest and IBT either last night or the night before, but hadn't spoken to them, and had no idea where they were headed.

"Okay, all of you keep checking. And call me if you learn anything or if Father Squid returns." Franny headed to the precinct.

♠

Maseryk was on duty so it meant Franny didn't get to march in, throw the missing joker file dramatically on the desk and announce, *"This case is no longer closed!"* For one thing he wasn't pissed at Maseryk the way he was at Mendelberg, and frankly the crew-cut captain intimidated him worse than Mendelberg.

Franny laid out the situation. Maseryk rubbed a hand wearily across his face. "Damn fool, I told him to back off, leave it to the professionals."

"Yeah, and the professionals closed it," Franny shot back, forgetting to be intimidated.

"Watch it," Maseryk warned. Franny folded his lips together. "The case is now active. Get on it. And find him. This is the kind of thing that can be like lighting a match in a tinderbox."

Franny returned to his desk. He felt a sense of grim satisfaction. Until he realized that he still was nowhere, no leads, and one of Jokertown's most revered citizens taken without a trace. Then he noticed Jamal had called. Maybe the SCARE agent would have something. . . .

Those About to Die . . .

Part Three

MARCUS OPENED HIS EYES. For a moment he could see nothing but shapes behind a thick Vaseline-like coating. He blinked and rubbed at his eyes with his knuckles, trying to clear them.

"Awake finally," a voice said. " 'Bout time."

The voice was strangely familiar, but he couldn't place it. He heard footsteps move away, a chair scrape, and a person exhale as he sat down. Marcus realized the sitting person had touched him. That's why he'd woken up. But it wasn't the same person who was speaking.

"You know you snore, right?" the voice continued. "There's operations that can fix that. Think about getting one if you ever get out of here. That's a big if, by the way."

Even before he could focus on him, Marcus knew that last line was said through a crooked grin. It didn't make sense, but he thought he knew who was speaking. "Asmodeus?"

"You remember me! I'm touched. I remember you too. Last time I saw you you were on the ground in an alley, twitching, drooling, two cops standing over you."

Marcus lifted up his T-shirt and scrubbed furiously at

his eyes. When he looked up again, the world was oily, but he could see clearly enough. Asmodeus, the philosophizing general of the Demon Princes, paced a few yards away. He moved with the same cocky posture Marcus remembered. There was the crooked grin, the crown of short horns that ringed his head, the profusion of acne on his cheeks. His wardrobe had gone up a few notches. Gone were the pinstriped trousers, suspenders, and undershirt. Instead, he wore a shimmering maroon suit, with black shoes so sharp they looked like dagger points.

The seated man looked like a nat. He wore a wifebeater undershirt. It was not an attractive look considering his paunch, sagging breasts, and the black hairs bristling from his shoulders. His round face looked deeply bored. His jaw worked in a slow, bovine mastication of a piece of gum. He seemed to be staring at a spot on the wall.

The room provided no clues to what was going on. Sparse. Small. Simply furnished. He lay on a bed, though his long serpentine section spilled off onto the floor. He had no idea where he was. Last thing he remembered was . . . His gaze snapped back to Asmodeus. "Where's Father Squid?"

"He's here. Wasn't really meant to be. Bit of a fuck-up, if you ask me. Those numbnuts were supposed to pick you up, not Squiddy. Anyway, looks like he'll be staying. You'll see him soon. Before anything, though, you gotta sit through the talk."

"I'm not sitting through anything," Marcus said. Venom washed into his mouth like a surge of saliva. He drew himself upright and began to slide toward the door. Asmodeus moved to block him. Marcus snapped, "I'll take your fucking head of if you don't get out of my way."

"No, you won't," Asmodeus said. "Dmitri? Show Snake-boy why he's gonna sit and be good."

The bored man stopped chewing. He didn't look at Marcus, but his features tensed with concentration.

Not impressed, Marcus leaned forward, fists balled to

knock the grin off Asmodeus's face. Before he could, he felt something crawl across the back of his neck. Tiny legs, sharp points that moved with the rhythm of a centipede. He tried to swat at it, but his hands wouldn't move.

"That's how it starts," Asmodeus said. "Wait, it gets better."

The creature cut into Marcus's flesh. He felt it saw on his skull, cutting a slice through his cranium from ear to ear. Marcus's whole being cried out to shout and writhe and fight, but he just stood, trembling. Something slipped fingers into the crease and wrenched the back of his skull away from his brain. Scorching breaths burned his skin as the lips of an unseen mouth pressed close, using the slit in his skull to speak into his head. It spoke a garbled language that made the air curdle. Marcus didn't understand, and yet he knew the horrors the mouth spoke because he could see them before him. The world melted around him, went dark and sinister. The voice spoke of the unmaking of the world. It spoke of rot and disease and misery. Marcus felt the speaker moving around into his center of vision. He felt the enormous bulk of it, and he knew that whatever he was about to see was horrible beyond imagining. Just seeing it would kill him. Would stop his heart. But the worst part was knowing that even with his heart stopped he would go on, and the horror would use him like a cat plays with her mouse. It would never end.

And then it did. It stopped. The speaker vanished. The dark, formless world disappeared. Marcus slumped forward, gasping.

Asmodeus's tongue played along the line of his teeth. "That's some fucked-up shit, isn't it? That little trip was courtesy of Dmitri." He tilted his head to indicate the other guy, who had resumed working on his gum, eyes vacant again. "That's what he does. He fucks with people's heads. Now that he's been in yours, he can visit you anytime he wants to. Doesn't even have to be in the same room as you. You step out of line, Dmitri here steps into your cranium and escorts you to hell."

Marcus slithered back onto his bed, leaned against the wall, eyes snapping between Asmodeus and Dmitri.

"Now, let's try it again," Asmodeus said. "Here's what you need to know. Listen carefully because I'm not gonna say it twice. You may be wondering where you are, and how and why you're here. The where part is irrelevant. You just are. Deal with it. Don't worry about how you are either. The why is a bit more of a thing. You're here because Baba Yaga wants you to be. This is all her baby. Because of her, you've been plucked from the streets of J-Town and offered a chance at fame and riches. All you have to do is beat the shit out of fuckers. That's all this is about. It's about tapping into that primal urge for violence. It's about being a man and proving it in the arena. You're gonna be a gladiator. Understand?"

"No," Marcus said.

"Don't worry," Asmodeus said, moving toward the door, "understanding is coming at you fast. Come on. Take a look at the compound. You better get something to eat, too." When Marcus glanced at the ace, he added, "Dmitri's not gonna fuck with you. Unless you act up."

As if dismissed by this, Dmitri stood, pulled out his iPhone, and began scrolling through his messages.

Leaving his room, Marcus's gaze turned upwards to the arching dome above the open space. Daylight shone through the material, bathing the green, garden-like space so completely that it almost seemed like they were outside. Insects buzzed among the flowering vines that ran up the rafters. Birds flitted about. Birdsong blended with the low, sinuous pipe music that floated on the air, exotic, meant to tempt and entrance. The scent of incense hung in the air.

It was almost beautiful, until he lowered his eyes and took in the tables and chairs, couches and plush rugs that crowded the main room. Amongst them, a motley collection of jokers lounged. Burly men. Dangerous-looking. Some of them were bandaged and bruised. Some played cards. A few watched baseball on a large flat-screen. Several browsed tables laden with food. One met his gaze, snarled. Judging by the growths all over his face and arms, he answered to the name Wartcake. Father Squid had called him Simon Clarke. They'd wanted to find the vanishing jokers. Now they had.

"This is the common area. Canteen. Bar. Place to hang out and shoot the shit. We're pretty much free to do whatever, until a bout."

A short-armed bartender mixed drinks at a bar. A small crowd gathered around it, talking, smoking. A gorgeous, nearly naked young nat woman started dancing to the accompaniment of cheers, her body all moving curves and lean arms and legs. Another climbed onto the lap of a grinning joker.

"We get treated well," Asmodeus said. "You could get some of that, too. Just bring it in the arena. Win, and get the crowd loving you and you'll get rewards, too."

Marcus caught sight of Father Squid. The priest moved slowly through cots of injured jokers, talking quietly with them as he checked their injuries. "This place can't hold us," he said, though his voice didn't carry the conviction of his words. "We're not staying long."

"Jailbreak, huh?" Asmodeus asked. His voice dripped with sarcasm. "Gladiator uprising? Shit, you really are clueless. My first day here a joker named Giles made a fuss. He started ranting, trying to wind us up, saying our power was in our numbers and we could smash this place if we wanted to."

"Sounds like the type of shit you used to spout," Marcus said.

Asmodeus grinned. "He was all right, but didn't quite have my gift for oratory. He got folks pumped. Dmitri could've taken him to hell, but this time Baba's thugs appeared. They dropped out of the ceiling all of a sudden.

Had Giles strung between three Tasers, jerking and twitching, before anybody knew what was happening. They took him away. When they brought him back he wasn't Giles anymore. He wasn't even a man."

"What's that supposed to mean?"

"He came back as that." The joker leaned close to Marcus's shoulder and stretched his slim arm out to point.

For a moment Marcus didn't know what he meant. There was nothing where he was pointing but a weird-looking chair. He almost said as much, but the words caught in his throat. Something about the piece of furniture made his skin crawl. It was strangely organic, as if it were all made of one substance, stretched and morphed into shape.

"That chair is Giles. Don't ask me to explain how. We all just knew. When it first came . . ." Asmodeus lowered his voice, speaking with hushed reverence. ". . . it even looked like him. You could see him in there. He was twisted, changed, but he was still alive. We could see him breathing. We could see his eyes move. Sometimes, at night, I heard him pleading. Not really words, but, just sounds of anguish. He's dead now, but it was a long time in coming."

Marcus tried to think of something flippant, but there was nothing in Asmodeus's face to indicate he was joking. He looked at the empty chair. Maybe his mind was playing tricks on him, but he could almost see a kneeling man, tilted backwards, arms frozen in a rictus of agony.

"Baba Yaga's into some serious shit," Asmodeus said. "It's not like what Dmitri does. Some of it's for real. It's why you're gonna fight when she says fight."

Once More,
for Old Times' Sake

by Carrie Vaughn

ANA CORTEZ WAS PLAYING hooky from work. She called in sick—first time ever, not counting the couple of times she'd ended up hospitalized *because* of work. On the phone with her boss, she sounded as pathetic and self-sacrificing as she could, saying that she couldn't possibly come in and risk infecting anybody else with whatever twenty-four-hour stomach bug was ravaging her system. She wasn't sure Lohengrin believed her, but she'd earned enough status over the last few years, he didn't question her. She *deserved* to play hooky.

What would she do with her day off? What any self-respecting New Yorker—transplanted, but still—would do: she went to a baseball game at Yankee Stadium. Not that she particularly liked baseball, but Kate would be on the field today, and Ana wasn't going to miss it for the world.

Except for the local favorites and the one or two who made the news in some scandal or other, Ana didn't know who any of the players were, didn't follow baseball at all, but she got caught up in the excitement anyway, cheer-

ing and shouting from her seat in the front row off third
base.

The player who won the Home Run Derby, Yankee
hitter Robinson Canó, was a local favorite, and the
crowd stayed ramped up for the next event. The special
charity exhibition was billed as a Pitching Derby—the
major league's top pitchers took to the field, facing home
plate and a radar gun, and pitched their fastest. 100 miles
per hour. 101. 99. 102. The crowd lost it when Aroldis
Chapman pitched 105—it had broken some kind of record, apparently. But the show wasn't over, and when the
last pitcher in the lineup walked onto the field, an antici-
patory hush fell.

The athletic young woman wore the tight-fitting white
pants of a baseball uniform and a baby-doll T-shirt, navy
blue, with "Curveball" printed on the back. No number,
no team affiliation, which was Kate all over these days.
Curveball, the famous ace who could blow up buildings
with her pitches, who'd quit the first season of *American
Hero* to be a real-life hero, who'd then quit the Committee, because she didn't need anybody.

The crowd never got completely quiet as they mur-
mured wondering observations and pointed at the
newcomer. Ana leaned forward, trying to get a better
look at her friend, who seemed small and alone as she
crossed the diamond and reached the mound, tugging on
her cap. She didn't face home plate like the others, but
turned outward, to the one-ton pile of concrete blocks
that had been trucked to the outfield.

Kate looked nervous, stepping on one foot, then
another, digging the toes of her shoes into the dirt, pressing the baseball into her glove. Her ponytail twitched
when she moved. Some traditionalists hadn't wanted
her here—were appalled at the very idea of a woman on
the pitcher's mound at venerable Yankee Stadium. But
this was raising money for charity so they couldn't very

well argue. Ana wondered how much harassment Kate had put up with behind the scenes. If she had, she'd channel her anger into her arm.

Ana's stomach clenched in shared anxiety, and she gripped the railing in front of her until her fingers hurt. Why did this feel like a battle, that Ana should be out on the field with her, backing her up? Like they'd fought together so many times before. Here, all Ana could do was watch. This wasn't a battle, this was supposed to be for fun. Gah. She touched the St. Barbara medallion she wore around her neck, tucked under her shirt. The action usually calmed her.

Finally, the ace pitcher settled, raised the ball and her glove to her chest, wound up, left leg drawn up, and let fly, her whole body stretching into the throw.

Sparks flared along her arm, and the ball vanished from her hand, followed by a crack of thunder, the *whump* of an explosion—and the pile of concrete was gone, just gone. Debris rained down over the field in a cloud of dust and gravel. The sound was like hail falling. The crowd sitting along the backfield screamed and ducked. Kate turned away, raising her arm to shelter her face.

Something weird had happened. Ana had seen Kate throw a thousand times, everything from a grain of rice to a bowling ball. She'd blown up cars and killed people with her projectiles. But she'd never erased a target like this.

Then the speed of the pitch flashed on the big board: 772 mph.

The announcer went crazy, his voice cracking as he screamed, "... that sound ... the sonic boom of a *baseball*! Oh my God, I've never seen anything like it! Unbelievable!"

Kate had also put a sedan-sized crater in the outfield, but no one seemed to mind. The crowd's collective roar matched the noise of a tidal wave, and the major league players rushed out on the field to swarm Curveball. A pair of them lifted her to their shoulders, so she sailed above them. Her face held an expression of stark wonder. The screen at the backfield focused on her, her vast smile and bright eyes.

Ana clapped and screamed along with the rest of the crowd.

It took two hours for the stadium to clear out. Ana lingered, making her way toward home plate, where Kate was entertaining fans leaning over the boards to talk to her. Signing baseballs, posing for pictures. Ana arrived in time to catch one exchange with a girl, maybe twelve, a redhead in braids and a baseball cap of her own.

"I play softball," she said, handing Kate a ball to sign.

"You pitch?" Kate asked.

"Yeah, but not like you."

"Chapman doesn't pitch like me. I bet you're good enough."

The girl shrugged. "I don't know. We didn't win the season."

"Keep practicing. That's what it takes. Work hard. Okay?"

The girl left smiling.

Kate saw Ana hanging back as the last of her admirers left. Squealing, she pulled herself over the barrier and caught her up in a rib-squishing hug. Ana hugged back, laughing. They separated to get a better look at each other. Kate was still grinning, as well she should be, but Ana noticed the shadows under her eyes.

"I'm so glad you could make it," Kate said.

"Are you kidding? I wasn't going to miss it. You ready for the party?"

Kate sighed. "I need a couple more hours. They want a press conference and a photo op for the charity. We raised seventy-five grand." Her gaze brightened.

"That's so great. How about this—come over as soon as you can, and I'll have a chance to pick up a few more things and get the place cleaned up."

"You promised me a gallon of margaritas. Is that still on?"

"Oh, you know it. A gallon of margaritas, a pile of DVDs—and all the gossip on that new boy of yours."

Kate blushed, but her smile glowed. "You got it."

Ana had brought home the tequila, limes, salt, and a bag of ice already. Now, she went for approximately a metric ton of burritos from the excellent taquería around the corner from her apartment. They had to eat if they were going to keep up their strength for more margaritas.

The Lower East Side walk-up used to be her and Kate's apartment, back when Kate was still on the Committee, until she quit and went back to school in Oregon. That had been a couple of years ago now, and they didn't get to see each other very often these days.

Her apartment was on East Fifth Street, a few blocks off Jokertown, in a neighborhood that wasn't great but wasn't awful. Ana liked the place. It wasn't pretentious, and she could maintain some level of normality. Like go to the taquería without anyone giving her a hard time or snapping pictures. With her straight dark hair and stoutish frame, she wasn't as photogenic as Kate, but she'd had her own share of publicity as the Latin American Coordinator for the UN Committee on Extraordinary Interventions. She didn't much *feel* like a public figure most of the time. So she stayed in her unassuming neighborhood. The street food was better.

At her building's front door, she paused to find her key one-handed, when a voice hissed at her from the stairwell to the lower-level apartment.

"Ana! Ana, down here!" She looked over the railing.

The joker wore dark sunglasses and had his top two arms shoved into an oversized jacket. His middle two arms held it tight around his torso in some futile attempt at a disguise. He made his best effort to huddle in the shadows, away from the view of street level, but the guy was over seven feet tall and bulky: the world-famous drummer for the band Joker Plague.

"DB? What are you doing here?" she said.

He made a waving motion, hushing her. "Quiet! Get down here, will you?"

She swung around the railing, and Drummer Boy pulled her into the shelter of the stairwell, making her drop the bag of food. "Michael!"

"Shhh! Sorry. Here." With a fifth arm emerging from the bottom of the jacket, he picked up the bag and shoved it at her. The contents were probably mushed. Maybe they could have burrito casserole. "Ana, I need to talk to you, can I come in?"

"Couldn't you call?"

"*In person*. Come on, at least can we get off the street?"

She hadn't seen him in almost a year. Normally, she'd be happy to see him, and they tried to get together the rare times they happened to be in the same zip code at the same time. He'd gotten her tickets to a Joker Plague show awhile back, and she'd love to do something like that again. But she really wished he'd called. What she *didn't* want was him still hanging around when Kate arrived.

She spent too long thinking, and DB continued cajoling. "I'm passing through town, and I really need to talk to you but I'm trying to keep a low profile—"

She raised an eyebrow and gave him a skeptical look. With six arms and tympanic membranes covering his torso, Michael Vogali, aka Drummer Boy, could never keep a low profile. Ever.

"Michael, what do you want, really?" she said.

"Can I crash at your place? Just for a couple of days. Please?"

Three hundred sixty-five days in a year, and he picked this one to show up asking for a favor. He was a friend, she didn't want to say no, but this *couldn't* be happening. This . . . this was not going to end well.

She winced. "You don't have anyone else you can stay with? Don't you own an apartment on Central Park or something excessive like that?"

"Never did get around to it," he said. "Our recording studio's in LA."

"You can't stay at my place, it's *tiny*."

"It's just for a couple of days—"

Exasperated, she blurted, "You can't because Kate's staying with me tonight."

He brightened. "She is? I haven't seen her in ages. Is she . . . I mean, is she okay and everything?"

She hadn't meant to say anything about Kate. "Are you *sure* you can't stay someplace else?"

"This isn't just about someplace to stay, we really do need to talk. And Kate . . . oh fuck, I didn't want to be the one to tell Kate, I was hoping you could do it after I'd talked to you—"

"What are you talking about?"

"Please, can we go inside?" He gave her a hangdog look that should have been ridiculous on a seven-foot-tall joker behemoth, but he managed to make himself endearing.

She rolled her eyes. "Okay. Fine. But Kate and I are still having our margarita night."

"Hey, that sounds like fun—"

"Michael!"

He raised his hands in a defensive pose and backed up a step. "No problem."

"Hold this." She handed him the burritos and found the key for the door. "Why didn't you just call me instead of camping out like a homeless person?"

"Because you'd be more likely to say yes if I just showed up on your doorstep?"

She growled and hit him on the side, generating a hollow echo through his torso.

"My walls are thin—you're going to have to cut down on the drumming."

"Sure, of course," he said, smacking a hollow beat as punctuation.

Oh yeah, was this going to end badly.

Kate and DB had quit the Committee at the same time, over the politicization of the group in the Middle East. Ana hadn't been there, but she'd gotten an earful when Kate called to tell her about it. She'd cried a bunch during that phone call—Ana might be the only person in the world who knew how torn up Kate had been over the whole thing. Ana had been stuck halfway around the world, on another mission for the Committee, and couldn't do a thing about it. DB had just been angry—he hadn't called Ana to vent. A bunch of the tabloids insisted that DB and Kate had run off together in some torrid romance, but that wasn't at all true. It was all getting to be old history, now. They'd moved on. Ana hoped they didn't revive the soap opera here tonight.

Kate's call from the downstairs intercom came an hour later, and Ana buzzed her in.

"I never thought they'd let me leave," Kate said, pushing into the apartment and dropping her bag by the door. "One more picture, they kept saying. Not like they didn't already have twenty million."

Ana stepped aside, closed the door behind her, and waited. Didn't take long.

DB stood from the sofa and sheepishly waved a couple of arms, while a third skittered a nervous beat that sounded like balloons popping. He'd taken off the oversized jacket and stood in all his shirtless, tattooed glory. "Hey, Kate."

Kate turned to Ana. "What's he doing here?"

DB stepped forward. "It's just for the night, I promise, I'm trying to keep a low profile—"

"I'm a pushover," Ana said, shrugging.

Kate glared, and Ana wasn't sure whom the glare was directed toward. "I hope you have those margaritas ready."

"Two pitchers, ready to go."

They headed into the kitchen, or rather the corner of the apartment that served as the kitchen. DB followed them, sidling along, as delicately as his body allowed. "So, hey, Kate. How you doing?" DB had been nursing a crush on Kate for years now. He wasn't any more subtle about it than he had been back on the set of the first season of *American Hero*. He'd gotten a little more polite, at least.

"I pitched past the sound barrier at Yankee Stadium today, how are you?"

"Um . . . hey, that's great. I think. I just happened to be in town, and, well, we really need to talk—"

Kate said, "Michael, Ana and I planned a night to chill out, with too much alcohol and a lot of TV and not thinking about anything. That's not going to change just because you're here, okay? I can't be mad about Ana letting you stay here. But can you just . . . leave us alone?"

DB sat back on the sofa, his arms folded together contritely.

Feeding everyone margaritas kept them quiet for a little while. Half an hour, maybe. The first DVD of the latest season of *Grey's Anatomy* was good for another hour or so, especially watching the episode where Meredith and Derek spent the whole time fighting over Derek's ethically questionable experiments using a new version of the trump virus on a collection of hideous joker patients. It was pretty awful.

DB chortled through the whole thing. "I wouldn't mind it so much if they actually used joker actors rather than nat actors with fucking rubber tentacles."

Ana agreed with him, but they had to have the rubber tentacles so they could take them off and declare them cured for five minutes before they melted in a hideous ooze of sudden-onset Black Queen.

But the episode finally ended, and in the quiet while Ana changed out DVDs, DB had to ruin it. "Okay, I know you're having your party and all, and I know I'm interrupting—"

Kate, nested on pillows on the floor in front of the TV, took a long drink of margarita and ignored him. Ana almost felt sorry for the guy. He was nice, usually; he'd take a bullet for his friends, and with their history that wasn't just a saying. But he was way too used to being the center of attention, and definitely wasn't used to being ignored by a couple of women.

"—but I really need to talk to you. This is serious. Seriously." The sofa creaked as he leaned forward, and half his hands drummed nervously.

Ana shushed him, got the DVD in and hit play, hoping that would shut him up. But Kate rolled over and glared. "Michael, what are you doing here? Isn't Joker Plague supposed to be on tour in . . . in Thailand or someplace?"

He brightened. "You've been keeping up with us—"

She glowered. "Crazy guess."

"The tour was last month. We're supposed to be recording the new album, but . . . I gotta tell you, it's not going well. I knew we were in trouble when all our songs started being about how tough it is being a band on tour. So I'm telling the guys, maybe we should take some time off, get back to our roots. Hang in Jokertown for a while—"

Kate turned back to the TV.

"—but never mind that. I was doing this signing in LA a week or so ago, and a fan brought me this . . . this *thing*. I think you really need to know that this is out there." He was serious—worried, even, reaching for something in the pocket of his oversized coat, draped over the back of the sofa.

The intercom buzzer at the front door went off.

Ana needed a minute to scramble up from the bed of cushions. Her first margarita was already making her wobbly. She really needed a vacation. . . .

"You expecting anyone?" Kate asked.

"No," Ana said, and hit the intercom button. "Hello?"

"Ana. It's John. John Fortune."

This had to be a joke. Someone had put him up to this. This was too . . . If it had happened to someone else, it would be funny.

"*What?*" Kate said. Both she and DB were staring at her. So yeah, they'd heard it.

She didn't want to argue. "I'll be right down," she said, and left before Kate and DB could say anything.

He was waiting at the front door, hands shoved in the pockets of a ratty army jacket. She couldn't say he looked particularly good at the moment. He was a slim, handsome man, with dark skin, pale hair, and a serious expression. The white lines of an asterisk-shaped scar painted his forehead. At the moment his hair was too long and uncombed, and he looked shadowed, gaunt, like he hadn't gotten enough food, sleep, or both.

"Hi," he said, his smile thin, halfhearted.

"John. Hi. What's the matter?"

"I need a favor." Oh, no, this was not happening. . . . He said, "Can I stay with you? Just a couple of nights."

Any other night . . . "This really isn't the best time. Can't you stay with your mom?"

He winced and rubbed his head. "I would, except she's trying to talk me into coming back to work for her on

American Hero. And that . . . I can't do that. I'm avoiding her."

"No," she said. "You sure can't."

"I know I should have called ahead . . . but it's just a couple of nights, I promise."

Whatever else she was, Ana was not the kind of person who left a friend standing on the street. She held open the door. "Come on in. Um, I should probably warn you . . ."

♠

Ana half expected Kate to be hiding in the bathroom, the only spot in the studio with a closable door and any modicum of privacy. But she was standing in the middle of the room, side by side with DB, waiting. Ana led John inside and softly closed the door.

John slouched, and his smile was strained. "Hi, Kate."

"Hi," she said, her tone flat. That was it.

"Well," DB drawled. "Look what the cat dragged in."

"Can it, Michael," Ana said. She drew herself up, hands on hips. She'd stared down diplomats from a dozen countries and addressed the UN Security Council. Surely she could lay down the law here. "You're all my friends and I'm not going to leave anybody stranded. But I would appreciate you all acting like grown-ups. You think you can do that?" Nobody said anything, so she assumed that was yes. "I'll heat up some food, we can have dinner. Like normal people." While she pulled food out of the fridge, she listened.

"How you doing?" John said.

"I'm okay," Kate answered. "You?"

He might have shrugged.

Ana hadn't been there when they broke up, but she knew it had been bad—Kate walking out while John was still in the hospital, recovering from having a joker parasite with delusions of grandeur ripped out of his forehead.

John had gone from being a latent, to drawing a Black Queen, to having his father die to save his life, to having an ace power in the form of a scarab-beetle ace living inside him—to nathood. And then his girlfriend broke up with him.

But Ana had heard both sides of that story, and John had screwed up as well. He'd never trusted Kate. He kept assuming she would run off with someone else, someone with power—someone like DB. And he threw that in her face. She'd told him she loved him, and he never really believed her, so she walked. Now, Kate had her first real boyfriend in years. Ana wondered how John felt about that, if he even knew. He had to know—Kate was a celebrity, the pictures had been in the magazines.

They'd all met in the first season of *American Hero*— Ana, Kate, and DB as contestants, John working as a PA for his mother Peregrine, producer of the show and arguably the most famous wild carder of all time. Those days seemed dream-like, surreal. Part of some fun-house carnival ride that ultimately meant nothing. So much had happened since then, but that was where it all started. The show was still going strong, riding high in the ratings; Ana didn't pay attention.

DB paced, pounding a double beat on his torso.

"You in town for anything special?" John said to Kate, as if they were alone in the room.

"Yeah, charity pitching derby at the All-Star Game."

"Oh yeah? Cool."

"You?"

"I've been traveling, I guess. Here and there."

This was the most gratingly awkward conversation of all time. Ana wondered if she could fix it by feeding them more margaritas. She went to the kitchen to get started on that.

"I figured you'd be staying with your mom," Kate said.

John rolled his eyes. "I'd have to spend all night hearing about how I should go back to work for her on *American Hero*."

"Oh, *no*," Kate said, with genuine outrage.

The drumming and pacing stopped. "Hey, maybe you can get the Winged Wench to explain *this*. Unless *you* know where it came from."

He held out a DVD case, which he'd retrieved from his coat pocket. Poor quality, low production values, with a photocopied cover shoved behind cheap clear plastic. The title: AMERICAN *HERO UNCUT, VOL. I.*

John gave a long-suffering look at the ceiling. "My mother had nothing to do with that. *I* had nothing to do with that."

Kate yanked the DVD case out of DB's hand and stared at it. "What the hell is this?"

Ana drifted over to Kate's side, to study the case over her shoulder. The image on the front featured DB, all his arms wrapped around the svelte figure of Jade Blossom, another of the first season *American Hero* contestants. Naked Jade Blossom, Ana noted. Her state of undress was obvious even through the shadowed, unfocused quality of the picture. Uncut, indeed—unauthorized footage from the reality show's seemingly infinite number of cameras.

Somehow, Ana couldn't be entirely surprised that such a thing existed. What did surprise her was not stumbling on the footage online somewhere. Now that she knew it existed, she probably wouldn't be able to avoid it.

Kate gaped for a moment, then covered her mouth with her hands and spit laughter. "I'm sorry. It's not funny. But it *is*." She might have been having some kind of fit, doubled over, holding her gut. "Karma's a *bitch*!"

"Look at the back," DB said, making a turning motion with one of his hands. "*This* is what I've been trying to tell you."

When Kate turned the case over to look at the back,

Ana almost turned away. The back showed three more pictures: two more of DB, captured in the moment with two entirely different contestants of the show. And one of Kate, her back to the camera, towel sliding off her shoulders as she stepped into the shower. The picture was a tease, of course. How much did the video actually show?

Ana couldn't tell if the red in Kate's cheeks was from alcohol or embarrassment. When Kate set her jaw and hefted the DVD case as if to throw it, all three of them reached for her, making halting noises. Glancing at them, Kate sighed, and merely tossed the DVD back to DB, without her ace power charging it. DB fumbled it out of a couple of hands before managing to catch it.

Kate said, "At least I can say there aren't any sex tapes of me. Unlike some people."

"You had your chance," DB muttered.

Kate glared. The TV played through the pause; two characters were making out in a hospital supply closet.

"Volume I," Ana said. "So how many of those are there?"

"Who the fuck knows?" DB said. "The guy wanted me to *sign* it for him."

"Whoever's doing these has to have access to the show's raw footage." She looked at John, inquiring.

He said, "Could be anyone with access to the editing process. Mom and Josh have a pack of lawyers working on it—you can imagine what it's doing to the *American Hero* brand. But there's not much they can do about it once the videos hit the web."

Ana went to the kitchen and stuck a plate of burritos in the microwave. Food. Food would make everything better. And more margaritas. If she could just get everyone commiserating over the shared trauma rather than making accusations, maybe she could salvage the party.

"I do *not* need this right now," Kate said, and started pacing. "Oh my God, I should tell Tyler . . . but if he doesn't know about it already maybe I shouldn't tell him. . . ."

"Who's Tyler?" DB said.

John smirked. "Haven't you heard? It's been all over *Aces!*. Kate's new boyfriend—she's dating nats now."

"John, don't be an asshole," Ana said. She'd had no intention of bringing this up while the love triangle from hell was in her five-hundred-square-foot apartment. She'd kill John for poking Kate like this.

Kate plowed on. "I told you then, I didn't break up with you because you lost your powers. I broke up with you because I couldn't keep . . . propping up your self-esteem. You kept making the whole thing about you."

"Wait a minute, boyfriend? What boyfriend? Who is this guy?" DB said.

Kate didn't answer, and Ana sure wasn't going to say anything.

DB continued. "No, really—we can settle this. Tyler, huh? I don't care if he's a nat or the king of Persia, I want to meet him. You know, just to make sure he's a nice guy."

"I can pick my own boyfriends, thank you very much," Kate said.

"Apparently not," DB said, pointing three arms at John.

Kate growled and cocked back her arm. Despite watching for it—hoping to minimize damage to the apartment—Ana hadn't seen whatever projectile she picked up; but then, Kate always kept a few marbles in her pocket, for whenever she lost her temper.

"Kate!" Ana yelled. "Cool it! No throwing in the house! Nobody uses *any* powers in the house! Got it?"

The ace pitcher froze, a static charge dancing around her hand. For their parts, John and DB had both ducked, because she kept turning back and forth between them, unable to decide who to target first.

Then her hand dropped. "You know what's real rich? That neither one of you can figure out why I won't go out with you." She stomped into the bathroom and slammed the door.

The microwave dinged, and Ana said, with false brightness, "Anyone want burritos?"

DB and John circled each other, but finally settled down, DB on the sofa and John on a chair in the kitchen. Ana shoved plates of food at them both, and miracle of miracles they ate. She decided against giving them any more margaritas, but took an extra-long drag on one herself before heading to the bathroom to knock on the door.

"You okay?" she said to Kate, angling herself away from the rest of the apartment, hoping the boys weren't listening even though she knew they were.

The door wasn't locked; Kate was sitting at the edge of the bathtub. Ana slipped in and closed the door. Leaned against it, just in case DB or John decided it was a good idea to try to sneak in.

Kate didn't look particularly angry or upset. She did look thoughtful, her brow furrowed and face scrunched up. Finally, she sighed. "It's better knowing it's out there than not knowing, right? I'm not really surprised, I guess. It's just . . . annoying."

Ana quirked a smile. "That's the worst thing you can come up with? Not murderous rage?"

"I'm too tired for murderous rage," Kate said.

"I'll kick them out. Say the word and they're gone," Ana said.

Kate sighed. "You can't kick them out. They're still friends. Let's go get some food."

They hugged, and Ana liked to think some of the tension went out of Kate's shoulders.

When they emerged from the bathroom, John was there, holding a glass full of margarita, which he offered to Kate. Giving him a thin smile, she took it.

DB was sitting contritely—as contritely as he could, anyway, slumping, his hands still in his lap—on the sofa.

"I'm sorry. I wasn't trying to upset you—I just thought you should know that these are out there."

"No, it's okay. You're right. Better to find out from a friend than in some random interview."

"Do I even need to ask if there's any footage of me on those tapes?" Ana asked.

DB winced. "They got everybody with that shower cam."

She thought for a minute. "Would it be wrong of me to be insulted if I *didn't* show up on an *American Hero* bootleg sex tape?"

"I think you need another drink," John said. He'd produced a second glass from somewhere, and she was happy to take it.

They couldn't argue when they were eating. Ana was starting to be pleased with herself and her diplomatic skills. But, inevitably, conversation started again and circled back around. Wasn't anything Ana could do to stop it.

"So much for the hero part of the show," DB grumbled around a bite of burrito. "Not like it's been about anything but politics and sex scandals since the first season. Nobody's trying to save the world."

"I'm trying," Ana said softly. The margaritas were a warm flush through her system, making her talk more than she usually did. "Maybe it doesn't look like much from the outside, when I spend most of my time in an office, but I'm trying."

Kate frowned. "Seventy-five K for children's cancer research has to count for something."

"It does," John said, maybe too eagerly. "At least I think it does." She gave him a tight-lipped smile.

DB said, "You guys hear what happened to Joe Twitch?"

Joe Twitch, another first season veteran. Being on the show hadn't helped him out at all, and he hadn't saved anything in the end. After falling in with a very bad crowd, the ace had been gunned down in some messed-up police shoot-out.

"Yeah," Ana said, and the others nodded in grim agreement.

Kate shook her head. "Let's hear it for first season alumni. God, we're a mess."

They weren't, not really. Ana had her work, Kate had her charity fund-raising. After leaving the Committee, John had done volunteer work overseas, and DB donated a chunk of his concert earnings to the International Red Cross and other refugee aid organizations. He didn't even publicize it. They were all trying, though it felt like spitting into the wind sometimes.

"You know who probably knows something about those videos?" DB said. "Bugsy. He's working for *Aces!* now, he knows everything. Right?" Bugsy, Jonathan Hive, another first season alumnus who now wrote for a tabloid. So maybe they weren't all on the side of angels.

"Not a bad idea," John said. "So who wants to actually call him?"

"We had a little talk awhile back," Kate said, not looking particularly pleased. "He wouldn't tell us even if he knew. But he's got his own problems going on, we don't need to bug him. Um. Sorry. No pun intended."

John smirked. "I'm sure you did talk to him, after that story he did on you and your new boyfriend."

"John!" Ana and Kate both declared, cutting off that track before it went further.

More eating. Ana wished for continued silence. The episode on the TV had wound down, and she wondered if she should turn the DVD back on, for a distraction. DB said to his plate, carefully, "I don't suppose you have that copy of the magazine with the story Bugsy did—"

Kate raised her fork to throw it.

"You really want to know where those bootleg DVDs are coming from?" Ana burst, interrupting. "Why not ask the guys selling them."

"And I suppose you know who that is?" DB said.

"Sure—there's one of those stalls on the Bowery, just a couple blocks from here. You know those creeps who sell bootlegs CDs and everything. I'm sure he's got some of these. Ask *him* where they're coming from."

DB shrugged. "Sounds good to me."

Ana suddenly wished she hadn't said anything, but everyone else embraced the plan. Plates and glasses went into the kitchen sink, leftovers went into the fridge, and DB shrugged on his overcoat.

"Aren't you hot in that?" Kate asked wonderingly.

"I'm incognito," he said, and Kate squeaked out a stifled, tipsy laugh.

In a very brief moment they were all on the stairs heading down and outside.

◆

Ana shouldn't have had that second margarita. Or was that third? Not that it mattered. This was a bad idea, drunk or sober. John caught her arm when she stumbled on the stairs, asked if she was okay. She was sure she was fine, really. Right?

After leaving Fifth, they walked a couple of blocks onto the Bowery. The street was busy—not late enough to have cleared out yet. The sky was dark, but headlights and streetlights and storefronts glared brightly. Some people marched, clearly on missions, to or from work or home or miscellaneous errands. Clumps of people moved together, laughing at each other, out for a night of fun. Like Ana and the others should have been, if they knew what was good for them. The Guatemalan woman who ran the mobile taquería that Ana liked leaned out the window of her truck and shouted in Spanish, and Ana answered, *bueno,* everything was just fine.

This close to Jokertown, no one looked twice at someone who had an extra limb or three or was covered with a layer of fur or scales. But people were looking at DB.

"That coat isn't doing *anything* to disguise you," Kate observed.

DB scowled.

Really, people were staring at all of them. And when people were staring at you in *Jokertown,* you knew you were in trouble.

She almost walked right past the row of storefronts and streetside booths, selling everything from knockoff handbags to cheap souvenirs. It was almost a carnival along this stretch. A guy playing guitar and singing on the corner of Bond had his hat out. Another block or two along the Bowery and you'd be in Jokertown's red light district. But this was where she'd seen the guy with the DVDs. Stopping to take stock, she glanced up the row, then pointed. "There it is."

The guy had wooden racks set up on folding tables, filled with CD and DVD cases that weren't fooling anyone. The covers showed the right images for all the latest hit movies, but they were obviously fourth-generation photocopies. The plastic was cheap, warped, already coming apart. The DVDs inside wouldn't be any more slick or reliable. Buyer beware.

The guy didn't do much business that Ana had ever seen. Downloading had replaced much of the pirate CD and DVD market, she imagined. But guys like this selling crap like this would probably never go away. Not everyone had a fancy computer.

The four of them lined up in front of the stall. The stall owner, or proprietor, or clerk, or whatever, blinked back at them with round, dark eyes. A joker, he had a bony fan of flesh sprouting from his shoulder blades, through a modified slit cut into his T-shirt. Leathery and wrinkled, they didn't look functional as wings, but who could tell.

"Hey, hey. Ana, right? Wha-what can I do for you?

Que pasa?" His accent might have been Puerto Rican. His smile was strained.

She opened her mouth to say something, then completely forgot what it was she'd been about to say. Some accusation. Swearing, probably. This man was a criminal, she stood for truth and justice, she ought to do something about it. Shouldn't she?

"Where are they?" DB said, looming. The guy cringed, stammered, and DB grabbed the collar of his jacket and hauled him up. "I know you're selling them, where are they?"

"Michael, calm the hell down," Kate muttered, hanging off one of DB's arms.

Ana spotted a Joker Plague CD that might have been used or might have been a bootleg; she decided not to tell the drummer about it. Stepping in front of DB, subtly edging him away from the stall, Ana reminded herself that she was an international agent for good and found her voice again. "He's asking about special stuff that isn't in the racks, that you sell under the table. Right?"

The guy shrugged. A line of sweat dripped from his hairline. "Yeah, I got a lot of stuff. I mean, there's, you know, the triple X stuff—"

She shook her head. "No. Well, sort of. Outtakes from *American Hero,* bootleg behind-the-scenes stuff. I guess some of it's rated X. . . ." She winced.

His eyes widened, and Ana swore if he said something about her being too nice a girl for that sort of thing . . . "You *sure* you want to look at that stuff?" he asked instead. "All'a you. I mean you seem like nice kids, and I haven't watched any of it myself—I'd never do that, you know—but I hear it gets kind of rough."

DB grumbled, "Don't tell me about it—I was there for most of it, Bat Boy."

The joker cringed.

Ana made soothing gestures toward them both. "We want to find out where the videos are coming from— who's distributing them, who's making them. Who might have access to the footage, you know?"

"I don't know any of that—I just get the boxes of 'em from the wholesaler. I don't even look, you know?"

"You have to look—you already said you had some. Can we see what you've got?" Maybe some of the other DVD cases would have identifying information on them, unlike DB's copy.

The joker wore a skeptical frown, but he crouched to pull a cardboard box from under the table and started pawing through it. "I'm telling you, most of what I got's just porn, not from the show. You interested in any of that? I got a bunch of stuff here, ace on ace, ace on joker—"

"Just the *American Hero* stuff," Ana said. John was looking on, interested. DB and Kate were fidgeting, their patience stretching thin. DB pattered a riff on his torso that made people up and down the block look over. Why any of them had thought they could do this without drawing attention . . .

The stall owner pulled DVD cases out of the box and laid them out on his table. They were just as awful as Ana could have imagined, with all seasons of *American Hero* represented, most of the covers featuring particularly photogenic female contestants in various states of undress. And those were probably the least prurient covers of the bunch, because as promised he was selling a bunch of outright porn as well as other reality-based sensationalism.

"What's that?" DB said, grabbing a pair of cases out of the guy's hand. They all leaned in to get a better look.

Large, yellow capital letters, in a bullet-ridden font spelled *JOKER FIGHT CLUB VOL. III.* The image behind the words was murky, showing poorly lit figures moving in a blur. Two men—jokers, large ones, with abnormal muscles and bison-like bulk, one with horns growing from his shoulders, one with claws on his arms, beat on each other. The one who faced the camera had blood covering half his misshapen face. This didn't look staged. It didn't look like special effects.

"Where'd you get this?" Ana said.

"I don't know, they just turn up." He looked scared now, his hands shaking as he tried to grab the cases out of their hands.

She raised a brow at him, skeptical.

DB picked three or four more of the *Joker Fight Club* videos out of the batch. "How can you even sell this crap?" he said, disgusted.

"I gotta pay rent, just like everybody else. Those guys in the fights—they're paying rent, too, wanna bet? You're a joker, you know how it is."

"And what?" Ana said. "These just magically show up in a cardboard box so you can pay your rent? Where do you get them? Who sells them to you?"

He cringed away, but Ana didn't have any illusions that she was the one intimidating him. DB was looming, fury in his gaze.

The guy's vestigial wings flopped weakly against his back. "These ones, the fight club ones, they come from a couple of *hombres* in a white van. They drop 'em off every week or so. They just dropped these off this evening."

"Here?" Kate said. "They were here?" The ace turned to Ana. "You think maybe it's the same people doing the *American Hero* DVDs?"

Ana shrugged. "Worth finding out. Where'd they go?" She glared at the joker, who pointed down the street.

"East. Turned on Houston." Straight into Jokertown. Ana could think of a dozen scenarios where some low-life gangsters in Jokertown had decided to go into video production and managed to snag the *American Hero* outtakes. Not to mention the other stuff. God, if there was a porn studio in Jokertown she didn't want to know about it. Who was she kidding, there probably was. Never mind.

"How long ago?"

"Hour, maybe?"

DB started shoving DVDs into his coat pockets with two hands. A third threw a couple of tens down on the table. "I'm buying the whole fucking mess," DB said. "Hand 'em over to my lawyers and let them have a crack."

"Wait, what—" The stall owner pawed at the money. "Who do you think you are?"

DB snarled at him in answer and stalked off. Ana, Kate, and John followed.

Ana thought the guy was lucky DB'd given him anything at all and not called the cops. The joker at the stall must have realized that because he didn't argue further. Not that anyone would argue with DB when he got into a mood like this.

Except for John, who should have known better. "So what, we're going to search Jokertown for a white delivery van? How does that make sense?"

"What do you suggest?"

"Exactly what you said, hand it over to the lawyers and let them sort it out."

"Because that's worked so well for you so far."

Ana walked with Kate, leaving the boys arguing in front of them. "Some party, huh?" she said, by way of apology.

Wonder of wonders, Kate smiled. "I'm hanging out with my friends. That was the point, right?"

"I wasn't sure wandering Jokertown at midnight was what you had in mind."

"We always joked about doing it when I was living down here but never got around to it. So, why not?"

"I think you wouldn't be saying this if we weren't quite as drunk as we are."

Kate giggled.

DB stalked ahead like a predator on the hunt; Ana hung back, looking down side streets and alleys. At one point DB stopped somebody—a round, rubbery walrus of a joker selling newspapers out of a cart. The guy looked half amused, half worried when DB demanded to know if he'd seen a van. Amazingly, the guy pointed a direction, turning them down another street off Houston and deeper into Jokertown. Probably just to get rid of the angry seven-foot-tall man in front of him.

Ana had paused to look down another side street when she saw it: *a* white van if not *the* white van. She could just make it out in the light from a streetlamp bleeding into the alley. The back doors were open, and two jokers were hauling a third into the back. The third guy, a huge, lumbering man with muscles layered on muscles, covered with ropy, elephantine skin, seemed to be sick. He wasn't standing on his own, and his head lolled to his shoulder. His friends were probably taking him to the hospital. She wondered if they needed help.

"Hey," Ana said. "Everything okay?"

The first two jokers—one of them slick-skinned with fishy eyes, the other with a second set of arms that were actually tentacles, or vegetative tendrils, or something green and sinewy—looked at her with round, shocky eyes. Instead of answering, they rushed, shoving their charge into the van and slamming the doors.

That was when she noticed the elephantine joker's hands were tied behind his back.

"Hey!" she yelled, while thinking that this was all about to go very wrong in a minute. "Hey, stop!"

DB and the others turned back to look at her. She shouted, "Somebody call the police!" She patted her pockets—she usually had her phone in her pocket, where was it?

Tires squealed, filling the alley with smoke and the stink of burning rubber, and the van roared backward, out of the alley, toward Ana. All she could do was stare.

Then she fell, yanked out of the way by three power-ful arms, and she crashed against DB's bulk as he pulled her in to the brick wall of the adjacent building.

"Ana, Jesus, you okay?" he asked, propping her up while she regained her feet.

Meanwhile, the van screeched into the street and made an awkward turn before racing down Suffolk. A couple of other cars slammed on brakes and wrenched out of the way. Nobody crashed, but car horns blared.

"The van, those guys in the van, they grabbed some-one, it's a kidnapping!"

Kate threw something. She must have had a whole handful of something, because half a dozen projectiles zipped past Anna, crashing into the retreating van with the pings of bullets. Something popped. The van kept moving, rocking on a blown tire.

DB ran after the van. Ana called for him to stop, but he didn't listen.

"Who are those guys?" John asked, joining her along with Kate.

Ana said, "I don't know, they just bundled some guy into the back of the van."

"Well, looks like a party," Kate said, and ran to fol-low DB.

John had his phone in hand, and Ana sighed with re-lief. "You call the cops?"

"On the way," he said. "Not sure what else I can do."

"You can help me keep Kate and DB from getting themselves killed."

She thought he might argue, but he snorted and took off running after the others.

Somehow, the van was still going, throwing off sparks from its naked rim; smoke poured out the exhaust. A couple of taxis swerved, tires screeching, but DB and Kate ignored the chaos. Kate cocked her arm back, threw another marble, but the projectile fell short and blew a crater in the street. DB's chest swelled, six hands beating a tangled rhythm along his torso, building, speeding, until he arched his back and let out a wave of sound, a sonic sledgehammer. Ana ducked and covered her ears.

The shock wave caught the van, which lifted off its back wheels, tipped, and tumbled to its side. There were screams, more screeching tires and confused taxis. People running, and Ana wondered how bad this was going to get, and what she could do about mitigating the collateral damage. Her instinct was to get to ground and build a wall—raise enough earth to cordon off the street, isolate the van, keep the kidnappers from escaping. And perpetrate a couple million dollars of damage to the city's infrastructure in the process. She could already hear the press conference after that. So, no. She felt suddenly useless.

She ran toward the van along with John, Kate, and DB. Sirens sounded in the distance. The driver's door was open, the fish-eyed joker driver hauling himself out with impossibly muscular arms. His whole body slithered, powerful and agile, springing to the side—now top—of the van. His huge mouth bared to show needle teeth. Bulging, lidless eyes rolled over his shoulder to look at his pursuers, then he jumped to the far side of the van and out of sight. Kate reached to the ground for a piece of debris and threw. Ana didn't see it land, but heard an explosion. A puff of smoke rose up from the next block. Kate and DB kept running. Ana and John stopped at the van.

"The other guy's unconscious," John said, looking in through the shattered windshield.

The back doors, crumpled and warped, had swung open. Ana looked inside to find two jokers, the elephantine guy and one other, equally muscular and tough-looking, hands and feet and tentacles tied up, mouths gagged. They'd flopped to the side of the van—now the bottom—unconscious. She hoped they were only unconscious.

The blaring sirens rounded the corner—two patrol cars fishtailing onto Suffolk. "Freeze! Everybody freeze!" one of the cops yelled through a loudspeaker.

The guy in the passenger seat of the van, the joker with vines for an extra set of arms, had woken up. Bleeding from a gash in his head, he managed to crawl to the back of the van and wrestle Ana for the door. Shoving, he knocked her back. He was holding a gun.

"John!" Ana called, dodging to the front of the van to take cover. "Cops are here! Where are Kate and DB?"

John pointed down the street, around the next corner. They'd gone after the driver. Great.

The order came again. "You two! Freeze!"

A shot fired from the back of the van. Cursing came over the loudspeaker behind them, the gunman fired again, and the orders to freeze turned into orders to put the gun down. Ana figured the police had better things to do than go after her and her friends.

"Go!" Ana yelled at John, and they took off, turning onto the next street.

The desk job hadn't been kind to her stamina. Not that she'd ever been in great shape, but she used to do better than this. Two blocks of running and she was heaving. John was ahead of her and pulling away.

Ahead, he hesitated. Rounding the corner in her turn, Ana stumbled up against him in time to see DB go down, screaming. He'd grabbed the fish-eyed joker—who was tall, it turned out. DB only had a few inches on him. The six arms should have given him an advantage, but the joker had done something, let loose some crackling bolt of energy, sparking like a Van de Graaff generator. DB went limp and fell, and the joker fled.

Ana's heart skipped a few beats and she had to concentrate to get her legs moving again. She was afraid of what she'd find when she reached him. "Michael!" she called when she did get moving again, and dropped to the ground beside him. The big joker groaned. Alive, at least.

John yelled down the street, "Kate, stop!"

"I can catch him!"

"He'll kill you!"

"What do you care?"

A pause, and he yelled, "What do you mean, what do I care?"

"Find me something to throw, damn it!"

"Michael?" Ana asked, hand on his uppermost shoulder.

"Wha . . . happen . . ." An arm went to his forehead, and the other five flailed as if attempting to tread water.

"The guy zapped you. You okay?"

"Ung . . ." He rolled over and vomited.

Now that she had time to use her own phone, she fished it out of her jeans pocket. "I'll call an ambulance."

"No, no, I'm . . . shit, I feel like a truck hit me. Don't call an ambulance. Where's the fucker?" He slowly rolled over, propping himself on one hand, wiping his mouth with another. Ana tried to help him up when it looked like he was going to fall over, and grunted with the effort. Guy was *big*.

"You *sure* you're okay?"

Something blew up down the next street. An explosion, followed by a pattering of debris. "The hell?" DB asked. Leaning on Ana, he managed to climb to his feet. He was trembling, and the tympanic membranes on his torso hummed with a sympathetic vibration.

"I don't think you should go running after them."

"Bullshit, I've been through worse than this." He took off, limping.

Another explosion sounded. "Was that one of Kate's?" DB asked.

"Yeah," Ana said, sighing.

"Should I be worried about her or the other guy?"

Good question. "John's looking out for her."

"That loser can't do jack shit." He limped, winced, rotated a couple of sets of shoulders.

"Give him a break, Michael."

"Why should I? He had it all. Kate—the most beautiful, most amazing girl in the world—she picked him and he threw it back in her face. He broke her heart."

She'd done a pretty good job of breaking John's, too, but DB wouldn't listen to that. He might be okay with him and Kate not being together now. But he'd always regret the might-have-been that he'd lost.

That wasn't why Ana winced and looked away, trying to turn the expression into a smile. "I suppose I can always go for runner-up."

"What? Ana, hey, that's not what I—"

"There they are." Ana trotted ahead.

They found John and Kate standing on the next corner, peering around to an empty storefront on Orchard. Periodically, she hurled debris—broken glass, smashed soda cans—at the building. She'd just thrown a piece of brick, which landed with another blast, a shower of concrete. John handed her the next projectile. They argued.

"You really think I don't care if you live or die?"

"John, no, that's not what I meant."

"Then what did you mean? Is that what you think about me?"

"You always make these arguments about you, you know that?"

"What arguments? We haven't said a word to each other in over a year!"

Ana interrupted. "Where'd the fish guy go?"

"Kate's got him pinned down there," John said. Sure enough, the fish-eyed man lurked in the shadows of the shop's interior, hanging back from Kate's wall of destruction. Occasionally, he waved his gun and random shots fired, pinging off the brick wall above them. They ducked back behind the corner, except for Kate, who hurled another missile. Another chunk exploded out of the store-front across from them, but the joker was still there, moving back into the building, gun in hand.

"I'm calling the cops, telling them we're here," Ana said, punching the number into her phone.

DB huffed. "As long as you do all the talking when they get here. You're the diplomat."

She wasn't, really. More like a bureaucrat. Pencil pusher, desk jockey. Babysitter?

The joker tried to make a break for it again, creeping up to a broken doorway. Kate threw, and the guy stumbled back in a panic. "I should just go in there and take him down," DB grumbled. "Drum him out of there."

"And have him blast you again?" Ana said. "No. We wait for the cops."

"If he doesn't shoot us all first," Kate said. "I can't get to him as long as he keeps hiding. Maybe if I bring the whole building down on top of him . . ."

She'd already gotten a good start on that.

"Sure hope they have insurance," DB said. He was grinning.

"Are you actually enjoying this?" Ana said.

"Beats a press conference," he said, and she couldn't argue.

Kate glared. "Are you guys going to help or just stand there staring?"

"I thought I was helping," John said.

"That's not what I meant—"

"Kate—"

The gunfire from the storefront had stopped. The street had gone quiet; a car horn from a few blocks away echoed, and a distant police siren sounded. No fish-like movement flickered in the shadows of the broken glass and brick wall.

"Did you get him?" Ana asked.

"No," Kate said. "He's gone." She growled and threw the piece of glass at the nearby wall; it popped like a firecracker and left a mark like a bullet hole. They ducked as debris pattered around them.

Kate pointed at John. "*You* made me lose him."

"*I* made you—"

The siren rang out behind them now, and a squad car came through the intersection, barreled toward them, and screeched to a stop a few feet away. Ana's first impulse was to run. Which said a lot about the situation, didn't it?

"What the hell are you people doing?" The first cop who stepped out of the car might have been a joker, or a nat with an unfortunate set of features—bulging eyes, scraggly hair.

His partner was definitely a joker. Her shape was enough off the human norm to draw attention, though she ended up being more fascinating than ugly. She was barrel-chested, rib cage hinting at huge lung capacity and vast stamina. Below that she was wasp-waisted, and her legs were powerfully muscled. She was shaped like a greyhound, built for running. No getting away from her.

And she was pissed off. "No. Oh, no, not you guys. Goddamn ace vigilantes. I *hate* ace vigilantes."

Both John and DB responded, earnestly, "I'm not an ace." Kate punched John in the shoulder, and he glared at her.

The four of them stood shoulder to shoulder, regarding the two officers. They looked like kids caught fighting on the playground: gazes on their shoes, scuffing at the concrete. Kate had her arms tightly crossed, maybe to keep her from wanting to throw something.

"Is it one of you who called in a kidnapping?" the nat cop said.

Ana stepped forward. "Yeah. John called it in, but I'm the one who saw it. In an alley off Suffolk. There were two of them, the guy they pulled into the back of the van was unconscious—"

"Can you describe the driver of the van?" she asked.

"Gray, pale, bald. Big black eyes. Fishy, almost."

"And he's got some kind of badass electric shock," DB added. "Beat the *shit* out of me."

The joker cop—Michaelson, the name badge on her uniform read—scowled. "That would be the Eel. We've been on his tail for a while." She exchanged a look with her partner; neither seemed happy.

"So that really was a kidnapping?" Ana said. "I wasn't just imagining it."

"Don't give yourself a medal just yet," said the first cop—Bronkowski. "Which way did he go?"

Kate hitched a thumb over her shoulder, to the corner and the next street. "Saw him running that way. I almost had him until I got distracted." Again, she glared at John, who glared back.

Michaelson spoke into the radio at her shoulder, and a garbled answer came back. It must have made sense, because she nodded. "Right. I'm going to need you all to come down the station—"

"But we didn't do anything wrong!" DB grumbled.

"—just to make a statement. You think you can do that?"

Yes, they finally agreed. They could do that.

Michaelson's radio crackled again, and she replied. "Right, on our way." Turning back to them, she admonished, "Let us catch the bad guys, and you guys get yourselves to the precinct. Don't make me come after you."

With that, she and Bronkowski climbed back into the car. The spinning red and blue lights splashed across them as the car pulled away. Ana squinted and ducked away at their glare. Kate groaned. "So we're going to spend the rest of the night at a police station? Some party."

"All the best parties end that way," DB said, chuckling.

Ana sighed. "At least we did some good. I think." Some tiny amount of good. Assuming the kidnapping victims in the back of the van were okay.

"Kate," John said, his tone earnest, and Ana wanted to smack him before he said another word. Couldn't he just let it go? "I really do worry about you—"

"John—" Kate stopped herself, closed her eyes. Maybe counting to ten. "I know. But I'm fine. Really. Can we just go talk to the police now?" She started walking.

"I could really use another margarita," DB said, following her.

"Yeah," Ana said. That second pitcher still sat in the fridge. If only they could get to it before morning.

John stared after Kate. "It's not like I'm trying to annoy her. It just comes out that way."

"Maybe you should stop treating her like she's different. Like she's some sparkly fairy ice queen. You know?"

He pursed his lips, confused, which she took to mean that he didn't. "I just—"

"John, let it go." He only slouched a little before squaring his shoulders, settling his expression into something resembling calm as he walked off after the others. Ana needed her own moment to gather herself.

The sharp crack of a gunshot rang. Instantly, instinctively, Ana dropped to the concrete even as she looked for the source. The others had done likewise—they all had experience with getting shot at. Another shot fired—and DB roared, falling back, a spot of red bursting from the sleeve of his coat. *Shit.*

Ana saw the flash of shining gray skin in the streetlight at the opposite corner. The Eel, crouching in hiding, leveling his gun for another shot at the trio walking half a block ahead of Ana.

He'd targeted them because they were the dangerous ones; at least the ones who *looked* dangerous. People tended to glance right past Ana. Just as well.

She shouted a wordless warning, and one hand went to her St. Barbara medallion, which she clutched through her shirt. The other she spread flat on the pavement.

This wasn't like digging into bare soil, tilling a garden

or drilling a well, actions that came as easily to her as touching air. The city was full of dirt, rock, soil, but it had a crust over it, concrete and steel, and she had to get past that to get to her power. She almost had to trick herself—technically, asphalt was earth, containing bits and fragments, if she could work past the tar and additives. Concrete *did* have a trace of soil in it.

She pushed, found the layer between the streets and sidewalks and tunnels underneath, found the substrate through which the city had insinuated its limbs and tendrils. Then, she *shoved*.

The street trembled with the sound of an earthquake. Pavement cracked, crumbled. A section of sidewalk rose on a pillar of earth, pressing upward from under the city itself—trapping the kidnapper on its peak. Debris rained down the sides, bits of concrete broke off and fell. The pillar climbed a full story high. The joker was trapped in the open, unable to flee, unable to move. He'd flattened himself to the broken sidewalk, gripping the edges, staring down with fearful eyes.

She could feel the city's infrastructure—pipes and conduits, straight concrete and steel running like veins through the earth—and avoid the obstacles, for the most part. Curl the earth around it, nudge it aside. As careful as she tried to be, a water main broke, and a geyser spewed from a crack in the street, spilling a river into the gutter.

Well, so much for minimizing damage. At least the joker was caught.

Except that he looked down to the crevice and the flood pouring out of it, gave a determined nod, and jumped.

It should have been a suicide move, except halfway down he changed, his body morphing. His clothing ripped and fell away as he elongated, his limbs shrinking, his head bulging. Now, he didn't just seem like some slimy sea creature, he *was* one, and he disappeared into the flooded crack in the pavement and into the sewer pipes. Gone.

"Damn, didn't see that coming," DB said.

The others had doubled back and now huddled in a crouch behind her, holding onto ground that had turned unstable. DB clamped a hand over a bloody wound on an upper shoulder. Seemed okay, otherwise. Ana sighed with relief.

"What did he think he was doing?" John said.

"Thought he could get the jump on us," Kate said. "Idiot."

"Doesn't matter, he still got away." Ana sighed.

DB looked at her. "You okay?"

Using her ace had burned the last of the tequila out of her system. Now, she was just tired. She brushed grit off her hands and sat back against the nearby wall.

Over the sound of gushing water, the wail of police sirens returned. This was going to take a little more explanation than last time. Perfect end to the night, really.

The patrol car arrived, splashing through the river of water now pouring down the street. It stopped, and the whippet-shaped Officer Michaelson stepped out, followed by her partner, Bronkowski. She regarded them, arms crossed. "Can't leave you clowns alone for a second, can I?" None of them had an answer to that, and she continued, "I'm going to need you all to come with me."

Ana looked to her friends, but they were all staring back at her like they expected her to do something. She sighed. "Officer, please, Michael's hurt—"

"Not *that* hurt . . ." he muttered.

"You want to argue with me, go right ahead, that'll give me an excuse to put cuffs on the whole lot of you."

"Bugsy would love that for *Aces!*," Kate muttered.

"At least someone would get something out of the night," Ana replied.

They could make a break for it. A couple of cops

against the Committee. Well, the scattered remnants of the original Committee, at least. And Team Hearts of *American Hero*. The more Ana thought about it, the lamer it sounded.

Two more squad cars pulled up, more cops spilling out—some with guns drawn. Who were the bad guys again?

A big—monstrously big—joker, with fur and horns to boot, trotted toward them. "Rikki, Bugeye, you guys got a problem here?"

Michaelson smirked at the aces. "I don't know, do we?"

They didn't.

♥

Ana at least talked Michaelson and Bronkowski into taking them to the Jokertown Clinic first, to get DB's arm looked at.

"Just another scar to add to the collection," he said. He had a gauze bandage taped over the wound. The bullet had just grazed him, and a nurse had cleaned it out and stopped the bleeding. He probably wouldn't even need stitches.

"You could have been killed," Ana muttered. Now that the adrenaline—and margaritas—had worn off, the danger was only now becoming apparent. They should have called the cops, and waited.

But no, then the two kidnapped jokers would be gone. Instead, they were lying on gurneys in the Jokertown Clinic emergency room, and they were going to be okay.

Daylight had started to press through the room's glass doors. The four of them sat in a row of worn plastic chairs in the emergency room waiting area, right where Michaelson told them to sit. The place smelled tired and antiseptic. Way too many sick and hurt people had moved through this room.

Michaelson and her partner had taken up position by the door. The muffled voice in her radio said something, and Michaelson relayed the information that the passenger in the van, the other joker, had been arrested. In the meantime, dawn had broken, and Ana really wanted to go home. When Kate smashed a hand against a wall, they all jumped. "Sorry," she muttered, studying the crushed insect on her hand. "I thought it was Bugsy. It's just a fly."

Now Ana was convinced she heard a buzzing in her ear and looked around expecting to see one of the reporter's green wasps reconnoitering.

After what seemed like half the night, the whippet-looking cop—Officer Michaelson—came over, along with a plainclothes detective. Young guy, but grim-looking, with a set to his jaw that might have been there awhile.

"I'm Detective Francis Xavier Black," he said.

Ana stood, brushed off her clothes, offered her hand for him to shake. "Ana Cortez," she said. "These are—"

"Um, yeah, I know who you all are," he said, in a tone that indicated he was chagrined about the whole thing. "Rikki tells me you tore up half the Lower East Side playing vigilante."

And what was she supposed to say to that? Should she call a lawyer? And wouldn't Lohengrin love that. . . . The others looked at Ana, like they expected her to play diplomat. They expected her to throw herself on that grenade, and after she'd fed them all burritos and margaritas.

"Why do I have to do all the talking and herding cats and crap?" she said to them, pouting.

"Because you're good at it?" Kate said.

Ana blinked at her. Really? Well. Okay then. She straightened and matched Black's gaze squarely. She'd met the president for crying out loud, she could face him. "We called the police as soon as we realized something was wrong. You'll have to tell me where the line between concerned citizen and vigilante is."

"Or I could have a judge do it," Detective Black said, shrugging.

"Give me a break," Kate muttered, slumping back in her chair.

DB, easily the biggest guy in the room, drew himself up and thudded his chest. The sound reverberated through the floor. "We were only trying to help."

Ana said, "I saw someone get hauled into the back of the van—it looked like a kidnapping. I wasn't just going to sit by and watch. I wasn't wrong, was I? That really was a kidnapping."

"And what were you doing wandering around Joker-town at midnight?" he asked.

Like he couldn't believe she would do something like that. "It's a free country."

Black sighed, and Ana got the feeling he'd been awake and working for a very long time. He said, "You weren't imagining it. There've been a spate of kidnappings over the last few weeks. We haven't had a lot of luck tracking down the victims or perpetrators. Catching Rance is a big break." Rance must have been the other kidnapper, with the extra limbs.

"So we actually helped," John said, brightening.

"Yeah, well, don't think you need to *keep* helping."

"Look," Ana said. "I can help put the street back to-gether. Free excavation services. Just let me know."

Black nodded, and Ana expected she'd be getting a phone call from the city before too long. Then he turned to DB. "You picked up some DVDs from a stall on the Bowery, right?"

"Yeah?"

"I'm going to need to take those into evidence, if you don't mind." He winced. Maybe afraid he was going to have to argue with DB, which would make anyone wince.

"Why?" DB said.

"Part of an ongoing investigation."

"Having to do with the kidnapping? What the hell is going on, really?"

He hesitated, as if debating how much he could share. "It's early yet, I'm afraid I can't discuss details. But getting those disks would really help." Ana nudged DB's shoulder, and the joker pulled DVDs out of his copious coat pockets without further prodding. He'd managed to stash a dozen or so.

"Thank you, Mr. Vogali, I really appreciate this," Black said. The detective sorted through them, looking at titles, and nodded in satisfaction. "You'll be free to go just as soon as you give statements to Officer Michaelson. Thanks again, and please—try to stay out of trouble. We really don't need any more paperwork." Offering a weary smile, he turned away.

Michaelson appeared with a stack of clipboards and forms. "You need to fill out reports and contact info. Are you willing to testify if this goes to court?"

Testifying in court seemed like the easy part at this point. At least Michaelson had stopped threatening to arrest them.

In the middle of filling out her statement, Ana's phone rang, and she fumbled in her pocket for it. Caller ID said Lohengrin. Great. She couldn't avoid this, only delay it, so she went ahead and answered. "Yeah?"

"Earth Witch," he said, his accent making the name sound lilting and exotic. "You're in the news this morning. What happened?"

Already? She groaned. "It's a very long story. Can I tell you later?"

Then DB's phone rang. Then John's. Then Kate's. The story must have hit the papers, the Internet, the morning talk shows, and everything in between, all at the same time. Ana caught sound bites of conversation.

From DB: "No, Marty, I'm fine. Everything's fine . . .

what do you mean, doing something stupid? I didn't do anything stupid!"

From John: "Mom, I wasn't trying to cause trouble . . . can we talk about this later?"

And Kate: "I'm fine, Tyler, really. No . . . yes . . . yes, it was kind of stupid, but I'm not going to apologize. See you tonight?"

Lohengrin was still talking, and Ana didn't really care that she'd missed half of what he was saying. ". . . return to the office, right now."

She took a deep breath. "I'm sorry, could you repeat that? It's really loud in here."

"I've arranged a press conference in two hours. You need to state on the record that your actions last night were in no way associated with the UN, and the Committee is not operating on American soil. I need you here for a briefing. After the press conference, I'm sending you to Mexico while this clears up."

Oh, for God's sake. She really wanted to feel like she was doing good—but did there have to be quite so many hoops for her to jump through? She pressed her St. Barbara medallion through her shirt and concentrated on being polite.

"I'm at the Jokertown Clinic right now—"

"Are you hurt?" To his credit, he actually sounded concerned.

"No, I'm just tying up a few loose ends. I'll get there as soon as I can, but it might take a while."

"Two hours, Earth Witch."

She hung up.

DB finished his conversation next, clicked off his phone, and regarded Ana. "How much trouble are you in?"

"Don't ask," Ana said, frowning. "You?"

"That was my manager," DB said. "The record label's threatening legal action if I don't get back in the studio. I need to go to LA and sort it out."

"I guess getting sued makes recording another album not sound so bad?" Ana asked.

"For now. But I'm thinking it may be time to go indy. Don't tell anyone I said that."

"Just keep an eye out for Bugsy, yeah?" They both looked over their shoulders at that one.

The others had finished their calls and caught the last bit of the conversation. "LA, huh?" John said. "I'm heading that way, too, looks like. I have a job interview."

Kate's eyes grew wide. "Not for *American Hero*—"

"No. Mom's charitable foundation needs a new manager. I told her I'd only consider the job if I applied for it just like everyone else."

"Great," Kate said. "I think."

"Hey Ana, can I put you down as a reference?"

"Sure, but a letter from Lohengrin might sound more impressive," she said.

"I think I'd rather have one from a friend."

They looked at Kate next, with expectation. She blushed. "That was Tyler. Just, you know. Checking in."

Ana tensed, expecting a jab from one or the other of the guys, and Kate's defensive reaction. But it didn't happen.

"Cool," DB said thoughtfully, and that was that.

John looked down the row of them, and wonder of wonders, he was smiling. It had been a while, Ana realized.

"You guys have an hour before we all go flying off?" he said. "I want to show you something."

An hour after returning to Ana's flat to wash up and retrieve some cash, they ended up standing in a row, staring at the newest waxworks diorama at the Famous Bowery Wild Card Dime Museum.

They'd caused a scene at the ticket booth on the way

in—how could they not? The four of them together, for the first time since before the famous press conference when Drummer Boy quit the Committee. Tourists snapped pictures on cell phones, and Ana cringed because the photo would be all over the Internet in seconds, and she'd get a million phone calls, and yet another summons to the office of Lohengrin to explain herself. But that didn't matter.

The joker at the ticket counter, a girl in her late teens with green scales and a sagging throat sac, wouldn't let them pay, no matter how much they argued about it. They finally let her give them tickets, but Ana shoved forty bucks into the donation bucket in the front lobby out of spite. Then John led them to a display that was so new it still had signs announcing its grand reveal. They'd stared at it for five minute before saying a word, when Michael declared what they were all thinking.

"That's fucked up," he said flatly.

They, or rather waxworks versions of them, battled the Righteous Djinn in Egypt. Seven feet of Drummer Boy stood in the back, mouth open in a scream, all six arms flexed, some mythological creature captured in sculpture. Curveball braced, as if on a pitcher's mound, her arm cocked back, ready to throw the stone she held. John Fortune held a commanding hand upraised; the smooth gem of Sekhmet was still imbedded in his forehead. And there was Earth Witch, her expression a calm contrast to the others, kneeling on the ground, lock of black hair falling over her face, pressing her hand down where a realistic-looking crack in the rock opened under her touch. The Djinn hovered above them all, laughing. His features were too plastic to make Ana think he was real. The wires suspending him from hidden rafters were visible. She could look at the image, detached, impassive, and not flash back to the scene as she remembered it, the sounds of screaming, blood soaking into sand, bullet ripping through her own gut. She didn't remember it hurting

so much as she remembered falling, and fading as the
world turned upside down around her. She pressed a
hand to her side, where the scar lay under her shirt.

They were all there: Rusty, Bubbles, Bugsy, everyone
who'd made the trip to Egypt to try and save the world.
An "In Memoriam" section featured Simoon, Hardhat,
King Cobalt. It all felt like it had happened to someone
else, in another life.

Two different artists had worked on the figures, and
one had clearly been less talented. The Drummer Boy figure was uncanny, every flexed muscle accurate, the rictus of his scream exact in its lines and tension. On the
other hand, Earth Witch might have been positioned to
be partially hidden because her face was unnaturally
smooth, the bend of her body slightly awkward. Ana
imagined that not too many people would notice, distracted by special effects: LEDs in Curveball's hand,
John's forehead, and the Djinn's arms seemed to bring
their powers to life. From hidden speakers, the sound of
a desert sandstorm hissed. The smell of baking, sandy air
came back to her, and Ana couldn't tell if her memory
generated the sensation, or if the museum really was pip-
ing in the chalky, throat-tickling smell.

Kate tilted her head, her brow furrowed. "Are my
boobs really that big?" The figure's chest bulged inside a
too-tight white T-shirt.

"No," John said.

Everyone looked at him. Kate crossed her arms, and if
she'd had any ace power at all in her gaze, John would
have been flayed.

Ana laughed. Then laughed some more, hand clamped
over her mouth, gut spasming in her effort to stop. They
were probably thinking she was crazy. She'd had a lot of
surreal things happen to her, even by the standards of
wild card Manhattan. But this had to win the prize. "I'm
sorry," she said, trying to catch her breath, hiccupping.
"It's just . . . it's just . . . never mind."

They didn't have much time left and cruised quickly through the rest of the museum. The Great and Powerful Turtles' shells suspended in procession, the depictions of history that had been old before any of them were born. There was a curtained-off "Adults Only" exhibit, one of the classic dioramas that had been here for decades. John stopped there. "That's . . . yeah. That's the one on my dad. I'll pass."

Put it like that, Ana decided she'd pass, too. They all did.

Outside, the bright afternoon sun gave her a headache. She had to be at the UN in half an hour, when what she really wanted was a glass of water and sleep. But she didn't really want to leave the others. She wasn't ready for the night to be over—even though it was the middle of the next day.

John said, "This is going to sound really weird—but I'm glad we could do this. You know—get together."

"Drink some margaritas, fight a little crime," Kate said.

DB added, "Like what, 'Team Hearts catches muggers for old times' sake'?" He scoffed, but Kate bowed her head and smiled.

At least nobody died this time, Ana thought, but didn't say it. She didn't want to ruin the mood. "Maybe we can do it again sometime."

They exchanged phone numbers and called cabs. Having reached a compromise with his mother that didn't involve *American Hero,* John agreed to return home for a visit before moving on. DB's manager had arranged a flight back to LA. Everyone managed hugs. Even Kate and John, though theirs was fleeting. Still, if those two could be civil to each other, maybe world peace had a chance.

Before folding himself into his cab, DB leaned over Ana—his immense body filled her vision—rested a hand on her shoulder, and kissed her on the cheek. His other hands pattered a beat. Straightening, he smiled. She was shocked, and embarrassed to notice she was blushing red hot. "Call me next time you're in town?" she said.

"You bet."

His cab drove off, and Kate stared at Ana. "What was that about?"

She couldn't even make a guess.

Ana and Kate shared a cab. Kate would stay at the apartment—catching up on sleep, if she knew what was good for her—while Ana went to work to try to talk Lohengrin off the ceiling. Not likely she'd succeed, but she'd try. "I'm sorry the night didn't really go the way I planned it."

"Maybe not," Kate said, and her smile was bright. "Still, it was a hell of a party."

Ana couldn't argue with that.

Galahad in Blue

Part Five

HE HAD MET CURVEBALL and Drummer Boy. And he'd been a complete zero, a modern day Joe Friday, just the facts, ma'am. He could have done something to make an impression . . . but no. At least he'd managed to take custody of the DVDs that Drummer Boy had grabbed.

By the time he got back to the Five, Joe Rance, small-time hood with a lot of arrests and a lot of pleas, had already lawyered up. Franny studied the multi-limbed joker in his cell. "Has he said anything?" Franny asked Sergeant Vivian Choy.

"He asked for a lawyer and then clammed up. That's the problem with career criminals," she said. "They get arrested enough times and *we* end up teaching them how to beat an interrogation. You get anything from the aces?"

"Not a lot. They did have these." He showed her the DVDs. Franny jerked his head toward the multi-limbed joker. "Is his lawyer still around?"

"No, Flipper had a court date."

"Great. I'll leave a message, and meantime I'll check these out," Franny added, gesturing with the DVDs.

"Take the player out of Mendelberg's office and plug it in in the conference room. The one in there is a piece of shit."

"Thanks."

Once he had everything set up Franny loaded one of the fight club videos. The images of the screaming spectators were almost more revolting than the two jokers locked in combat in the ring below. Under the bright lights the blood seemed garish, almost fake. The people watching weren't rednecks in T-shirts and jeans. They wore tuxedoes and floor-length gowns. The lights glittered off diamonds and gold cuff links, and glistened in their sweat-damp faces. Discreetly attired waiters moved through the crowd carrying silver trays with champagne flutes.

Franny was too new in Jokertown to be able to identify many of the jokers who passed beneath the camera's unfeeling lens. If Father Squid were here, he would have known them. Franny decided to ask for help from Dr. Finn. Some of these people had probably passed through the clinic.

He picked up another DVD, the handwritten label read *And the Beat Goes Down*. Franny loaded it. Drummer Boy's broad back and hips pumped accompanied by harsh grunts, and a woman's shrill cries. At one point they rolled over placing the woman on top and Franny recognized Tiffani, one of the contestants from *American Hero*'s first season. Face flaming, Franny quickly ejected the DVD, feeling like a Peeping Tom. He picked up another one—*Bath Time* was the title. He watched Jade Blossom squeeze water down her back as she lolled in a bathtub. The next cut was of Curveball, one long shapely leg extended out of the water as she scrubbed down with a loofah. He kept watching that one. He tried another, and another. The disks were a mix of the fight club and sex tapes from *American Hero* featuring Drummer Boy fucking an astonishing number of the female contestants.

He stood and paced around the conference room table. Did the *American Hero* disks qualify as evidence? He knew he needed to watch the fight disks, but this stuff? His stuttering thoughts settled, and he picked up a fight club disk and a sex disk and compared the printing on the titles. It looked like the same hand had lettered both. So maybe the same cameraman? But it wasn't like he'd signed his work, so who would know? He needed to talk to somebody associated with the making of *American Hero*. He knew Peregrine had something to do with it.

The door to the conference slammed open, and Sergeant Taylor, who was normally on the desk, rushed in. His eyes were wide, and his usually drooping wings were fluttering with agitation.

"Detective! You're wanted! At the holding cells!"

"Why? What?"

"You can see faster than I can explain," Homer said.

Franny ran. There was a clot of people gathered around the door of Rance's cell. Franny pushed through them, and checked at the sight of Joe Rance slumped on the steel toilet, orange jumpsuit around his ankles.

Gordon the Ghoul knelt at the man's side holding one wrist. The extra, vine-like appendages between his waist and his real arms were blackened and wilted as if a fire had swept down those faux arms. Gordon climbed back to his feet and dusted off the knees of his slacks with an embroidered handkerchief.

"What happened?" Franny demanded of nobody and everybody.

"Somebody made him dead," the pathologist answered.

"Yes, thank you. I gathered that. How?"

Gordon rolled the body off the john, and inspected the blackened posterior. "Electrocuted. Got him right in the ass."

"God *damn* it!" Franny swung his fist at the wall, only

to have it caught by a giant paw tipped with vicious claws.

"Don't," Beastie said. "You'll just hurt yourself."

"I never even got a chance to talk to him!" Franny took several deep breaths, fought for control. "Did he say anything? Anything at all?"

Head shakes all around.

"Should have let me squinch him down, and put him in the castle," Jessica Penniman said. Slender and delicate with flyaway blond hair, she didn't match anyone's idea of a cop.

Vivian Choy glared at her. "Hard to question a suspect when they can barely talk because their vocal cords are the size of threads."

"Harder when they're dead," Jennifer snapped back.

"Stop it," Franny ordered. Amazingly both women did. Gordon motioned to a couple of orderlies, who entered the cell and loaded the body on a gurney. "I'll have the autopsy report for you tomorrow," the medical examiner said as the sad little parade passed by. "But I'm pretty confident I won't find anything more."

Franny went to his desk and began writing up the report. The death of a prisoner in custody would bring in internal affairs, and lawsuits would follow. He could just imagine the reaction of the precinct brass to this FUBAR.

Aside from the bureaucratic shit that was about to hit the fan, there were very real consequences for his case. This was the first real, clean break they'd had, and now the suspect was dead. He asked Bronkowski and Michaelson to stop by his desk to see if Rance had said anything to them during his arrest. Typically Bugeye refused, but Michaelson agreed. Unfortunately Rikki had nothing to add. "He was pretty woozy," she said, as she fidgeted in the chair next to his desk. "Look, if there's nothing else, I'm beat. My shift ended hours ago." She stood up, and stretched her whip-lean body. "Sorry Eel got away from us. If he hadn't, Rance would still be alive."

Franny sat, drumming his pen on his desk. It was a safe bet that Eel was behind the murder. Franny pictured the sewers beneath the city, a highway, albeit a disgusting one, for Eel. He could travel everywhere, enter anywhere. And Franny was the lead investigator on this case. He wondered if his home address was obtainable online? Probably, everything was. He pictured himself vulnerable, sitting on the toilet taking a crap. His sphincter tightened. Do they still sell chamber pots, he wondered? A bucket would work too. He resolved to stop at a hardware store before he went home that night.

He realized he had left the DVDs in the conference room when Homer had burst in. Franny went to collect them, and stood holding them for a long moment. All hell was about to break loose over this murder. He really didn't have time to call Peregrine right now. Could he ask Stevens? Would his supposed partner be willing to do that for him? Then Franny realized that he knew someone who had federal clout, and who had actually been on *American Hero*. He returned to his desk, and called Stuntman. The agent answered on the first ring with a terse, "Norwood."

"I confiscated some DVDs this morning," Franny began. "Some of them show my missing jokers fighting in a kind of gladiatorial arena, but others are from the first season of *American Hero,* and they're . . . well, let's just say somebody had pinhole cameras where there shouldn't have been cameras. What's clear is that the same person prepared both the fight club DVDs and these Contestants Gone Wild DVDs from *American Hero*."

"Am *I* on any of these DVDs?" Norwood's voice was low and rather dangerous.

"Not that I saw. I just thought given that you were on the show you might have contacts."

"Why can't you do it?"

"I've got problems. A prisoner died while in custody." Franny wasn't going to say more, but he knew a shit-storm was about to break over his head, and he had a feeling he was going to get blamed for what had happened to Joe Rance. "One of the people kidnapping jokers. This could have broken the case. He could have told me where they were taking them. Where they are now! They're in that ring, and it's brutal. Some of them have to have died." Disgust at his own impotence choked off the words. Worse, Franny realized he'd shown weakness and admitted to police incompetence to a Fed. He waited for the inevitable insult.

Instead there was a long silence, and Norwood said quietly, "I'm sorry. I understand these are your people being taken. I'll talk to Michael Berman, he actually runs the show, see what I can find out."

"You'll let me know what you learn?" Franny asked.

"Absolutely."

"I'll make copies of the DVDs and send them over to you." Franny hung up.

It was late afternoon by the time he'd finished copying the DVDs and sent them to Norwood, finished his report, talked to internal affairs and Rance's public defender.

"Well, that's unfortunate," the joker lawyer wheezed asthmatically. "Rance told me he was open to making a deal in exchange for immunity."

That little tidbit added to Franny's sense of despair and the stunning headache that had settled behind his eyes. He realized it was nearly six P.M., and he'd had nothing to eat since the night before. He started out in search of dinner, only to be waylaid by Apsara. "Remember, to-morrow night, Starfields, eight o'clock. Dinner with my parents. They're looking forward to meeting you. And wear your dress uniform."

"That's just for funerals and parades," he said, his headache intensifying.

"They don't know that, and you look very handsome when you wear it." She started away with that swaying dancing gait.

But Franny had had it. Three long strides and he caught her by the upper arm. "No." He pulled her aside and said in a low voice, "I'm going along with this for your sake, but I don't like it, and I'm not going to act like a clown."

Tears welled up in her eyes and trembled on the ends of her lashes.

"Forget it, Apsara, the tears won't work. And what does your phi think of all this?" It was low of him, but it had the desired effect.

"You're right," she whispered. "Be yourself, Frank."

"I could recommend the same to you," he growled.

Those About to Die . . .

Part Four

THE DOOR SWUNG OPEN and the guard prodded him forward and he slid out onto the smooth floor of a small arena. He blinked under the bright lights, barely able to make out the ranks of expectant faces that ringed him. They stared at him from behind a wall of thick glass. Above it, a crosshatch of netting enclosed the space. Whatever this was, he was trapped in it.

The guard shoved him forward, and then retreated back through the door. It closed, trapping Marcus in the oval. *This can't be happening,* he thought.

He'd told himself that again and again since he'd woken up in that small room with Asmodeus and Dmitri. He'd said it several times to Father Squid as they talked. The priest—kindly, grave, the membranes of his eyes sliding closed and then opening again—had assured him that it was, in fact, happening. "We are trapped in a garden of evil," he had said. "Have courage, son."

Marcus gaped at the spectators. Men and women in suits and fancy dresses, champagne glasses in hand. Fat men grinned their pleasure. Beautiful women rubbed up next to them, bejeweled and gaudy. Some of them clapped. A few shouted at him, jeers or encouragement—he wasn't sure which.

Set apart from the others, a private box hung above the netting. An old couple inside of it. The woman looked like some ancient librarian with shockingly red hair. What the fuck was she doing here? The man was a twisted monstrosity in a wheelchair, with wires and tubes running all over him, connecting him to the machines that crowded behind him. Attendants hovered around him as if he might croak at any moment. He looked like he was close to it. His gaping mouth drooled. His face twitched. His palsied hands squeezed in on themselves. Head cocked to one side, eyes closed, breathing labored: he was a monster, a knotted deformity of a man.

Lining the wall at the back of the box was a row of big-shouldered men in black suits and dark sunglasses. They looked like some Hollywood versions of Russian gangsters on steroids. It went without saying that they were packing.

Who were these people? Why were they here and what did they want from him? Asmodeus may have explained it, but it still seemed mad and unreal.

A voice spoke over the commotion, announcing him. "IBT in his debut bout, ladies and gentlemen. Vigilante of Jokertown. Serpent of the sewers. Villain or hero? You be the judges. Place your bets."

This can't be happening.

The door at the other side of the oval swung open. Through it, Marcus saw a figure in silhouette. His heart hammered. The figure was like something dredged out of his childhood nightmares. It emerged into the light, a perversion of a centaur, horrific in a way that made Marcus's skin crawl. From his torso up he was humanoid, but beneath he merged into a bulbous, arachnid body, with eight long, segmented legs.

The announcer spoke over the new tumult of applause. "The Recluse, ladies and gentlemen. Reluctant combatant with a deadly sting. Veteran of three bouts. A battle of half men, the first ever such bout in the entire history of gladiatorial combat. Betting remains open until the first contact . . ."

The lights above the audience faded to black, leaving just the ring alight. The announcer spoke on, but Marcus stopped hearing him. He stopped hearing anything, or seeing anything but the spider-man. He watched him through ripples in the air, like heat waves. They distorted his vision, but they also brought waves of clarity. Crystal-clear images and understanding.

The spider-man circled to the left. The sharp tips of his legs skittered across the floor with audible clicks and scratches. At first, it looked like he was trying to run, searching for an exit. Marcus knew that was a ploy. The more he watched him, circling to stay away from him, the more he saw the man was sizing him up, testing him, trying to trick him. He kept saying something. Marcus saw his teeth gnashing together. He swayed crazily, his arms lashing at the air. His eyes flashed cold and savage, cut with highlight and shadow cast from the harsh lights.

He's insane, Marcus thought.

The guy kept up such a frantic scurrying that Marcus felt trapped, pressed up against the glass wall that hemmed him in. He bunched his coils beneath him, and hovered above them, looking for a way to attack. His tongue trembled in his mouth, venom-soaked and ready to dart out. But he couldn't get his aim set. The guy's upper body wouldn't stay still. He was trying to hypnotize him with the motion, confuse him.

This fucker wants to kill me.

Marcus surged at him, trying to get a good shot at the guy's face. His venom needed to hit skin, not the man's shell-encrusted legs or hairy underbody. Marcus shot, too early, poorly aimed. His tongue darted out a full ten feet. It nailed nothing but the air beside the spider-man's head.

He snapped it back. He swung his momentum into a hay-maker. His fist would have caught the man's jaw per-fectly, but, before it did, one of those sectional legs clipped it at the wrist. The blow slammed Marcus's arm down onto the stone floor, yanking his body with it.

Marcus writhed on the floor, trying to wrench his arm free as his opponent's bulbous, hairy black torso loomed over him. He punched at the joker's underbelly with his free hand, slamming it again and again. It responded by pressing him down, rising and turning and pressing him down again. It was sickening. When it rose a third time Marcus caught sight of a jagged barb protruding from the underbelly. All the pressing and rising was just to keep him down while he moved into position to strike.

Marcus's flesh tore as he ripped his arm from under the leg that pinned it. His torso corkscrewed him out of there just as the barb slammed down against the stone that had been beneath him. He rose up so fast that his head spun. He saw a blurred image of the spider-man. The man's face craned up to follow him. Marcus took his shot.

His tongue impacted with the man's face with all the force he could muster. It hit hard as a fist, snapping the joker's head back. Marcus loosened the muscles so that his tongue lapped venom all over the man's cheeks, across his lips and into his nose. And then his tongue snapped back into his mouth. It only took a second.

The spider-man careened away. His legs skittered even more wildly as he clutched at his face with his hands, crying in delirious pain. Marcus followed him. He held his damaged arm snug to his body, but struck blow after blow with his other fist, punching from high up on his coils, fast, snake-like. He kept at it until the spi-der legs collapsed in a jumbled splay. The man fell un-conscious on top of them. Marcus shouted for the fucker to get up and take more of a pounding.

The lights above the crowd flared. Where there had

been darkness a moment before, the close-packed people reappeared. They rose to their feet applauding. They laughed and shouted and pumped the air with their fists. Their eyes were wild with glee.

The announcer's voice returned. "The Infamous Black Tongue, ladies and gentlemen! The Infamous Black Tongue! Now that was a show, wasn't it?"

Marcus's eyes settled on the elderly couple in the private box. They were the only two not caught up in the frenzy. This time, it was the woman who drew his attention. As horrible as the deformed man was, the woman was somehow more frightening. She stared back at Marcus, arms crossed, eyes hidden behind elaborate glasses, her red hair in a snug swirl atop her head. Her face betrayed no emotion that he could fathom. Compared to her, the screaming crowd looked positively sane.

"It's not your fault," Father Squid said. He sat across from Marcus, a table between them.

Marcus pushed morsels of egg around his plate with a fork. "So you keep telling me."

"I saw the entire fight. They made us all watch it in the common room. It was horrible, but the man in that arena was not you. It was a perversion of you. I can see that even if you cannot. Trust me." The priest managed to convey calming empathy through his eyes, and with the shape and movement of his dangling tentacles.

Marcus tried not to see it. "I trust you," he said, "but you shouldn't trust me. Not anymore. I would've killed that guy. I don't know why, but . . . I hated him. I still do."

"You would not have gone that far," Father Squid said. "It's this place. Somehow it turns men's natures, brings horrible things out of them. It's not your fault, though." The priest reached across the table and tried to place a sucker-covered palm on the young man's hand.

Marcus pulled away. "You haven't been in the arena. You don't know what it's like."

The older man pulled his hand back. "I will soon."

"What?"

"I have been matched to fight tomorrow night."

"Against who?"

"That I don't know."

"But they won't be able to make you fight. Not you!"

"They can put me in the arena, but I will strive not to give in."

"If anyone can resist it you can!" The thought buoyed Marcus like nothing else had. Father Squid would beat them by not fighting. He could see it: the priest standing with his arms crossed, proud and defiant, staring down that old lady. And if he could do that, maybe Marcus could too. "You can beat it."

The priest ducked his head, seeming unnerved by Marcus's sudden enthusiasm. "I will try, but I have violence in my past, Marcus. I fear it's not buried as deeply as I would like."

♦

That evening, as he lay staring at the ceiling, his mind crowded with thoughts, his door cracked open. Of all the things he might have imagined would step through the door, the girl that slid into view wasn't one of them.

As far as he could tell she was a nat. A jaw-droppingly beautiful one. Beauty wafted in with her like a scent that he inhaled through his eyes. Fashion model–slim, firm and soft in the right places. She wore jeans so tight they looked like she'd been dipped into them. Her shirt opened all the way down the front, a gauzy-thin, semi-transparent material. He could just see the curves of her breasts. Her large eyes were spaced widely, but they were more striking for it. Icy blue, sparkling, they studied him with a frankness that set his heart racing.

"I am for you tonight," she said. "You must have fought well, yes?"

Marcus couldn't say a word.

She considered him for a long moment, and then asked, "Is your tongue really black?"

Marcus had never heard a sexier question.

Her name was Olena. She sat beside him on his bed. The threads in the stitching of her jeans sparkled gold when she moved. She was Ukrainian, from a city called Poltava. "You know it?"

Marcus pursed his lips, frowned as if he was trying to place Poltava.

"It's on the Vorskla," she said. Her accent reminded him of when his sister used to imitate Natasha Fatale from the *Rocky and Bullwinkle* cartoons. It would almost have been funny, except that she was too earnest, too beautiful, for him to possibly laugh at. "Is a river. Vorskla. You should know it." She punctuated this by stabbing out her small hand and slapping him on the shoulder. "You live in New York, yes?"

Marcus nodded. He almost specified Jokertown, but the name died on his tongue.

"Do you know famous persons?"

"Not really." Seeing disappointment in the way she bit the corner of her lip, he added, "I . . . I'm a little bit famous." He chose not to say "infamous."

"What makes you famous? Are you rapper?"

"Ah . . . no." He had no idea what to say. He was famous for beating up a crooked cop? For living in sewers? For roaming around at night looking for thugs? "Just for . . . getting in trouble."

This seemed to please her. She laughed and swayed into him. "You're bad boy, aren't you? I can tell you are!" Her head dipped coyly. For a moment her face was hidden behind a screen of her long black hair. Then she parted her hair with a hand, scooped it clear, and swiped it over her shoulder. "Show me your tongue."

Initially, Marcus refused, but she insisted. She seemed fascinated, first staring into this open mouth and then making him demonstrate his talent. She clapped with pleasure when he shot his tongue out and nailed the far wall.

"Is your 'little snake' as long as that?" she asked, sliding a hand over his torso.

Marcus felt an instant erection press against the scales of his groin.

She pulled her hand away and changed the subject. "Where would you take me in New York?"

An easy enough question, but it stumped him. Where would he take her?

"Not just your apartment," she cautioned. "Not just there. I need to see places. United Nations. Broadway. Liberty Statue. Where else?"

To his relief, she didn't make him answer the question. She went on talking about the places she wanted to see. Not just in New York, but at random points all across America. Marcus tried to listen, but he couldn't understand who or what she was. Where had she come from? How was it possible that she was sitting here on his bed chatting with him like it was the most normal thing in the world? Why was she speaking as if they had a future together, filled with voyages to amazing places? He wanted to know, but he didn't want to ask. Asking might kill whatever spell he was living in.

"Are you a good man?" she asked.

Marcus's stomach knotted. "I try to be."

"I know you are. I can see it in you. You won't hurt me, will you?"

"No, I would never—"

"Asmodeus is not a good man. He hurts me. He wins and then hurts me. I say I don't want to go to him but he always chooses me. That's not so good for me. A better thing is that you fight and win and have me. Be a monster at fighting. A monster for me. Then we will do things to make you happy. All the things you want. You know what I mean."

His face must've indicated that he didn't.

Olena slipped off the bed onto her knees, sliding her hands across his scales. She smiled and whispered, "I show you."

♥

"We should be in there," El Monstro said, pointing at the screen. "Front-row seats, baby. Wanna see the blood splatter." He punctuated this by smacking one of his massive, plated fists into the palm of his other hand.

The Somali girl who was oiling his horns drew back to accommodate his movements. She was beautiful, brown-skinned and lithe. Marcus had never heard her speak a word. He wondered if she even understood English.

El Monstro had just sat down beside Marcus, saying winners should sit together, shouldn't they? Eight feet tall, plated, with an oddly benevolent smile: Marcus couldn't figure him out. He'd been in here longer than anyone but Asmodeus. He was thriving here, enjoying the violence and the raw pleasures it afforded him. At least, outwardly he was. At times, Marcus saw a timorous quiver beneath his arrogant facade, as if every now and then he forgot who or where he was. Or maybe it was that every now and then he remembered. Once, during a melancholy moment, he'd mumbled something about his mother. Marcus didn't hear what, and he didn't ask for him to repeat it.

Marcus pulled Olena tight against his body. She repositioned her arms around his neck, leaned in and nibbled his ear. He felt the room's lecherous eyes on her, and on the other girl. The jokers didn't even try to hide their lust. If it wasn't for Baba Yaga's rules and Dmitri's talent,

Marcus was sure he'd be fighting them all off. El Monstro seemed to thrive on the jealous attention. Marcus didn't, but he couldn't miss seeing the fight. And he wanted Olena with him. It had only been one night, but he wanted her beside him forever and ever.

Everyone in the gladiator compound had gathered to watch Father Squid's first bout. Chairs and couches had been pulled together before a large-screen television. The buffet table lay ravished behind them. The mood was festive, edged with menace, but festive nonetheless. None of the spectators had to worry about their own lives tonight. That was on the priest and whomever he was going to fight. Nobody knew who that was yet—somebody brought in special for it, apparently.

"Look at them," El Monstro said, nudging Marcus's shoulder. "They're like wolves licking their chops. And they say we're the savages!"

The large screen panned across the expectant faces of the audience. Men and women, old and young, different races and features: they all shared the same expression. They looked possessed. Their noses flared as they breathed. Their eyes bulged. The sight of them made Marcus's skin crawl.

Asmodeus entered the room. He stood in the door a moment, staring at Marcus. Or . . . that's what he thought until the joker's eyes shifted and met Marcus's. He glared at him for a long moment, and then he moved into the group to take a seat. Before he met his eyes, Marcus realized, he'd been looking at Olena.

Onscreen, the camera shifted to one of the combatants. The joker shook out his muscle-bound shoulders, snapped his hands, and flexed his fingers. He shouted and stomped, his enormous eyes trembling with rage. Marcus tensed. The guy was hard not to recognize. Marcus had last seen him emerging from the white van.

"Ladies and gentlemen," the announcer intoned,

"tonight's main event features two debut performances in our arena. Aleksei the Eel, a joker of incredible physical strength, a fighter just recently snatched from the mean city streets. Formidable—and horrible—to look upon. There's more to him than brawn. He's endowed with a high-voltage touch. Aleksei the Eel, ladies and gentlemen!"

Wartcake said, "That's how the ugly bastard caught me. Fucking shocked me." Others spoke up as well. It seemed that many of them had had run-ins with the Eel.

"Why's he in there?" John the Pharaoh asked.

Asmodeus answered. "He screwed up when he nabbed the squid. Was supposed to just get snake-boy, here. Add to that selling DVD's on the side, and wreckin' a van and slugging it out with a bunch of fucking aces. Baba Yaga ain't happy. She's teaching him a lesson."

Marcus didn't say anything. He just glared at the screen.

The announcer described the fighter facing him as an agent of righteous retribution, a killer who hides beneath the robes of a saint, a man with a past mired in unspeakable violence. "Some know him as a saint, but saint and sinner; what's the difference? Ladies and gentlemen, the Holy Redeemer!"

Father Squid appeared on the screen. He stood motionless, his arms slightly raised to either side, like a gunfighter awaiting the moment to draw. His gloved hands hung loose. His cloak draped him and covered his head, but the lights illuminated his face. The camera even drew in near enough to show the sway of the tentacles covering his mouth as he breathed. His expression was impossible to read.

It began abruptly. Bellowing, Aleksei barreled forward. Father Squid stayed immobile as the hulk charged. His head hung forward. It didn't even look like he saw the guy rushing toward him, not until the last minute. Just as Aleksei reached him, Father Squid shifted to one side, dodging Aleksei's headlong attack. It was a swift, efficient motion, just enough to send Aleksei stumbling into the wall beyond him. He bounced off it and whirled.

Father Squid strode away. His steps looked as heavy and ponderous as ever, but there was a grace to him that Marcus hadn't noticed before. The priest circled and shifted as if his body was remembering the motions for him. He kept Aleksei at arm's length, near enough to talk to. That's what he was doing. Marcus couldn't hear what he was saying, but he saw his tentacles shifting and flexing as he spoke.

He's going to do it, Marcus thought. Look how cool he is. How calm.

Gesturing with his arms, Father Squid made some argument that Aleksei kept trying to punch through. Aleksei shook his head savagely. He spit and hissed and pressed to get in striking range. "The squid's a coward," Wartcake said.

Marcus snapped, "He's no coward. He's just above this shit. He's not going to fight for those fuckers."

This got him a few jeers and insults, but mostly they all just watched the fight. Aleksei was all testosterone-pumped, muscle-bound rage. He threw wild, powerful punches, changeups that went from high to low, swinging wide or jabbing for the torso. His fists sparked with electricity. His ugly face contorted as he concentrated.

For his part, Father Squid moved with an uncanny precision. He backed and dodged, slipped his head to the side, twisted from the torso. No matter how he tried, Aleksei couldn't land a blow. Father Squid didn't move any faster, but it seemed he knew what his opponent was going to do just before he did it. He swatted the joker's punches away with sharp, karate-like motions, his body taking on stances Marcus had never imagined the old priest capable of. Once, he caught Aleksei's fist in his gloved hand. Judging by the way the big man scowled, Father Squid must've squeezed it painfully. Just for a moment, though, then he flung it away.

"Squid's getting pissed," El Monstro said.

Don't, Marcus said to himself. *Don't give in.*

Aleksei landed a punch in Father Squid's gut. The priest lurched over around it, and Aleksei slammed another fist into his temple. The electric force of it hurled Father Squid's body backwards. He rose just as Aleksei bore down on him. He snapped out a hand, catching Aleksei's arm at the wrist. He twisted around, keeping a grip on the arm while clipping the man's legs with his body and using his momentum to trip him. The joker flew heels over head. Father Squid planted his feet and pulled. The arm popped out of its socket. It was a sickly thing to watch, the unnatural way the body and arm moved in opposite directions. Father Squid let go and backed away. He looked horrified at what he'd done. He stared with bulbous eyes as Aleksei squirmed across the stadium floor, helpless.

"Finish him," Asmodeus said, mouth open, tongue sliding across his teeth.

Shaking his head, Father Squid stepped forward. He made soothing gestures with his hands. He reached out, and Marcus knew he was trying to position Aleksei to slip his arm back into its socket.

Yes, he thought. *Show them.*

He didn't get a chance to.

Aleksei transformed. In the blink of an eye, he became an eel. Eight thick, muscular, slimy feet of one. His jaws opened and he lunged up at the priest's face. Father Squid blocked with his forearm. The eel bit into it and thrashed, yanking the priest off his feet. The crowd went wild, roars so loud Marcus could hear them through both the television and through the actual walls themselves. He watched, unsure what to feel, his stomach tied in knots.

After a few frantic moments, Father Squid got the eel

pinned beneath his thighs. He gripped the joker around the neck and banged his head on the floor. He banged it hard, over and over again.

Grimacing, Marcus shut his eyes.

Ties That Bind

Part Three

THE CONDO WAS NORMALLY quite roomy. One bedroom with a king-size bed for them, one bedroom for Isai, two large bathrooms, and a modern open-plan layout for the rest. It worked great for their family—or at least it had, until Kavitha's family showed up on their doorstep and moved in. Two parents, two sisters, and their husbands, all bunking on air mattresses in the living room. Glorious.

"He was here in New York, Michael," Kavitha's mother said in British-accented English. "That was where he called us from last. The phone records are clear."

"Yes, I know," Michael said, trying to be patient. Sandip's parents had hired an investigator when the kid had first gone missing, but the man had turned up nothing. So far, neither had Michael. It wasn't technically his jurisdiction, but he'd squeezed looking for Sandip into every free minute at work. You did that for family; the other cops understood and covered for him when they could. But phone records, bank records, Internet, nothing. Michael had walked the streets, checked his contacts, but with no luck. As if the kid had dropped off the planet.

"I know Sandip was here in New York; we saw him then." Was he still here? Michael had no idea.

"So, I tell it to you again," she snapped, regal in her silver sari and hair in a perfect bun, despite four nights sleeping on the floor. "And you will listen!"

Michael could only nod in response. He didn't have a lot of moral ground to stand on, given his living situation, which Kavitha's parents were handling with a fierce lack of acknowledgment. They had barely spoken to their daughter for years, ever since she'd gotten pregnant by a black guy and decided to keep the kid. But for this, for their only son, they'd finally broken the silence with a vengeance. Family was the most important thing to Kavitha, Michael knew; it had broken her heart when they'd turned so cold. But she wouldn't betray them now, no matter how they'd treated her. It was one of the things Michael loved about her—he knew that no matter what, she would be loyal to family forever. Which loyalty now included him, Isai, and Minal. And as for her parents, Kavitha might never forgive them, but she'd still feed and house them until Sandip was safely found.

Now Michael stood in front of Kavitha's mother, trying to swallow his own anger at the kid who had driven the whole family to distraction by disappearing. He was probably running around with some gang, pretending to be a hero. But he couldn't say that to this tiny old woman, wrapped tightly in her shawl and shivering, clearly out of her mind with worry for her youngest child. When he found Sandip, he was going to strangle him. But he couldn't tell her that; what Michael said out loud was only, "Don't worry, Aunty." She frowned at him, and he wasn't sure if it was for the fatuous reassurance, or if she thought the "Aunty" impertinent. What was he supposed to call her? He couldn't use her name—he was sure she'd think that was rude. This whole situation was impossible. "I'm sure he's fine."

If Michael was honest with himself, he had to admit

that he was worried about the kid too. It was only two years ago that his own daughter had disappeared. Just for a few hours, but he'd thought his heart would stop. If Sandip would just pick up the damn phone and call.

♣

He couldn't spend all his time looking for the kid, not if he wanted to keep his job. Most of Michael's days were spent on the street, talking to contacts, trying to figure out how the art smugglers were getting their pieces into New York. He'd nailed down almost every other part of the case—he knew who was doing the smuggling, where the pieces were coming from, who was buying. The one thing missing was the point of connection, the person or place that moved pieces from thief-seller to buyer. As soon as Michael found that link, he'd be able to make an arrest. Not that anyone at the station would care—everyone's attention was focused on the missing jokers now. His punk partner was getting all the glory on what had turned out to be a much bigger case than anyone had expected. Michael glared across the desk at Franny, at just the wrong moment—the boy happened to look up, caught the glare, and then ducked his head back down, flushing.

Michael felt a surprising pang of guilt. He had been kind of hard on the kid; Franny wasn't that much older than Sandip. Children, all of them, playing at being men. And Franny had a massive stack of papers in front of him; that couldn't be fun.

"Hey—you want a hand with that?" Maybe it was time for a peace offering. They were supposed to be partners, and the truth was, it was Michael's job to watch over the kid, help him out.

But Franny just spat out a brusque, "I can handle it."

Not even a thanks in there. Fine. If Franny was determined to drown in paperwork, Michael didn't need to extend a helping hand. He already had one kid to rescue.

When he got off this shift, he'd go hit the streets again. Someone had to know where Sandip had disappeared to. Jokertown wasn't big enough to hide a kid forever.

♠

They'd canceled dinner with his parents last Saturday; this week, Minal had decided to invite Michael's parents over to their place instead. She said it was time the parents met, that since Kavitha's parents were here, they might as well take advantage. Get some good out of the situation. Neither Michael nor Kavitha were enthused about the idea, but Minal was insistent.

There wouldn't have been room to seat everyone, but Kavitha's sisters and their husbands had finally decamped this morning, pleading jobs and other commitments. Her middle sister was just getting to the uncomfortable stage of pregnancy, and had sounded relieved to go home and sleep in a real bed again, instead of bunking on an air mattress on the floor. Kavitha's father was making noises about work responsibilities as well, but so far, her mother had held firm. And so here they were, waiting uncomfortably for Michael's parents to arrive. Minal, busy in the kitchen, had banished everyone from her domain, and so they sat, awkwardly, in the living room. Thank God for Isai.

She had started part-shifting lately—just enough to sprout feathers on her head and arms, to turn her nose into a beak. Michael worried that her nose was turning more beak-like with every day, even when she wasn't shifted—if she transformed too often, would the changes become permanent? But try to tell a five-year-old not to do something fun; it was impossible. And no one had the heart to discipline Isai right now in any case.

"Ammama! I can't find the birdie!" She leaned against her grandmother on the sofa, book in hand. Isai's current obsession was hidden picture puzzles, and Kavitha's mother was remarkably good at them. She could find any hidden object with just a glance—she was equally good at finding dust. The one thing she couldn't find was her missing son.

The phone rang, shrill and loud. Had someone turned the ringer up? The sound made Michael's head ache. Kavitha jumped up and grabbed an extension. "Hello?" Hope in her voice—not that any of them really expected Sandip to call, but you never knew. But then she just walked away, out of the room, listening to whomever was on the other end of the line. Apparently not Sandip.

And then another ring—the doorbell. Michael's turn to jump up, this time to open the door. His mother bustled into the room, dripping rain from her coat. He turned to help her with it, but she ignored him, heading straight for Kavitha's mother, who had risen to greet her. His mother's wet bulk engulfed Maya in a huge embrace. "I am so sorry," she said, her voice thick with its Korean accent, but even thicker with sympathy. And Maya's stiff formality broke down completely; the tiny woman was sobbing now, in his mother's vast arms. Hugely muscled, from long hours over decades of wrestling wet clothes at her laundromat. Strong and warm, the kind of arms that could hold you up when you were drowning.

Michael's heart was aching now, along with his head, but Minal had been right to invite his parents here. His dad was slipping off his own coat, closing the door behind him. And even though Michael couldn't remember the last time he'd hugged his father, in this moment, it seemed natural to rest a hand on the old man's back, to feel the warmth of skin under the thin shirt, as he ushered his father into the room. Michael knew in that moment that if he were the one missing, even as a grown man, his dad wouldn't rest until he found him again. He had to work harder to find Sandip. Maybe after dinner, he'd go out again, talk to some more people.

Kavitha came out of the hall, the phone still in her

hand, to see her mother straightening up out of his mother's embrace, tears still running down her face. Kavitha's face was stricken, and thank God for Isai, bewildered Isai, who asked loudly, "Is it crying time?" And his father scooped her up and leaned his head against hers, saying, "No, sweetheart, baby girl. Crying time is done for now. Now it's hugging time, okay? And as soon as your Mama Minnie tells us all that yummy-smelling food is ready, it's gonna be eating time. Sound good?"

Isai loudly agreed. Michael took his mother's wet coat that she was finally shrugging out of; Kavitha pulled herself together enough to explain that the studio had called to remind her that she only had one more week of rehearsal time before her show was due to start. She had to get back to work tomorrow morning, for at least a few hours. That started her father talking about business again; import/export problems, ever-higher taxes, lying and cheating employees. It was never pleasant listening to Kavitha's father complain about his work, and Michael caught Kavitha wincing at a few of the worst comments. But it was still a relief to talk about something normal, and at least his mother was happy to join in, commiserating on the travails of the small business owner.

Somehow, the mundane details carried them through to dinnertime, when Minal's food on the table and their faces around it seemed like a blessing. Michael had never expected to see his parents and Kavitha's together, not really. But they got along surprisingly well—Kavitha's mother even laughed at a few of his father's wry jokes. If they got married, maybe this would be normal, would happen often. That might actually be nice.

He just had to find Sandip first.

Galahad in Blue

Part Six

AS HE'D EXPECTED THERE had been a long, tense, and unpleasant conversation with Deputy Inspector Maseryk about the death of a prisoner while in custody. After it was over Franny returned to his desk and went through all his notes on the joker kidnappings. Another person had been reported missing. A schoolteacher named Philip Richardson. The kidnappers were no longer taking just the lost, the discarded, and forgotten.

His now almost constant headache was back, pounding in his temples and behind his eyes. He closed his eyes, but all he could see were images from the fight club DVDs. The blood, the fists, the contorted faces of the men fighting in that arena. There had to be something he'd overlooked, a thread that might lead to the taken.

Michael came in at one point. His eyes were sunken and he looked exhausted. Franny opened his mouth to ask if his partner was all right, but Michael seemed to just look right through him, and he walked past without even a grudging hello, and headed straight to Slim Jim's desk. Franny swallowed the words.

Adding to his misery was the fact that tonight he'd

agreed to have dinner with Apsara and her parents. He'd started to head to the file room about ten times to cancel, but then he'd think about the shitstorm that would cause and he'd return to his desk unable to face one more person who was pissed at him. Apsara had wanted him to go with her to the Hyatt to collect her parents but Franny refused. He would meet them at the restaurant. That would give him another hour to work.

Norwood still hadn't called back. The agent probably wasn't going to follow up on the *American Hero* thing. Why would a fed do something to help a local? Franny's sense of being abused deepened. He decided he was being stupid and paranoid. Jamal had gotten him the info on the Russian thugs.

He slumped in his squeaking, broken-down chair. *So much* American Hero—*Curveball and Earth Witch and Drummer Boy, Peregrine's son, and of course Jamal, the first season winner, and the tapes . . .*

Various Wikis listed all the contestants who had actually made it onto the show. There were some jokers—the preponderance were aces, and why not? Hollywood liked attractive people, most jokers weren't very attractive. He watched an online video showing some of the humiliating tryouts. *Tryouts.* He checked his watch. It was only four o'clock on the West Coast. He called the studio that made *American Hero,* and after only a minimum amount of runaround he was connected with an efficient assistant who e-mailed him the full list of everyone who had ever auditioned for the show. He ran down the list. Nearly every one of the missing had auditioned for the show.

He put in another call to the SCARE agent. "Jamal, found another link with *American Hero.* Most of the victims auditioned for the show. There's got to be a connection. Please call me once you've talked to Berman."

◆

Starfields was one of Manhattan's better restaurants, and it didn't hurt its caché that the owner, Hastet, was a real live alien, a woman from Takis. Actually she was now the only alien on Earth, since Dr. Tachyon had departed. The menu was eclectic and rather than the traditional large plates of food served in most American eateries, Hastet specialized in what Franny thought of as Takisian dim sum. Small plates, exotically spiced and unfailingly delicious. You ended up ordering a lot of them to fill up, and were presented with a large bill at the end of the meal. That wasn't something he was looking forward to. It was unworthy of him, but he was really hoping that Apsara's dad would pick up the check. Then he wondered if *he* ought to offer to buy dinner? Ugly thought.

Franny was waiting in the lobby when the elevator doors opened to reveal the trio. Apsara's mother was an older version of her daughter and just as beautiful. Her father was bald, with a slight paunch, but neither condition detracted from his strong, powerful features. Apsara looked adorable in her police uniform. Franny suppressed a sigh. He stepped forward to meet them, and felt gigantic. At five foot ten he towered over all three.

Introductions were made, hands were shaken, and they moved from the lobby into the restaurant proper. Franny paused for an instant before stepping in and scanned the people in the restaurant. He mentally assessed and dismissed the patrons as any kind of threat. He then took a good look at his surroundings. The ceiling was painted space-black and gold and silver stars twinkled against the dark background. Hastet herself, looking neat as a pin and dressed in traditional Takisian clothes, escorted them to a booth.

He'd read that at one time the waiters had dressed in colorful and flamboyant styles in imitation of Tachyon, but the Takisian doctor had been gone for almost two decades and that affectation had ended. Now the waiters wore black pants and white shirts with bow ties. Hastet supplied them with menus, while a waiter filled water glasses, and another shook out napkins and laid them in their laps.

Mrs. Chiangmai looked at him over the top of a menu and said in her softly accented voice, "Detective Black."

"Frank, please."

She inclined her head with the grace of a dancer. "Frank. Apsara has been telling us of some of her cases. They sound quite hair-raising. How dangerous is this for my daughter?"

Apsara cast him a pleading glance. He wasn't exactly sure what she wanted so he made a guess. "The truth, Mrs. Chiangmai, is that we almost never draw our guns, much less fire them. I'm not saying it can't be rough, but it's not normally life-threatening." The next glance was grateful. He'd guessed correctly.

"And what's your job like now that you've been promoted?" Mr. Chiangmai asked. "Apsara tells us you are one of the youngest people ever to make detective."

Because of politics, he thought, but he kept his remark as neutral as possible. "Less active. I mostly interview people now."

"Do you like it?" Apsara asked.

He thought about it. He knew he was supposed to, but he had made a discovery. "I liked walking a beat. Seeing my people. Hearing about their days. But this is the career path if you want to make captain."

"And you do," Mrs. Chiangmai said.

"My father was a captain. In fact, captain of the precinct where I work."

"A lot to live up to," Mr. Chiangmai said.

Uncomfortable, Franny looked away. The conversation swirled around him. Apsara spinning tales. He recognized them as recent cases handled by both detectives and uniformed officers in the 5th Precinct. With luck her parents would not know enough about protocol to tell she was fibbing, or not pause to wonder how she had taken part in so many arrests.

He lost interest in the conversation thread. Found himself thinking about Abigail. He'd promised her he'd help and he was no closer to a solution for the Croyd problem. Back when Abigail had first gotten involved with Croyd Franny had abused his position to look up the file on the man. A file that extended back into the 1950s.

Some of the old-timers in Jokertown claimed that Croyd had actually been around on Wild Card Day back in '46. The length and age of the file suggested it might be true. The crimes listed were mostly B&Es and larcenies. Then as the years had passed and Croyd had become a fixture in Jokertown a degree of sympathetic understanding for the man's plight had taken root in the minds of the officers of Fort Freak. Croyd's ace meant he really couldn't hold a job, and none of the crimes he committed were so very bad. Or so the argument went. But if Croyd acted on his threat and killed Mick and Rick there would be no turning a blind eye. Croyd would go to jail.

Franny again scanned the restaurant. Croyd could probably remember when the waitstaff were all dressed up like faux Tachyons. Hell, he probably remembered Tachyon himself. Remembered when Aces High, on the top floor of the Empire State Building, was the pinnacle of wild card chic. When the Astronomer and Fortunato had battled in the skies over Manhattan, the day Franny's father had died.

He's also very suggestible. Dr. Finn's words came back, and with it an idea. A crazy idea, but it was the first one Franny had that didn't involve him trying to subdue, handcuff, and keep Croyd locked up until the ace fell asleep.

"Uh huh," Franny said agreeably when the cadence of

Apsara's voice indicated she'd asked him a question. From the puzzled look on her parents' faces it hadn't been the right response. "Would you excuse me a moment?"

Franny slipped out of the booth and went to the men's room. He washed his hands, splashed water on his face, and stood staring into the mirror. Would Abby think he was crazy or just stupid if he mentioned his idea for dealing with Croyd? He realized he did not want to sit through a meal while Apsara hosed her parents. They seemed nice, and he didn't want to be a part of it. He also wanted to go call Abby and put his plan in motion *right now*. And he had the perfect out. Duty called.

He returned to the table. "I just got a call about a case I'm working on," he explained. "I'm afraid I need to leave."

"We certainly understand when duty calls," Mr. Chiangmai said expansively. When the older man spoke the words aloud it almost embarrassed Franny into staying, but only almost.

It was also clear from Apsara's ice-dagger stare that she didn't.

"So, what do you think?" Franny asked Abigail after he had outlined his plan. Since Franny had bolted before eating they were seated in a booth at a burger joint. A french fry liberally coated with ketchup hung forgotten in Abby's hand.

"I think it's either completely mad, or madly genius."

"I'll need your help to pull it off."

"The theater's dark tonight, nobody around, and I don't think the director will mind if I borrow a few things from the costume department." She cocked her head in that way she had that reminded him of the cardinals that visited the bird-feeding station at his mother's house in Saratoga. "But rather than *ask* maybe we'll just assume it's okay."

"Better to ask forgiveness than permission?" Franny suggested.

"I like that. I think it shall become my motto."

They polished off their burgers. Abby reached for her purse. Franny held out a hand. "Let me get this."

She glared up at him from beneath her bangs. "This is *not* a date."

"Absolutely not," he hurriedly agreed. "But you're a starving artist, and I got a promotion."

"Well, all right then." He thought she looked relieved.

Three hours later, in the stairwell of a Chinatown apartment building Abby helped him into the costume they had "borrowed" from the Jokertown Rep. It had been used in a performance of *Cyrano,* and however chic it might have been in 1680 Franny knew he looked like an idiot.

Abby tugged the shirt ruffles from beneath the wide cuffs of the long paisley coat so they hung over his hands. The knee-high boots were too big, causing him to shuffle, which was probably appropriate given the shoulder-length gray wig Abby had provided. The coat and matching pantaloons were both too small, which had him breathing in shallow gulps. The drooping feather in the musketeer's hat fell into his eyes, and he blew it away in irritation. Abby had her knuckles stuffed in her mouth trying to hold back giggles.

"Okay, ready?" Abby asked.

"No. If anybody sees me in this getup I'll . . . I'll . . ." Words failed him.

"Nonsense, you look . . . you look . . ." Giggles overcame her again.

"Yeah, that's what I thought," he said sourly.

They left the stairwell and went down the hall. Standing outside the apartment door they could hear both a television and a radio playing inside.

"Maybe he's asleep, and that's why both are on," he whispered.

Abigail shook her head. "Probably not, he tries to stay stimulated when he doesn't want to sleep," she whispered back. "Okay, good luck. He shouldn't see me here, or he'll know something is up."

"You'll rescue me if this goes pear-shaped, right?" Franny asked plaintively as she hurried back toward the door leading to the stairwell.

She flashed him a smile and a thumbs-up. Franny gave himself a shake, faced the door, tried to take a deep breath, and palmed the pass key he'd obtained from the building super by flashing his badge. He tried not to think about how many laws he was breaking. He slid the key into the lock, opened the door, and swept into the room.

His first impression was that smells could have weight and heft. The room reeked of pizza, fried chicken, beer, and man sweat. A hulking figure, hollow-eyed, skin like bumpy rock, and dressed in baggy sweatpants and a T-shirt jumped out of a recliner and curled his fingers into fists. The individual digits vanished and the hands became solid, skin-colored sledgehammers.

"Greetings!" Franny said. He swept off the feathered hat. "I am a Takisian anthropologist, and I have been sent on behalf of the Star League to seek your help in determining if Earth is ready to join our glorious hegemony." Croyd gaped at him. *Nobody would buy this bullshit.* Franny eyed the massive hands. Yep, he was going to die. Desperate, he plowed on. "We have determined that you are the human who can best accomplish this task as you move in circles both high and low."

A frown knotted Croyd's brow. "What does that mean?"

"Criminal and not criminal," Franny explained.

"Did Tachy send you?" Croyd asked.

"Uh . . . yes . . . yes, he did." Franny prayed that Croyd wouldn't ask for any details regarding the alien doctor.

Croyd turned away. "I can't. I gotta deal with these bastards who are kidnapping jokers." He paced the room, his footfalls heavy on the linoleum floor. "They're coming for me. But I'd be happy to do it after I kill these guys."

"Not necessary." Franny removed a small pocket recorder. "This device will not only record your interactions with the citizens of this world, but it will protect you from any kind of assault."

Sweat trickled through Franny's sideburns beneath the ridiculous wig. Given Franny's shitty luck Croyd would get mugged while carrying around the recorder. Then he would come find Franny and pound him into the ground like a tent peg. One the other hand Croyd looked like an Easter Island statue right now. No mugger in his right mind would assault that. But in Jokertown *right mind* was a sliding scale.

Croyd rubbed a now semi-normal-shaped hand across his face. The rasp like rock on rock could be heard even over the radio and television.

"Well, that's fine for *me,* but they'll take somebody else. Nope, I gotta kill them."

"No! You don't. They're not involved." Croyd turned back to face him, the eyes buried deep under that protruding brow line were suspicious.

"And how the hell would you know? I'm supposed to be the expert on this community. At least according to you."

"We've been monitoring Jokertown from space. They haven't taken anybody."

"If you can watch from space then why the hell do you need me?"

"We can't . . ." His brain felt like it was frantically

picking up and then rejecting ideas. "Can't . . . hear what they say."

Amazingly Croyd bought it. He grunted. "Okay. So, what's in it for me?"

Frantically Franny considered. "First human . . . delegate to the League." He hoped it didn't sound as lame to Croyd as it did to him.

"I'd get to go into space?"

"Yes, on a spaceship." Franny winced.

Fortunately exhaustion and the level of drugs in his system made Croyd less discerning than the rock he resembled. "Cool," he said. He took the small recorder. "And this will really keep me safe?"

"Absolutely. Guaranteed. Just turn it on and walk around."

"Okay."

"And please, don't kill anyone while you're working for me. It would make it a lot harder for me to present you as a League delegate. Well, I must go."

Franny hurried to the door. "Hey," Croyd called. "How'd you get in?"

"Alien technology," Franny said, and fled. He knew he needed to get clear fast so he opted for the elevator rather than shuffling to the stairwell.

Thankfully there was nobody in the entryway. Franny dropped the key through the mail slot on the manager's door, left the building, and pulled out his cell phone to call Abby, and tell her where to meet him. He heard footsteps approaching, and he withdrew to the stairs leading down to the basement apartments.

"Hey, you!" came the never to be mistaken, high-pitched voice of his former partner Bill Chen. "Step out here where I can see you. What are you doing?" The powerful beam from a cop's flashlight blinded Franny.

Yes, Franny decided, he had the worst luck of any living human. Bill lived in Chinatown, and of course fate would put Franny in his path right as Bill was coming off duty. "Relax, Bill, it's me," Franny said, stepping out of the shadows, and pulling off the hat and wig.

A grin split the big face as Bill took in his appearance. "Halloween's not for months."

"Costume party."

"You know what you need? Some *bling*." And Bill un-limbered his nightstick, whistled, and pointed the stick at Franny. Franny tried to dodge, but the too-big boots tripped him up. An instant later he was surrounded by a pink glow shot through with stars and glitter.

"Tinkerbill! You *dick*!"

Abby turned up at that moment. Bill looked from her to Franny and back again. Gave a snort of laughter.

"You kids have a nice night," Bill said and sauntered away.

Those About to Die . . .

Part Five

MARCUS HAD A PRETTY good burn on. He was working his biceps, slow curls with the dumbbells. He looked down at the taut bulges of muscle, trying to focus, trying not to think about Father Squid, or Olena, or the fights, or Dmitri's mind trips. He wasn't having much success, but it was better to be doing something than lying on his cot. He didn't notice that Asmodeus had entered the workout room until he spoke.

"It's not all about muscle," Asmodeus said. He strolled toward Marcus, his slim, lanky body at ease. "I don't work out. Don't need to. Five bouts, me on top every time. Bet you wonder how I do it, don't ya?"

"Fuck you."

A tick of annoyance flashed across the joker's smug visage, gone just as quickly. "I thought Olena was taking care of that for you. But then again she's not yours anymore, is she?"

Marcus glared at him, hating the fact that his mouth even formed her name, hating the way he grinned and let the tip of his tongue show. He knew what was going to happen before he did it, but he couldn't help himself.

He surged at Asmodeus, propelled by the long muscles of his tail. His weight-heavy fists swung up from his sides. He nearly smashed one of the dumbbells into the joker's spotty face.

"Dmitri!" Asmodeus called.

The name was enough to freeze him. The ace strolled into the room, looking bored as ever. He leaned against the wall. His dead eyes fixed on Marcus, though without a spark of genuine interest.

"Yeah, they sent me with Dmitri," Asmodeus said. He pulled up a stool and leaned back against it. "I'm not here to shoot the shit. Baba Yaga didn't much like the way you handled your last fight. She wants me to school you."

Resuming his curls, Marcus muttered, "I won, didn't I?"

No one could dispute that. The fight hadn't lasted more than a few minutes. The joker facing him looked like one of the ogres in that old animated version of *The Hobbit*. He had come at him with his massive mouth open, teeth like curved daggers. Marcus swiped his feet from under him with his tail. He pounced on his back while he was down and pounded his face into the floor. He could still hear the joker's teeth snapping on the floor and saw them spinning away, dragging thin tendrils of blood. He'd bashed his face to pulp and hadn't seen the guy since. Marcus wanted to feel more sorry about it than he did. It was wrong hurting someone like that. He knew that, but he didn't quite feel it. Part of him found beauty in the broken teeth, the thin lines of bloody spittle they left behind.

"Yeah, you fucked him up real good, but Baba Yaga wants us to fight. Not to kill each other. And you could've made more of a show of it. That's what I do. I string them along a bit before closing the deal. It was that shit with the audience that pissed her off, though."

It hadn't been enough to destroy the ogre. Marcus had been too enraged. He turned from beating on the guy to raging at the audience. He smashed into the glass. He bounced off of it and came back pounding and shouting. He thrust himself straight up and ripped and yanked at the webbing above the glass. He almost believed he could get through it. If he just tore hard enough, found a weakness. If he could've gotten through, he'd have ripped the spectators apart. He'd have torn at them, bit them, crushed them. Only when Dmitri entered his skull and dragged him into his own personal hell did he stop. It had been far worse than the first time.

When he came out of it, alone in his room—Olena nowhere to be seen—he'd nearly lost what sanity he had left.

"You do something like that again and Dmitri's gonna spend a long time in your head," Asmodeus said. "Bet. Just get your act together. Use your anger; don't let it use you. Master that, and you'll do all right. There, that's my charity work done." He stood. "I gotta go rest. Got a fight tonight. When it's over . . ." He grinned. ". . . I'm heading to Poltava. Nothing like Ukrainian pussy, is there?" He strolled away.

Marcus watched him go, feeling like each step he took away slammed another nail into his heart. Just as he reached the threshold, Marcus called out to him. "Hey! Who are you fighting?"

The joker spun on his heel, amusement—and challenge—in his eyes. "Why do you want to know?"

♠

Marcus's knuckles were sore from the knocking. Strange how he could pound flesh without a problem, but something as simple as knocking on a door made him wince. It wasn't just the physical sensation that hurt.

"Father, it's me! I'm not leaving until you open up."

No response.

Behind him, life in the compound went on. Jokers

lounging, tossing insults at each other, posturing. Girls. Drink. Amusements. In some ways it was all the same as when he'd first beheld the place. Things were changing, though, slowly, gradually, almost unnoticeably. The more they fought, the more the gladiators found the violence of the ring staying with them.

For Marcus, it was like a smell that clung to him. Sometimes he didn't notice; sometimes he caught the scent and his muscles tensed and his face went hard and any and everything seemed like an insult. He'd bashed Wartcake in the face with his tray at the buffet table and would've done more, had he not felt Dmitri's creeping touch coming over him. Afterward, he couldn't even remember what had angered him. More and more, the trigger didn't matter. Just the urge toward violence did.

Making it worse was that he didn't have Father Squid to turn to. The night of his fight the priest came back stunned, shaken to the core, shame-faced and silent. He'd stayed in his locked room ever since. Marcus had tried getting him out several times. He'd been refusing to eat or interact. Not even Dmitri's mind tricks seemed to affect him. He was beyond it all. Marcus had heard him praying. Once, he heard a repetitive thwack! thwack! thwack! He didn't want to imagine what that meant.

Leaning in to the door, he said, "You can't stay in there forever."

Nothing.

"You think you're the only one that feels like an animal?" Marcus snapped. "I got news for you. All of us feel that way! Some like it. I don't. But . . . I'm getting tired of fighting it. You know? It's hard. It's easier to give in." He paused, clenched his fist again and touched his knuckles to the wood. "What about all that stuff you said to me? How it wasn't my fault. How it was this place that drove me crazy. If that's true about me it's true about you, too."

There was a noise behind the door, a snuffling and

murmur that he couldn't make out. It sounded like some sort of prayer.

Annoyed, Marcus said, "Whatever, Father. I'm getting on with it. Just so you know, I'm fighting tonight. Didn't even have to, but I want to. Yeah, I do. They took Olena from me. You probably think that's for the best, but you've never been in love."

The praying cut off abruptly.

"We got something. It's real. It's not like you think it is. She's the only truly good thing in this place, and they took her from me. If I don't do anything, Asmodeus is going to . . ." He couldn't get the words out. "I'm not gonna let that happen. That's why I'm fighting tonight—for her. What else do I have to fight for now?"

Out of words, Marcus felt the urgency drain away. He sighed and pushed himself away from the door. "Anyway, that's all I wanted to say. I'm going. Guess I'll see ya when I see ya."

He turned and made it only a few steps away before he heard the door open. Father Squid peered through the crack, his face haggard, streaked with tears. "Marcus . . . You're wrong about me. I did know love once. I would've done anything to keep her safe, or to punish the one that . . ." He cut off. He blinked and inhaled a long breath and said, "Come in, son. I'll tell you about it. I'll tell you about my Lizzie. And you can tell me about your Olena." He drew back, leaving the door open for the young man to enter.

♦

"Stupid move, kid," Asmodeus said. "Stupidest thing you've done yet."

The joker was slick on his feet. He moved as if sliding across ice, deceptive, graceful. In his skintight jeans and white T-shirt, he could've been a dancer in *West Side Story*. Only he wasn't singing.

Marcus pursued him. He slithered with a purposeful fluidity all his own. He wanted to pound him, to feel his fists thudding against his face. Backing Asmodeus up to the ring wall, he snapped his tail around to one side, to keep him from fleeing to the left, and then he curved in from the right. He released his tongue. It shot from his mouth sopping wet with venom.

Asmodeus blocked it with the palm of his hand. The impact thwacked wetly, spraying his face and knocking his arm back. He spun away, shaking the sting out of it. Good luck with that, Marcus thought. His venom would work just the same. Skin contact. That's all it needed. Marcus kept his sinuous curve around the joker, waiting for him to weaken. He wanted to see his face register the venom, and then he would come on swinging, beat the crap out of him, and then end it.

Asmodeus looked at Marcus. There was no awareness of his impending doom on his face. He grinned and wiped the moisture from his forehead. "Your venom's crap," he said. "It's nothing to me but the stink of your breath. I've got a bit of reptile in me as well. I produce my own venom. Comes out in my semen." His grin widened. "The ladies love it. Olena more than most. Says my spunk lights a fire inside her."

Marcus lunged, swinging his fists with everything he had. Asmodeus tried to leap over his tail, but Marcus swiped his feet out from under him. As he fell, Marcus landed punches on the back of his head. It was sloppy, ugly fighting, but he kept at it, battering the joker until he was on his knees. Marcus grabbed him by the hair. He raised his head up, ready to drive him face-first into the floor.

Asmodeus began to convulse. Surprised, Marcus let him go. Maybe the venom was working now. On all fours, dry heaves racked the joker, making him look like a cat coughing up a hairball. As much as Marcus wanted to kill him, he wanted everyone to see how pathetic he was. He wanted Olena to see his humiliation.

Asmodeus, in one terrible cough, expelled something from his mouth. It hit the floor with a clank. He picked up the object, sprang to his feet, and slashed at Marcus's chest. A knife. The blade opened a slit from shoulder to shoulder. It wasn't deep. He punched at Asmodeus. The joker ducked under it and landed a jab on Marcus's chin. As he spun away, his knife sliced a gash to the bone on Marcus's forehead. It gushed blood.

Laughing, Asmodeus danced away. He gestured toward the audience, raising the knife and waving it about. "Here's my talent, kid," he shouted. "Give me enough time and I could cough up a samurai sword. That would be overkill in this situation."

The two engaged again. Asmodeus slashed and dodged, landing kicks every now and then. Marcus didn't want to risk his tongue, so he worked in close, pounding at him. He knew he was getting cut, but he didn't feel it. He could barely see, but it didn't matter. His own voice inside his head screamed at him to kill. It shouted and cursed and banged on his brain. The noise was incredible.

Asmodeus sank the blade into Marcus's tail. The pain of it threw him sideways. He couldn't see anything but blood, no matter how he tried to wipe his eyes free. In a moment of sheer panic, he realized he might lose. Ignoring the man's blade, Marcus grabbed blindly for him. He pulled him into an embrace, bashing his bloody head into Asmodeus's face. He pushed him down and wound his tail round and around him. Asmodeus thrashed and yelled, but Marcus got his arms pinned. His coils slid around him. He let go of him with his arms and just coiled and coiled, squeezed and squeezed and squeezed. . . .

♥

When Marcus awoke, he thought, *I killed a man. That can never be undone.* Was he changed by it? He wasn't sure yet. He hadn't meant to kill him. Not really. He wasn't sure what he felt. In the arena everything was different. Outside the arena . . . well, it was getting harder to tell the difference. Even Father Squid had admitted as much. Thinking of the priest, a flush of shame warmed his face.

Olena sat on the edge of the bed. She was fully clothed, leaning forward with her head clutched in her hands. She must've sensed that he was awake. She didn't turn, but she said, "Baba Yaga makes a promise to you."

Reaching out, Marcus touched her back.

Olena snapped, "No! You can't touch me."

"Why?" Marcus sat up.

"Because of Asmodeus."

"I took care of him. He doesn't matter anymore."

"He does matter. Baba Yaga is mad. You weren't supposed to kill him."

"He had a knife! He was going to kill me. Everyone saw that. I was . . ." Marcus tried to believe his own words, but it was hard to get them out. ". . . defending myself."

"But you didn't have permission. She didn't say you could kill him. That made her mad. Oh, she was mad. You don't even know."

"So what? What do I care if she's mad at me? She's an old—"

Olena shot to her feet and turned to face him. "Stupid! She's not just mad at you. She's mad at me. She thinks I made you do it. I didn't. I didn't say to kill him!"

"Okay," Marcus said, trying to soothe her. "I'll tell her that. I'll say it's not your fault."

"You don't understand nothing. She was going to kill you, Marcus! I begged for your life. You don't know how I begged. She didn't listen to me, but the crowd—to them she listens. The crowd went crazy. They loved watching you kill. They want more. They'll pay so much. So much. Enough that Baba Yaga thinks again. She thinks of something better than killing you. I tell you how it is. She made a promise to you, and told me to tell it. That's why I'm here. To tell you." Looking through a tangle of black hair, Olena looked miserable. And beautiful. Beautiful like nothing Marcus had ever seen before. "She said you have one more fight. She said . . ."

When she hesitated, Marcus slipped his body forward and grasped her arms, gently. "What did she say?"

She pulled away from him. She struggled to get the rest of the sentence out. ". . . it must be a fight to the death. 'You and the other troublemaker,' she said. 'Why not put them against each other?' She will make big money from it. High rollers coming in from Moscow. Billionaires from China. Vietnam. They want to watch a big death match. Is the only way for you to live. Is the only way for me to live. But, Marcus, if you fight, and win, she'll let us both go. That's what she said."

Marcus didn't hesitate in answering. The words just came straight from his heart to his mouth. And that was it. He was committed.

The Big Bleed

Part Seven

"DIVERSIFIED CONTENT."

Going by her voice alone, the assistant was a young woman, no older than early twenties, filled with attitude. Or so it seemed to Jamal Norwood when he called Berman's office.

Jamal identified himself. "I'd like to speak to Mr. Berman."

"And you are?" There it was again! As if Jamal had interrupted her at curing cancer or, more likely, repairing her nail polish.

"Jamal Norwood, also known as Stuntman. Mr. Berman knows me."

The assistant sighed, as if the effort of doing her very basic job was some kind of imposition. "Hold on."

The waiting music turned out to be hundred-strings versions of past Berman television theme songs. Which suggested to Jamal that Diversified was more than just a vanity card, Berman, and an assistant—that it might be a real production company.

The former producer of *American Hero* had his office in the Brill Building on Forty-ninth and Broadway, just north of Times Square. The eleven-story structure had been home to various songwriters, Broadway impresarios, and jumped-up television producers for the past seventy years. Jamal's SCARE research turned up a fifth-floor office number belonging to a Diversified Content, a name that was a perfect fit for Berman's smarmy self-conceit.

A bit of shoe leather reconnaissance would have told Jamal whether or not it was a real operation—DC was listed as a company that had "under twenty" employees, which could mean nineteen, or one. One employee would be easy to deal with. A dozen or more and Jamal's off-the-books operation would be outed.

He had considered an ambush interview at Berman's Upper East Side condo, especially since getting that home address had been a greater challenge. (The condo was owned by another of the producer's endless supply of personal service entities.)

But ambushes were tough to accomplish when you were in a hurry and your window of available time was narrow. Yes, you could stake out the man's condo and catch him on his way to work, if you had that time—which Jamal didn't.

The other option was to hit him coming home—but that could just as easily have been ten P.M. after a business dinner as seven.

He didn't want to spend three or four hours lurking without payoff.

A quick cost-benefit analysis convinced Jamal to simply phone the man at Diversified. And here he was, on the speaker. "Jamal Fucking Norwood!"

Jamal wondered who else was in the office with him. "Do I have a new middle name?"

"That's been your middle name since 2007," he said, laughing. "To me."

"Oh, good, I was afraid this was going to be contentious," Jamal said.

"You knew it was dangerous when you called me," Berman said. "What's on your mind? Is this about your new gig? Gonna say good-bye to being a G-man?"

"What new gig?"

"I hear you're top of Cinemax's want list for *I Witness*."

Jamal was momentarily stunned to silence. It wasn't impossible that Berman would know about the script—scripts floated around Hollywood like dandelion puffballs. But even Jamal didn't know that the project had been set up at Cinemax . . . which made it slightly more attractive as an alternative to SCARE. Assuming Jamal was ever strong enough to be Stuntman again. "No," he said, hoping his voice projected more confidence than he felt, "I'm still working for the national interest."

"Schmuck. What's on your mind?"

"I need to ask you some questions. About an investigation."

Suddenly Berman was off speakerphone. "Did I miss your transfer to the IRS?"

"Would it speed things up if I said this was an audit?"

"Not a chance. You'd have to get in line for that." Jamal heard thumping on a desktop—Berman obviously turning the phone or re-arranging some item. "If it's not my money, it's what?"

"There are some DVDs floating around that are going to cause someone to go to jail. And they all tie back to *American Hero*."

Jamal had the satisfaction of shutting Berman up for an entire ten seconds. "Well, then, it obviously behooves me to share what I know with law enforcement. When do you want to talk?"

"Let's start with right now."

"Let's revise that to two hours from now, my place."

"Okay." Berman rattled off an address that matched what Jamal had discovered.

Then, without a good-bye or even a parting shot, Berman was off the phone.

Which was good. Jamal needed to lie down for an hour. Of course, what he really needed was a shower to remove the taint of a conversation with Michael Berman.

The moment Jamal emerged from the cab at Berman's building, he was forced to make a further adjustment in his evaluation of the man's current success.

Berman's condo was in a building at 675 Madison Avenue, near Sixty-second a block east of Central Park. The building looked like an expensive hotel, the effect enhanced by its ground-floor tenant, a high-end English lingerie store. Jamal could easily picture Berman stopping on his way into or out of the building, window-shopping the models . . . possibly telephoning their agents while he smudged the window with his nose.

Jamal found the entrance, which was discreetly tucked to one side, and a doorman who granted him access to the elevators.

On this May evening, Michael Berman, creator and executive producer of *American Hero,* former CBS vice president of reality programming, current asshole for life, was still on the south side of forty—which, to Jamal Norwood, seemed impossible. He was one of those creatures that grew like mushrooms in Hollywood. More clever than smart, greedy to the point of idiocy, entirely lacking in moral standards, over-sexed, operating on the principle that what was theirs was theirs, what was yours was negotiable, possessing only a single useful skill . . . the ability to give an audience the things it wants.

Things that are bad for it. Empty calories. Heroin.

He opened the ornate door, and showed that the years had not been kind. True, he was wearing his Berman casual uniform of pressed jeans and tailored white dress shirt unbuttoned a button too far. But he had gained weight: his paunch strained the lower third of the shirt. And he had lost what little hair he had possessed in *American Hero* days. Then Berman had rarely been seen without a baseball cap.

"Boy," he said by way of greeting, "and I thought I looked like shit." Jamal knew that he had gained weight, too—thank you, hotel and restaurant food. And while there was no hair loss, he was moving slowly and looking sickly.

But then, strangely, Berman offered Jamal a hug.

"Checking for weapons?" Jamal said.

"Come on, man, we're foxhole buddies."

"From opposing armies."

Berman pointed an index finger at Jamal—his way of saying, *good one.* He indicated that Jamal should take a seat in the beautifully furnished living room, all white floors and rug, glass and white furnishings. "Something to drink or eat?"

"No thanks. On duty."

"That's it, remind me that I'm in a world of trouble."

"Since when do you need a reminder?"

Another finger, as Berman yelled, too loudly for the space, "Mollie, darling!"

Not unexpectedly, Berman wasn't alone.

"This is Mollie Steunenberg. Mollie, Jamal Norwood, the Stuntman. He's also an agent of SCARE, so be careful what you tell him."

Mollie offered her hand. She was a plump little redhead, maybe a year past twenty, wearing heels that were higher than absolutely necessary and a greenish summery dress that was so short as to be unappealing to anyone this side of a recent parolee. Someone had probably told Mollie that redheads should wear green. *Not that green, young lady.*

"Hey," she said, tiredly, nicely completing Jamal's mental portrait of Berman's bored assistant.

Berman flopped onto the couch. Jamal carefully lowered himself to the nearest chair. It felt good to sit.

"So, nasty DVDs," Berman said. "And you think I had something to do with them."

"The only thing every scene has in common is you."

Berman rocked his head from side to side, like a metronome. It was as obvious a tell as an eye blink from a nervous poker player. With Berman, it meant: I'm actually going to be honest. "Look around me, Jamal, and ask yourself this: what possible value would there be in my involvement in naughty outtakes from my shows? You don't get rich off stuff like that. And I'm rich."

Shit, Jamal realized, what if Berman wasn't the source? "If not you, then—"

Berman turned to the redhead. "Darling, who was I just complaining about five minutes before Agent Norwood called me?"

"You want the short list?"

"Don't fuck with daddy, baby." He was getting impatient.

"Joe Frank," she said.

"Joe Frank!" Berman said, turning to Jamal and gesturing, as if to say, *problem solved.*

"Okay, who's Joe Frank?"

"Mollie, tell Agent Norwood who Joe Frank is!" Berman smiled. "Because I can't fucking bear to talk about the cocksucker."

"Joe Frank," Mollie said, "is the cameraman Michael fired off *Jokers of New Jersey.*"

"What the hell is that?"

Mollie answered without being prompted. "Our new History Channel series about jokers trying to make lives for themselves as waitresses or plumbers or truck drivers—"

"In New Jersey?" Jamal said, finishing for her, wondering what that had to do with history—and whether or not there was suddenly some connection to Wheels.

"Tell Agent Norwood why, darling." Suddenly Berman stood up. "No, better yet, *show* him."

Like a hostess turning letters on a game show, Mollie tottered over to the big-screen, high-def television and expertly called up a display that showed nine pictures-within-picture, each one a fixed camera within the *American Hero* house in the Hollywood hills that Jamal knew so well.

"As you may recall, Agent Norwood, our various reality series locations are filled with cameras, all capturing unique footage that is then brutally and skillfully edited to create the fine entertainment that American audiences have come to expect from Diversified Content. But there's always a lot left over. Hours and hours of footage, most of it tedious beyond belief." Here Berman smiled. "Some of it rather private and salacious."

Mollie aimed the remote, and one small picture filled the screen . . . Jamal Norwood emerging from the shower, naked and semi-erect. "Look away, Mollie," Berman said, smiling wickedly. "I wouldn't want your love for me to be affected by the sight of Agent Norwood in his . . . natural state."

Jamal was too ill to be embarrassed. He was also growing tired of this hound and horse show, though he was impressed that Berman had been sufficiently frightened that he'd created an actual pitch. "There's more to this than just aces gone wild," Jamal said. "These things are also snuff films."

Berman did his head tilt again. "I fired Joe Frank because we caught him copying raw files on *NJ2*, Jamal. I have no idea who else he was working for or had worked for. I just know that he was a cheap motherfucking sleaze." He smiled again. "And when I say that, you know it's bad."

Before Jamal could respond, Berman turned to Mollie. "Get Agent Norwood our file on Joe Fucking Frank, please." Then he stood up, terminating the interview.

At the door, Jamal accepted a thick letter-sized envelope from Mollie's hands. For an instant, he felt something tingly and life-affirming. He had been dismissing Mollie Steunenberg as a truck stop waitress who had probably slept her way into a job in New York and a tawdry relationship with Berman.

Nothing about her had changed . . . but Jamal decided that her freckled nose was actually rather appealing, that she had a pretty voice, and maybe that green wasn't wrong.

"Thanks, darling," Berman said, dismissing her.

He did watch her go, and worse yet, caught Jamal watching her totter and wriggle back into the living room. "Just for the record, I'm not sleeping with her," Berman said, using the most normal voice Jamal had ever heard from the man.

"So noted."

"Just in case you want to take a shot . . ."

"Thanks."

Then the old Berman was back, clapping him on the shoulder. "Hear much from Julia these days?"

Jamal blinked. For the second time today, Berman had managed to make it clear that he knew too much about Jamal's business. "We're in touch," he said, neutrally. "Do you know her?"

Berman made his *oh, come on* face. "I know everyone I need to know, right?" He sipped his drink. "Nice girl." Smirked. "Petite. Bit of a mouth on her."

"Never boring."

"I bet you really want to get back to Hollywood."

"It's crossed my mind," Jamal said. There was no point in trying to game Berman: the man possessed a freakish power of perception that could have qualified him for wild card status.

And Jamal suddenly wondered if Mollie Steunenberg didn't have a power, too.

Jamal needed the cab ride back to the Bleecker to gather his strength.

With what felt a lot like his dying breath, Jamal tapped the auto-dial for Franny. Thank God, he picked up. "I just left Berman," he said.

"And yet you live."

"Barely," he said, meaning it in a way that Franny couldn't know. He gave him the recap. "Consider the source, who happens to be a pathological liar . . . but the DVDs came from this Joe Frank individual. Berman was kind enough to give me his address and phone, in case I was motivated to contact him."

Franny gratefully thanked him for the information. "I'll handle this particular numbnuts."

"Let me know how it goes."

All he wanted to do was lie down.

Maybe forever.

But first a shower: he truly needed it now.

Galahad in Blue

Part Seven

THE GARROTE WAS DEEPLY embedded in the skin of Joe Frank's throat. Frank was an older man, maybe late fifties, early sixties with a face lined by the sun and years. Rivulets of blood filled the wrinkles on his turkey-like neck. His blackened swollen tongue protruded from between purpled lips, and his eyes were open and staring.

"Son of a bitch," Franny said.

The small apartment would have been pleasant if it hadn't been trashed. Cushions on the chairs and sofa had been ripped open, books and DVDs and a few VHS tapes were pulled off the bookcase.

The moment Jamal had provided him with the cameraman's name and address Franny had headed straight to SoHo to find a door that swung open at his first knock, and a body. It was only that unlocked door that had Franny inside. Joe Frank's murderer hadn't cared enough to close the door behind him, much less lock it. The man's contempt and confidence had saved Franny the trouble of a warrant. The only plus in this shit sandwich.

Franny called in the crime, and while he waited for criminalistics and an ambulance to arrive he donned gloves and began to search the apartment. He doubted he would find anything. The thoroughness of the search conducted by Frank's murderer extended to every room. In the kitchen every cabinet, cereal box, and canister had been emptied. In the bedroom the mattress lay on the floor looking like a gutted white whale. Every drawer, every article of clothing had been searched. In the bathroom Franny's shoes crunched on broken porcelain from the shattered toilet tank lid.

The evidence techs and a coroner arrived along with a detective from the 9th Precinct. He was not happy with Franny, and indicated that he found Franny's rather disjointed explanation of why he was even in Joe Frank's apartment to be less than compelling—though he didn't phrase it that way. What he said was far more terse, and expletive filled. He promised his captain would be calling Franny's captain.

Before he headed back to the 5th Franny swung by the street corner where the aces had confiscated the DVDs. He wasn't surprised when he found the bootleg DVD seller had vanished. Probably decided things had gotten too hot. Or he was dead too.

When Franny returned to the 5th Homer was quick to tell him that Captain Mendelberg wanted him in her office—pronto. "And she is *pissed*." He drew out the word with obvious relish.

"What the fuck were you doing in SoHo?" she asked the moment Franny stepped into the office. Her ears were waving more than usual.

"Ummm, well, I had a tip."

"From who?"

Franny knew her eyes were always bloodred, but did they seem redder than usual? "Umm, Agent Norwood."

"And why, pray tell, are you taking tips from a Fed?"

So, he tried to explain. About *American Hero,* and the audition lists, and the DVDs, and how all of that led them

to Berman, but the longer he talked the more convoluted
and confusing it seemed even to him.

"So when Jamal ... uh, Agent Norwood got this cameraman's name he did the right thing and turned it over
to me ... and ... I ... went ... there ..."

Mendelberg was staring at him. Kept staring at him.
"Get out of here, and try to do some work that might
actually result in us finding our missing citizens!"

"Yes, ma'am."

♠

The fifth martini was going down a lot smoother than it
had any business doing. Franny and Jamal sat in a booth
at a cop watering hole just outside Jokertown on its
northern edge. "The Ninth is ruling it a home invasion,"
Franny muttered into his glass.

"Yeah, so many burglars carry a fucking garrote,"
Jamal said, and took another sip of his beer.

"Yeah."

"Dead end," Jamal said.

"Yeah," said Franny.

"I think that bastard knew he was dead when he sent
us his way."

"He? Who? Huh?" The amount of alcohol he'd consumed was making it hard for Franny to untangle all the
pronouns.

"Berman. I think he knew the cameraman was dead
when he gave me his name," Jamal said.

"Throwing him under the bus."

"Exactly."

"But we can't prove it."

"I know. We can't prove a goddam thing."

Franny sat quietly for a moment, feeling the alcohol
buzz through his bloodstream. "We know from the
DVDs that the missing jokers are fighting in an arena ...

somewhere. And we know people are betting on the fights."

"Yeah. Like dog fights."

"Uh huh, but a really different crowd than you find at a dog fight. Tuxedos, fancy dresses, bling, but fancy bling—diamonds and rubies and emeralds and stuff." Franny's tongue felt thick. "Berman's a big Hollywood guy. He could be in that crowd. Instead he's providing them with the names and abilities of jokers—or so we think. So maybe he's working off something."

"People bet on *American Hero*," Jamal said thoughtfully. "How could we find out?"

"My undergraduate degree is in accounting," Franny said. "Then I went to law school—"

"And then you became a cop. You're an idiot."

"But lucky for us, an over-educated one."

Ties That Bind

Part Four

"KAVITHA! I NEED TO talk to you!" Minal was hollering down the hall, giving Michael a headache. This was not a great way to start the day. He stumbled out of bed, to hear Kavitha shouting back, "After rehearsal!" and disappearing out the door. God. She'd spent almost the entire day yesterday at the studio, and now she was gone so early? It wasn't even six A.M. yet. He wasn't even sure they turned on the AC in her building at this hour of the morning.

"Michael, I know you don't like dealing with money, but we have to talk about this," Minal said, walking up to him, frowning, hands balled on her hips. Finances always gave him a headache—maybe the residue of all those years of hearing his parents worry about money, about whether the laundromat would make enough to see it through another month. It had been such a relief when Minal, capable Minal, had taken over the family finances. "She spent way more than her discretionary budget allows for yesterday."

"Minal, that's not my problem. Take it up with Kavitha." Michael was relieved that it really wasn't his problem. He had enough to worry about. He was going to go back and re-check the docks for Sandip on his lunch break today; he'd thought of a few more places worth looking at.

Minal thumped him gently on the arm. "I tried to talk to her! You saw—she just ran away from me."

Maya Aunty came out of Isai's bedroom, the child rubbing sleepy eyes and holding her grandmother's hand. "What is the problem? Why all the shouting? I would be happy to give you children some money."

"No, no, Aunty," Minal said hastily. "We have plenty. It's just important to stick to a budget, you know? Kavitha has always had trouble with that, but we've been working on it—I thought we finally had an agreement. She was being so good, but now—"

"It's a difficult time," Maya Aunty said quietly. Isai let go of her hand and climbed up into Michael's arms for a good morning hug. He buried his face in her unruly hair and took a moment to enjoy the fierce embrace of his daughter. This part, he loved.

Minal sighed. "I know. She probably bought herself some new clothes to cheer herself up. Although I haven't noticed any shopping bags."

Isai slid down impatiently and went to give Minal the same monster hug treatment. Michael said, "Maybe she was embarrassed. She might have left them at the studio." It was sort of charming, actually—he could imagine Kavitha there, surreptitiously trying on clothes in front of the big glass mirrors. Something red and slinky would look so great on her, although that wasn't really her style. Maybe when all this was over, he would buy her something she could wear out to dinner, with his ring on her finger. He was pretty sure Minal already had plenty of slinky red dresses. Although it might be the better part of wisdom to get her a present too. A man didn't survive this long with two girlfriends without learning a few things.

Minal sighed in reluctant agreement. "I suppose we can talk about this later. C'mon, sweetie." She settled Isai more comfortably on her hip. "Time for morning potty and teeth brushing."

Morning potty was another thing Michael was happy to leave to Minal, along with the financial headaches. Right now, all he wanted was coffee. "Coffee, Aunty?" That, he could take care of.

Yesterday, Kavitha's mother had finally explicitly told Michael to call her Maya Aunty. It was a huge concession, and won only after her husband had decamped. He had tried to persuade her to come too, saying, "What is the point, *kunju*? The boy will come home when he wants to come home—it's not up to us."

She had responded, "You! You are the one who drove him away! Go, go now. I will stay, and make sure that he comes home."

And so Maya had stayed, moving into Isai's bedroom, giving them back their living room. A bit of breathing space, and even some grandmotherly babysitting— whatever her prejudices, Maya had been completely won over by her grandchild. And Isai, for her part, adored her new grandmother. It was endearing, if bizarre, to see the old woman crooning over her grandchild, singing old lullabies in Tamil while preening the girl's shape-shifted feathers.

So things were relatively quiet at home, and quieter at work too—no new snatches. There were reports of similar incidents overseas, but nothing in America recently. Yesterday, he'd found the final link in his smuggling case; it was all over, except for the paperwork. Michael was going to keep looking for Sandip, of course, but he was still hoping Sandip would find his own way home soon. Michael was almost ready to relax—until he was ambushed in his own home.

Maya dug into her dressing gown pocket. "I do not want coffee. I want to know, what is this?" she hissed, holding up a little red box, practically shoving it into Michael's nose.

"Where did you find that?" Michael whispered, with a glance down the hall, to where Minal was in the bathroom with Isai. The door was closed; she shouldn't hear anything, as long as he finished this quickly. Follow a question with a question, that's what he'd been taught—keep them on the defensive. Easy to say, hard to do, especially when your heart is racing.

"I wanted to wash your jackets and coats yesterday; winter is coming."

Not for months! "You don't need to do that, Aunty," Michael said, automatically.

She frowned. "If I don't, who will? At least that girl"—she always referred to Minal as *that girl*—"can cook, but none of you clean properly. You live in filth."

Michael was glad neither of the women were around to hear that—Minal would probably shrug and move on, but Kavitha would be hurt. She was just beginning to mend her relationship with her mother, but it was a fragile peace—she wasn't up to taking much in the way of criticism yet. Michael had had enough of conflict in the last month to last him a lifetime.

Yet here Maya came with more. "So what does this mean?" She flipped the box open, letting the two rings sparkle. One was a vintage ring, lots of tiny little diamonds in an intricate setting, for Kavitha, who loved old things. And the other was a single large-ish diamond, flanked by two tiny rubies—that one was for Minal; he'd thought she'd appreciate a flashy rock to show her old street friends. Neither ring was terribly expensive, but the best he could afford on a detective's salary.

"It should be obvious, I think," Michael said, striving for calm.

"For both of them?"

Quiet certainty, that was the tone to use. He needed to sound sure of himself, even if he wasn't. Maya would leap on weakness like a shark on its prey. "Yes."

She raised a diminutive eyebrow. "So what are you waiting for?"

"What?" He felt as if she'd just punched him with that tiny little hand.

"How long have these been sitting in your pocket?"

"Umm . . . a while?" Had it really been less than a month since Sally had gotten that promotion? The weeks with Black as his putative partner seemed endless.

Maya snapped, "A while? Do you know how far we could have gotten in planning the wedding in a while?"

Michael frowned, bewildered. "You mean—you're happy about this? You wouldn't mind if your daughter married a man who was also marrying someone else?" This was not the reaction he'd expected.

Maya frowned right back, and stepped even closer to him. He wanted to step back, but he was enough of a cop to stand his ground. He wasn't going to be pushed around by a little old lady, even if she was his almost-mother-in-law. Maya said, "It's not the marriage I would have chosen for her. But the important thing is that she get married. She is so old."

Michael winced. Another thing Kavitha didn't need to hear.

Maya continued, "Besides, the marriage is your affair. The wedding is mine. I will have to hurry if we want to reserve elephants for next summer. We cannot get them any earlier, I am quite sure."

"Elephants?" Michael felt as if she'd added a set of brass knuckles to the fist she was punching into his gut. Metaphorically.

She sighed. "Well, of course, elephants. In the old days, we would have had to go back to Sri Lanka for a proper wedding, but now, things are advanced. You can get anything you need here. The elephants, thali necklace, saris, saffron and jasmine, a priest willing to perform mixed marriages . . ."

"There isn't going to be a Hindu priest," Michael protested. His parents would freak out if the wedding wasn't Catholic. God, he hadn't even thought of that. But Maya just flipped her hands in his face.

"Details, details. You let me worry about that. Me and your mother—we'll sort it out. Don't worry about the money—we have plenty saved up. I was going to spend it on a luxury cruise, since I didn't think the girl would ever get married, but cruises can wait."

"Aunty—"

She stopped him, with a raised hand in front of his face. "Michael. Do you love them? Both of them?"

It was so strange—the last few weeks had been so crazy, there hadn't been any time for fun, or romance, or even sex. And he still couldn't really imagine the life to come, when he was married to two women, until death did them part. He was pretty sure that wasn't a wise choice for an ambitious man who wanted to go far with his career. But when she asked the question, Michael was surprised to find that none of that mattered. Because the answer was easy, it just slipped right out, grounded in a bone-deep certainty. "Yes."

Minal with her cooking and sexiness and the practical competence that got the four of them through their days; Kavitha with her beauty and grace, her passion for family and commitment to lofty ideals. Michael loved them both to death, so much that it was easier not to think about it. He wasn't sure a man should love a woman, especially two women, so much.

"So ask her, *kunju*," Maya said, her tone suddenly gentled. "Ask them both. Life is short, and unpredictable. You must take happiness where you can. If the past few weeks have taught me nothing else, they have taught me that." Her eyes were bright, but her voice was steady.

"I'm sure Sandip will turn up," Michael offered weakly.
He wasn't sure of any such thing.

Maya just pushed the ring box into his hand, shook
her head in that strange South Asian gesture that meant
yes—no—and it's in the hands of the gods all at once,
and turned away, her shoulders erect and unwavering.

God. Michael swore, if he had a dozen like her on the
force, he'd clean up this dirty city in a month.

Just ask them. Okay. What the hell had he been waiting for?

◆

Michael had thought about how to do it. He couldn't ask
one of them first, and then the other—that would be too
strange, and might lead to problems. It had to be both at
once, and the only time he had alone with them both was
at night, once Isai and Maya had gone to bed. But he'd
also eventually realized that he couldn't ask them in
bed—it would be too weird. Like saying "I love you"
right after an orgasm—no one could take it seriously. So
not in bed, but after Maya and Isai were asleep. Which
meant during dishes, which they usually did at the very
end of the day, after picking up the disaster of scattered
toys. It wasn't the most romantic time ever, but it was
the best he could do.

Usually Michael washed, Minal dried, and Kavitha put
away. It was fast and efficient, but tonight Michael left
Kavitha to wash the dishes and disappeared into the
front hall. The box was waiting in his jacket pocket, the
rings still safe inside. He took it in a hand that was suddenly shaking—it was funny; he'd faced down more than
his share of bad guys, some of them with guns, some of
them twisted by their wild cards into something scarier
than a gun. Yet here he was, the big bad black cop,
shaking.

Michael took a deep breath, steadied his hand, and

then turned and walked back down the hall, into the kitchen. He'd left the room with everything calm; he came back in to find the women bent over the sink, snapping at each other in lowered voices, clearly angry, but also careful not to wake Kavitha's mother or the child.

"Are you serious?" Kavitha asked, her hands still furiously washing dishes. "You're going to abandon me now? We still have no idea where Sandip is." Her voice was sharper, more shrill, than Michael had ever heard it. He felt a pang of guilt that he wasn't looking harder for her brother. Although he had his doubts that the kid was even still in New York. Maybe he'd managed to cross the border, go back to Toronto, to hang with his friends. Wasn't that the sort of thing teenagers did?

Minal took a plate from her and rubbed it dry. "I'm not trying to abandon you. Gods, I know you're a performer, but do you have to be such a drama queen? Don't you think it would be easier, if I weren't here? Spring semester will be over in two more days—I can take the summer off, head out of town for a month or two. It won't be so crowded here; you won't be tripping over each other."

Kavitha said flatly, "You just don't want to deal with my mother anymore."

Minal sighed. "Look, I won't claim it's easy talking to her, especially when she so carefully avoids discussing our relationship. But it's not that. She's actually kind of sweet, in her own way. I just don't want to make her life harder right now."

"You think I do?" Kavitha's hands stilled in the soapy water of the sink.

"Oh, God. That's not what I was saying! Michael, will you tell her, please? Can you explain what I meant?" Minal turned to him, finally seeing the box in his outstretched hand. "Oh, shit."

Kavitha turned too, her open mouth abruptly closing. He didn't want to know what she'd been about to say.

He didn't know what he ought to say. This wasn't how he'd pictured this going.

Well, he wasn't going to put the box away, not now. He popped it open, so the rings were visible, and slightly awkwardly slid to one knee in front of them. "Umm . . . I love you. I love you both. Will you marry me?"

Minal looked at Kavitha, then back at him. "You idiot. Your timing sucks. But yes, of course. Yes." She grinned widely, and reached a joyful hand out to Kavitha. "Sweetheart? Marry us?"

Kavitha swallowed, and took a step back, pressing up against the porcelain sink. It seemed like an endless awful time before she said, "I'm so sorry. I can't. No."

The Big Bleed

Part Eight

AFTER THE WORST TWENTY-FOUR hours he could remember, Jamal returned to his Bleecker Street room at eleven P.M. Tuesday night.

And found Sheeba waiting for him.

"The logical question," he said, panting as if he'd climbed the stairs rather than ridden the elevator, "is how the hell you got in here."

"I'm a federal agent? It gives a lot of leeway with hotel managers. And when that fails, I can fly. Remember. You should sit down."

The suggestion was unnecessary: Jamal had already collapsed in a chair.

"Here's where I also say, 'whassup?' " He barely managed his street black voice. "If this is an intervention, you should have my parents and my girlfriend, too."

"You've got a *girlfriend*?" She shook her head. "Jamal, you aren't well. You've been running off and not telling anybody where—"

"—On my own time."

She held up a hand. "No malfeasance is suggested."

"Christ, Sheeba, you've been in management too long—"

She bristled. Of course, Jamal had used "Christ" improperly. "I just want to help."

"While getting in my business."

"That seems unavoidable, since your business is our business."

"Well," Jamal said, "this wasn't really a sin of commission as much as omission. I'm tired of hiding it."

They had done Memorial Day duty with the Rodham campaign, then up early on Tuesday for Holy Roller— again; his appearances seemed to require double Secret Service and SCARE detachments—and no release from duty until ten that night.

With the late Wednesday, Jamal had been able to visit Dr. Finn at Jokertown Clinic—the doctor had asked him to come in Thursday the week before, but there had been no time. "You appear to be suffering from muscular deterioration."

"Do you know what or why or whether anything can be done?"

"No to all of those, at least provisionally."

Had he felt strong enough, he would have lunged across the desk at the doctor. "Mind if I ask what the fuck you have been doing?"

If Finn was disturbed by Jamal's vehemence, he didn't show it. He merely indicated the files spread out on his desk. "Eliminating other factors, mostly. Environmental, chemical—"

"So this is something in my wiring."

"It appears to be." The centaur paused, as if searching for something positive to offer. "You may be the first of your type."

"So after this kills me, it will be known as the Jamal Norwood Disease? Do I get to address the crowd at fucking Yankee Stadium, too?"

"Mr. Norwood, it is difficult and progressive, but not . . . dire." He cleared his throat. "I would advise you to take a much less . . . active role in your work, possibly go on leave. Help us with tests and conserve your energy."

There had been more, but Jamal could no longer remember it. It all added up to . . . telling the Angel everything that had happened to him.

By the end, Sheeba, bless her, was blinking back tears and reaching for Jamal's hand. "Oh my God, Jamal. This sounds awful."

"Try feeling it."

"We feel it," a man said from the bedroom doorway.

Carnifex himself entered. Jamal couldn't decide which annoyed him more: the fact that Billy Ray was part of this . . . or that he hadn't even thought to look and listen. "That was pretty sneaky."

Ray chose not to acknowledge the rebuke. "Here's the deal: you're on medical leave until further notice."

Jamal was looking at the floor, feeling nothing but relief as Ray continued: "I'm going to light a fire under our medical people and get you into Johns Hopkins. I can't believe you've been dicking around with the Jokertown Clinic all this time."

"They're sort of the world's specialists in folks like us."

"They give Band-Aids and aspirin to jokers, Norwood. They may have some sympathetic docs there, but that place is as far from a world-class research facility as you are from being a first-rate agent."

Typical Billy Ray: never pass up a chance to step on a subordinate.

He stood up. Sheeba did, too. "Jamal, is there anything you need tonight?"

"Sleep," he told her, quite truthfully. "It will be nice not to have to hit the road tomorrow."

♥

Billy Ray and Sheeba had not mentioned it, but Jamal assumed that being on leave would mean loss of access. *So use it while you've got it.*

The first thing to do was follow up on a promise he'd made to Franny, to search the intel database for Joseph Frank—

Well, no. First thing was, open a beer and pour it into a glass.

Then repeat.

It didn't make him feel stronger, but he did feel *better*.

Then it was back to the computer, playing cyber sleuth. Jamal was surprised to find that, in the past fourteen months, Joseph Daniel Frank had made a number of exits from the USA and entrances to the Republic of Kazakhstan.

It further developed that Mr. Frank had been involved in a disturbance—a drunken dispute with a prostitute that resulted in a beating and an arrest (in Kazakhstan, likely the same thing)—three months ago.

In the city of Talas. Talas. Not Astana, the capital.

Talas, specifically at a casino-nightclub named Maxim's.

What was in Talas that would draw Michael Berman's cameraman there repeatedly over the past year-plus?

What would a real cyber sleuth do here? Well, since the one given was that Joe Frank, and by extension, Michael Berman, had to be involved in something illegal, Jamal ought to search for criminal enterprises or individuals that could be tied to the city of Talas, of course.

That turned out to be a rich vein. Kazakhstan was an oil producer, with oil producer–level corruption. Drugs, whores, counterfeiting, human trafficking, all on a significant scale—especially for a city with a population under fifty thousand.

Drilling down in each category, Jamal built up a list

of names and links that he saved in another file. By the time he had gone through the primary areas of criminal activity, he realized one name showed up in all four: a party known as "Baba Yaga."

There was no file on Baba Yaga, just a name and a list of activities that filled a page. All agencies were on record as welcoming further details—

God bless those foreign crime lords. They were always coming up with cute names for themselves. Johnny Batts. The Vicar. Of course, Jamal himself was known as Stuntman and he worked with the Midnight Angel—

Whatever. The name "Baba Yaga" was familiar to Jamal from some childhood book or movie, so he called up Wikipedia for a refresher even as he pictured some slick-haired, black-eyed young thug out of *Scarface*.

Oh. It turned out that Baba Yaga was a witch or a hag. Didn't sound like the kind of name a young male hood would choose . . . unless that young male hood had a terrific sense of humor, which was not usually part of the ensemble.

Male or female, Scarface or hag, this Baba Yaga owned an establishment named Maxim's. Which happened to be the establishment where citizen Joseph Frank got in trouble with a hooker.

Jamal sat back. Detective Francis Xavier Black was going to find this useful. Which was a good thing, because Agent Jamal Norwood was down for the count, out of the game, on the disabled list.

Likely for the rest of his short life.

No Parking

Mon–Fri 7–9am 3–5pm
Except Buses

No Loading Except Authorized
Commercial Vehicles

Mon–Fri 9am–3pm Except Wednesday
With Pass—1 Hour Limit

Snow Emergency Route/No Parking
Odd Side During Snow Emer.

No Parking 3–5am March/November
No Standing Other Times

---

by Ian Tregillis

WALLY GUNDERSON SIGHED WHEN he saw the conglomeration of parking signs. They were bolted to a single streetlight, like a profusion of fungus on a steel tree. His steam-shovel jaw creaked up and down as he read each line to himself, trying to decipher Jokertown's byzantine parking regulations. He scratched his forehead. It sounded like a railroad spike dragged across an iron skillet.

No *standing*? What the heck did *that* mean?

The blare of a car horn broke his concentration. A hairy lizard leaned from a window of the delivery truck idling behind Wally's rusted and battered '76 Impala.

"Hey, Tin Man!" she yelled. "Move it!"

He glanced at his watch. *Crud*. He'd be late picking up Ghost again. The adoption committee got sore about stuff like that.

He didn't have time to cruise around for a different spot. But Wally wasn't very good at parallel parking—it would take just as long shimmying the car back and forth to ease into the spot. Plus, he felt pretty badly when he scraped the other cars. So he used a shortcut.

Wally hopped out of the Impala. The lizard lady lay on her horn. He waved at her. Crouching alongside his car, he reached underneath to grip the frame in one hand. He paid careful attention to his hands, knowing from experience that if he wasn't careful he ran the risk of accidentally rusting through the chassis. Then, after wrapping his other arm over the trunk, he gave the car a solid shove.

It skidded sideways seven feet and slammed against the curb. It went straight into the gap, but Wally overshot. The Impala bounced over the curb, cracked against the parking meter, and scraped a Toyota on the rebound. The Toyota's car alarm shrieked. The parking meter toppled to the sidewalk with a crash.

"Nuts," said Wally. "Not again." The delivery truck sped past him.

He surveyed the damage. The meter had been felled like a tree in high winds, complete with a little clump of concrete at the base like the root ball. The LCD window in the meter blinked nonsense patterns of static hash before fading to black, like the last gasp of a dying robot. He couldn't open the Impala's passenger door, which now sported a large dent. He'd have to pound it back into shape later.

From the glove compartment, he fished out a notepad, pen, and roll of duct tape. Wally scrawled a note of apology on the pad, tore off the sheet, folded some money into the note, and taped the package to the broken meter. Duct tape worked better than masking tape. This he'd learned through trial and error.

People were staring. Wally gave a guilty shrug, then headed at a fast walk toward the Jerusha Carter Childhood Development Institute. He glanced at his watch again. The fast walk became a jog. The pounding of his iron feet left a trail of cracks in the sidewalk.

Things would have been so much easier if he could take the subway. But sometimes it got crowded, and when that happened people got shoved up against him, and when that happened the seams and rivets of his iron skin could hurt folks. Didn't matter how careful he was.

As he passed the Van Renssaeler Memorial Clinic, a flash of yellow caught Wally's attention. He paused at the entrance to the Institute, his hand resting on the door. A boxy three-wheeled cart turned the corner a few blocks up. It was painted blue and white like a police car and had a yellow strobe on top. The cart puttered along the row of parked cars. It eased to a stop alongside a Volkswagen. The driver strutted out, brandishing a ticket pad. A dishwater blond ponytail poked from the brim of her hat.

Wally sighed. "Aw, rats. Not her again."

Ghost hadn't yet finished her counseling session when he arrived. She sat cross-legged on the floor in one of the glassed-in side rooms along the courtyard, talking to one of the Institute's child psychologists. The doc saw Wally but kept her attention on Ghost. Wally's foster daughter didn't see him. He tiptoed away.

Ghost had resisted the counseling for quite a while; it had been a relief for all involved when she started engaging with the teachers and staff at the Institute. For the longest time she trusted only one adult, and that adult was Wally. He'd rescued her from the life of a child soldier in the People's Paradise of Africa, where she had been an experiment: infected, traumatized, brainwashed, trained to kill. But she was also a little girl who liked Legos, Dr. Seuss, and peanut-butter-and-mango sandwiches.

More and more, she was a little girl. But traces of the soldier remained. And probably always would.

A few of her classmates played in the courtyard. They shouted and waved at Wally. He knew most of them; he and Ghost had been coming here since before the Institute opened. There was little Cesar, whom he'd known as long as Ghost, and who faced similar counseling issues; Moto, the boy who exhaled searing gouts of flame when he got excited, or frightened, or a case of the hiccups; Allen, whose mother and father were both in jail; Jo, who always wore the top half of a cow costume and refused to say anything except "Moo" and "Dickwad." Some of the children had come from Africa, like Moto and Cesar, though not with Wally. Others had come to the Institute in the intervening years.

The world was full of troubled kids. But you couldn't save them all. Wally had learned that the hard way. No matter how much he wanted to, he couldn't forget the smell of the mass grave in Nyunzu, where his pen pal had been murdered. Failing Lucien was the worst thing he had ever done. The shame made Wally so sad and angry that sometimes he wanted to punch the whole world.

He swallowed the stone in his throat and waved to the kids. "Howdy," he said.

An immense baobab tree shaded the sandbox. Wally laid a hand on its bark. "Hi, you," he whispered. The surrounding building shielded the tree from wind, but sometimes it seemed as though the leaves rustled in response to his greeting. The baobab smelled of rain, and jungle, and a lost friend. It made Wally smile, but it also made him feel lonely. Sometimes it felt like his ribs were still shattered, pushing spurs of bone to pierce his heart. But he tried not to let it show.

Wally knelt in the sandbox. "So what kind of trouble are you guys getting into today?"

"Moo," said Jo. Her cotton cow ears flopped up and down. "Dickwad. Moo."

"She says she's glad you're back," said Cesar. "I'm moving to Brooklyn!" he added. "I'm going to have a room and my own bed and everything. And they even said I could have a birthday party! You'll come, right?"

"Heck yeah, pal. We wouldn't miss it for the world."

Moto sniffled. His tears wafted across the courtyard like smoke from an extinguished candle. Wally put an arm around him. The heat from his breath seeped into Wally's skin, conducting through the metal across his back and sides, to soothe an old surgery scar/weld. It felt good.

The poor kid didn't get many hugs. Wally also knew, from what Ghost told him, that Moto had been bounced from his third foster home. Another accidental bedroom fire. His foster parents lacked the patience to sleep in shifts.

"Hey," he said. "You know what Ghost asked me the other day? She asked if we could throw a party for your birthday. Would you like that?"

The sniffles trailed off. "Really?"

"Well sure, why not?"

Moto hugged him again. Wally made a mental note to buy another fire extinguisher.

When Wally sifted his fingers through the sand they came back covered with random phrases: "The joy a." "A rainbow it axe." "Shadow the the running barn to under." A few days earlier another foster parent had brought a set of refrigerator poetry magnets for the kids' message board. At least half of these were already scattered in the sand.

Wally didn't understand poetry. He didn't read much.

Allen saw the magnets stuck to his iron fingers and tossed the letter "H" at his chest. It stuck with a muted *click*. Wally could feel the tug of the magnet through his coveralls, like a faint buzzing in the rivets of his sternum.

"Gosh," he said. "That tickles."

Moto saw what Allen had done and flung a handful of magnets and sand at Wally's shoulder. He blinked the sand out of his eyes to see the letters "R," "G," and the word "cattle" stuck to his forearm. Moto covered his mouth when he giggled; little tongues of flame fluttered through his fingers. Then Jo got into the act. Wally lay sprawled in the sand while the kids climbed over him. Laughter and the stink of melted plastic filled the courtyard.

Wally had to pluck the magnets from his scalp a couple of times. They made his head feel funny, like he had a mild fever, or as if his brain were stuffed with cotton. The game went for a few more minutes until Ghost's session ended. Her therapist followed her into the courtyard.

"Moo," said Jo.

"Hi, Ghost," said Cesar.

"Huh," Ghost said, and shrugged.

The therapist beckoned to Wally. He rolled gently to his feet, careful not to pinch little fingers or toes under his bulk. He hugged Ghost just as gently, but more firmly.

"How was your day? I broke another parking meter."

She shrugged, and then became insubstantial to pull away from his hug. She floated to the sandbox, toes dangling an inch above the ground, before settling to earth alongside Allen. It had been a while since she'd been so withdrawn. Wally wondered if he'd find her standing over his bed in the middle of the night with a knife in her hands, like the haunted little girl he'd met in the jungle.

"Okey-dokey. You guys just hang out for a sec," said

Wally. He followed the doctor into a cloister alongside the courtyard. "What's going on, Doc?"

The psychiatrist wore her hair pulled back, and the scarf around her neck matched her earrings. She looked fancy, like somebody on TV. Her name tag read "Dr. Miranda." She shook her head.

"Yerodin threatened a classmate with a pair of scissors today." Yerodin was Ghost's real name. All the adults at the Institute used it, but she hated it when Wally called her that.

"Awww, cripes," said Wally. He ran a hand over his face and added "new bedspread" to the mental shopping list, just under "fire extinguisher." "How come?"

"She's been acting up all week. Since we told the children that Mr. Richardson was ill."

Wally remembered Richardson. Ghost talked about him a lot. He taught math, and sometimes he gave the kids rides on his carapace. He could fit three or four of them on the flat of his back, between pairs of detachable legs. He kind of reminded Wally of Dr. Finn, except more like a bug than a horse. He also told really corny jokes, which Ghost loved.

"Well that's a bummer. What's he sick with?"

Dr. Miranda lowered her voice. "That's what we told the children, but he hasn't called in sick. N-nobody has seen him since last Friday."

Wally said, "She's been doing real good at home, you know. Real good."

"Well, she wasn't today. She still reverts to using sharp objects when she feels angry or frustrated."

"Okay. I'll have a talk with her." Wally frowned. "Will this affect the adoption?"

She started to answer, but then her face crumpled into a scowl a second before Jo started to bawl.

"DickWAAAD!"

Wally turned just in time to see Ghost, scissors in hand,

stuffing a trophy in her pocket: a cotton cow ear from Jo's costume. The sobbing girl didn't pull away when Ghost pulled the second ear taut and opened the scissors.

Wally vaulted the cloister railing. He crossed the courtyard in one hard stride. But rather than pulling Ghost away, or lifting Jo out of reach, he gave the blades a gentle flick of his finger. They dissolved into a fine orange mist. Ghost floated away.

"Cripes, kid," he called after her.

Wally spent a few minutes consoling Jo. "Don't you worry. We'll fix your ears right up. You'll hear good as new, okay?" Wally couldn't sew. But maybe he and Ghost could learn together. That sounded like a good idea.

"Moo," said Jo between sniffles. "Moo . . . moo . . ."

Wally found Ghost with Dr. Miranda. Silently, they packed up her teddy-bear backpack, plastic bag of dry cereal, and Dr. Seuss book. The doctor gave Wally a Look as he led Ghost down the corridor. His feet left deep imprints in the carpet, but not as low as Jo probably felt.

He said, "That was a pretty crummy thing you did."

"I don't care," said Ghost. "She's dumb. I hate her."

"No you don't. She's your friend. Remember the time I forgot to pack your juice and she shared hers with you?"

"No."

"Really? I know a guy, an ace like us, and he can tell if somebody is lying or not. But when he does it to you, it feels like having a hundred spiders crawling all over your body." Ghost shrugged. She'd spent a lot of time in the jungle. Creepy-crawlies didn't bother her. "But they don't bite like normal spiders. No. You know why? Because . . . they . . . *tickle*!"

Wally reached for her, careful to miss as she squealed and danced away. She took his hand as they stepped outside. Good. Maybe she'd open up a little bit.

Ghost stopped to stare at the flashing lights when they reached the street. The meter maid's cart flanked Wally's dented Impala. She pointed at Wally's car, then at the parking meter, while two more police officers listened.

One of the cops was a petite woman. Her tag read "Officer Moloka." Her partner was a huge hairy guy who towered over Wally. With his wolf snout and long black claws, he looked like a drawing in one of Ghost's books.

"Uh-oh," said Wally.

The hairy guy, Officer Bester, nodded to him. "Hi, Rustbelt." Ghost giggled at his deep voice.

Most of the 5th Precinct knew Wally by sight. NYPD sometimes provided security for Committee events in the city. Wally didn't recognize the officers, but he waved anyway. "Howdy."

The meter maid wheeled on him, red-faced and sweating. "You! Why can't you park like a normal person?"

"I'm real sorry about that meter. Did you get my note?"

"Your note? This is—" She pointed at the broken meter so strenuously that she had to grab her hat with her other hand. "—destruction of city property!"

"Yeah. Those things aren't cheap, Rusty," said Officer Moloka.

"Sorry."

"Don't you know it's illegal . . ." The meter maid trailed off. "What is that on your face?"

Wally's fingertips scraped along his jaw and forehead. He found a blue plastic "E" stuck to his left ear, and the word "barrel" over his right eyebrow.

"You really want us to take him in, Darcy?" asked the furry cop.

The parking lady seemed ready to choke. Ghost hid behind Wally's legs. "He—the—it's—city property, and he's a repeat offender! This is how it starts, the death of the city. First it's jaywalking and littering, then it's people ramming parking meters just for fun, and then it's a short slide to lawless anarchy. This," she said, again gesticulating at the destroyed meter, "is the bellwether of the decline of a civil society!"

The policewoman sighed and crossed her arms. Her partner leaned over to look at Wally's license plates. "Diplomatic plates. If we issue a citation they'll just appeal and have it rescinded."

"He does this on purpose. He's hiding behind his job!"

"Oh. You mean them fancy plates? I didn't even want those," said Wally. "But Lohengrin insisted."

He was trying to agree, but that only seemed to make the meter maid—Darcy—more angry. Or, at least, the color of her face turned a darker red.

She said, "Do you see what I mean? Practically boasting about his ability to flout the law. And he does! Broken windshield, broken taillight, parking beyond the allotted length of time at a broken meter, destruction of city property."

"Write him up if you want," said Officer Moloka, "but we can't walk him down to the precinct. First, I don't want to be the one who has to explain to the chief why the UN is breathing on the mayor who's breathing on him. And second, he's got his kid with him." She winked at Ghost.

The meter maid flipped open her pad and clicked her pen. Officer Bester said, "Your funeral, Darcy."

"I'm doing my job." She started to fill out the ticket, paused, and waved her pen at the cops. "And I'm going to find that van, too."

"Whoa, whoa. No." Officer Moloka shook her head and waved her hands as if trying to fend off somebody with bad breath. "Those guys are dangerous. They won't balk at hurting a meter maid—"

"Parking enforcement officer!"

"—and they won't be intimidated by a parking ticket."

"Yeah," said Officer Bester. "If you see them, call the cops."

"I *am* a cop."

The other police officers waved good-bye to Ghost and returned to patrolling their beat. The hairy one turned around and made a face at Ghost. She giggled.

"I won't try to get out of this ticket," said Wally.

Darcy wrote out the citation, tore a carbon copy from her pad, took the magnet from Wally's hand, and used it to stick the ticket to his chest.

"You'd better not," she said. Wally waited until her cart puttered away to haul the Impala out of its parking spot. He really needed to learn how to parallel park.

"That was funny," Ghost said when the coast was clear.

The run-in with the parking lady caused Wally to forget all about Ghost's trouble at school until he saw the severed cotton cow ear on the floor alongside her bed when he tucked her in. Wally was too heavy to sit on the edge of her bed without causing her to flop onto the floor, so he knelt beside it. Ghost handed him *Green Eggs and Ham*.

"Read it, Wallywally. With voices," she said.

"Tell ya what. I'll read a little bit if you tell me about what happened at school today." He picked up the scrap from Jo's costume. "This wasn't very nice."

"I hate Jo. She's dumb."

"No you don't. Tomorrow you'll forget all about it and want to be pals again. But she won't forget it, because you hurt her feelings real bad. She'll remember you as a mean person. You should tell her you're sorry."

Ghost looked away. She went insubstantial, as she sometimes did when she wanted to run away from trouble. But she didn't float away through the ceiling. Good kid.

Wally asked, "Is this about Mr. Richardson?"

She rematerialized. "He's gone. He didn't say good-bye." Her voice broke; her accent grew thicker. She sounded much more like the girl she'd been when she first arrived in New York when she added, simply, "He was nice."

Ghost still didn't trust many adults, but she talked about Richardson from time to time. That counted for a lot.

Wally read to her. He did the voices.

Later, he took out the telephone book. Richardson, unfortunately, wasn't an unusual name. There were several Richardsons in and around Jokertown. But one of those had to be Ghost's teacher. A guy like that, if he worked in Jokertown he probably lived nearby, too.

It took half an hour to work his way down the list of telephone numbers. The first number he called belonged to a man—or a woman, it was hard to tell—whose voice sounded like two people speaking not quite in unison with each other. They (he? she?) didn't know any schoolteachers. The second number rang fifteen times with no answer. When Wally called the third Richardson on the list, he got an earful from a lady whose telephone number was apparently quite close to that of a popular Chinese takeout place and who was pretty sensitive about wrong numbers. The fourth number belonged to Mr. Richardson-the-teacher's cousin, but she said she didn't keep in touch and hadn't spoken to him for a while. She gave Wally her cousin's telephone number, apologizing that it might be out of date. It was the number that rang without answer. Wally gave her his name and number and asked her to please have Mr. Richardson get in touch if she happened to hear from him.

Ghost floated through the wall from her bedroom just as he was hanging up. She mumbled to herself in a language Wally didn't understand; it was spoken only in the PPA. Her fingers curled as though clutching a knife hilt. He had to wake her because his hand passed through her shoulder when he tried to lead her back to her bedroom.

She yawned. He carried her back to bed, wondering about her dreams.

It seemed part of Ghost would always dwell in the dark jungles of the Congo, in a land of mass graves and Leopard Men. Some wounds healed; some turned into scars.

She had enough of those. He wanted to be a good foster dad for her. That meant protecting her from new scars and new traumas when he could. He couldn't always be there; the world was a big place. You couldn't protect everybody all the time. But the way he saw it, this meant it was important to save Ghost from the little hurts of life when he could.

He thought about it while preparing for bed. He took a fresh pad of steel wool from the box under the bathroom sink. As he scrubbed himself, Wally decided it wouldn't take more than a couple of hours to stop by Richardson's place. He'd find him before picking up Ghost tomorrow.

He touched the photo of Jerusha Carter on his bedstand. It wasn't a real photo—he'd printed it from the *American Hero* web site. It was all he had. But it was something.

"Miss you," he said, and turned out the light.

♠

On weekday mornings, Ghost took the subway to school with Miss Holmes, their neighbor across the hall. Miss Holmes was a bat-headed physical therapist who worked at Dr. Finn's clinic, next door to Ghost's school. Sometimes she let Ghost ride on her shoulders, and when she did Ghost practically disappeared between the enormous hairy ears.

Before they set off, Wally said, "Remember our talk last night? About Jo?"

Ghost looked down, scowling at the thin fuzz atop Miss Holmes's head. "Yes."

"You're a swell kid. See you later, gator."

"Not now cacadile!" Her English was pretty good, but sometimes Ghost had trouble remembering rhymes.

Wally stood in the hallway, watching and waving until they got in the elevator. Then he went back inside and called the Committee offices in the UN building up near Forty-second Street. He had plenty of vacation built up, so taking a day off was easy. They were happy as long as he wasn't running off to a remote corner of the world on a personal mission.

After copying Mr. Richardson's address from the phone book, he retrieved his fedora from the coat closet and headed out. The hat had been a gift, so it actually fit. And it looked snazzy. Wally had watched enough black-and-white films to know how detectives dressed. A good detective also knew where to go for information. Nero Wolfe had Archie, Nick Charles knew all sorts of guys . . . But Wally could do them both one better. He knew Jube.

Jokertown existed in a perpetual state of frenzy. It had been an exciting but difficult adjustment when Wally moved here, until he accepted that venturing outside the apartment inevitably meant navigating a scene of low-level chaos. The cacophony of traffic—idling delivery trucks, car horns, a siren in the distance—washed over him. Sometimes, when she was nearby, he could barely hear Miss Holmes's echolocation, like a high thin screech just at the edge of his hearing. He stepped into the street to make room for a lady pushing a walker and towing a little girl who floated like a balloon on a string tied to her mother's wrist. She gave him a grateful nod. He must have been getting better at it, because he didn't find himself dodging and jostling as many people as usual.

A sheen of thin, high clouds cast a faint haze across the sky. It was early June, so the garbage cans waiting for pickup along the sidewalks weren't quite as ripe as they would be in high summer. His stroll took him past the Italian bakery a couple streets down; he bought a bag of bombolone pastries dusted with powdered sugar. They reminded him of eating beignets in New Orleans. He munched as he walked the few blocks to Jube's newspaper stand.

He could have driven, he supposed, but a good detective beat the pavement. A good detective had a feel for the streets and could read the city's mood through the soles of his feet. Weren't they called gumshoes for a reason? He stuffed the wax paper from his breakfast into an overflowing garbage bin that smelled of sour milk. The odor faded, masked by the more pleasant scent of buttered popcorn as he approached the newspaper stand across the street.

"Howdy, Jube." He waved at the walrus sitting behind the counter.

"Wally Gunderson. You've been a stranger." The tusks made it sound like he was speaking around a mouthful of food. Or maybe it was the cigar doing that. "I ever tell you the one about the two Takisians who walked into a bar? The third one ducked."

Wally scratched his chin, trying to remember. "No, I don't think I've heard that one. How does the rest of it go?"

Jube blinked. His cigar paused in mid-roll from one corner of his mouth to the other. Little puffs of ash wafted down to dust his bright Hawaiian shirt with spots of gray. "You know what? Never mind. Anyway, you haven't been around much."

"Yeah. It's lots of work, raising a kid. Hardest thing I ever did."

Jube's stand normally did a brisk turn of business. He had a trickle of customers, but it wasn't busy as usual. Was it Wally's imagination, or were there fewer people on the streets? Jube made conversation while unwrapping a bundle of tabloids and making change for customers. "How is she?"

"So-so. She's pretty upset. One of her teachers stopped coming to school. I was kind of wondering if maybe you knew him? You know everybody around here."

Folds of blubber jiggled when Jube used a penknife to cut the twine on the bundle. He unwrapped the papers and plopped the pile on a corner of the counter.

"Not everybody," he said. "But could be I know him."

"Philip Richardson? He's the bug guy with six legs, kind of shaped like Dr. Finn, but not a horse. Kind of a strange-looking fella, but real nice."

Jube fell silent for a moment, that awkward kind of silence that people sometimes got when Wally said something. Then he said, "'Strange-looking,' he says. Uh-huh. You do know this is Jokertown, right? Two fifty."

The last part he said to a translucent shadow in the shape of a woman; she was wrapped in what appeared to be twinkling Christmas lights. They chimed. Three one-dollar bills appeared on the counter, and then a tabloid floated up, folded itself, and disappeared into the silhouette. "Keep the change, Jube," said a whispery voice. The ethereal woman faded into the play of light and shadow on the street.

"Anyway, you ever seen him?"

"Sounds vaguely familiar. You sure he's missing?"

Wally told Jube about what they'd said at school.

Jube adjusted his hat (Wally thought it was called a porkchop hat, though he couldn't figure out why) and shook his head. "Guess they got another one. Getting so nobody's safe anymore."

"Who got another what?"

"The fight club. What else could it be?"

"The what club?"

For the second time in a few minutes, Jube just stared and blinked at him. He seemed to do that a lot. Wally wondered if it was a walrus thing.

"You know, the joker fight club? Videos, death matches. That one."

Something about what Jube said, or the way he said it, momentarily reminded Wally of the PPA. The humidity, the sting of rust eating his skin like slow acid, a line of rippling V's in the water as a crocodile cut across the river . . . *Death matches?*

He shook off the chill. "I don't read much."

Jube made a pained sound, a cross between a rumble and a sob. *Here it comes,* thought Wally. People always got real judgmental when he admitted that. Except Jerusha.

"Wally, Wally, Wally . . . You're killing me here. How can you say that to a poor newspaper vendor? 'Doesn't read,' he says. Gah."

"Sorry. Maybe you could fill me in a little bit?"

Jube asked, "You're not pulling my leg, are you?"

Wally shook his head. It didn't take long for Jube to fill him in on the basics. Learning about the cage match videos put Wally back in Africa again: the flapping of buzzards, the hum of mosquitos, the smell of quicklime and rot as he excavated a mass grave . . . So many dead kids, black queens and jokers stacked like firewood.

"Wally? *Wally!*" The cigar stub came flying out of Jube's mouth. It left a trail of ash and slobber across the counter.

The front of his stand had crumpled. Wally looked down. His hands had curled into fists, each containing a chunk of wooden newsstand. *Rats.*

He said, "Hey, I'm real sorry about that."

Jube waved it off. He fished the cigar stub from between two stacks of newspapers and shoved it back into his mouth. "Don't worry about it. Occupational hazard, serving this community."

Wally barely heard him. He was thinking about Ghost, and Jo, and Cesar, and Moto, and Miss Holmes, and Allen, and Lucien . . . All the folks everywhere who couldn't defend themselves. He'd seen plenty of that working for the Committee. Guys like Mr. Richardson, decent folks just trying to get by. Dying, or forced to do horrible things, just because they were jokers.

Forced to fight and kill. Just like Ghost.

It wasn't fair. It wasn't right. The seed of an idea sprouted in the back of Wally's mind.

"How many of them videos are there?"

"Beats me." Jube shrugged. "I won't sell that filth."

"Who all have they taken?"

"Well, that's the question, isn't it? Some folks, like your kid's teacher, might disappear for any number of reasons. We'll never know unless somebody spots him in a video."

"Oh."

"But others . . . I hear they got Infamous Black Tongue. And you know Father Squid? He's missing, too."

"Gosh." Even Father Squid?

"Yeah, the creeps. Shining Moira, Charlie Six Tuppence, Nimble Dick, Morlock & Eloi, Glabrous Gladys . . ." Jube leaned forward, whispering, "I hear they even tried to snatch the Sleeper, but they botched it and now he's looking for them."

Looking for them. Wally's seedling idea grew.

"You wouldn't happen to know where folks are getting snatched, would you?"

"Not thinking of doing something stupid, are you?"

"I just want to see what's going on."

"These people are dangerous, Wally."

"I can be, too. Breaking stuff is just about the only thing I'm good at."

"You're not a killer."

"Don't have to be." Wally looked around, over both shoulders, as he said, a little loudly, "I'm a real good fighter, though. Pretty tough."

Jube sighed. "Yeah, I hear things. It's happening all over. But maybe, I don't know, this is just street talk, maybe there are some places that folks try to avoid these days." He gave Wally a rundown of the rumors.

"Thanks, Jube. This is swell of you." Wally bought a paper, tipped his hat, and turned to leave. He stopped. "Hey, by the way. Do you know where I can buy a fire extinguisher?"

◆

Richardson lived in an apartment building on the north side of Jokertown. Kind of a long walk, but Wally was glad he chose not to drive. Every minute he spent outside was a better chance of getting snatched. He tried to look like a potential victim.

It was a tough sell. Few people thought it was a good idea to mug a guy made out of iron.

The way Wally figured it, if the fight club bums were snatching regular people from the street, they weren't accustomed to dealing with somebody who had lots of experience fighting for his own life, and defending others'. He'd be back by the time school let out this afternoon.

But just in case . . . He called the school, and left a message saying he might be late picking up Ghost. They arranged to have Miss Holmes bring her home.

A good private eye knew disguises, too. Wally decided that he'd be an old friend of Richardson's. What kind of person would be easy to snatch? He thought about this long and hard before deciding that maybe they belonged to a crossword puzzle club together. That seemed like a good fit for a schoolteacher. And maybe Richardson missed their last meeting, and so Wally was going to his house to collect his membership dues so that the club could buy more pencils. *Yeah*, thought Wally, *that's pretty good*. Mechanical pencils, really sharp ones, and separate clicky erasers. Crossword people probably went through lots of those. Oh, and newspaper subscriptions. Maybe they got a bulk discount or something. Jube could help with that.

It was a good fake identity. Lots of detail. The creeps running the fight club would probably get a kick out of snatching somebody real brainy like that.

He stopped to loiter on several street corners along the way, talking loudly to himself. "I'm nervous," he would say. "I don't like being out on the streets by myself," he would say. And then, with a sigh that he hoped conveyed both fear and weakness, he'd sum it all up: "I sure hope I don't get kidnapped."

There were no takers.

The walk to Richardson's apartment took Wally past Squisher's Basement, a joker-only place Jube had mentioned. It was situated under a clam bar, so Wally decided to stop in for an early lunch. The place had just opened but it smelled skunky, like bad beer, and fishy, like the bottom of a Styrofoam cooler after a long camping trip. The bartender stared at Wally through shafts of mustard-colored sunlight leaking in from the dingy windows at sidewalk level.

"Wow. Rustbelt? Never seen you in here before."

Wally shook his head. "You must have me confused with somebody else. I don't think that Rustbelt fella, whoever he is, wears a hat like mine. I'm just here to eat lunch and do the crossword puzzle. I'm real good at those."

Wally ate a mediocre hamburger, washing it down with a bottle of skunky beer while he pretended to do the puzzle. A few folks, regular customers, drifted in and out.

"Gosh," said Wally. "I'm having a hard time with the puzzle today. Probably because I'm so nervous about getting kidnapped."

He cast furtive glances around the room, checking to see if this projection of vulnerability caught undue attention from anybody. But most of the other customers seemed to ignore him. One fellow got up and shuffled to a table farther away. Wally found that promising. As his gaze followed the guy across the room—he made squelching sounds as he moved, and his body jiggled like a water balloon—he thought he might have glimpsed somebody staring right back at him. A big gray guy covered in round nodules of stone, sort of like a concrete wall frozen in mid-boil. But Wally spent another forty-five minutes writing random words in the crossword grid, and the stone man never looked once in his direction.

♥

He wasn't far from Richardson's apartment when a yellow flash caught his eye again. A parking enforcement scooter idled alongside an expired meter.

Officer Darcy finished her ticket before he caught up with her. So he trotted down the street, waving and taking care not to dig gouges in the sun-softened asphalt with his hard feet. He made eye contact with her in the rearview mirror. Her cart puttered to a stop.

"Howdy," he said. "I just—"

She gave him a nasty look. "Save your breath. You're not getting out of those tickets."

"What? No, I—"

"But if you keep trying, I can cite you for interfering with a police officer in the course of carrying out her duties." She put the cart into gear and started rolling forward again. Wally walked alongside her. It was easy; she didn't go very fast.

"I didn't come over here to do any of that. I know I deserve those tickets. I just, well, I feel real bad about the whole thing. I wanted to say I'm sorry."

Darcy's cart jerked to a halt. The suspension creaked as it rocked back and forth. "What?"

"I know I'm real bad with parallel parking. I swear I

don't break those meters on purpose, okay? And I'm going to talk to folks and get it straightened out with them fancy license plates. I never wanted 'em anyway."

Wally wasn't sure, but her eyes looked a little wider. Her lips made a little "o." Like she was frightened or surprised or something. He hoped this didn't count as interfering.

"Wow," said Darcy. "Nobody has ever apologized to me for getting a ticket before. Not once."

"Well, probably nobody breaks as much stuff as I do."

"That's true," she admitted. Wally strolled alongside while she studied meters. They had to wait for a giraffe-necked lady in a convertible to pull out of a parking spot.

Darcy squinted at Wally. The bridge of her nose crinkled up when she did that. "Are you wearing a fedora?"

"Yeah. Pretty nifty, huh? I saw it in a Humphrey Bogart movie."

"Nobody wears fedoras anymore. Not since forever."

"Private detectives do." Darcy twisted her lips in a little moue of doubt. "Anyway," said Wally, "I like hats. I used to have a really neat pith helmet, but I lost it."

"How'd you lose it?"

"Not sure," said Wally. "But I think it was the crocodile."

Darcy cocked her head. "You are very strange."

"I've heard that. Usually they use the term 'weirdo.'"

She snickered at that, but saw the look on his face and looked guilty. "Anyway, what's this about being a detective? We both know you work for the UN."

"Yeah," he said, "but I took the day off."

"Well, at least you're not driving. Or parking."

"Nah. A good detective pounds the pavement."

"And why, I ask entirely out of idle curiosity even though I'm sure to regret it, are you a detective today?"

Wally tapped the side of his nose with a finger. *Clang, bang.* "I'm working the case of the missing jokers," he said quietly.

"Do you know what the term 'vigilantism' means?"

"No. But it sounds like a real good crossword puzzle word. How do you spell it?"

"Are you for real?"

"What?"

They went down the street, crossed an intersection, and kept going. Darcy didn't say much. She was pretty focused. At one point, when they encountered a double-parked two-seater with its blinkers flashing, she muttered to herself, "Look at this clown. Why do people think that turning on their hazard lights will make them immune to tickets?"

Darcy opened up a little more when he asked her how she liked being in the police. It meant the world to her; he could tell. Justice meant a lot to her, too. Her eyes went a little wide when she said that word, "justice."

And she said it a lot. She had this whole long thing about justice and civil society and police as guardians of order. It was pretty interesting, though Wally didn't catch all of it, and it all came out in a smooth rush like she'd said it a hundred times. Secretly he was a little glad when she trailed off.

A white van eased past them on the narrow street. Darcy lifted her sunglasses to watch it. Her gaze followed as it rolled away.

"What's wrong?" She didn't answer, too busy squinting at the van as it dwindled in the distance. "You want me to stop that van? I can, you know."

For a second there, it looked like she was considering it. "Nah," she said.

The van turned a corner. She shrugged, put her sunglasses back on, and went back to work. Wally asked, "What was that all about?"

"Probably nothing," said Darcy. After a tired sigh, she said, "There's a van I kept citing. I'd written well over a dozen tickets. It was always illegally parked . . . double-parked, or blocking a hydrant, or in a loading zone . . ."

"Do they bust up parking meters?"

"No, they're not like you. You don't tear up your tickets and toss them on the ground." Veins pulsed in her neck and forehead. Just talking about it got her upset. "Once I found a pile of shredded tickets in the gutter."

"I guess you have to mail them, huh?"

Her voice went flat. "Can't. Fake plates. They're not in the system. No registration, no address. They even filed the VIN off the dash."

"That's strange."

"Illegal is what it is."

They crossed another street. Wally poked a finger under the brim of the fedora to scratch his forehead. He tried to think like a detective. It was hard.

"I guess I don't get it. Why go to all that trouble of having a made-up license plate just to avoid parking tickets? He could learn to park better and then he wouldn't get them in the first place. Or why even bother with the plates at all?"

Darcy's nose crinkled up again when she stared at him. "You're kidding, right?"

"No."

"It's not about the parking tickets, Wally. The plates look legit because they don't want to get pulled over. Probably because they don't want anybody to see what's in the van. I wouldn't be surprised if it belongs to the same people who are kidnapping jokers."

He stopped. "Really? That's super!" But then he thought about it a little more. This detective thing was hard. "Uh, I still don't get it."

Darcy sighed. "If they stop to grab someone, or drop something off, they have to do it when and where the opportunity arises. So they park illegally." She explained it patiently, and didn't make him feel dumb. He liked that.

This was great. He'd been on the case less than a day and already he'd made his first major break in the case.

Granted, it was really Darcy who'd made the break-through, but Wally didn't mind. Good detectives always forged a relationship with the police. He'd managed that much.

"Wow. You found the kidnappers!" He frowned. "How come you haven't arrested them?"

"Last time I ticketed the van was before we recognized the probable connection to the fight club. Before those aces busted it up . . . and half of Jokertown." She shook her head, mumbling, "Right through my fingers . . . Could have stopped them way earlier . . . some police officer . . ."

All of a sudden, she looked really sad. Wally said, "You'll catch 'em."

"I'm not so sure. I followed it once, after I realized the plates were bogus."

"Oh yeah?"

"It turned down an alley. Narrow, dead end. But when I came around the corner, it was gone. Where the hell did it go? But people still keep disappearing so they must have gotten a new ride. I keep looking, but . . . ."

Darcy sounded so dejected that Wally tried to hide his disappointment. "Huh. Well, better luck next time."

She fell silent after that. Not entirely sure why he kept at it, other than that it seemed Darcy was pretty neat, Wally tagged along while she checked meters and wrote tickets. One guy who received a parking ticket got pretty steamed and called Darcy all sorts of mean things. Wally didn't like that at all and told him so. Darcy seemed even sadder after that, so he walked with her for another half mile, until she demanded that he buzz off and leave her alone. It was demeaning, she said. "Chauvinism masquer-ading as chivalry," is what she called it.

But she also said, "Thank you."

♣

Mr. Richardson's place was a bust. Wally rang the bell a whole bunch, and circled the block about ten times, each circuit beginning and ending with Wally sitting on the stoop in case Richardson went out or came home. But Wally never saw him. No mysterious vans, either.

Each day, Wally visited another spot on Jube's list. Each day, in spite of his disguise, and much to his disappointment, he wasn't kidnapped. And Ghost grew more sullen with each day Mr. Richardson didn't return to school.

Wally had decided to pack it in for the afternoon, and was turning his thoughts to the weekend and fun places to visit with Ghost, when he noticed somebody following him. Well, not really following. More like keeping pace with him across the street. The big gray guy across the street paused every time Wally did. He hurried when Wally hurried; he dallied when Wally dallied. Wally pretended to start to cross the street before turning the corner instead. Behind him, the blare of a car horn told him somebody had darted through traffic. Wally stopped to study his reflection in a storefront window but it didn't work as well as it seemed to in the movies. He bought a hot dog from a jellyfish with a street cart, and took his time scooping relish and mustard on it. The other fellow drew steadily closer. He was covered in chunks of rock like a walking fireplace. Wally had eaten most of the hot dog before he recognized the guy from Squisher's Basement.

This is it! thought Wally. *They're coming for me.*

He tried to hide his excitement. It was difficult pretending to not notice as his kidnapper drew closer and closer. Wally concentrated on looking vulnerable.

"Gosh," he said aloud. "I don't feel so good. Maybe I'm coming down with something. I feel pretty weak."

But the stone guy never made his move. Was he waiting for the van to arrive? Wally walked slower and slower. He faked a couple of sneezes. Even that did no good.

Finally, feeling impatient, he decided to pretend to be lost. He gazed up at a street sign and made a show of being confused. Then he looked around, as if needing directions.

"Gosh. Where am I?" he said.

The gray rock guy approached him. He held something that resembled a little digital voice recorder. It seemed pretty sinister, he decided. Wally wondered what that thing really was, and what it really did.

"Hey," said the rock guy. "Can I talk to you?"

It's working! thought Wally.

"Sure, fella. I hope you can help me. I'm pretty lost." Wally looked around. *Maybe it would be easier to kidnap me if we weren't out in the open.* "How about we step into that dark alley over there and talk?"

The stone man stopped dead in his tracks. "Oh, I'm not falling for that! I know who you are. And I won't let you take anybody else!"

"Hey, pal, I just want directions—"

The stone man punched Wally in the face with a boulder fist.

Sparks rained on the sidewalk as Wally stumbled backward, toppling a streetlight. It hurt like heck. The gray guy was strong. Wally shook his head, dazed, while the streetlight clanged to the ground and other people on the street quickly scattered.

"You can't hurt me!" yelled the other guy in a voice like an earthquake. With his other fist, the one that hadn't clobbered Wally, he waved the recorder in Wally's face. He jumped up and down, gibbering, "You can't even touch me!"

Uh oh. Had the kidnappers seen through Wally's disguise? If he was going to get taken to their secret hideout, he needed to impress them, make himself irresistible. He'd show them he could fight pretty well before letting the other guy win.

"No, please, I don't want to go with you," said Wally.

He leaped to his feet, and blocked another punch with a wide sweep of his forearm. With his other fist he landed a jackhammer blow to the kidnapper's stomach. There was a loud *crack* and another burst of incandescent sparks like the dying embers of a Fourth of July firework. It knocked the wind from the other guy; his breath smelled like hot ash.

"Oof." The rock guy fell to one knee. He glanced at the recorder. "Lying alien bastard," he groaned. It crumpled in his fist, and then he sent the pieces whistling over the rooftops.

Wally wound up for a kick, but the other guy lunged. The tackle threw Wally against a mail truck. It crunched like a soda can and toppled over, blocking the street. They wrestled atop a mangled heap of metal and glass. Each punch and kick threw sparks like a Roman candle as iron scraped against stone. A chorus of shrieking car alarms echoed up and down the street.

"I know you're one of them! Following me everywhere, reporting everything I do," said the rock man. His eyes darted around really fast, like he had trouble keeping still. "Bribing my dentist, eavesdropping through my fillings! Poisoning my thoughts with fluoride!"

He kept up a steady stream of paranoid ranting, even as Wally slipped in a pair of incandescent jabs to the chin and chest. The kidnapper grabbed Wally by the shoulders and kept slamming him against the flattened truck until it felt like his rivets were coming loose.

Wally got a knee up. One hard flex sent the other guy skidding down the sidewalk with a fingernails-on-blackboard screech. He pulled free of the twisted wreckage of the mail truck and got to his feet just as the other guy wrenched a big blue mailbox from the sidewalk with the groan of tortured metal and popping of broken bolts. He swung it at Wally. Wally slapped the blow aside with an open palm. The mailbox exploded into a cloud of rust and fluttering envelopes. The bright orange rust eddied into his opponent's eyes. He flinched, coughing. Wally used the opening for a solid roundhouse to the jaw.

The kidnapper's head snapped around. The shower of sparks ignited a pile of mail.

The other guy kept twisting, and took advantage of the momentum from the blow to land a high spinning kick to Wally's ribs. It sent Wally sprawling across the street. He landed on a compact car. Pain lanced down his side from shoulder to hip. A shiny dent now creased his old surgery scar. He didn't feel like fighting much more.

"Oh, no," said Wally. "I'm feeling pretty woozy now." Which he was. It didn't require any acting to make a show of stumbling to his feet. His ears rang. The ringing turned into sirens.

The kidnapper ran away. Wally tried to give chase but tripped over the flattened mail truck.

He was still lying there when the police arrived.

♠

It was a tight fit in the squad car, but this time they did take Wally to the precinct. The kidnapper was long gone, but they hauled Wally in on charges of disturbing the peace, destruction of city property, mail tampering, and reckless public endangerment. He wondered what would happen when the adoption committee heard about this. At least the police let him call Ghost's school, to arrange to have Miss Holmes take her home again.

The booking officer, whose name sounded like Squint or something like that, kept a large dollhouse on her desk. That seemed strange. She wasn't very interested in Wally's side of the story. She didn't appear to be listening at all until Wally mentioned that the whole thing happened because he was defending himself from one of the fight club kidnappers. And suddenly the police were *very* interested in Wally's story. Particularly in his description of the kidnapper. They put him in a room and left him waiting.

The room had two chairs, a wooden table, and a water cooler with a little tube of paper cones hung alongside it. A window with broken venetian blinds gave him a view of the station house. The precinct was a busy place. All sorts of people—uniformed officers, plainclothes detectives, lawyers in suits, criminals and suspects—passed back and forth outside the room. Wally even glimpsed Darcy at one point. He knocked on the glass and waved at her; she seemed disappointed, but not surprised, to see him.

Wally pressed a paper cone full of cold water against his bruises. It helped to numb the ache. He wondered what Ghost and Miss Holmes were eating for dinner. He drank the water, laid his head on the table, tried to ignore the rumbling in his stomach, and closed his eyes. He hadn't quite fallen asleep when a voice roused him.

"I'll be goddamned . . . Wally Gunderson."

The voice was vaguely familiar. Wally sat up. And then he blinked. There were two men in the doorway. One he recognized.

"Cripes," he said. "Stuntman?"

The man standing across the table wore a suit. Moving like a man in pain, he flipped open a thin leather case about the size of a wallet. "It's Agent Norwood now. I'm with SCARE. More or less."

Heart sinking, Wally stared at the badge. He couldn't remember what SCARE stood for but he knew it was a pretty big deal. "Gosh."

The other guy leaned across the table, extending a hand to Wally. He looked tired too, but in a different way from Stuntman. "Mr. Gunderson, I'm Detective Black." He glanced at Stuntman. "And shouldn't you be in bed?"

"Yes. But I've got to hear this story."

Stuntman closed the badge case hard enough that the breeze tickled Wally's face. He tucked it back into a breast pocket.

"Howdy." *Detective?* "Is this about the mail truck?"

The men shared a look. Stuntman rolled his eyes and shrugged.

"Uh, no," said the detective. "Agent Norwood is helping me investigate the Jokertown kidnappings."

From his suit pocket Stuntman produced a narrow notebook. The kind with a spiral wire along the top. Clicking a pen he pointed it at Wally. "I'm just dying to hear how *you* of all people got mixed up in this mess."

Wally told them about Ghost's teacher, his conversation with Jube, and his decision to infiltrate the fight club by letting himself get kidnapped.

"This is the most idiotic thing I've ever heard," Stuntman said.

The detective frowned at the agent, then said to Wally, "What you were trying was very dangerous, Mr. Gunderson. People are dying in that ring."

"That's why I'm doing it. Somebody has to stick up for them folks."

Stuntman rolled his eyes. "You're moderately famous, and apparently well liked," he said, "for reasons I've never understood. Did it never occur to you that they might choose to avoid nabbing a minor celebrity?"

"Father Squid is way more famous than I am. Everybody in Jokertown knows him."

Wally imagined he could hear the grinding of Stuntman's teeth. "We're aware of that."

"And anyway," Wally continued, "I was undercover. With a special hat and everything. So they didn't know who they were grabbing."

"You're made of metal and covered in rivets. What kind of disguise did you think—"

"Tell us about this disguise," prompted the detective.

Wally explained the made-up crossword puzzle club,

and how they needed to find Mr. Richardson so that they could afford more pencils.

Stuntman laughed. It wasn't a friendly laugh. "You know, I used to wonder if the rube thing was just an act. I'll never wonder again."

Detective Black shot another sharp look at Stuntman. "Please continue."

"No, wait," said Stuntman, struggling to get the laughter under control. "Let me make sure I get this down." He clicked the pen again and jotted something in his notebook. "Crossword puzzles. Genius."

"Zip it," Detective Black snapped. He turned back to Wally. "Keep going, Mr. Gunderson."

Wally did. When he got to the part about the botched kidnapping, the detective sighed. He said, "Big gray guy? Covered in stone? Fists like boulders?"

"Yep."

"Ranting and raving?"

"Uh huh."

The detective ran a hand over his face. To Stuntman, he said, "That wasn't a kidnapper. That's Croyd Crenson."

Stuntman stood. He and the detective conferred in the corner, whispering. Wally caught the words "sleeper" and "Takisian." Stuntman came back a moment later, and sat with a sigh of disgust. He glared at Wally, shaking his head. Finally, he said, "I swear to God. You make hammers look smart."

Wally said, "Well, I don't know about this Croyd fella, but he sure seemed suspicious to me."

"Of course he did," said the detective. "He's blitzed out of his mind on speed." He shook Wally's hand again. "Thank you for your time, Mr. Gunderson, and please leave the police work to the police. You could get hurt." He walked out, muttering, "Paranoid delusions, fists like sledgehammers, and now he's blaming *me*. Wonderful . . ."

Stuntman closed his notebook, and threaded the pen through the spirals. "Thanks for wasting our time."

"Can I ask you a question?"

"That is a question."

"I was just wondering if you ever get tired of always blaming other people when things don't go the way you want. I mean, that must be a pretty lonely way to live."

"What the hell are you talking about? I turned my short turn with celebrity into a good career." Stuntman spoke with a hollow pride that didn't touch his eyes. He still looked tired. "I was smart about it."

"I dunno. You still seem like a pretty angry guy."

"Holy shit. Did you just call me an angry black man? You, of all people?"

"No, I think you're a mean person who is also black." Wally remembered a conversation he'd had with Jerusha. It seemed like yesterday. They were piloting a boat down a river in Congo, and talking about their time on *American Hero,* which even then had seemed like a jillion years ago.

I didn't say that stuff.

I know, Wally. Everybody knows it.

"You never fooled anybody," said Wally.

Stuntman made another show of checking his watch. He yawned. "Let me know when you get near a point."

Wally thought about that. What was his point? He hadn't thought he had one; he was just curious, because it seemed like a crummy way to live. But then he realized maybe he did have something to say. "If you hadn't done what you did all those years ago, my life would be a lot different. Actually, maybe lots of lives would be different. Because of you I went to Egypt, and then so did some other folks, and that's how the Committee was formed. And then I got to know Jerusha and I met Ghost and now I'm adopting a kid and everything. I miss a lot of folks—" Wally struggled to force the words past the lump that always congealed in his throat when he thought about Jerusha. He thought about Darcy, too. "—And it hasn't fixed everything for everybody. But, I dunno, I think maybe my life would be a lot lonelier if not for you. So, thank you."

Stuntman stared at him as if he'd just grown another head. He stood. "We're finished here." He left without another word.

"You know what?" Wally called after him. "You're still a knucklehead."

♦

"Gosh," said Wally to nobody in particular in his loudest speaking voice, "those joker kidnappings sure do worry me. I hope those cage match guys don't decide to make me fight because I'm so strong. I have a kid at home."

He pitched his voice so that it carried over the music; past the rotating stage where a bored-looking lady covered in goldfish scales half danced, half strutted around a fireman's pole; and even into the darkened corners where ladies danced privately for solitary drinkers.

Early afternoon at Freaker's was one of the most depressing things he'd ever witnessed in Jokertown. Nobody here looked particularly happy.

The bartender, a man with tattoos covering both his arms and most of his neck, wrapped a dirty dishtowel around the lid of a jar of pickled pearl onions. The tattoos shifted as he heaved on the jar.

"Do you need help with that? I'm pretty strong." Wally studied the room from the corners of his eyes, adding, "Strong enough to be a wrestler or something, probably."

He gave Wally a Look. "Thanks, tough guy. I'll manage." The jar lid came loose with a wet sucking sound. Wally caught a whiff of vinegar.

"Can I have another beer please?" And then, to cover up the "please" he added, "I don't know how many I've had."

That wasn't true. He'd nursed that first bottle for an

hour and a half. But he wanted the kidnappers to think he'd be easy to grab. He didn't like to drink alone. But it was important to blend in. All part of being a detective. Still, it was embarrassing, picking up Ghost from school with beer on his breath. Even worse when it was beer from a place where ladies took their clothes off. He was glad his mom and dad couldn't see him now.

"Yeah," said the bartender. "That higher math is hard."

The bartender set another bottle in front of him. The crinkled edge of the bottle cap made a screeching sound against the pad of Wally's thumb as he flicked it off. The cap tinkled on the bar. The bottle foamed up.

One of the dancers sidled next to him. She leaned on the bar. She had a feline face, and wore a bikini that didn't cover very much.

"Neat trick," she said.

"Oh, sure. I do that lots. It didn't hurt or anything—" He looked around the room again to see if anybody was listening, which is how he noticed she had more lady parts than he assumed was normal. The rest came out in an embarrassed cough: "—Because my skin is so tough."

The dancer purred. *"Really?"*

She ran a finger down his arm; the purring got louder. "Tell me. Is your skin this hard all over?"

"Well, yeah. It's—" And then he realized she was doing that thing where somebody appeared to be talking about one thing but was actually talking about a totally different thing. Wally blushed so furiously that it actually hurt his face. She watched him, waiting for an answer, but he focused all of his attention on his beer. He took a swig, clutching the bottle so hard that it cracked. The dancer sighed, rolled her eyes at the bartender, and walked away.

The beer ran over his fingers. He flicked them dry, earning a dirty look from the guy sitting a couple barstools down. Wally hadn't seen him come up to the bar. Now his shirt was stippled with dark spots where flecks of foam had soaked into the fabric. Great.

"Oops. Sorry about that, fella."

The guy glared at him with huge iridescent eyes like those of a housefly.

Wally said, "Here, I'll buy your next one."

The other guy shrugged. "Won't argue with that." He took a stool closer to Wally. Wally caught the bartender's eye and put another bottle on his tab. The dancer lady returned not long after that.

It was a long, embarrassing afternoon, and by the end of it Wally was no closer to finding the fight club.

Somebody knocked on their door just as Ghost was nodding off for the night. Wally placed the Dr. Seuss book he'd been reading to her on the bedside table next to the sippy cup of water, tiptoed to the door, and turned off the light. Another knock came while he stood just outside Ghost's bedroom, listening for the long slow breaths that told him she'd fallen into true sleep. Only when he was certain she'd stay asleep did he go to answer the door.

Darcy stood in the hallway. He didn't recognize her right away because she wasn't dressed like a police officer.

"Cripes," he said. "I mean, howdy."

She shrugged, more to herself than to him. She said, "Do you have a minute?"

Wally beckoned her inside. "I just put Ghost to bed," he said in a half whisper, "but we can talk in the kitchen."

Darcy shook her head. "I'm sort of in a hurry here." Wally paused. She said, in a rush, "I think I've found the fight club kidnappers. Do you want to come and help me catch them?"

Wally straightened up so quickly he nearly ripped the doorknob off the door. "Holy smokes, yes!"

♣

It took another half hour before they were under way, and Darcy fidgeted the entire time. First, he had to put Ghost back to sleep, and then he had to go across the hall to speak with Miss Holmes. Wally didn't know what he would have done without her willingness to watch over Ghost. He made a mental note to buy her a cake or maybe cook a casserole for her to say thank you. He wondered if she liked eating Tater Tots. He knew a good recipe for Tater Tot casserole.

But eventually he and Darcy were under way. They took his car. She directed him west, to the very edge of Manhattan.

"How'd you find these guys?" he asked.

"I've been spending my off hours reviewing footage from traffic cameras."

"Gosh. I didn't even know that was a thing."

"It is a thing. But it took about two hundred hours before I found a pattern."

Holy cow. Two hundred hours? That was . . . Wally tried to do the math in his head, but he couldn't do that and drive at the same time. Anyway, it was a *lot* of days.

"Wow," he said. "That's pretty neat."

"It wasn't as fun as it sounds," she said. But she sat a little straighter, puffed up by the fact of his amazement. "You have no idea how many vans drive through this borough every day. But only one that can disappear and reappear. Turn here."

He did, saying, "I'm real happy to lend a hand. But I thought you weren't real keen on my acting like a detective. You had the fancy word for it. Vigil-something."

"Vigilantism." Darcy sighed. "Yeah. Well, once I uncovered a possible lead on the van, I realized I had two problems. I knew I needed help. But maybe you remember what my colleagues said a few days ago: 'If you see them, call the real cops.' If I tell anybody about this, I'll get shoved aside, and if it turns up anything useful they'll forget I was ever involved." She practically vibrated with irritation. "The second problem is that this place we're approaching is, technically, outside of my precinct's jurisdiction. The right way to do this would be for me to notify Detective Black, but that would kill hours because he insists on doing everything by the book." Wally remembered the detective. He seemed pretty nice, all things considered. Darcy continued, "Franny would contact the other precinct, and explain the situation, and then they'd have to come to some agreement. And maybe the captains would have to talk. They'd have to do some handshake deal to let us come in and do a bust inside their precinct, or more likely they'd insist on having their own guys do it. But you can imagine how much enthusiasm this case receives outside of Jokertown. Missing jokers? Ha."

Wally said, "So you called me instead."

"I'm bending the rules a little, yes." She paused. Fidgeted again. "I've never done that before."

Wally smiled to himself. "How does that feel?"

"Like I want to write myself a ticket with a big fine."

Wally stopped smiling. "You, uh . . . I guess you must really want to catch these guys."

"Yes."

♠

Darcy directed him to a junkyard situated partially beneath a section of the old elevated West Side Highway, right on the Hudson. *West Side Auto and Scrap,* according to the sign over the entrance to the yard. The sun had just set past the New Jersey refineries when Wally parked his car outside the tall fence surrounding the property. The residual glow of sunset turned the underside of a low cloudbank pink and orange, casting enough ruddy light to turn Wally's iron skin the color of rust, and to show him that the junkyard was quiet.

A breeze whistled through the Slinky-curls of barbed wire atop the fence. Much of the yard inside was given over to stacks of smashed-up old cars, some of which were five or even six high in places. The ones at the bottom were a little older, and more pancaked than the ones on top. Few were car-shaped; many had been crushed into squares. Once in a while a stack creaked, or groaned, or rattled. Wally chalked that up to wind, or maybe rats. But aside from the wind, and the constant thrum of traffic along the highway, the yard was still. The dying firelight of sunset silhouetted a tall crane deeper in the yard. The front offices of the junkyard appeared to be housed in an old double-wide mobile-home trailer. Nobody came or went. And as the salmon-colored glow of sunset faded from the clouds, turning the sky a mottled violet gray, no lights came on in the trailer.

The shadows felt heavy. The weight of Darcy's focus gave everything a hard edge.

Wally wasn't sure how big the yard was. Maybe the secret club was deeper inside. Or maybe there was a secret entrance, like a trapdoor, and it was underground. The junkyard would be a swell place to hide something like that. The entrance could even be in one of the cars, maybe the trunk. That's what he would do. He decided to keep an eye open for big cars that hadn't been squeezed into boxes.

They eased out of Wally's car. Wally threw the driver's-side door closed a half second before noticing Darcy had been careful not to make any noise with her door. She winced at the noise.

"Sorry," he whispered.

They tiptoed to the gate, which was chained and padlocked. Wally pinched a chain link in both hands and gently twisted it open. But the squeal of tortured metal wasn't much quieter than it might have been had he simply snapped the chain apart. Darcy winced again.

The gate creaked. Wally tiptoed into the deepening shadows of the junkyard with Darcy right behind him.

Within the warren of crushed cars and scrap metal, the sporadic breeze smelled like gasoline, mud, and the river. His feet clumped against the earth where the passage of heavy machinery had compacted bare soil. They kept to the shadows, slowly circling behind the trailer until he could approach it from the side with the fewest windows. Along the way, he did see a number of cars that hadn't yet been crushed into boxes, but they were so banged-up anyway that the doors and trunks didn't want to open unless he heaved on them or rusted out the hinges. He found no secret passages.

Darcy was light on her feet. He couldn't even hear her footsteps and she was right next to him. She whispered something about misguided chivalry, but he still insisted she stay behind him. Wally figured he made a pretty good shield for her.

They crept up to the trailer and crouched beneath a window. Darcy was too short to see over the sill. The pane was too grimy and the interior too dark for him to see anything when he peeked inside. But if there was any evidence connecting the junkyard to the joker kidnappings, surely it would be in the office. Wouldn't it?

Darcy whispered, "Wait!"

But the lock was flimsy, and Wally had already twisted the handle right off the door. Darcy crept back, pressed herself against the trailer. Wally eased inside.

It was even darker here than outside. A flashlight, he realized, would have been a very good idea. He was debating whether to go back for the one in the glove compartment of his car—did it have batteries?—when the *click* of a desk lamp replaced darkness with sterile white light. In the moment before Wally tumbled from the trailer, squeezing shut his dark-adapted eyes, he glimpsed a few cots.

Darcy had disappeared.

Wally tripped. There was a *thud* as somebody leapt on him and smeared Wally's face with goo.

The darkness that swallowed him smelled like cough medicine.

◆

He awoke outside. He knew he was outside, and not still in the trailer, because his face was coated with slime and dirt. His arms didn't work right when he tried to roll over; he flopped around like a walleye gasping for air on the bottom of a canoe. Everything tasted like an overdose of cough drops. He almost managed to sit up, but then the ground shook with the rumble and rattle of heavy machinery starting up, so he toppled over again, head spinning.

Spotlights, like big construction lamps, now flooded the junkyard with silvery light. More dirt, he noticed, was caked into greasy handprints on his lower legs and ankles.

"Can't believe he's already getting up," somebody said. "That dose would've put a rhino into a coma."

"Yeah, well, better luck next time," said a woman's voice. "Let's just get—" She was interrupted by the sound of sporadic gunfire. Wally knew that sound.

"Shit," she said. "The Iron Giant brought friends. Screw this noise."

Wally managed to lever himself up to his knees, swaying like a ship on high seas. He glimpsed a short woman with curly auburn hair sprinting toward a white van. But then a slippery foot on his back shoved him down again. A cloud of dust went down his throat. He coughed.

"Hey!" the other guy called after her. "You can't take off until I've taken care of this."

Somebody else was yelling now, too. It sounded like Darcy's voice. She had a pretty voice.

The rumble of machinery grew louder. Shadows slid across the ground, dark tendrils skimming across oil puddles and weedy slabs of broken concrete. Then there was a clink, and the rattle of chains. The crane, Wally realized.

A weird but somehow familiar tingly sensation took root in his belly, spreading through his chest to his arms, legs, and head. It differed from the medicinal wooziness; this felt like somebody had pressed a tuning fork to the roof of his mouth and it was vibrating his brain to pudding. He tried to roll over to see what was happening, but his arms and legs refused him. He couldn't think straight.

He'd felt this sensation before. Where?

For a moment he felt lighter . . . almost like he was floating. But then the ground fell away, all in a rush, and somehow he was falling *up* until his head and back and arms clanged against something large and flat. His body rang like a gong. Then he remembered.

Oh, yeah. When the kids stuck those magnets to my head. This felt the same, only times a million. Probably because they used this magnet to pick up cars. It made his brain feel cottony, like he had a bad fever.

The crane whined and whirred as the magnet retracted. Wally dangled high above the junkyard, splayed against the magnet like a fly on flypaper. His view of the yard bobbed back and forth, like the carnival rides he and his brother used to take on the midway at the Minnesota State Fair. Back before Wally's card turned.

It took most of his strength merely to bend his elbow, straining and contorting just enough to press his fingertips to the surface of the electromagnet. But he didn't touch metal. The working surface was laminated with a thin plastic coating. He couldn't make it rust. His arm slammed back against the magnet.

Oh, crud.

The crane arm lurched. Wally left his stomach behind. And then he was soaring across the yard: over Darcy, who crouched behind a car, reloading her gun; over a half-naked man with a towel around his waist, running away from her; past the trailer and the van parked behind it. He remembered there was something important about a van . . . But the magnet scrambled his brain and made everything feel gauzy and surreal, like dream logic.

The woman he'd glimpsed on the ground leaped into the driver's seat of the van. A cloud of exhaust coughed from the tailpipe. She must have floored it because the tires kicked up large clods of mud. The van spun around the trailer.

"You bastards!" screamed the little Gandhi guy.

Wally watched helplessly while somebody pulled him through the van's open side panel.

Wally became aware of a new sound, a thrum and a whine, like the groaning of a giant hydraulic press. Wally wondered where they were taking him. The crane swept him past more stacks of crushed cars.

Crushed cars.

Oh.

But he couldn't get smushed. Who would take care of Ghost?

The fright and worry hurt worse than any punch, any gunshot, any crocodile bite.

His struggles caused the magnet to swing like a pendulum. But each time he managed to wrench one arm or leg free of the magnet, it banged back when he went to work on another limb. He didn't have any leverage.

The crane pivoted. The maw of a giant press came into view. It was large enough to hold a big car, like Wally's Impala. The lid was a thick slab of steel on massive hinges, and the sides of the empty crusher comprised thick steel plates on massive hydraulic arms. That steel had been laminated, too. The whole thing stood on a pair of retractable legs, so that it could rock back like a dump truck to tip out the crushed cars. A generator rumbled off to the side. Wally caught a whiff of diesel fuel.

Another gunshot *crack* echoed through the junkyard. The crane jerked to a stop, which sent the magnet rocking wildly on its chain. Wally's head spun. Between the magnet, the spinning, and the diesel fumes, he felt like he might puke.

The van picked up speed. But it wasn't heading for the gate. Instead, it was barreling straight toward a wall of cubed cars. The magnet spun. Wally glimpsed Darcy again, now creeping to the other side of the crane. When his vantage spun around again, the van had almost reached the wall, but . . . Wally wasn't sure because the magnet made his brain all fizzy and he really wanted to puke and also he was dizzy. But he watched while something that sure looked like a tunnel or hole opened up to swallow the van. He expected a big crash, but instead the van just disappeared as though the wall of cars was fake, like a hologram in a movie. The magnet spun. He blinked. When he opened his eyes again, the van was gone.

Somebody shouted. The crane lurched back into motion, once again leaving Wally's stomach behind. The press drew closer. There was another *crack,* closer this time, followed by the *ping* of ricochet.

The crane stopped again. Somewhere, a distant voice said, "Wally!"

He thought about that. *Oh. That's me.*

"Uh, hello?" His voice sounded weird, like it was full of marbles. The magnet tugged on his jaw, making it hard to shout. "Up here."

The tingly sensation stopped as abruptly as somebody turning off a light switch. But before he had time to think about what that meant, the ground leaped up to hit him in the face. He belly flopped on the edge of the compactor. He bounced, crashed against a car cube, and skidded to a stop with one arm wrenched under his back.

"Ouch," he said.

It took a bit of work but eventually he managed to lever himself into a sitting position propped against one of the car cubes. The metal felt sticky, somehow, which was a little weird. The residual effects of the magnet and the goo crammed up his nose left him woozy. His eyelids made a weird clicking sound when he blinked. He was still sitting there, trying to clear his head, when Darcy walked up a few minutes later. She knelt beside him.

"Are you hurt?"

"I don't think so." His voice came out slurred. It felt like his teeth were trying to jostle each other out of the way.

Darcy sat with him while his head cleared. When he could think a little better, he asked her what happened.

"They got away," she said. "*Again*. And I'm probably going to be fired."

"Gaaagghhh—" It was hard to talk because his jaws kept repelling each other. He tried again. "Gosh, I don't know. I'd be in a real jam if not for you. I bet the Committee could help you out."

Darcy stood. She stared at the fence gate where they had entered the junkyard on their failed secret errand.

"You found the fight club," said Wally.

She frowned. "I'm not so sure. We found a few folks and a van. Big deal." She made a twirling motion with one finger in the air. "And anyway, they're all gone now. Where the hell did they go?"

"Oh, I saw the whole thing from up there. They drove away through the magic tunnel. Have you seen my hat?"

"I think that magnet scrambled your brain. You should probably see a doctor."

"Oh." Well, at least he wasn't getting smushed into a bloody cube.

She helped him to his feet. He tried not to lean on her,

but she was stronger than she looked. "I think I should take you home."

Wally said, "But my car."

"No way. You are in no condition to operate heavy machinery. Not even yourself."

"Oh. Okay." They stumbled toward the outer gate. The door on the trailer hung wide open, and a pair of tire tracks had cut deep furrows in the dirt. They led straight to a wall of cars, which struck Wally as weird, though his head was too fuzzy to figure out why.

Darcy noticed the tracks, too. She stopped to study them. She stared, unblinking.

Then she said, "When you're feeling better, I want you to tell me exactly what you saw."

"Okay," he said. "Do you like kids?"

She shrugged, which made him wobble. "I guess. Why?"

"Good. I think you should meet Ghost," he said.

Galahad in Blue

Part Eight

TO MOST PEOPLE FORENSIC accounting sounded about as exciting and interesting as watching paint dry, but it was actually something Franny enjoyed. Back at the precinct he began by drafting a request for a warrant. He then called over to the courthouse to see who was signing warrants that day.

Turned out it was Samuelson, which was great. He was a decent enough judge, but when he wasn't hearing cases he got blow jobs from hookers in his office. Which meant he liked to keep his office hours free of work. A stupid man might have solved the problem by refusing everything, but Samuelson wasn't stupid, and he knew that constant denial would lead to challenges and questions, and have the opposite result of what he wanted. The judge also knew that most warrants did result in lowlifes getting hauled in, and lowlives and their overworked public defenders usually didn't challenge how a warrant got issued. Which meant he was a good bet to sign off on this rather shaky house of cards that Franny had constructed.

As Franny walked down the hall of the courthouse,

warrant tucked into a folder briefcase, he hoped that the judge wasn't an aficionado of *American Hero,* and had never heard of Michael Berman. The warrant really was a fishing expedition, but like Jamal, he fully believed that Berman was in this up to his neck.

Franny had timed it so he walked into the back of Samuelson's courtroom just as the lunch break was called. The judge's furry caterpillar-like eyebrows drew together in a sharp frown when he saw Franny enter. Spectators, a bored city beat reporter, and the families of the victim and the accused shuffled for the big double doors. Only one person remained seated, a very tall, very leggy woman with hair a shade of red that was found nowhere in nature, black leather miniskirt, blouse with a plunging neckline, and stiletto heels. Yep, the judge was going to want to get Franny and his warrant out the door, and fast.

A sharp gesture, and Franny walked down the aisle and approached the bench. "What have you got, Detective?"

"Warrant for forensic accounting." Franny slid the paper across the bench.

"Come in my chambers."

Franny followed the judge through the doors behind the bench. It was a cliché of a judge's chambers—overstuffed armchairs, bookcases filled with weighty tomes that, judging from the dust, weren't getting touched. No reason to with every case online and available now. A sack lunch sat on the polished mahogany surface of the desk. The pungent smell of corned beef, kraut, and mustard hit his martini-abused gut, and Franny swallowed nausea.

Samuelson sat down behind his desk and flipped through the warrant. "Nice job," he said as he scrawled his signature.

"Thank you, Your Honor."

"Don't make a habit of this."

"No, sir."

Franny and the leggy redhead exchanged nods as they passed in the doorway.

♥

Back at the precinct Franny put in calls to the IRS and faxed over the warrant. Once he had access to Berman's tax returns he would be able to bootstrap into Berman's bank accounts, and payments from those accounts would lead him to the credit cards. "And then we'll see what you're made of, Mr. Berman," Franny said to the fax machine as the final page of the warrant slid through.

"You know, it's never a good sign when you're talking to mechanical objects," Beastie Bester said as he lumbered in, heading for the copy machine.

"Yeah, well, when nobody, including my partner, will talk to me I'm all I'm left with." Franny hadn't meant it for it to emerge quite so plaintive.

"You could have turned it down," Beastie said gently.

"No, I couldn't have. I have my own traditions to live up to."

Eventually the material on Berman's finances landed in his e-mail inbox. Franny got himself a cup of bad precinct coffee. He began to dig into Berman's life as sketched by the producer's finances. First Franny looked over the W-2s and W-9s. Hollywood had been very good to Mr. Berman. Next he looked at bank statements for the past six months. Money flowed into the bank account and out just as quickly. There were a lot of overdraft charges.

He went back to the tax returns. The IRS had given him five years. What Franny found were gambling losses claimed as deductions against gambling winnings. That sent him digging into the credit card statements. There were a lot of charges at casinos in Las Vegas, Cannes, Atlantic City, Monaco, and *Kazakhstan*. Where the murdered Joe Frank, cameraman for Michael Berman, had also traveled. Franny went back to the bank statements and found ATM withdrawals at various gambling venues. Judging from the number of withdrawals, Berman had lost a lot more than he'd won.

Franny called Berman's bank and had the good fortune to end up with a representative who was a Badge Bunny. Once he'd scanned and e-mailed a copy of the warrant she was more than happy to help him, and was very disappointed when she discovered he was in New York City and she was in Houston. After an hour where his ear went numb she had given him online access to all Berman's checks for the past five years.

What he found had him jumping out of his chair, and pumping the air in triumph. Berman was a liar. He hadn't fired Joe Frank. As late as two weeks ago he had been writing checks to the cameraman. He was picking up the phone to call Jamal, when Deputy Inspector Maseryk walked up and dropped a file on his desk. "That big Committee ace Rustbelt and one of our meter maids have been playing detective, and they nearly got Gunderson killed."

"I told him not to," Franny said.

"Well, he didn't listen, and I'd like an actual detective to follow up. Maybe they'll have something useful. God knows we need something. I just hope it's not another of Darcy's fantasies."

"Yes, sir." Maseryk walked away and Franny slowly replaced the receiver. What he was doing with Jamal and Berman was strictly off the books. This was his actual job. And maybe the big ace did know something.

Wally Gunderson walked toward Franny's desk, the floor shuddering under his weight, and Franny watched in dismay as paper clips, sets of keys, staplers, and anything made of metal went sailing through the air to land like a flock of futuristic butterflies on the exposed metal skin of Rustbelt's face, neck, hands, and arms. Cops were yelling, and snatching at their suddenly airborne items. The big iron ace batted in alarm at the clinging objects and only succeeded in having them attach to each other in long strings that dripped from his fingertips. "Ah shoot," he said in his deep Minnesota accent.

Rikki, her over-developed chest heaving in alarm, rushed up waving her arms like a modern-day Chicken Little. "The computers," she yelled. "The computers."

Franny suddenly realized what she was ranting about. Rustbelt's magnetized skin was probably wreaking havoc on the hard drives. He reached up, placed his hands on Rusty's shoulders, turned him around, and propelled him back out of the precinct. The big head with its steamshovel jaw drooped. "I'm sorry. I guess I got all magnetized by that magnet."

"Not your fault," Franny said as he plucked metal detritus off Rusty, and set it in a pile just inside the door. He spotted a coffee vendor's cart on the far side of the street down by the corner. "We can sit on the bench at the bus stop. I'll buy us some coffee."

"Sure," Rusty said, as he plucked off an overlooked paper clip.

"How do you take it?"

"Lotta cream and sugar."

Franny sprinted down the street and bought a couple of cups. Joining Wally on the bench Franny took a swig, and felt his gut rebel. He stared down into the black depths, and realized he had been subsisting on coffee for the past few weeks.

"What did you need from me, Officer?" asked Rustbelt. "Darcy wrote everything up, and I sure hope you fellas aren't gonna fire her. She works real hard to be a good policeman."

Franny set the cup on the sidewalk next to him. "Well, that's not my decision, but I'll certainly put in a word for her. I did read Darcy's report, but it's a little . . ." He considered the twenty-seven-page-long report filled with an exposition about the decay of cities, analysis of traffic patterns, traffic camera logs, parking violations, and a detailed sketch of a junkyard, and finally settled on a neutral word. ". . . detailed. I just need to hear what happened when you reached that junkyard. Darcy's report was a little vague on exactly how the perps got away." Franny's pen was poised over his notebook.

"There was a tunnel, and this skinny guy wearing a towel. And he stuffed some stuff up my nose, and I got all woozy. Oh, and this red-haired woman. She was driving the car when it went into the tunnel."

"Was she a joker?"

"No, just a girl."

"Girl. So she was younger?"

"Yeah, I guess."

Franny asked a few more questions, but it seemed he had exhausted Gunderson's store of useful information. Vaporlock was old news. What was new was the woman, and the use of a clear ace power.

The bus pulled up, the doors opened, and the driver glared at Franny and Rustbelt. "Let me guess, you're just passing the time?"

"Sorry." Franny stood. Shook hands with Wally. "Thank you, Mr. Gunderson."

"Did anything I told you help?"

"I think so."

"May I tell Darcy? She's feeling real low right now."

"Sure," said Franny. He returned to his desk and his computer to search for aces who could open tunnels. It didn't take long to find one.

♠

He called Stuntman. "Berman's got a gambling problem," Franny said. He paused for breath while Jamal gave a low whistle. "And Berman hadn't fired Joe Frank. He was still writing him checks as late as two weeks ago."

"Son of a bitch lied to me."

"Yep, but that's not the best part. I think I know how the jokers are being taken out of the city." Franny told Jamal about Rustbelt's testimony. "So, I went looking for an ace with a power like that. There is one. She was on *American Hero*, Tesseract. I looked up what 'tesseract' means. It's a four-dimensional analogy to a cube. I found some YouTube video of Tesseract doing her thing. She can make an opening in, say, Los Angeles, and reach through to Paris, or Beijing, or somewhere. She can make these openings big enough to walk through, probably even drive through."

"You have a real name?"

"Oh, yeah, sorry. Mollie Steunenberg." There was silence from the other end of the line. A silence that went on for so long that Franny thought they'd been disconnected. "Jamal? Hello?"

"I'm here. Mollie Steunenberg is Berman's assistant."

"Oh, holy fuck."

The Big Bleed

Part Nine

"YOUR GUY JUST ARRIVED. He's got the girl with him."

"Thank you," Jamal Norwood said. "We'll be there as soon as possible." Then he clicked off. He didn't want to be on the phone with Jack Metz any longer than necessary. Not that he had anything special against Upper East Side building managers, but this one was off-scale creepy.

He had proved to be useful, however. Metz's call meant that Michael Berman was back in the city with Mollie Steunenberg, aka Tesseract. Jamal knew it was unlikely to be for long.

It was early morning, mid-week, rainy, colder than it should be in New York this time of year. Jamal's physical and mental state matched the grim weather. He had been dozing, dreaming strange dreams about being chased down a street by the missing joker Wheels, feeling that he was late, ill-equipped, in danger.

On waking, he considered phoning Julia, something he had not done in over a week. But what would he tell her? *I'm feeling great!* Every conversation he could imagine ended in a lie, or a very uncomfortable revelation.

So he didn't. He distracted himself by watching TV with its news of the various campaigns, growing bored as the same stories repeated.

Eventually he turned to a movie channel and, to his amazement, caught the last half hour of *Moonfleet*, a cheap adventure feature he had worked on early in his career. In spite of its title, it had not been sci-fi, but rather a period piece about pirates and smugglers in the Caribbean (though the confusing title likely contributed to *Moonfleet*'s failure . . . that and an unappealing cast and incoherent script). Stuntman Jamal Norwood had one major gag in the piece, as a sailor who goes aloft during a storm only to have the yards break, plunging him to the deck of a ship.

Who was that young man? So eager, so fit, so certain he was making all the right decisions, making money, making himself into a star—

Right now Jamal merely wished he possessed that young man's health.

◆

Franny picked him up a block from the Bleecker. "You're getting good at all this paranoid shit," the detective told him.

"A little too late."

"Don't be a pessimist."

"Don't be a cheerleader."

It was the middle of rush hour, a murderous time to be traveling from Jokertown to the Upper East Side. "I don't suppose you can use your siren," Jamal said.

"Sure, but it won't do us any good." They were completely gridlocked trying to reach the FDR. Eventually it did, and to Jamal's relief there were no unusual traffic problems.

As they turned into the building's parking lot, Jamal

suddenly feared a Murphy's Law moment, that they would drive right past Michael Berman and Mollie Steunenberg heading out for a latte or breakfast—

Fortunately, no. Perhaps less fortunately, the attendant at the lot seemed all too aware of their business. "You know, my favorite TV series is *Baltimore Stakeout*," he said. "How do you get into that kind of work?"

"If you have to ask, you're not qualified," Jamal snapped.

They met up with Metz, who was as eager as a five-year-old on Christmas Day. "They're up there! You can hear voices."

"You actually saw them, though, right?" Jamal said.

Metz nodded.

Within minutes, Jamal and Franny were heading up the service elevator. Jamal carried a Watchman tuned to the cameras they had hidden in the apartment the night before, toggling from one view to the other. They were cheap Radio Shack–style equipment that couldn't be monitored remotely and of the two men one was too busy to man the cameras 24/7 and the other was too sick. No, the cameras were there because of Tesseract and her power. Both Jamal and Franny knew they needed to grab the girl first. Otherwise she'd be gone, and Berman with her. Jamal could see Berman and Mollie in motion in and out of the living room and hallway. They were out of view for minutes at a time, presumably in the kitchen, bathroom, bedrooms.

Jamal loathed stakeouts and had not prepared for this one. Thank God Franny seemed to be . . . the police detective had not only suggested hauling two folding chairs up the elevator, he produced water and an energy bar without asking. "I hope this doesn't take all day," Jamal said, knowing that he was now grumbling like a man twice his age.

They had deliberately chosen the back hallway as a site

for the second camera because it gave them their best opportunity to surprise Tesseract and grab her.

"We should have miked the place."

"Well, we didn't," Jamal said. "So we wait."

Their planning for Operation Grab Michael Berman had been complicated because they were skirting the edge of legality. "I don't suppose you have any black bag team you could activate," Franny said. "To find this shit and install it."

Had Jamal still been on duty with SCARE, he could easily have given the task to just such a group—right after Carnifex signed off on the warrant and the budget. "Haven't you created a team of Jokertown irregulars?"

"Not yet," Franny said. "And if this goes tits up, not ever."

Then there had been the question of warrants. "I can get one," Franny had said. "Might take a day, or at least hours. What about you?"

Jamal shook his head. "Right," Franny said. "Hard to do that when your bosses have no idea—"

"—And you're on medical leave."

They could just have gone ahead, warrantless. But, eager as he was to put Berman, and by extension this whole gaggle of joker-nabbing criminals, out of business as swiftly as possible, Jamal was unwilling to allow those arrested under U.S. law to skate because he and Franny acted like movie cops. "Do what you can as quickly as you can."

While Franny worked the warrant issue, Jamal trolled through the audio and video shops on Eighth Avenue in search of surveillance gear—which turned out to be easy to acquire, though a bit hard on his credit card.

That night he left a message for Franny, then collapsed. When he awoke, yesterday morning, Franny's message was: "Warrant in hand; good to go."

♥

Shortly after twelve-thirty P.M. Jamal and Franny heard raised voices from inside the apartment, Berman yelling something at Mollie and receiving a blistering answer in return. "All right," Franny said, "I withdraw my petty complaint about lack of audio surveillance . . ."

Wearing a T-shirt that displayed two of her more notable features and a pair of shorts that would, if worn in public, have gotten her arrested in certain communities, Mollie stormed into the hallway carrying a bag of garbage.

"Showtime!" Jamal whispered. Franny displayed a pair of handcuffs. "Double-locking Smith & Wesson," he had told Jamal earlier. "Bought them for twenty-five bucks!" He unlocked them—

—As Jamal pushed the door open, smiling and saying, "Hey, there!"

The girl was stunned into silence and immobility as Jamal wrapped her up—not the most unpleasant act he had performed in the past few weeks—allowing Franny to cuff himself to her, his left wrist to Mollie's right.

Now Mollie found her voice. "What the fuck?" she shouted, writhing and struggling and trying to slap Franny with her left hand.

Her voice brought Berman—in rumpled khakis and an *American Hero* T-shirt—into the hallway.

Jamal was ready for him—"Hi, Michael!"—diving at the producer and slamming him against the wall in a hammerlock, an action he had wanted to take for at least five years. He got a second pair of cuffs on Berman. "In case you're wondering, you're under arrest."

Berman had sufficient composure to say, "Do you have a warrant?"

Franny slapped the warrant on his chest. "Read, weep."

♣

They hauled Berman into the living room. Jamal shoved him into an expensive-looking leather chair while Franny took Mollie to the couch. "Why are you doing this?" she asked the detective.

"So you don't pull your Tesseract trick."

"I don't need my hands."

"True. But if you go, you'll be taking me. And I'm guessing you don't want that."

"What if I need to pee?" Mollie said.

Hearing this, Jamal laughed out loud. "Then you'll still have Detective Black for company."

Suddenly the girl seemed less eager.

Berman had been complaining ever since being slammed against the wall. "This is brutality, plain and simple. I don't care what your warrant says."

"We don't care that you don't care," Jamal said.

"What's the charge?"

Jamal turned to Franny. "Detective?"

"Dealer's choice. Fraud, murder, accessory to both, terminal assholeism." Franny grinned at Jamal. "It was hard to narrow it down—"

Berman finally lowered his voice. He looked at Jamal, too. "Hey, Stuntman, who'd a thunk it?"

"You mean, who'd a thunk that you'd wind up in cuffs someday, Michael?" Jamal said. "Only every fucking person you ever met."

That actually seemed to sting Berman. He turned back to Franny. "Okay, what? You take us downtown? Is that the drill? When do I call my lawyer?"

"We could talk first," Franny said. "Isn't that right, Jamal?"

"I believe that Mr. Berman's cooperation at this time would be looked upon with some sympathy."

Berman seemed to think this over. Then, a dangerous smile—one that Jamal recognized—appeared on his face. "All right, then, yeah. A little conversation between friends." He cleared his voice and looked at Jamal. "Would you like to record this?"

Jamal set his phone on the table between them. "We'd love to."

"I am offering my full, voluntary cooperation here," Berman said. "Mollie, you're a witness."

"Wow," Mollie said, stretching a single syllable into a four-second snarl of sarcasm.

Berman held up his cuffed hands. "May we lose these?"

"What," Franny said, "you can't talk without using your hands?"

Jamal laughed. "He's telling the truth!"

♠

So Jamal uncuffed Berman, who flexed his wrists and got slowly to his feet. "Time for the aria. You may recognize this."

"Jamal—" Franny said, a bit alarmed.

Jamal just waved a hand. "Watch and listen." He knew that for Berman, presentation and salesmanship truly over-rode all other concerns, even personal safety and dignity.

The producer faced them, hands clasped, eyes closed.

Then he opened them. "Okay, picture this. A talented, rich, ambitious, handsome young man with a flaw. A very human one . . . he wants money and power, not just for themselves. But for what they can give him. Which is love, right? What everyone wants. Picture Tom Cruise."

"Oh, you wish!" Mollie said.

Franny was still nervous. To Jamal he said, "Okay, what is this?"

"He's *pitching*!"

"He's *trying* to, Detective," Berman said. He actually seemed angry at the interruption.

"Continue," Jamal said.

"Thank you," Berman said. "Let's give our hero a

name—Gene. Gene could never accept that he would be loved for who he was or what he wanted to be . . . so he went for the money. So, yeah, he's a bit of an unsympathetic character. But so was Rick in *Casablanca*. Or Charles Foster Kane. You don't have to like Gene, you just have to want to see how far he goes . . . the depths he will descend to." To Jamal he said, "He makes a lot of money."

"So I recall," Jamal said, knowing that Berman was playing him, but not especially concerned. He had always found the producer to be fascinating. How low *would* he go?

"But no amount of money is ever enough, right? Just like you never have enough love or—" And here he leered at Mollie. "—or sex—" Which made Mollie shudder.

"And earning it through work is ultimately unsatisfying. So Gene begins to gamble."

"Like every other rich asshole in Hollywood," Franny said. Jamal laughed: Mr. Police Detective was getting into this!

"It starts with sports, then gets into . . . more interesting sports. Cock-fighting, then the human equivalent. Fights to the death, especially with jokers. Insane visuals, tragic moments, and large amounts of money changing hands. Then, and here's where Gene's arrogance rises to the level of a Greek tragedy—which is pretty highfalutin for a Hollywood pitch, but you'll see why it works. He bets on his own television series, one of those survival game things in which spy cameras and crazy competitions are edited into episodes week by week, so audiences can vote on their favorites.

"This series becomes hugely popular, and there is betting everywhere, especially in Europe. Now, you can't just go to Vegas and make these kinds of bets, not for interesting amounts of money. You've got to find a place with a Wild West sensibility, or in Gene's case . . . Wild East. A casino in Kazakhstan." Berman glanced behind him. "If I'd had a few moments' notice, I could show you some visuals."

"If you'd had a few moments' notice, we wouldn't be here," Franny said.

"Gene goes big for a female winner whose name is probably not important—only to have her walk off the show! There's a little twist for you . . . she just changes her fucking mind, typical woman, something Gene can't control—making a far less-suitable male contestant the winner."

Jamal cleared his throat. "Less suitable?" He couldn't let Berman's comment pass without challenge.

Berman continued to play the game. "Let's just say, less suitable for our hero's purposes."

Jamal wanted to get to the point where Berman actually incriminated himself. "Michael, so far we're just taking our character down," Jamal said. "I like a good wallow as well as anyone, if the scenery is good and the dialogue is snappy."

"Oh, the scenery is fantastic. A bleak landscape in Kazakhstan, and set against it a city of mystery. Known as Talas when it was a major stop on the ancient Silk Road you'll now see it written as Taraz or Tapa3, but it's the same place filled with history and secrets. And there are dangerous secrets in this casino palace in the middle of it. Beautiful Russian hookers for eye candy. Handsome Eurotrash men in tuxes. And wild bad guys like Dmitri, who is this huge fat guy, always wears a T-shirt, one of those sleeveless ones, even on the casino floor. Oh, and he chews gum. All the time. What makes him dangerous is his ability to crawl into your head. Fucks with you, makes you afraid. So afraid you freeze up."

"Noted," Jamal said. "But Dmitri isn't the star of your movie."

Berman smiled. "Nowhere near. He's just one of many threats. There is one far more dangerous, and the most unlikely villain you can imagine. Picture an elderly woman, call her Baba Yaga—"

"Michael," Mollie said, warning the producer. She had suddenly begun to pay attention.

He ignored her. "Obviously, given her business, she's not an ordinary old lady. Terrific casting possibility here, though. I'm thinking of one of those English actresses who were sex symbols a generation ago—"

"Wait!" Franny was laughing. "Your big villain is the world's scariest seventy-year-old woman? What does she do, whack you with her walker?"

Berman laughed. "Good one, Detective. Actually, no. Baba Yaga is an ace. She . . . changes people. And not in a good way. We're talking about furniture. So, at the same time Gene suffers a series of losses—huge amounts of money he can't pay—rather than transform him into a footstool, which she threatens to do, she comes up with a way he can pay her back: by using his skills and his team to, uh, recruit jokers for death matches at her casino. Next thing Gene knows, he's in business with a pretty young woman who possesses an amazing talent, one that allows her to move pretty much anywhere. There's a nice symmetry there too—this girl was also a contestant on our hero's show but in a later season. Ties everything together, you know? Anyway, this is the end of the first act.

"This team identifies interesting jokers and grabs them. Not by themselves, of course . . . Baba Yaga wants people she trusts at every step of the process. So Gene and his girl—"

"I was never your *girl*," Mollie snapped.

"I'm talking about the girl in this movie," Berman said, smoothly. "The jokers would be held in New Jersey until they had enough to fill a van for this talented girl to ship them to Kazakhstan."

Franny said, "Hey, is that where Father Squid is?"

"Who?"

"A very large joker who looks just the way the name suggests," Jamal said. "He's a priest."

Berman snorted. "He's not part of the pitch."

"He's an important figure in Jokertown," Franny snarled. "It's important for us to find him."

"I can . . . imagine a joker like that in Kazakhstan. So, sure, he's part of the cast, part of this new crew. Better fights, more money. Everybody's happy!" Then he lowered his voice. "Until one stupid cameraman sells footage of the fights."

Jamal had felt two different emotions as he listened to this presentation. First was amusement at seeing Berman in action—the producer's version of begging for his life and using the tools that have worked for him all his career.

Second was the satisfaction of having the dots connected for the missing jokers and dead cameraman Joe Frank. "Is there some point in the story where our hero fucks up?" Jamal said. "Where he is confronted by the police and possibly a handsome superstar of a federal agent, and he gives up the cameraman only to learn that he's been killed?"

Berman blinked. "The hero is stuck. He knows that the cameraman is in, shall we say, a tenuous situation, quite likely to be a victim of Baba Yaga's temper. But he has no choice, does he? He's trying to buy time—"

"What's act three?" Jamal said. "How does he get out of this?"

All during the pitch, Berman had been on his feet, moving between the couch and the television. Now, however, the producer was kneeling in front of the cabinet beneath his television, rummaging through various DVDs.

Until he came up with a gun, which he swiftly pointed at Franny. "This is how," he said, pulling the trigger.

Before he could react, there was a flash to Jamal's left—a change of light as, strangely, the couch seemed to open up and swallow Franny and Mollie. But only for a fraction of a second; the couch was in place again, spewing fabric as Berman's bullet blew through it.

Berman was training the weapon on him, but now Jamal was in motion, moving faster than he had in months. He slammed the producer into the entertainment unit, hurting himself in the process, but ensuring that Berman was unable to fire the pistol again.

He was ready to pummel the man . . . years of frustration made him want to smash the smug criminal bastard's face. But Berman was moaning, already defeated.

Franny appeared, dragging Mollie with one wrist, holding his weapon with the other. They had simply walked into the living room from the back hallway. "Do pitches usually end like this?" Franny said.

Jamal had no answer for that. After securing Berman's pistol, he pulled the producer to his feet. Berman groaned and stretched his back, which surely hurt like hell. "Michael, what did you think would happen?" Jamal said.

"Shoot the cop, then you. Then out of here."

"I'd bounce back."

"Sure. But not for a few minutes." *Possibly not ever,* Jamal thought.

"It's time we took Mr. Showbiz and his tape downtown," Franny said.

"What about me?" Mollie was blinking tears and now looked about fifteen—and frightened.

"What *about* her?" Franny said.

"We take her in, book her, she gets a lawyer. No way any lawyer is going to let her help us. And we need her to get the jokers. Or worst case, she gets bail and she's in the wind."

"So a little sin of omission," Franny said.

Which is how Stuntman wound up handcuffed to Tesseract.

♣ ♦ ♠ ♥

Ties That Bind

Part Five

KAVITHA HAD SAID NO to his proposal.

"Why the hell not?" was what Michael had said in response, which in retrospect was perhaps not the most tactful way to persuade a woman to marry you. But he'd been genuinely shocked—he'd never actually thought she'd say no. And worse, Kavitha had refused to tell them why, even when Minal had started crying. And Michael had tried not to shout, but the discussion had gotten a little . . . heated, and they must have gotten pretty loud, because Isai woke up, and then Maya Aunty, and somehow it was two A.M. before they got everybody back to bed, and he'd just given up and collapsed. Minal wore his ring, but Kavitha didn't, and that was just wrong.

Maybe Michael couldn't find Sandip, but he could at least find out what was going on with his girlfriend. If he couldn't stalk his girlfriend, what good was it being a cop, anyway?

♦

Michael called in sick to work the next day, *after* he'd left the condo.

She spent the morning at the studio, but at noon she left and didn't head for home. It was easy, following her. She might have ace powers, and jet set with the Committee on occasion, but Kavitha was still a civilian at heart. She didn't even look behind as she left the studio, walking a path that wasn't taking her home to the condo. And when she finally ended up in a frankly terrible part of town, she headed straight into one of the dingiest motels on the street. Michael waited a few beats, and then followed her in. She might see him, but at this point, he knew enough to confront her if he had to. He was going to get the truth out of her, one way or another.

He was in time to see the elevator doors closing, and to watch the indicator go up, up, up. Third floor. Michael took the stairs, as fast as he could, glad he'd kept up with the station's physical requirements, and emerged from the stairwell just in time to catch her disappearing into room 328. At that point, he abandoned all subtlety— because what the hell? Why in God's name would his girlfriend be meeting up with someone in a dingy motel? Was this why she'd refused to marry him?

There was just one likely explanation, but it made no sense. Michael found himself with one hand on the door, the other on his gun, fighting a sudden murderous rage. It was one thing to date more than one person—it was an entirely different thing to have one of them cheating on you. If she'd just *told* him that she wanted to see someone else—well, Michael still wouldn't like it, but he wouldn't feel the need to pound somebody's face in. He didn't think.

"Open up!" he shouted. "Police!"

The door suddenly swung open, with his fist still raised to pound again, and Michael almost fell inside before catching himself on the door frame. Kavitha stood just a

step away, and there, legs and feet hanging off the end of
the motel bed was . . . her brother. His torso swathed in
bandages, looking like death warmed over, with terror
in his dark brown eyes.

Michael took a quick, steadying breath. Carefully, deliberately, lowered his hand from the butt of his gun,
suddenly ashamed of the urge that had put it there. And
then he asked, in as calm a voice as he could manage,
"Will one of you *please* explain what is going on?"

They didn't fall over themselves to explain. Not at first.
The silence grew quite deafening, until Kavitha finally
said, "Sandip. Tell him." She moved over to sit by her
brother and took his hand in her own slim hand. She pet-
ted it gently, reassuring him, and finally, the kid opened
his mouth to speak.

"They're killing jokers. Killing *people*." The words
came stumbling out, and suddenly, shockingly, the kid
was crying, big gasping sobs from deep in his belly, tears
streaming down his face. Kavitha grabbed a towel by the
side of the bed and started dabbing at his cheeks with
practiced motions, as if she'd done this before. As if she'd
been doing this for days.

"Tell me what happened," Michael said, in his calm-
est cop voice. On one level, he couldn't believe Kavitha
had kept this from him—but he held the anger down,
waiting for the facts.

And the story came spilling out. Sandip had been re-
cruited a few weeks ago by the kidnapping squad; one
of the disgruntled Tamils he'd tried to join up with had
been a joker involved in the scheme. Sandip knew the
basics of how to handle a gun, part of his revolutionary
aspirations, though he'd never shot one outside the range.
He didn't mind waving one around to scare people,
though. Especially given how much money they'd paid
him to do it.

"And not just money. Free drinks, as many as I wanted,
and women too. Fucking gorgeous women just waiting

for us. *Machan,* you should have seen the setup they had over there." The kid's eyes were wide and glassy.

"Over where?" Michael asked sharply.

Sandip huddled in on himself, and Kavitha put a protective hand on his arm. "I can't remember. They never really told us anything, but I heard some of them talking about it. Some tiny country, something stan?"

This was important. He had to tell the captain, as soon as he got the whole story. The kid was still babbling. "I don't know where it was, I'm sorry. I'm sorry!" He kept going on about how cool it had seemed, at first. Sandip had thought he was living the dream. And then they'd let him see the killings.

Now he was crying again as he talked, the words stuttering between jagged sobs. "I mean, they *told* me what was going on, but it's different when you see it. They said joker fight club, I figured it was gangsters, big guys, fighting it out to prove their manhood, y'know? Those were the kind of guys I was helping to grab. But the first real fight I saw, it was this little man, with glasses—he looked like a schoolteacher. Like the guy who taught my freshman history class. I kind of hated Mr. Matthews, but I didn't want to see him ripped apart into little pieces! The other guy started chomping on what was left of his stomach, and that's when I knew I couldn't keep doing this." Now Sandip was crying so hard that he couldn't talk anymore, and Kavitha took up the story.

"That's almost all of it," she said. "When they came back to New York on that trip, he took off. Got shot in the shoulder, but got away. He was too scared to go to the hospital, so he called me. It was the day your parents came for dinner. I snuck out that night, took some of our money, and rented him this place. Got medicine, bandages, dug the bullet out of his shoulder, patched him up and prayed that he'd survive it. You should have seen the shape he was in." Her voice was high, trembling.

Michael couldn't believe what he was hearing. "A

week. You've kept this from us for a week?" No wonder she'd been wound up so tight; keeping secrets wasn't in Kavitha's nature. It must have been killing her to lie to them like this. That didn't make him any less angry. Rage was churning in his stomach.

"Michael." Kavitha stood up, came two steps closer, close enough that he could smell her fear. Although, perhaps wisely, she didn't touch him. "I knew you'd have to arrest him, send him to jail for a long, long time. But he's just a kid. That's what they do, you know." Her voice was shaky now, close to breaking. Kavitha took a deep breath, trying to steady herself. "To keep the brutality going—they take children, and make them part of their battles. We can't punish the children for what the adults have done."

Michael shook his head. His chest felt as if it were being stabbed with knives. He'd never thought heartbreak could feel so literal, so real. "Kavitha, you know better. He participated. Sandip is old enough to know what he was doing when he took those people to their deaths." She'd always been so committed to doing what was right. It was part of why he loved her. He'd known how she felt about family, but he'd thought she was better than this.

The boy was quieter now, doubled over and hugging his knees, swallowing his sobs.

She spread out her hands, helplessly. Despite everything, Michael was struck once again by how beautifully she moved. "He's my little brother," Kavitha said. "You should have seen him, bloody, with a bullet in him. He asked me to help him. I thought if I hid him for a little while, until it was all over . . ." She trailed off, clearly not sure what possible good ending there could have been.

If she had only come to him right away—he could have found some way to make it right. To protect the boy; as a juvenile, if Sandip had come in and told his story right away, maybe Michael could have saved him. But now it was too late. "You lied to me for a week. You let these bastards continue their operation unimpeded. How many people did they grab, in the last week?" He could see the words hitting Kavitha, see her bracing against their assault.

How could they come back from this? Michael realized that she was never going to wear his ring, not now. He couldn't offer it to her after this, even if he understood on some level why she'd done it. He couldn't keep living with her; he could barely look at her. Oh, Isai. Sweetheart. This was going to tear their little girl apart. And Minal—would she still marry him? Or would he lose her too? If he made her choose between them, Michael didn't know who Minal would pick.

Kavitha stepped back, away from him. Let her hands fall to her sides. "What are you going to do, Michael?"

She knew the answer; she knew him too well. "What I have to."

Michael said the words, feeling the weight of them fall like a knife between them, cutting the ties that bound them together. "Sandip Kandiah, you're under arrest. You have the right to remain silent. Anything you say or do can and will be held against you in a court of law . . ."

Those About to Die . . .

Part Six

STANDING JUST OUTSIDE THE arena, hidden behind the doors that opened into it, Marcus told himself, *Just one more time.*

One more, and this is all over.

He knew he would hate himself for it later, when he was far from here and could look back. But that would be then. This was now. He had to get out of here. With Olena. He would do this for her, and then they would be free. They'd hide somewhere nobody knew him. It wouldn't matter where, because he'd have Olena.

Just one more death, and then never again.

The music died down and changed tempo. The announcer called for the crowd's attention. "Ladies and gentlemen, it's been an amazing night so far," he claimed, "but now it's time for the main event—a death match. Not since the time of the ancients, of Rome's mighty glory, have gladiators risked their very lives in the arena. But this bout goes even further back than that. Back to the very beginning. Back to the Garden of Good and Evil."

A different voice cut in, speaking a different language.

Russian, Marcus guessed. And after that still another language, perhaps Chinese.

Marcus thought, *The world's watching,* but he hoped that wasn't true. Both for himself, and for what it meant about the world.

The English announcer picked up again, saying the first competitor, ladies and gentlemen, showed his murderous talent just days ago. He comes armed with the weapons the wild card virus gave him. Welcome him, ladies and gentlemen! *The Infamous Black Tongue!*

The doors in front of Marcus flew open. The rush of sound trapped in the small, claustrophobic space hit him like a physical force. He slithered into the bright lights of the arena. As soon as he was through, the doors shut behind him, trapping him inside. That was all right, though. He knew the way out. To kill. And he knew this arena. It was a friend. He passed through a rippling wave of tension in the air. Like heat but not. Like a scent but scentless. He sucked it in, feeding off it, filling himself with the rage he was going to need.

His eyes darted up to Baba Yaga's box. She was there, like always, with the twisted old man beside her. But this time someone sat on her other side, looking uncomfortable and nervous. And beautiful. Olena. She wore a tiny, tight red dress, and had her hair pulled up. She could've been a model, or a starlet on the arm of some Hollywood actor. He hated that she was so close to that evil woman and that horror of a man. Hated that the black-suited guards lined the back wall, a half dozen of them, staring at the arena from behind black sunglasses. They shouldn't be anywhere near Olena. He closed his eyes, reminding himself that once this was over she was going to be his. He would take her away from all this. That's what mattered.

When he opened his eyes again, Baba Yaga reached over and set a hand atop Olena's. She held it there, watching Marcus. The message was clear.

When the commotion died down the announcer continued. Facing the serpent would be a soldier of death disguised in godly robes. For years he pretended to be a man of the cloth, when he was really a man of the blade, a soldier of fortune with a past soaked in blood. They all knew the name he went by now. They'd all seen him in action.

As the translations rattled on, Marcus pulled his thoughts, and his eyes, away from Olena. *A man of the cloth?* he wondered. That didn't describe El Monstro. Or Nimble Dick. Or John the Pharaoh. Or any of the jokers he thought they'd match him with. They couldn't mean . . .

A door on the other side of the arena opened. A hooded figure lumbered through.

No! Marcus thought.

As if refuting him directly, the announcer shouted, "Bring in the Holy Redeemer!"

No, they can't do this!

The door slammed shut behind the priest. Father Squid reached up and pinched back his hood with his fingers. He stared at Marcus. He didn't look surprised. He didn't look horrified. But Marcus couldn't say what emotions did lie in the dark depths behind his large, round eyes.

"Ladies and gentlemen," the announcer intoned, "the serpent and the holy man! Only one of them can leave this Garden of Good and Evil alive. Who will it be? Which one should it be?" He reminded them that they could place bets electronically right up to the moment of first contact. That was the first thing that hushed the crowd, as many heads turned down to their mobile phones.

Father Squid approached him with his heavy steps.

"What are you doing here?" Marcus snapped. "You're messing up everything. You can't be here!"

The priest shook his head solemnly. "I'm the only one who should face you, Marcus."

"This a death match!"

"Who better than a priest to face death with?"

The man's calm annoyed Marcus. His fists turned to stones. Resentment surged through him. "Stop talking nonsense."

Shouts and jeers rained down on them, the audience urging them to fight.

"Marcus, God put us in this ring together. Nothing happens without his will. I understand it now."

Marcus wanted to grab him and shake him. He almost punched him. He wanted to. He was ready to. That's why he was here, to beat someone down. To kill. But . . . he couldn't make his fists do what they'd have to. He thought, *This is Father Squid.*

Father Squid looked away from him. He let his eyes range over the crowd. "We're not here for them. We're here so that you can become the man you are destined to be."

And then Marcus understood. The realization hit him with a physical force, stunning him, but also clearing the clutter from his mind at the same time. "You . . . you volunteered to fight me, didn't you?"

"I'm here to give you the last thing that I can. It's the only way you'll get out of here. Kill me, Marcus. Give in to the rage that you're holding back. Just this one last time."

The announcer piped up, saying something to the audience. Marcus concentrated through the announcer's voice and the crowd's taunts and the urge inside him to lash out. It was still there. He still breathed it in. It still egged him on. Just start it, his body seemed to be saying. Start it, and let death happen. He fought to get a word out. "Why?"

Father Squid closed the short space between them. He grasped Marcus by his forearms. Marcus tensed. His coils bunched, every inch of him screaming to unleash. The crowd roared, thinking something was finally going to happen.

The priest spoke slowly, clearly. "Because I led you into this hell. Because I've had my life, filled as it was with crimes—and with wonders. But for you, Marcus, the meaning of your life and work on this earth is before you. You can yet be a great man. I've always seen it in you, from the very first time I saw you—a frightened, angry fugitive, seeking help but not knowing how to ask."

"But you—"

Father Squid tugged on his arms, sharply. "Because there's no other way! And, as God sees and knows and plans all, this must be what he plans for us. No matter what you do, I absolve you. Now fight me!" The priest let go of Marcus's arms, pulled back, and slapped him.

The blow tossed Marcus to the side. Fury rushed through him. He swung back, fists cocked, poisonous saliva flooding his mouth. The crowd loved it. They rose to their feet.

"Kill me!" the priest bellowed. He slapped him again. "You have the rage. I see it in your eyes. Do what your body wants. Fight. Hate me, Marcus, for standing between you and your love. Kill me, and go with her and be free. Cut the bullshit and do it, Marcus!"

Marcus almost obeyed. He was so close. Father Squid was right there in front of him, offering the path to everything Marcus thought he wanted. Freedom. Olena. But hearing profanity come from the priest's mouth was another slap, one that brought with it a memory. Marcus saw the spinning of a teacup, thrown from his hand, chipped by his frustration. He heard that curse word, but to his shame it was his mouth that uttered it. A word said in anger. A teacup thrown. Chipped. He'd always regretted that. Always been ashamed of it. Always wished he could take it back.

"It's the only way out of here for you, and for me," Father Squid said, shoving him with one powerful arm. "I cannot take my own life, but I can give it. I give to you. It's okay, Marcus. Really. I'm not afraid. I will face my reckoning. If God allows it I'll see my Lizzie again, and that will be the greatest gift of all. What are you afraid of? Just do it. Poison me. And then do it. I'll feel nothing, if that's what you're worried about."

Marcus could poison him. He knew that. The father's aquatic skin, he figured, would absorb his venom in an instant. And then what? Break his neck? Choke him? It could be done, but knowing that he could just confirmed that he wouldn't. It was strange, how calming that realization was. He was going to lose everything. He would never have that life with Olena. He would likely die in the moments to come. He wouldn't have that future that Father Squid imagined for him, but he felt a resigned satisfaction at all of this. He could stay true to himself. He could go forward into his last moments without shame. He could make both Olena and Father Squid proud. That mattered more than anything else. The only thing he couldn't do was what the priest asked him.

Marcus glanced up at Olena. He saw in her face that she understood, looked more concerned than ever. Even from a distance, he could see her lower lip quivering. Slightly, ever so slightly, she shook her head. That was what Marcus needed. He slid forward and grasped Father Squid by the arms, just as the priest had done to him a moment before. "You really loved her, didn't you?"

"Lizzie?" the priest asked, coming in close to support him. "Yes, with all my heart. Loving her has kept me human. She was in every act of kindness I did."

"I'm sure she's waiting for you. You'll see her again, but not by my hand. That simply cannot happen. You mean too much to me."

As he spoke, the priest's facial tentacles went slack. He closed his eyes. When he opened them, they were again the ones Marcus had always known. Calm. Sad. Wise. A tear escaped one corner and trickled down into his tentacles.

Turning from him, Marcus projected his voice to cut

through the crowd's commotion. "No, I won't do it. This man, he saved me. You understand that? When I was nobody, miserable, lost: he took me in and taught me I could be something. And you want me to kill him? No, I won't." He turned to Baba Yaga. His tongue quickened. "And fuck you, bitch, for starting all this. You got nothing on me. Not anymore. Not when you ask me to do this."

The old woman had risen from her seat. The crowd, looking from the players in the ring up to the standing woman, hushed.

Glaring down at Marcus, Baba Yaga's lips moved. She said, "Kill him if you want to live. If you want the girl." Her voice was just a whisper, but Marcus heard her clearly enough. Or did he see the words on her lips? Or just feel them, pressed from her mind to his? Whichever it was, there was power in that voice. Command. That voice could have told him to do a lot of things and he would've, especially for Olena. But this one thing he wouldn't do. Marcus shook his head.

Baba Yaga stared down. It was nearly impossible to hold her gaze. Marcus had seen hard men. He'd faced monstrous jokers. He'd killed men who wanted to kill him. But none of them had a face as deathly fierce as this old woman. The anger in her eyes pummeled him, seared him.

Watching must have unnerved the crowd. Whispers passed through the audience. Uncomfortable shifting. A few rose and then stood, unsure what was happening. One man, sounding drunk, said this wasn't what he paid for. The woman next to him shushed him.

"Marcus," Father Squid said, "you could still—"

"Never," Marcus said.

"I only wanted a future for you."

"A future with your blood on my hands? Never."

Baba Yaga's voice was small and cold, and yet reached them clearly. "You defy me? Foolish boy." She puckered her thin lips. She sucked in her cheeks, leaned forward, and spat.

The spittle fell through the wire mesh and down toward Marcus. Such a small action from such a small woman. *Pathetic,* he thought, *if that's the best she can do.*

Father Squid smashed into Marcus's side and shoved him away.

The small gob of spit landed where Marcus had been a moment before. It splattered on the side of Father Squid's cheek. The priest yanked his face away, but not quickly enough. He pressed his fingers to his tentacled cheek. He staggered. His body went rigid, fingers jerking spasmodically. His black eyes bulged, as if a great pain had bloomed inside him and he just then understood it.

Marcus slid toward him. He reached out, but Father Squid twisted away. He walked a few stiff steps before one of his legs buckled. In the complete hush of the arena, Marcus heard the snap of bone breaking. Not just once but again and again, a whole concussion of fractures. Father Squid went down. At first he grasped his leg, but he let go when it began to bend and twist. And then his other did the same. His head snapped back, banging against the floor. His torso bulged as if living things were moving beneath his skin. He rolled over and tried to push himself up. A wave rolled up his spine, audibly snapping vertebrae as it did. His arms and legs wouldn't support him. They were shattered, rubbery things, writhing.

And then he did rise, but not by his own power. The terror on his face made that clear. His body levered up from the floor, slowly, excruciatingly, supported on legs that were no longer legs. When he was upright, his eyes found Marcus. With great, trembling effort, he said one long, drawn-out word. *"Lizzzzzzzzie . . ."*

Before he was finished, the name rose into a scream. His torso snapped back from his middle and he became a molten form morphing out of all recognizing. His face went liquid. His eyes held their shape but they swam within the shifting chaos. His mouth was still a mouth and it screamed and screamed . . .

Until it stopped. Until all the horrible motion ceased. Marcus stared, recognizing what stood on the floor beside him, but not believing it. In the silence of the arena, Marcus—and everyone else—stared at the strange structure that was and wasn't Father Squid. The priest had been transformed into a prayer bench, complete with padded platform for the knees and an upper shelf for the faithful to lean against, heads bowed. Trapped in material that wasn't exactly flesh but wasn't wood or metal or plastic either, the father still breathed. His mouth stretched wide across the front portion of the bench. He saw still, through eyes that no longer had a face. Instead, they looked up from the shelf on which one of the faithful might tent their hands in prayer.

Galahad in Blue

Part Nine

FRANNY HAD FLASHED A badge at a cabbie, and shoved the handcuffed Berman into the back of the cab. He hadn't been gentle. They had wasted weeks, even shut down the investigation when all the while this man had held the key. And had kept silent while people died. Thinking about Father Squid and all the others trapped in a nightmare had Franny's hands clenching in impotent rage.

Wingman goggled at him as he blew in the door of the precinct, shoving the producer ahead of him. "Book this asshole."

"Okay. For what?"

"Attempted murder, assaulting a police officer, kidnapping, conspiracy . . . hell, being an asshole for that matter. Captain?"

"He's in," Homer said, still looking poleaxed.

Franny nodded. Homer called down to Sergeant Squinch and took control of Berman. Franny pushed through into the bullpen. Michael Stevens, seated at his desk, looked at him. Strain had etched lines around his eyes. He looked like a man who had lost everything. Franny ignored him, strode across the room to the office door, gave one pre-emptory knock and walked in. Maseryk looked up, a Jovian frown creasing his forehead. Surprisingly Mendelberg was also there, seated in a chair across the desk from the older man.

"Black, what the fuck?" the joker woman asked.

"I know where they're holding our missing jokers," Franny said. The two captains exchanged glances.

"Yeah, we do too," Mendelberg said.

Maseryk shot her a glance. "That might be a bit of an overstatement. We know they're someplace that ends in stan."

"How did you? Never mind . . . I've got more than that. They're in Kazakhstan, in a town called Talas," Franny said.

"Kazakhstan," Mendelberg repeated as if she were tasting the word.

Looking down into those bloodred eyes Frank remembered how Mendelberg had shut down the investigation, browbeaten him for arguing. He couldn't control it, he snapped, "Do you want me to spell it for you?"

That brought Maseryk out of his chair. "You better fucking climb down, Detective."

Mendelberg surprised him. She waved it off. "It's okay, Thomas." She turned back to Franny. "Where did you come by this?"

"Berman. He's being processed right now."

"You arrested him," Mendelberg said slowly.

"Yes."

"Why?"

Franny laid out what had occurred at the condo. For a moment the two captains just blinked at him, then Mendelberg reverted to form.

"Why is a SCARE agent involved in an NYPD investigation?"

"He had resources I . . . why are we talking about Norwood? Why aren't we—"

"Tell me everything," Maseryk ordered.

"That could take a while."

"Give me the *Reader's Digest* version."

So Franny walked them through it all. How the dead joker on a rural highway in New Jersey linked up with a SCARE investigation of smuggling. How the body led to the dog-training facility. How Jamal had run the names of the dead Russians that linked them to the KGB, how the DVDs had led to an *American Hero* cameraman, which had led to Berman, and how Berman had provided to the mysterious and very scary Baba Yaga the names of jokers who had auditioned for *American Hero*. "It sounds like there's a lot of former KGB goons so we better have SWAT—"

"Are you listening to yourself?" Maseryk interrupted. "This is Fort Freak. NYPD Fifth Precinct. We don't have jurisdiction in Brooklyn, much less fucking Kazakhstan."

"And even if we could act how the hell would we get there? Flying carpet?" Mendelberg chimed in.

"We've got that handled."

Maseryk came out of his chair again. "You are not going to cause a diplomatic incident. And neither am I."

"So what? We're going to do nothing? These people are being killed." Franny clenched his teeth before even more intemperate words could emerge.

"Black, my first partner here, thirty years ago, taught me one hard lesson: when in doubt do nothing. Otherwise you're sure as fuck going to make things worse." The captain continued, forestalling the objections he saw rising to Franny's lips. "Now, nothing doesn't mean nothing. The first thing we're going to do is contact the State Department. Then I'll get on the horn to the UN, see if I can reach Lohengrin and the Committee. Your buddy can tell his people at SCARE. We rattle enough cages this Baba Yaga may shut down the operation."

"And bury the evidence. Literally." Franny spun and headed for the door.

"Black! Where are you going?" Mendelberg yelled after him.

"To do something."

"You walk out of here . . . it's your career," Maseryk warned.

"It's my soul if I don't."

Conversations in the bullpen were subdued. Franny realized the reality of a fight if not the details had penetrated to the assembled cops. Michael intercepted him before he reached the door. "I'll go with you," he said.

"How did you . . . ?"

Michael shrugged. "There's a place in the hall where every word from the captain's office comes through the vent. My dad showed me. I'm your partner, Franny. I haven't been a very good one up till now. Let me see if I can do something about that."

Franny read the shame and the sincerity in Michael's eyes. Jamal was sick, barely on his feet. Having another person . . . Franny shook his head. "You've got a kid. And I've heard you're getting married."

"Maybe not," Michael muttered.

Franny didn't have time to inquire. "Look, I appreciate it, but no. Now I've gotta go before the brass finds some way to arrest *me*."

Those About to Die . . .

Part Seven

MARCUS HAD TO DRAG his eyes away from Father Squid. They seemed heavy as stones. He lifted them and found Baba Yaga. She stood with her arms crossed, her lips pursed and her cheeks sucked in against the bones of her face.

You bitch, Marcus thought. At first it was a whisper. *You bitch.* But then, as he watched the smug satisfaction that lifted the corners of her lips, it became a scream. *Biittttcccchhhh!* All the rage and anger and confusion and determination to kill that he had overcome with Father Squid surged back into him with a vengeance. Poison-laden saliva flooded his mouth. He didn't think about what he did next. He just rose and did it.

He propelled himself upwards and crashed against the mesh that trapped the fighters in the ring. He pressed it up, his tail flexing beneath him. When the strained tension of the mesh pushed him back he fell with it. Gripping the mesh in his fists, he yanked down savagely, using the weight of his long body.

Dangling from it and looking through the lacework, he saw Baba Yaga turn to one of her guards. She jabbed her finger, indicating Olena. The burly, black-suited man stepped up behind her. He pinched Olena's shoulder in one hand. Using his other, he caressed her chin with the barrel of a handgun, lifting up on it to make her rise. She looked terrified.

Marcus shot upwards again, and then yanked down again. Up and down again, more frantic, failing with each attempt. The guard was leading Olena away. The announcer was saying something. It sounded like he was ridiculing Marcus. The crowd, watching him thrash, began to relax again. A man decked out in African garb pointed at him, smiling. A red-haired woman in a tight black dress stood and thrashed in imitation of Marcus. Another man followed Marcus with his upheld cell phone, his freckled face tight in concentration as he tried to take a photo.

Hating them all, Marcus roared up into the mesh with renewed fury. He clenched it in his fists and wrenched his body around, his snake portion twisting him with all the force of his long, trembling muscles. He felt one section of the mesh give, just a single ringlet cord where it looped through one of the thick glass panels. He sensed it like a spider in its web. He let go and dove for the weak spot. He slammed his head and one arm through. Straining and cursing, he squeezed the other shoulder through, and then he wriggled like mad.

Marcus landed on the African man, driving his shoulder hard into the man's chest. The audience panicked. No laughter now. Shocked faces, people crawling backwards, shouting out, running for the exits. As much as he wanted to rage at them, Marcus had a different target. He squirmed toward Baba Yaga's box. He punched the man with the cell phone as he passed him and elbowed others out of the way.

Reaching up and grabbing the low railing of the box with both hands, he came up and over, face-to-face with a cadre of armed guards. Baba Yaga stood beside the wretched old man. Her face was wrinkled in concentration. Her lips puckered and her cheeks sucked in as if she were trying hard to gather enough saliva to spit.

For a terrible moment Marcus thought she was going to do to him what she'd done to Father Squid. The horror of it—even though he'd rushed to it—froze him in place. He watched her lips move.

She didn't spit, though. She was trying, and the guards were waiting for it. That was clear enough. Marcus realized she couldn't do it again! Her power had limits. There was exhaustion in her eyes. She clutched at a chair along the wall with one hand, needing its support just to stand. She gave up trying to summon her power and, said, flatly, disdainfully, "Shoot him, you idiots."

Marcus ducked under the box as the barrels of several Uzis fixed on him. He skimmed beneath it and shot up from the rear. Curling and coming up fast, he grabbed Baba Yaga by the shoulder. He spun her, and launched his tongue at her stunned face. It hit with a wet venom *thwack*. The impact snapped her head back and flung her arms out. She fell into her guards, who scrambled awkwardly to support her, encumbered by their weapons.

Having poisoned her good, he didn't wait around for the spray of bullets he knew would be coming his way. He slipped back over the railing and dropped down into the stands. He landed hard. He glanced through the glass at the prayer bench that was the still-living Father Squid. He hated leaving him, but there was no choice. The father would want him to escape and live. So he was going to.

Gritting his teeth, he squirmed, whip fast, through the aisles and over seats. *Olena*. She was his last bit of business here. Get her, and get out. That's what mattered.

Many were heading, like him, for the exit doors. It was chaos. When bullets started to fly from Baba Yaga's box it only got worse. They tore up the seats and ricocheted off railings. Marcus weaved wildly, all curves, the point of his tail snapping behind him. He slithered over a row of cowering Japanese businessmen. He shoved a fat white man in a pinstriped suit out of his way, and bowled right through the blond, slinky, barely clad harem of women following an Arab-looking man in a long, shimmering robe. Someone behind him screamed, a high, piercing screech of agony that cut through all the other noises. Then the screamer died, battered down by the barrage of gunfire.

Marcus kept going, telling himself that nobody in here was innocent. They had come here to see people die. They may have gotten more than they bargained for, but who was to say they didn't deserve it?

When a man and woman, holding hands as they ran, went down right in front of him, Marcus realized the shots had come from the other side of them, from the mouth of the tunnel. The woman's long, auburn hair floated above her as she fell. Through the trailing screen of it, Marcus saw the shooter. The guard took aim with one hand, while his other clamped down on Olena's wrist. She twisted and yanked, making it hard for him to set his shot.

Marcus arched his body over the fallen couple. He reared high as he climbed the steps up to the guard. His tail cut a sinuous weave beneath him, a sidewinder motion that clearly unnerved the guard. He fired at Marcus's torso several times, only managing to graze his shoulder. And then, just before Marcus reached him, he lowered the gun and shot at his tail. Two bullets punched through his scales. The pain was instant, molten, as if red-hot iron prods had been slammed deep inside him. Roaring at the pain of it, the tip of his tail lashed at the shooter, catching his legs and flipping him. Marcus squirmed over him, pressing down as hard as he could. He bent and poison tagged him.

That done, he looked up at Olena. He stopped, unsure—now that he'd reached her—what to do. He stared at the perfection of features that was her face. She was too beautiful. Too beautiful for him, at least. He with venom on his tongue, blood on his fists, with the guilt of a murderer a searing brand on his flesh.

Suddenly, it felt impossible that someone like him had any claim on someone like her. He was speechless.

Olena stepped toward him, a hand held to her lips as her wide blue eyes took in the blood glistening on his scales. The concern on her face was exquisite, almost too generous to be believed. "Marcus, you are shot."

Marcus managed to say, "I'm okay." He wasn't sure it was true. His tail hurt with each pulse of blood through it. It took effort to keep the rhythmic surges of pain from showing on his face. "Olena, will you . . ." He hesitated. She watched him. "Can we get out of here? Will you come with me?"

The crowd had begun to squeeze around them, pressed against the wall, nervous but still frantic to escape down the tunnel. Olena scowled at them. "Yes. Get me away from these ones." She bent and retrieved the guard's handgun. With a few quick motions, she popped it open, checked something, and then slammed it closed again. Marcus didn't know what she'd just done, but clearly she knew a thing or two about handguns. Weapon raised in one hand, she beckoned him with her other. "Come. We go."

He didn't need to be told twice.

The Big Bleed

Part Ten

"THEY SAID NO."

Franny had returned from his delivery of Berman to Fort Freak with the bad news. He slumped on Berman's couch, accepting a glass of water delivered to him by Jamal and Mollie, who moved like participants in a three-legged race.

"What kind of 'no'?" Jamal said. "'No' as in 'not now,' or 'not without SCARE'? Or 'no' as in 'never'?"

"'No never nada.' The only thing Maseryk promised to do was tell SCARE so they could put the jokers on their to-do list."

"That's just what I didn't want."

"Well, will it make you happier to know he was going to add State, the Committee, the mayor's office, and I believe parks and rec?"

Jamal just closed his eyes. *Christ.*

"You two really know how to make a girl feel protected," Mollie said. "God." She tried to cross her arms, a gesture rendered impossible by her linkage to Jamal.

For the first half hour, Jamal had not found being handcuffed to Mollie Steunenberg to be a complete burden. She was pretty and bouncy and not wearing more clothing than necessary. Being free from Michael Berman improved her mood, too: she never reached flirty, but she had gone some distance from sullen.

But only for the first half hour. Four more half hours had passed, and now both of them were utterly sick of each other's company. "I don't like this any more than you do," Jamal told the girl. Her attitude had helped him make a decision. "Our only way out is forward."

"What the hell does that mean?"

Jamal turned to Franny. "We do this ourselves. Now."

He didn't have to spend much time or energy on the proposal, which was helpful, since he had diminishing amounts of both. For Franny, the pitch was simple: "Every hour that passes, some citizen of Jokertown dies."

For Mollie aka Tesseract, it was this: "The only way you're ever going to be free of Baba Yaga and the rest of her gang is if we take them out."

"Can we kill that old bitch?"

"It will probably come to that."

She was suddenly happier than Jamal had ever seen her.

The first sensation Jamal felt upon stepping through Tesseract's "door" from Berman's apartment into the gladiator compound inside Maxim's was dizzying vertigo.

Had Mollie bothered to consider the fact that the spatial orientation in New York, Eastern Time Zone, was radically different from that of Talas, Kazakhstan, Asian Crazy Time? Was it even possible? Or was this his illness at work, not only robbing him of his bounceback, but of *any* mental or physical resilience?

No matter. Jamal took in the huge digital television screen mounted above a wet bar, showing chaos in the arena itself. A camera operator was struggling to locate the action (*for whom?* Jamal wondered) as what looked

like Snake Boy's torso slithered through a crowd of glit-
terati, knocking them sideways while zapping them with
his poisoned tongue.

Nice.

Adding to Jamal's disorientation were the smell of the
gladiator's quarters—heavy on cologne, perfume, and
cigarette smoke—and the sound—hideous bass-heavy
rap. Lounging on couches or bellied up to the bar were
maybe a dozen jokers and twice that number of attractive "hostesses." And, holding a drink, his arm around a
tall nat woman with un-nat breasts, Dmitri . . . fat,
sleepy-eyed, sloppy, menacing.

Then Franny and Mollie walked in—looking as
though they were holding hands like high school sweethearts, though most high school sweethearts weren't
joined by handcuffs.

And, to quote Big Bill Norwood, a great deal of Hades
came unmoored.

The jokers all sprang to their feet—those that had feet.
Their eyes went wide—those that had eyes—with surprise
or amusement. "What the hell is this?" growled an eight-
foot-tall man-mountain joker Jamal knew as El Monstro.

Only Dmitri seemed to appreciate the situation. Shoving his goddess to one side, he smirked and turned his
menacing attention to the intruders.

"Franny!" Jamal shouted and pointed. "Cap him!"

But Franny hesitated. And in that moment, Jamal felt
as sad and sick and weak and afraid as he'd ever felt in
his life. Worse than the day he'd broken his leg on the
football field. He thought of Julia crushed, his parents
dead, his own life ended. He wanted to crawl into a hole
anywhere but here—*Dmitri at work*. Knowing what to
expect in no way lessened the effect.

But that foreknowledge gave Jamal a few precious seconds of lucidity, and enough energy to raise the Glock. He
snapped off three rounds that caught a surprised Dmitri
in the back, shoulder, and, as he turned, in the face.

Down he went in a spray of blood and cranial matter.

"Oh my God!" Mollie was almost hysterical, and Jamal couldn't blame her. Franny stared. "Sorry, cop training." Blinking hard, he forced a smile. "I wanted to tell him to throw down his gun . . ."

Jamal stared at dead Dmitri. It seemed that someone else had pulled that trigger. There was no time to reflect, however. More goons with guns would be here soon. "Hey, people," he shouted. "We are here to take you back to New York!"

The unfortunately-but-appropriately-named Wartface was giddy about being rescued. "About fucking time! Can I hit anyone before we go? I've got a list!"

"Sorry." Jamal turned to Tesseract. "Do it!"

Without a word, Mollie opened a "door" to Fort Freak. They should be safe there, and it would allow the cops to remove them from the missing-persons list . . . once they calmed down. "There's the exit. Move!"

There was a mad rush. First the hookers, then the jokers flopping, crawling, hopping after them. They piled through the door, and Jamal imagined the chaos at the other end of the journey.

Two goons appeared from a side door, guns blazing in spite of the presence of at least two joker-gladiators. Jamal ducked: he knew these idiots were just spraying rounds. He squeezed off three rounds that were aimed no better, but served to force the goons to take cover.

As he reloaded, Jamal had a sudden surge of energy. Maybe he *was* some kind of adrenaline junkie, happy only when moving, chasing, shooting. It certainly fit the persona of Stuntman the ace from SCARE and Hollywood. Maybe he was seeing the endgame. All they had to do was grab the rest of the jokers—

Franny and Mollie were forced to duck as a lucky shot from one of the goons passed between them, shattering a mirror on the wall. Franny had finally lost his inhibitions, unleashing a spray of covering fire that silenced both goons.

Mollie was crying, whether out of fear or anger or the residual effects of the Dmitri mindfuck, Jamal couldn't know. He wondered what these Tesseract shifts did to the girl—God knew that bounceback drained him, even when he was healthy.

El Monstro had been lingering off to one side (his height made it impossible for him to truly take cover). Now the eight-foot-tall joker abruptly headed for the arena door. Jamal grabbed him. "Hey, big guy, where are you going?" He nodded toward the "door." "New York is that way."

"I'm not going. I like it here!" El Monstro insisted.

For a moment Jamal was furious—this was just the latest entry in a long litany of stupidity he had endured since learning about Wheels and the missing jokers. He was out of time, out of patience. He was not going to let this big goon stop him from completing this mission, no more than he had let Rustbelt stop him from winning *American Hero*! He trained his Glock at El Monstro's vast mid-section. "Look," Jamal said, "I don't know what they've done to your head here, but you're going through that door."

With no apparent windup, no warning, El Monstro simply swung one of his giant arms and metal fists toward him. It was slow, but still too fast for Jamal Norwood to dodge.

The massive fist slammed into the right side of his face.

It was worse than his first deliberate jump from a tall building, in *Halloween Night XIII*. He had time for the sickening realization that there was going to be no bounceback, that Stuntman was falling fading dying.

Galahad in Blue

Part Ten

EVERYTHING SEEMED TO SLOW down.

Franny's vision narrowed to a tunnel that showed him only Jamal's face, blood flying from his mouth, his right eye dangling loose, the deep indentation in the side of his skull. The agent seemed to collapse in stages, until he lay on the floor like a broken toy, casually discarded. Mollie was screaming in his ear, trying to hide behind him, yanking at the handcuffs that joined them.

Franny yelled. It wasn't even words, just an incoherent sound of rage and grief and denial. He brought up his gun.

And suddenly the dragging weight on his left arm was gone. He whirled in time to see Mollie, a paper clip clutched between her fingers, step backwards through an opening that afforded him a brief glimpse of the Eiffel Tower, flipping him the bird. Then the doorway snapped shut.

Of course the door to Fort Freak was also gone.

Trapped. Panic clogged his throat.

The whine of a bullet past his head brought him back

to the precariousness of his situation. Franny dove behind a sofa. He heard El Monstro yelling to the remaining guards, "I'll get him."

Despite his ringing ears from all the gunfire Franny
could hear and even feel El Monstro's footfalls as he
closed on him. He leaped up and vaulted over the back
of the sofa. He snapped off a few shots at the last remaining guard on the catwalk overhead, who ducked
into cover.

El Monstro was closing. It wasn't that he was particularly fast, but he was so big that each stride covered a
lot of ground. The buffet table was on Franny's left.
Franny's eyes flicked across the offerings—deli meats,
bread, cheese, a mound of caviar, a soup tureen set on a
hot plate. The handle of a ladle invited someone to try a
bowl.

Franny snatched out the ladle brimming with hot soup.
The smell of paprika hit his nose. About half spilled as
he whirled, but there was enough left in the big ladle for
Franny to flick into El Monstro's face. The big joker
howled, and clawed at his face and eyes. *Guess it was hot
not sweet paprika,* Franny thought inanely. He closed
with the big joker, screwed the barrel of his gun into El
Monstro's ear, and pulled the trigger twice.

Until this day he had never actually fired his gun
outside the range. Most cops went through their entire
careers and never fired their piece much less killed someone. Now Franny had killed a man. A man he'd supposedly come to rescue.

It wasn't like in the movies. It wasn't even like watching Jamal shoot Dmitri. His knees suddenly felt like
they'd been replaced with rubber bands, and he found
himself sitting on the floor. A bullet creased the air where
his head had been only seconds before.

There was no time for shock or regret. If he was getting out of here alive he needed to take care of that ass-

hole on the catwalk, and find his way to the outside. After that—well, he'd think about after that once he got that far.

Access to the catwalk wasn't immediately obvious. There was another burst of gunfire from above that sent Franny scrambling for cover, but someone on the high ground always has the advantage, and Franny found himself knocked sideways from the force of the bullet that slammed into his left shoulder.

The shock wore off all too quickly, and the pain hit. It was worse then anything he'd ever experienced. When he broke an arm playing hockey, slashed his leg on a sub-merged tree while swimming in a lake that summer at camp nothing could match this searing agony. Franny screamed and fell to his knees.

Despite the torment some part of his brain kept work-ing. *He needs to think you're dead.* Franny collapsed on the floor, the pistol hidden beneath him. With luck the goon would leave, or come down to make sure Franny was dead.

At which point Franny would kill him. Or try to kill him. Only, God, he didn't want to kill anybody else. Ever.

Blood was trickling from the wound. Franny could feel his shirt becoming wet and sticky. He listened to his heartbeats like a slow deep drum in his ears. The pain flared and ebbed also in time to that primal clock. Franny gazed into the staring eyes of El Monstro prone on the floor near him. He wanted to look away, but didn't dare move. He wanted to close his eyes, but didn't dare risk it.

Overhead Franny heard an agitated conversation in what he guessed was Russian. Two sets of footsteps. A door closing. Franny counted another thirty heartbeats and then cautiously climbed to his feet. Nothing. Press-ing a hand to his shoulder he staggered to Jamal, knelt and, pressing his fingers against the SCARE agent's throat, felt for a pulse. There was none. He hadn't expected to find one. Not with the side of the agent's skull crushed in in that horrifying way.

"Eternal rest grant unto him, O Lord, and let perpetual light shine upon him. May the soul of this faithful departed, through the mercy of God, rest in peace, Amen." Franny lifted his head, crossed himself, pulled the cross from his collar, kissed it, and tucked it away. "I'll get you home to Big Bill and your mom and Julia. I promise," he said softly. It was stupid. It wasn't like Jamal could hear. But it did give him a purpose, and jolted him into motion.

Franny moved to the buffet table, shook out a napkin, folded another into a pad, and made a makeshift bandage. Got it tied using one hand and his teeth. Next task: Find a way out. He searched through bedrooms that smelled of sweat and jizz and perfume.

Eventually he found a door that looked like it might lead to stairs that would lead to the catwalk. It was locked. He went back and found the body of one of the goons either Jamal or he had shot. The man had taken a header off the catwalk, and his legs and neck were bent at odd angles. The Uzi was undamaged. Franny carried it back to the door. Bracing the gun against his hip, he held down the trigger. Bullets whanged and bounced, but eventually the lock gave up.

Up the stairs. There were a couple of doors off the catwalk. Franny picked one at random. It put him in a long hallway pieced by doors. At first he edged up to them, then took five-second looks inside, the Uzi at the ready. They were all empty and they all appeared to be offices. Computers that would have been old in 1990 sat on desks.

At the end of the hall was another closed door. Franny leaned against it. Partly to listen, partly because he needed to lean on something. Through the thick wood he faintly heard shouts, screams, and gunfire.

He really didn't want to face any more gunfire, but he couldn't wait for Baba Yaga and her goons to regain control. He had to add to the chaos and use it to escape. He sucked in several deep breaths, then pushed open the door.

He was in the casino proper. The usual dings and rings of gambling machines were muted. Many of the slots had been knocked over. Extremely well-dressed people were running in all directions. Women's discarded shoes littered the carpeted floor. Franny even spotted a forlorn toupee dangling off a chair like a dead squirrel. The room reeked of cordite and cigarette smoke.

Across the large, chandelier-hung room he spotted IBT writhing toward elaborate double doors. His tongue shot out like a lashing whip, leaving behind convulsing people. A young woman ran at his side, gripping his hand while with the other she held a pistol that she used with murderous skill.

"*Marcus!*" Franny yelled, but over the screams and gunshots and the crashes as people tore open cash boxes behind the cashier's stands he wasn't heard.

That looked like the way out so Franny followed in the snake-man's wake. He passed through a lobby with a coat check area, and a bench where a large man with a suspicious bulge under his shoulder was slumped. The mark of IBT's tongue was on his face. The doors were standing wide open.

Franny stepped out as a battalion of police cars swarmed up, lights blazing and sirens blaring. A loudspeaker blared out instructions in a language he didn't understand. But he was a cop. He could guess. He threw down the Uzi, and put his hands up, bit back a cry of pain as it hurt his wounded shoulder. "I'm a cop! *American. Police officer!!*" He reached slowly into his pocket to pull out his badge.

Somebody shot him.

The bullet ripped into his side. Franny fell. He heard people yelling. He vaguely felt hands rifling his pockets. The face of a young man holding aloft a saline bag, the swaying roof of an ambulance.

Darkness.

Galahad in Blue

Part Eleven

Epilogue

GETTING SHOT HURT.

Getting shot twice . . . well, that should have hurt twice as much, but it seemed like more. Ten times as much, at least.

The treatment after the fact hadn't been much better. The Kazakh police had handcuffed him roughly, despite the blood leaking from him. Since he had a bullet in his shoulder, and another in his side, he had lost all macho cred by screaming. That penetrated the language barrier and they had taken him to the hospital, where the personnel had seemed overwhelmed by the number of gunshot and poisoning victims as well as some old joker hunched in a wheelchair, a creature as hideous as he was pathetic.

Franny hadn't been sure what to expect from a Kazakh hospital, but it wasn't all that different from an American facility. He had been taken quickly into surgery, and awakened in a private room. He had a feeling this wasn't the norm, but the presence of two large, very unsympathetic Kazakh policemen at the door made his status crystal clear.

He kept demanding to see the American ambassador and kept being ignored. He'd then tried using the fraternity of law enforcement to generate some sympathy from his guards. That hadn't worked either. Maybe because none of them could understand a word he was saying.

He decided to get dressed even though his bloodstained shirt was gone; he didn't feel terribly effective clad in an open-back hospital gown. But when he opened the door, he found himself looking down the barrel of his guards' submachine guns. Franny had a brief moment of thinking the perps in New York would sure as fuck be impressed if he had one of those instead of his service pistol.

One guard snapped out something in what sounded like Russian. Or maybe Kazakh. He had no fucking clue. Franny indicated his bare if bandaged torso. "Hey, how about a shirt? T-shirt? Anything?"

The guards looked at him with disinterest and shut the door again.

Franny returned to the bed, sat down, tried to think. It was a hopeless effort. His thoughts kept returning over and over to those chaotic moments when Jamal had been killed. His throat felt tight, and he swallowed hard for a couple of seconds. He had liked the cynical SCARE agent. *I got Stuntman killed.*

He was now totally alone. When he failed to check in Maseryk would probably figure out where he'd gone. Maybe eventually someone from the NYPD or the State Department or SCARE or somebody would ride to the rescue.

"I got most of the jokers home," Franny said aloud to the room.

The room wasn't impressed.

The door opened, and his guards entered accompanied by a man with a secretive face and slicked-back brown hair that made Franny think of an otter. His suit was expensive. He wore a Rolex, and the wire from a radio earpiece ran down into his collar.

The guards grabbed Franny's arms, and frog-marched him out of the room. It hurt his shoulder and his side and he yelled. "Hey! What are you doing? Where are we going?" He was being hustled down the hall. "I demand to see the American ambassador! I'm a police officer, you can't—"

The man in the suit slapped him hard across the face. Franny chewed on the bright coppery taste of blood and shut up.

"Baba Yaga wishes to see you," the man said in a voice that had one of those unidentifiable but superior European accents.

A flock of moths seemed to have taken up residence in Franny's gut. He could feel a subtle trembling in his legs. Okay, he was going to die. He didn't have to face it whimpering like a girl. He stiffened his spine, glared at the otter, and said, "*I'm* under guard, but she gets to send fucking errand boys? She's a fucking criminal. Why aren't these guys—" He jerked a thumb at the two cops. "—on *her* door?"

"Because she is a respected member of the business community here in Talas, and you are American cowboy cop who is very much out of his jurisdiction."

The otter pushed open the door, and for the first time Franny faced the woman behind all of this madness.

She was a small, wizened figure, her dyed red hair shockingly bright against the stacked pillows. She seemed fragile until she lifted heavy eyelids, and gave Franny a piercing look out of the coldest, most calculating gray eyes he had ever seen.

He was pushed inexorably forward until he stood at the side of the bed. The two guards backed away. Baba Yaga's wrinkled lips worked.

. Baba Yaga spoke. "So, this is the hero," she said, in English. Franny stared at her wondering what Berman had meant about furniture and footstools? "Stupid, stupid, boy," the old woman went on. "You have no idea what you have done. He is waking. And we are all dead now."

Franny swallowed. "We?" he said. "Who, we?"

Baba Yaga laughed and pointed at Franny. "You." She touched her breast. "Me. Them." Her gesture encompassed the otter and the cops and set the gem-encrusted rings to flashing. "Talas. Kazakhstan. Eventually . . . the world."

Somewhere far off, in a distant part of the hospital, people began screaming.